To Grasp A Shadow

Jack Gauntlett

To Grasp A Shadow

Jack Gauntlett

JANUS PUBLISHING COMPANY
London, England

First published in Great Britain 2006
by Janus Publishing Company Ltd,
105-107 Gloucester Place,
London W1U 6BY

www.januspublishing.co.uk

British Library Cataloguing-in-Publication Data
A catalogue record for this book is available from the British Library

ISBN 1 85756 681 5

Cover Design: Dave Valance

Printed and bound in Great Britain

To all those who were unaware, not so
long ago,of the perils we were facing
and the shadows they cast.

God moving darkly in men's minds
Using their passions as His tool
Brings freedom with a tyrant's chains
And wisdom with the fool.

John Masefield

November 1965 – London

"Yes I know him", she said and hesitated, "why do you ask?"
"How long have you known him?" he asked, ignoring her question.
"About two years I suppose." She tried to appear noncommittal.
"Where did you first meet?"
"At a party at my father's house... look, what is this all about?"
"Did you like him?" His questions were brusquely given and she was beginning to feel apprehensive. She seemed to be at that point in a conversation where it became interrogation.
"Yes."
"How much?"
She hesitated. "Yes, very much. Look, I don't really know why I've come to answer these questions." She looked down at her hands which were entwined in her lap.

He looked up from the paper that he was periodically noting upon. "You know the government department that I represent; well, we are concerned about the disappearance of Ronald Cameron." He stated it baldly, not attempting any preamble.

She felt the blood flush to her face and a quiver of something akin to nausea grip her inside.

"Disappearance... but I spoke to him only the day before yesterday... he was on a train going on a visit to Moscow... he phoned me from Cologne station."

"Yes, we know about that," he said, his eyes searching her face, "he was a member of a party organised by Intourist to see the October Revolution celebrations in Red Square."

"Yes, I know," she replied, "we had spoken about it and it had been organised for some time." She glanced up at the man sitting in the armchair by the window. His back was to the light and the bright late

1

autumn sunshine prevented her from discerning his features clearly. He had been present throughout but had not contributed to the conversation at all.

She had presented herself at these offices in Whitehall through the urgent summons of a phone call this very morning. She tried to remember the actual words used when a secretary had rung... something about Ronnie, and that he needed some help.

"Look, I'm sorry Miss Robinson, but I have to tell you that your friend Ronald Cameron has gone missing from the party."

"Missing, but how...?"

"He apparently left the train at a halt stop just after Smolensk and has not been heard of since."

She felt sick and it wasn't her time of the month that was causing it. "How do you know so quickly that this has happened?" Her mouth felt dry.

"The party are on a group visa and if anyone is missing it quickly affects the whole tour. The party has been held in Moscow until something can be sorted out." The man behind the desk looked up from his notes,"there were two of them who went missing." He said it slowly and, she thought, deliberately.

"Who was the other? " She asked. She felt a curious reluctance to hear the answer.

"The other who was with him was his wife's brother."

This time the blood came into her face with a burning that was so intense that her breathing was affected. She gulped seemingly for air that didn't come.

"His wife...?"

"Yes, didn't you know he was married?"

"No," she shook her head and tried to stop the tears from welling in her eyes. It was unsuccessful.

"Would you like a glass of water?" The kindly way it was asked prevented her from speaking and she shook her head. She took a handkerchief from out of her handbag and blew her nose.

"I'm sorry," she said, apologetically.

"That's quite all right, it must be a shock," he referred to another sheet of paper. "He married during the war... a Russian girl, but had to leave her in Russia... she was twenty then, he looked up, which makes her thirty-nine now."

She met his gaze. "He never told me about a wife," she spoke softly and she noticed the man in the armchair lean forward slightly, as if to hear better. "How do you know about me?" She suddenly realised the implications of what she had said.

"We searched his flat in Poole and found letters from you." He spoke matter of factly but in that short phrase she understood how suddenly naked she felt.

"My letters..."

After a pause he said, "It seems that you were very close to him."

Her eyes were cast down and she whispered, "Yes."

"Did he feel the same way about you?"

She looked up as if to re-establish some sort of authority within herself, "Yes, he did; I have many letters from him that tell me of his feelings."

"But not marriage." He said it as a fact and not a question.

"No," she tried to sort out her words before she said them, partly, maybe, to convince herself. "He said I was so young compared to him, he was over double my age and we needed time to think about this."

"Were you lovers?"

The question that she knew had been coming was none the less brutal when it came. "Not physically, no." She hesitated briefly, "You see, he always said that he believed the majority of married couples didn't have the intimacy of mind and soul that we had together. He always said that we were lovers..." she tailed off, "and I always considered myself his lover."

The man behind the desk was silent for a few moments. "When did you next see him after that first meeting?"

"He rang me up the following week, the Thursday I think, and suggested that we go out for a meal." She began to feel a relief that the questioning had come off the more intimate level. "He arranged at the house to collect me that evening and he took me to a little Italian restaurant in the Old Brompton Road."

"Can you remember what you talked about?"

"Not really, no... it was two years ago... general things... I just got the impression of him as a nice gentle guy who was considerate and polite and who was interested in what I had to say."

"Were you surprised that he invited you out to dinner after such a brief meeting at a party?"

"No, not at all, in some way I was expecting him to call me."

"Why was that?"

"We got on really well, we seemed to have so much in common," she paused, "despite the fact of our difference in ages he had time to listen to me and hear my point of view on things."

"Did you know then that he had been in the Navy during the war?"

"He made a passing reference to it, I think during the party, something about the wine we were drinking was similar to one he had 'liberated' from a bombed-out auberge on the outskirts of Antwerp."

"Were you flattered by his attentions towards you?"

"Flattered yes I suppose so; I saw him as a man who had experienced so much of life. A life that I was just starting out on. He had so much to give and yet he seemed very reticent... almost shy." She shrugged, "He didn't push himself at all. He made me feel equal to him, he put me completely at ease from the first." A wave of memory and emotion caught her and she feared she was going to cry again. "I liked him from the start." She ended lamely.

The man looked up from the desk and his scattered papers, smiled and said, "fine, Miss Robinson, I think that's all we need to talk about just now. I'm most grateful for you coming and your prompt attention to our summons."

She got up and shook his proffered hand. He went to the door and opened it for her and she took the stairs down one flight to the ground floor. She went out into Whitehall, blinking mentally at the sudden rush of traffic noise that engulfed her.

She was in her second year at London University reading History and was living in a flat in Kingsbury, North London, with her friend from school days, Rachel. Rachel worked in a bank in the City of London and although they both lived under the same roof it was only rarely that they were able to be at home together. This evening was one of those rare events. As Nina put the key in the door she was greeted by a cheery call from Rachel in the kitchen. Rachel was petite and dark, with long ringlets of hair that seemed to have a life of their own as they bounced about her head. She demonstrated this as she came into the hall to greet her.

"Nina how lovely to see you, didn't expect you back for hours." They embraced and Nina noticed the faint scent of expensive perfume as they brushed faces. She had always admired Rachel for the graceful femininity she seemed to exude. Beside her Nina somehow felt much more gauche and awkward. Nevertheless, despite this feeling, when they went out together, people seemed to notice, men particularly, the beauty of one reflecting off the beauty of the other. Rachel was dark and small, Nina was blond and, although not big, was more fulsome in her figure. The contrast between the two girls complemented them both.

They both went into the sitting room. "I've just made a cup of tea, I'm sure you need it," said Rachel. Nina flopped down onto the settee and kicked off her shoes.

"I think I need a gin but I would love one, thank you."

"How did the interview go?" Rachel poured out the tea.

"It was curious and in some ways alarming." Nina told her the salient details of the visit to Whitehall and Rachel listened with an intensity that at the time Nina didn't think unusual but in retrospect puzzled her.

December 1943

The I class destroyer pitched into the grey sullen sea and the creamed waves heaved over the bows. The ice from the freezing water was building up on the fo'castle and the gun turrets, making the ship top heavy. As she went down into the troughs the officer of the watch noticed that she was more sluggish as she came up into the next wave. He spoke into the telegraph as he huddled more securely into his duffel coat.

"Watch officer here, get the ice party out again."

Within minutes heavily clad ratings were scrambling about the decks, slipping and holding on where they could. Steam hoses were being used to quickly disperse the ice but axes were soon needed to preserve the steam.

Ronald Boyd Cameron was unaware of all this activity going on over his head as he sat hunched before the radio set that was installed in a console in front of him. The earphones clamped over his head shut out the crashing and groaning sounds of the ship's hull as it progressed through the waters of the Barents Sea. On his occasional visits on deck he could imagine the escort vessels of the squadron clustered around the thirty or so merchant ships on the grey sea. In fact, reality was often different from this picture he imagined. Very often ships could not see each other. They only knew of each other's presence by the occasional fleeting glimpse of another ship through the rain squalls and clinging spray that momentarily parted. However, he knew by the messages that came through the vibrant static via his headphones that there was a cluster of ships in the area. Depending on the weather and enemy activity, the area occupied by ships in the convoy could vary by many miles of sea space.

On this convoy the Royal Navy were escorting an assortment of merchant ships carrying war materials to Murmansk. The ships were low in the water, heavy with holds full of complete Spitfires, Hurricanes, spares and general supplies. There was also one oil tanker, which had in close attendance two frigates.

This was the second convoy to Russia that he had been on and as a humble ordinary seaman, albeit in radio communications, he was getting acclimatised to life on board ship. His one fear, apart from the fears that he didn't dare express, was the ever present threat of seasickness. He found the stuffy, oil-fumed cabin with its constant movement an absolute nightmare. On his first voyage he honestly didn't think he could endure one moment more than the ten days it took for the convoy to reach its destination. However in between retching into a bucket he found he was able to find some almost hidden strength to perform his duties adequately. He dismissed the next voyage from his mind. He thought wryly that the ship might be torpedoed anyway so such fears were pointless. The taking of one day at a time was absolutely necessary, indeed he soon realised that each moment was all he could cope with.

His growing up in London before the war was now such a detached experience that he couldn't believe he was the same person. In those moments when there appeared a period of relative calm back in Plymouth, he would pause and take out the photo of Babs, the girl he was dating before he was called up. The slightly wrinkled picture showed the face of a young, dark-haired girl smiling hesitantly into the camera. The summery printed dress she was wearing made her appear as if she was a flower growing out of the field she was sitting in. There was evidence of a picnic around her and, looking at the picture, he could scarcely believe he had once inhabited such a world of bliss.

As the radio activity was momentarily stilled he reached into the alcove where he kept his few personal things and looked again at her photo. A wave of comfort came over him as he gazed at the picture and he allowed himself a slight smile as he was transported back to the joy and freedom that he experienced with her. A sudden babble of morse came into his headphones. An SOS was coming from one of the merchant ships and he scribbled down the message. He was back to reality as he put the note into the canister and the canister into the vacuum pipe that sped the message to the plotting room above him.

November 1965
As Nina talked to Rachel about the interview she felt a despondency settle upon her. How could he deceive her like this? They had always been so close. Two years she had known him and he had never given a hint of a wife. It wasn't that she was amazed, she was but this feeling was overtaken by an intense disappointment in him. There was something within her that she knew was precious and special that she was keeping for him and now he had destroyed all that. At a stroke he had cast all her specialness back in her face. That unique bond that he kept talking about was an empty farce. He couldn't love her if he counted her so slight in his counsel. Yet the more she thought the more she came to realise that perhaps the fact that he was married was the reason they had not become physical lovers. Perhaps the moral sense he had prevented him from adulterating her in that way. She was taking comfort from that thought the more she talked to Rachel. "Perhaps he loves you more than you think," Rachel said.

December 1943
The escort squadron of four cruisers and twelve destroyers had set sail from Plymouth on 10th December. They had slipped their moorings in the dim light of a murky dawn. The rain was sleeting down as he took a deep breath of the freezing air and he took his last look at the naval dockyard as it disappeared into the mist. He shivered and went below decks and made his way to the radio room. He opened the steel door and stepped over the ledge into the small

cabin. Able seaman Earnie Watts was there, headphones on and transmitting. He noticed again, with that familiar thrill of revulsion, the oil-fumed fustiness and warmth of this all too familiar room. The engines were beginning to produce the power that would propel this destroyer to its cruising speed of fifteen knots and he felt the vibration in the walls and floor as the ship settled itself into the flow of the sea. In three days, after sailing up the west coast of England, they would be into the Firth of Clyde ready to rendezvous with the thirty or so merchant ships that were assembling there. After that the convoy would steam up over the north coast of Scotland, north of the Shetlands and set the course eastwards towards the inhospitable territory of Russia. The ten days it would take to steam the two thousand or so miles to Murmansk through the North, Norwegian and Barents seas would be fraught with three particular hazards. The German Airforce, U boats and, by far the most fickle of enemies, the weather. Sometimes, ironically, the weather was not the enemy, in fact if the weather was severe enough the two other enemies would be nullified.

According to the weather forecast for the next ten days, within the area in which they would be operating, they would have to expect a colluded front with frequent snow showers with a low dipping onto the Norwegian coast. However, he knew there was something special about the enemies on this trip because the German battle cruiser *Scharnhorst* was threatening to break out from the Alten Fiord with escort vessels of unknown quantity.

November 1965

Nina bent down and picked up the mail from the mat. She recognised instantly Ronald's writing on an airmail letter. She hurried into her bedroom, closed the door and, trying not to be too hasty, tore open the envelope. She noticed the postmark as being from Cologne, dated 31st of October. She read:

My darling Nina,
By the time you get this letter you may be wondering what has happened to me. I know that my absence from the train will be noticed and that certain elements will contact you at some stage. Before anything else happens I must set the record straight and tell you something about myself that I am afraid I

have so far kept from you. Ever since we met two years ago we have felt something special between us and, despite the variance in our ages, a common bond has grown up and a love that seems to be growing. I have written to you in the past trying to tell you how much I feel for you and how much I love you and you have graciously returned my love and this I count as one of the greatest privileges of my life, that someone as beautiful as you could love me like that. Because of this I owe it to you to explain my present actions. You probably know by now that I married a Russian girl towards the end of the war. For various reasons, not least the obstinate nature of the Russians, I could not bring Anna back with me and she had to remain in her homeland. You can probably imagine the trauma and ache behind those simple words. She was to me the most perfect, wonderful girl that I had ever met or indeed imagined, until I met you that is! She is the reason why I have now gone missing behind the Iron Curtain. Her brother was over in the U K as part of a trade delegation and he made contact with me, he told me that she was ill and that their parents had just died and that if I wanted to see her again there was a way it could be done. She apparently convinced him to make contact with me and, although he is taking a risk, he knew she wanted to see me again. These are the reasons why I am now in Russia and although I don't know the way things will work out I do know that I want you to know beyond anyone else what is happening. Whatever happens, please know that I love you beyond all things. You are what is important in my life now and until I get this resolved with Anna I feel my life is on hold and that I can't go on with you in any truthful sense until I know. For the moment, my darling, that is all I can tell you, but until we meet again, for assuredly we will, I remain your true lover and friend forever.

Your Ronald xxxxxxx

Nina's tears fell onto the pages as she read the letter for the third time. Now she felt and knew from that moment how much she needed him. The hours that had preceded this moment had been the most difficult of her life but somehow there was vindication in these pages.

As she pondered his precious words she knew she had to go back to Whitehall and try and find out what it was that made them so interested in him.

November 1965

She was very reluctant, as she ascended the stairs to Witherspoon's office. Was she doing the right thing? Was her curiosity likely to endanger Ronald's future? But she had to know what was going on. Somehow she had a feeling that the more the Foreign Office knew about Ronald the safer he would be. She couldn't rationalise this but it somehow brought her some comfort. It also helped in the sense that she needed to share this letter with the authorities who had perhaps doubted her true relationship with him. Perhaps her feminine intuition needed to assert her authority in the situation.

Witherspoon greeted her politely as he rose from his chair behind the desk. His handshake was firm and he gestured her to the armchair by the window. He seated himself in the swivel chair and said, "So you have had a letter from Ronald Cameron?"

"Yes," she replied, bringing the letter out of her handbag and handing it to him.

He took the letter and began reading. She watched his face closely, noting a slightly embarrassed expression as he turned the pages. He looked up quickly now and again as if to see how closely she was watching him. He finished and laid the letter on the table, rather reverentially she thought, as if in deference to the sensitive nature of the contents. He looked up and smiled.

"Thank you for letting me see this, it gives us a more balanced view of the situation," he paused. "It makes it difficult for Her Majesty's government anyway; the fact that he has disappeared in the middle of Russia and until we receive some indication from the Russians we will not know how to proceed. They, of course, are doing all they can to trace him but the fact that he has gone missing with a Russian citizen will, I imagine, make it more difficult to find him."

Nina swept her hair back behind an ear, a mannerism that Ronald, she remembered, found appealing. "They will go to be with Ronald's wife won't they and the Russians will find him there?"

Witherspoon shrugged, "Maybe; I am sure they will look into every possibility." He looked at her keenly and hesitated as if uncertain

about what he should say. "There is another possibility."
"What is that?" Nina said.
Witherspoon leaned forward, his elbows on his knees, his hands together under his chin. "During the war he was involved in communications, his job as radio operator in destroyers chiefly. He was privy to some pretty sophisticated equipment and after the war carried on in marine survey, particularly in regard to radio electronics."
Nina sensed that words were being carefully chosen.
"Because of the nature of this business," Witherspoon continued, "he had to sign the official secrets act, a continuation of his wartime commitment. He is still under these strictures now and his presence in Russia is, shall we say, inadvisable."

10th January 1944

The grey sombre skyline of Murmansk appeared in the dim dawn light. There was a light scattering of snow showers blurring the vision of the watchers on the cruiser as the grey battle ship came to its mooring astern of a merchant vessel that was tied up at the dock where cranes were already lifting out crates of aircraft spares.

It wasn't the custom for warships to come into the dock area of Murmansk. Only the merchant ships were allowed to dock alongside to use the unloading facilities. Normally warships moored at buoys in the River Kola nearer the mouth of the Kola peninsular closer to the port of Poljarnyj.

However, the line of official Zim limousines with the Soviet flag displayed on the front wings were unusual and the cluster of Russian military personnel in evidence around the dock area were conspicuous, not only by their presence, but by the attentive attitude to the Royal Navy cruiser. As soon as the ship was secured and a gangway installed, the phalanx of Army and Navy officers were piped on board and shown down to the captain's cabin. What went on in the privacy of the cabin was not apparent to the ship's company then but the evidence a few days later resulted in events that would change some of their lives profoundly.

November 1965

She remembered the words, "I'm lost without you," that he had sent to her on the Tuesday before he went off to Russia. As the days went by and she didn't hear any more news, those few words seemed to burn into more of her thought processes. As the days turned into weeks and she felt no diminution in the effect of those words, she came to the realisation that all the words of endearment that he had expressed to her in letters and on the phone were growing into her psyche. They were becoming part of the very fabric of her existence. He had always been the one who initiated the love that they expressed to each other. She had somehow just gone along with it but now that he wasn't here to express his feelings she made the remarkable discovery that she was taking on the initiative of responding to him and ironically he wasn't here to receive it. Somehow she now had to take on the responsibility of keeping their love alive. It all rested on her to accept all those loving words and translate them into herself so that the foundation of their love had a permanent basis in her heart. It was now her turn to recognise the love that had been born in them to come into a grown-up state of maturity.

It was now three weeks since he had disappeared in Russia and as she lay on her bed in the early hours of that November morning and sleep refused to come to her aid she suddenly felt wave after wave of sheer warmth and joy suffuse every fibre of her being. She hadn't particularly been thinking of anything but in that state of apparent blankness of mind had come this wonderful experience of euphoria. She couldn't describe it as anything else, it was so concrete, so definable, so solid that she knew it was real. At that same moment of joy had come the recognisable identity of his love for her being born into her. She knew he was alive and at that moment she realised the immense nature of the love he had for her. Tears flowed down her face and she sobbed into the pillow. She wasn't aware of how long she was in this state but eventually the shuddering of her body eased and the outward flow of emotion left her empty of all but exhausted peace and happiness. As her eyes opened and she sensed rather than saw the early grey light of the winter morning, she tried to come to terms with what she had just experienced. It was as if she had had a visitation of some angelic presence. She wasn't religious but if she had been this would have been her initial response. As she lay there she knew she had been changed in some indefinable way. She no longer felt anxious or frustrated when she thought of him, only an extremely warm peaceful attitude of mind that was literally filled with love. A love that was not sentimental or facile but vigorous, strong and, yes, indestructible. She knew that was it, whatever happened, whatever transpired, she knew of a certainty that this love could not be destroyed. She knew he was now the other half of her. That true essence of love, being joined to one's lover. To be the same flesh in body, mind and spirit.

Witherspoon opened the file in front of him. He peered over his glasses at her. "We have just had another," he paused to give emphasis to the word, "request, from the Russian government. It appears that they require more information regarding Ronald Cameron's service in the Royal Navy during the war."
Nina shrugged, "I don't know much about it, he told me a few stories about his life on board ship but that was really all."
Witherspoon flicked his pencil in a pensive fashion against his lower lip. "Did he ever tell you about any trips he had ashore?"
She tried to think and had been trying ever since he went missing and so far nothing seemed to come clear. "He did once mention in a very offhand way that he had gone ashore and met an officer who was the medical officer off one of the other Navy ships."
Witherspoon looked at her, "I wonder why he mentioned that?"
"I don't know, I think it was in reference to a man's name. We had been talking about names, something about if we had any children," she paused,' "I was teasing him I think, it wasn't a serious conversation." She blushed slightly and looked down at her hands in her lap.
"Can you remember the name?"
She looked up. "It was Brian Anstruther-Plowman."
Witherspoon made a note on the file. "Can you think of anything else in reference to him?"
"No, it was just his name."
"An unusual name, I must admit," responded Witherspoon.
"There was also," Nina paused as Witherspoon looked up, "I don't know if it's relevant at all."
"Don't worry about whether you think it relevant, just tell me and I will work it from there."
"Well," she continued, "they had a concert party on one of the Navy ships. The Russians sent a group of sailors to dance and sing songs."
"Did he mention anyone, particularly, that he'd met then?"

"No I don't think so," she was silent for some moments and Witherspoon was just going to interject when she spoke, "is that where he could have met his wife?"

Witherspoon shrugged, "It's possible, however, it seems that the Russians were very careful about who they allowed to make contact with Navy personnel." He was surprised at her abrupt question and realised that in this question and answer session she was thinking, if not ahead, at least level with him.

"If they first met then it couldn't have been easy to maintain contact," he spoke, but it seemed to her that he was almost thinking aloud.

"Do you know how many trips to Russia he made?" She spoke quietly.

"It seems three, according to the Admiralty that is."

"And he was not in Russia any other time?" She spoke it more as a statement than a question.

"No, not as far as his Navy records go."

"Did his ship stay long in Murmansk when he was there?"

"According to the practice at the time, although the merchant vessels went through to the docks at Murmansk, the Navy escorts stayed at the mouth of the Kola river, which was some way from Murmansk itself."

Nina took a cigarette that Witherspoon offered her and inhaled deeply. She remained silent as she watched the smoke drift up to the ceiling. She looked back at Witherspoon, "Do you think that what he did in the war explains his disappearance now?"

Witherspoon gave a hint of a smile, "I think all our past actions are a reason for our present situations."

12 January 1944

Under the grey sullen sky that hung like a blanket over Murmansk, the British battle cruiser in its grey paintwork seemed to merge into its surroundings almost completely. Ronald Boyd Cameron stood at the ship's rail watching the activity on the dock below. This was his second visit to Murmansk and as his gaze moved over the murk of the skyline his heart did not rejoice that he was here again. A Russian convoy of military trucks drove slowly along the wharf and stopped, the lead vehicle level with the gangway of Ronald's ship. At about the same time a Royal Navy escort party appeared at the top of the gangway and went down to meet the convoy's personnel. The sailors were dressed in their blue combat uniforms complete with white gaiters and were carrying Lee Enfield rifles. They quickly formed a cordon around the end of the gangway and stood guard at the first lorry as it's tailboard clanged open. For the next three hours a series of heavy boxes with rope handles were unloaded, two men to a box, and carried up into the ship.

November 1965

Nina sat in the cinema not really seeing the film at all. It was *Lawrence of Arabia* and its impact was by no means tedious but her mind was 90 per cent occupied with her recent interview with Witherspoon. She had come to the cinema straight after seeing him, somehow wanting a place that was dark and secret and where she could be hostage to her own thoughts without interruption. How was it that she was now so completely absorbed in her thoughts of Ronald? He had been in her life just two years and yet he represented now such a complete passion for her. There were, particularly, three things that dwelt in her mind about him. This apart from the neatness of his body, which if she wished to analyse, consisted of his strong forearms and large hands, narrow waist and broad shoulders. She tried to bring her mind back to the more esoteric thoughts of him but sitting in the dark of the cinema she found it to be extremely difficult. She took out another cigarette, lit it and took a deep inhalation. She must not dwell on those achingly intriguing parts of him that she missed so astonishingly badly. The appeal of him was strong to her now, as she contemplated a possible life without him. There was a nausea within her as a powerful meloncholy swept through her. How could she bear to be without that gentleness, that compassion, that obvious cherishing of her that she adored in him. Those three things that she considered to be the most desirable of gifts within a man. Yet that nagging doubt that lingered, of his omission to tell her of his Russian wife, still hurt. His letter was wonderful but she guessed there must be many things that he couldn't tell her in it. She had the feeling also that there were things that Witherspoon didn't tell her that were resounding in their absence. Again she knew that she had to be strong in her love for Ronald. It was as if this was her test of how much she really loved him. Not to doubt but to know of a certainty that he hadn't deserted her and would return. For some reason that she could never explain afterwards her mind was brought back to the film.

Lawrence had just brought back one of his party who had been left in the desert. He had gone back for him and found him half dead in the sand. To the amazement of his Arabs, Lawrence had risked his own life and the success of their expedition in order to save an apparently 'insignificant' life. In answer to the fatalistic Arab sentiment of 'it is written', he had replied, 'nothing is written'. He had demonstrated that if we believe in something no matter how hazardous, we must act. But she didn't know how to act. If there was something she could do, tangibly, something definite, she would do it. This was her problem. Her life, her motivation for life, had suddenly left her. She had been denied that life force that had been the centre of her existence for the last two years.

If she had been prepared for his disappearance she could have come to terms with it and more easily made provision for this loss. One moment he was there in her life, the next he was gone. She was ready for his absence for the trip to Russia, which was only going to last two weeks, and she was geared up for that, but now the prospect was unknown.

For two years they had been in constant communication, either on the phone, by letter or by being physically together, this all too rarely. He had become her centre. She realised with a shock that for all this time, by almost daily contact, she had talked to him, confided in him and they had shared their mutual love and affection for each other. As she sat in the darkened cinema she seemed to be staring into a dark void that had opened its malevolent emptiness within her. She was immediately appalled. The pain of this realisation of loss was immediate and despairing. How could such an essential part of herself be now gone? Her mind, which had included so much of him, now was numb, seemingly incapable of coherent thought. Surely something so basic, so important to her existence, couldn't disappear so comprehensively and so easily. She realised as she looked at the film that her vision was blurring with the tears that were now filling her eyes and flowing down her face.

November 1965

He looked across at Anna on the bed and saw the beautiful face that he'd once adored with such a passion, sunk deep in a dreamless sleep. Her long blond hair hung straight, masking her high cheek bones and framing the pale yellowing skin stretched tight over her thin face. Her mouth, which had inspired a thousand kisses, had lost its heart shape and been reduced to a thin straight line of suffering. The dark shadows under her eyes spelled out the draining of the life force within her. He held her hand, it felt cold and clammy to his touch. She stirred and the fluttering of her long eyelashes seemed to tell him of her attempt to see him.

"It's me my darling, your Ronald." He spoke softly, hardly daring to disturb the sepulchral quiet of the clinic's sick room.

January 1944

"How do we address the evil within ourselves?" The ship's chaplain was standing on a box overlooking the assembled ship's company. It was church parade on the first Sunday after they had arrived at the mouth of the Kola river.

Ronald thought about this. "What evil was there inside of himself?" In view of the obvious greater evil they were fighting in this war, what was in himself was surely of little account. It depended, he supposed, on whether this evil was answerable to anything or if it just existed on its own, independent of any force outside of itself. Was there a good that was opposite to this? If something is evil it presupposes, he thought, that there must be a positive opposed to the negative of evil. Words from the chaplain broke into his thoughts. "We will now sing 'Fight the Good Fight with All of Our Might.'"

November 1965

As the nurse came in to check and change the drip feed into Anna's arm, Ronald's thoughts returned to the first time he had seen Anna. It was on board the Royal Navy cruiser and she had come on board with about fifty other Russian sailors to perform, for the benefit of Anglo-Russian relations, a number of songs and dances. The cruiser had made available her ample hanger space below decks where a concert party could be held. Anna was playing the balalaika and in her naval uniform with her blond hair tied back, she looked, to him, the archetypal Russian beauty. Even more so because the severe nature of her uniform seemed to presage the vibrancy of her need to break out from its restraints. Ronald saw this from the first row in the audience. He could not take his eyes off of her. To him, he would acknowledge this now, with his limited experience of women, she was utterly adorable. She seemed to represent all that he would ever need in an ideal female companion, lover and friend. He was close enough to see the intense blue of her eyes, the slight moistening of her lips as she concentrated on the music. With all that he was going through in his work in the ship, the arduous nature of the voyage and the continual strain of not knowing when the next emergency would arise, the vision of this girl brought balm to the very core of his soul. In his very youth, he was only nineteen, he suddenly felt, as he looked at this girl, an immense wave of what he could only describe as home-sickness. She seemed to represent home and all that that meant in warmth and safety and comfort. All those things that he was missing now but, in fact, hadn't realised that he was missing. They were things that he longed for but had never experienced. They were an ideal that his deepest longings sought after but had failed until now to identify. If only he could meet her.

As the concert went on the need to meet her became overwhelming. The music and the dance became frenetic yet he was only conscious of her as the energy swirled around her. His gaze on her became so intense, so inviolate that only a blur of vague substance seemed to form the periphery of his vision. The clarity of her was the centre of all that he wanted to know in life. Nothing could ever again intrude on this sacred mystery of her. He felt complete, he had come home, he couldn't be hurt again now he had seen his beloved.

January 1944

When the concert was over to wild applause from the assembled ratings, Ronald noticed that she, as she bent down to pick up some music sheets, looked straight at him. As if drawn by an invisible hand, he left his seat and went over to her. He smiled and offered his hand as introduction. She smiled in return and grasped his hand and it was from that moment Ronald knew they were together. He still did not know how this happened and in some ways he didn't want to analyse it too much. He only knew he would accept it with a grateful heart.

He hadn't realised how much could be said through the eyes and through the shape and movement of the mouth. She had an amazingly open face, her expressions were immediate in their meanings and, as she looked at him, she seemed to pour love into him. Indeed, love had found its home in her and by her expression, particularly through the eyes, it flooded out to suffuse him, surround him and, he knew with a certainty, change him forever. She didn't have much English and in many ways speech would have spoiled the absolute dependence he had in watching her every movement. And to watch her was such a delight to him, he adored every gesture, every nuance of her body. She moved with a grace and fluidity that enchanted him and every one of his senses. To touch her brought to his body an ecstasy of joy. Just to rest his fingers onto hers and look into the limitless depths of her eyes gave him a view of what he imagined heaven to be like.

November 1965

As he was holding her hand and looking into her adored face, she died. It wasn't a dramatic death, only a slight sigh and she was gone. He knew it straight away. Even though her eyes weren't open something essential seemed to go from her. He discerned a slight but sudden twitch in her hand and knew that the pulse that was there a moment ago had gone. The utter sadness within him as he bowed his head seemed to find its home in his stomach and the sudden sickness at the centre of him threatened to spill out into the room. Yet nothing physical manifested itself apart from a vast emptiness that now replaced the sickness.

February 1944

It was her birthday, she was just nineteen. He looked at her naked body as she showered in the small cubicle adjacent to the bedroom. The soapy water ran over the curves of her breasts and down her thighs and buttocks. Her slim body glistened. He mused as he looked at her and worshipped the thought that he didn't need to envy the water that drenched her because he had already touched every part of her himself. He was blissfully happy as he stretched his body on the bed in that luxurious awareness of his muscles and the part they had played in the making of love to Anna. He thought of the miracle that had allowed them to be together as they were. Somehow he had been able to secure a visa from the Russian authorities to be able to have a shore posting and to be part of the Navy's contingent ashore in Murmansk, monitoring the plethora of radio signals issuing from German-occupied Norway. They had made use of every opportunity to be together, mainly through the good offices of Anna's brother, who had, with his wife, a small flat in the town. When he and his wife were working nights at the munitions factory they had been able to use the space that wasn't being used. She called from the shower, "Ronnie, please hand me the shampoo."

He arose from the bed and handed her the bottle. He watched as she poured it over her head and he reached out and began massaging it into her hair. Her hair was silky and so blond it was almost milky white in some lights. It reminded him of the golden straw colour of ripened wheat of the fields of his grandparents home in East Anglia. He poured water over her head as she closed her eyes and put her head back. He kissed her eyes and her lips and his body trembled as she took the closeness of his body into hers.

November 1965
He found the letter as he shuffled through the desk. He recognised his own writing on the envelope, it was dated January 1949. He opened it with trembling fingers and began to read the words he had written sixteen years previously.

My darling Anna,
How can I put into words how I feel about you and about our situation. We have been apart physically now for five years and there has not been a moment in those endless years when I have not thought about you. More than that, you have become the very fabric of my mind. You inhabit every one of my thought processes. I yearn for you, my body and my mind long for the touch of you. To be able to touch you and to see you has become the foremost ambition of my heart and my whole life is completely centred on you.
I wonder how you are, how you are feeling, what thoughts you have as you wake in the mornings. Do you think of me? Or am I reduced to that outside fringe of your thoughts where they no longer hurt you? I try desperately to dismiss thoughts of you to

20

that outer fringe of my mind where the torture of this love I
have for you no longer terrorises me by needing you so much.
But I cannot. You are such a part of me that it would be like
cutting half my soul away to dismiss you from me. I don't want
that sort of annihilation.

So I am determined to renew my efforts through the British
consul in Moscow to bring you out. I know that your English is
improving amazingly because of your letter. I think it was
nothing short of a miracle that the letter got to me via BAP.

The letter ended with further endearments which made his eyes fill
with tears.

First Special Administration of the KGB
Central registry for secret police agents and anti-Soviet elements
Suspects – designated potential enemies ASE-SI (svyaz s inostrantsami–connection with foreigners), one who has any personal
contacts abroad. In practice 'suspects' are often sentenced to detention in camps by Special Board without any trial.

November 1965
Nina answered the phone, it was Witherspoon. "Can you come over
to see me, I have some more information for you that might help."

Witherspoon flicked open the file. Nina noticed a certain gravitas in
his expression. He smiled briefly from the corner of his mouth.
"It seems that your friend is more involved than we first thought, we
have had a message from…" he paused and looked again at the file,
"that area and we know more about his wife."
Nina's heart gave an extra beat.
"She has spent a certain time in a detention camp," he turned over a
page. "In the late 1940s she was incarcerated in a camp in the
Siberian region."
"Why?" asked Nina. "What did she do?"
"It seems she became another statistic of the Soviet system. She was
designated as a potential enemy." Witherspoon continued to consult
his papers. "Under their 'so- called' judicial system, she was entered
as an SI 'a svyaz s inostrantsami'."

His Russian pronunciation made Nina feel eerily that there was another world that was going to intrude rather more forcibly than she perhaps wanted.

"Which means that she had 'connection with foreigners'. This, in the Soviets' eyes, means that she can be held in a camp without trial." Witherspoon looked up. "She was held apparently for five years and then released," he consulted his file, "in February 1954, just after Stalin's death."

"Why was she released then?"

"It was apparently after his iron hand had disappeared; they reviewed her case; in fact, quite a number were let out of the camps then." Witherspoon shrugged, "I can only surmise."

Nina spoke softly, "Would Ronald have known this?"

"I don't know, the information we have at present doesn't allow us to know that." He pursed his lips, "If he did, of course, then his subsequent actions could have more meaning."

"What do you mean, his subsequent actions?"

"It seems he was involved in a cultural exchange to Moscow in June 1951. It was part of a music lovers' society that had arranged a week's trip through Intourist, the Russian state travel department. This, if you remember, although you were very young at the time," he paused to give a half smile to Nina, "was when Burgess and Maclean defected to Russia. In fact, they slipped across the channel in May 1951, after their spying activities had been uncovered." He offered Nina a cigarette, she took one and he lit it for her, leaning across his desk.

She inhaled deeply. "You are not suggesting that Ronald had any connection with that?"

Witherspoon eased himself back in his chair." "You have to understand that there is a great veil of secrecy involved where Russia is concerned. At this moment we are not at all sure what was happening then, or indeed, even now."

Despite her tender years, Nina had a woman's intuition to know that she was being led into new revelations that could have far-reaching implications for her life.

Witherspoon continued, "As you know, we have been making enquiries regarding Cameron's ship's chandlers business and we discovered the other day that he has been working on a device that could be of great benefit to navy ships of many different persuasions."

"What is that?" Nina asked.

"You know that during the war he was a radio operator on destroyers and towards the end of the war new equipment was coming into the ships that benefited greatly the operating ability of these ships to find their enemies. We believe he is in the process of, shall we say, refining this equipment. However, this is all above board; he has a contract with the Admiralty to work on this. It is just," he paused, "it is just his disappearance in Russia now could be difficult in view of what he is working on."

"But you knew he was a member of the party going to Moscow last month, why didn't you advise him not to go?" Nina stubbed out her cigarette.

"For some reason," Witherspoon spoke softly, "he used an assumed name and a forged passport."

"A forged passport!" Nina tried to keep her surprise out of her voice.

"Yes, he had the passport of a certain Earnest Watts who had been his shipmate on the Russian convoys but who had subsequently been drowned when his ship was torpedoed in the Med. We traced Cameron through this connection."

Nina wondered with incredulity at the amount of time and effort Ronald must have expended to arrange all this. She was silent as the implications came rushing at her.

November 1965

The drawer in the desk yielded further evidence of Anna's life. An envelope contained photos of himself and Anna taken on board the freighter *Islay Mist*. They both looked so happy and young and the captain who had married them was smiling broadly behind them.

March 1944

Igor Morozov pressed the button on his intercom that connected to the office of his adjutant.

"Bring the file on Anna Kruglov."

The Peoples Commissariat of Internal Affaires (NKVD), which had come from the original Extraordinary Commission for Combating Counterrevolution and Sabotage (Cheka) in 1917, was bustling with activity on this late March morning in 1944 in Moscow. The snow was piling up against the windows as a bleak north wind scattered the few pedestrians crossing the vast square outside the substantial walls of the Kremlin.

An NKVD Army of Special Purpose commanded by General I.I. Maslennikov had just recently played a major role in breaking the German 'Blue Defence Line' in the Kuban and the Taman peninsula and the operations of special police were being monitored by the department. This required intense communications activity by Morozov's office and his staff were correspondingly occupied.

Although Anna Kruglov's activities were marginal compared to the need to "neutralise" the newly liberated territories, Morozov felt that his diligence over apparently minor cases had earned him a justified reputation as a candidate member of the Politburo. He saw from her file that she had been categorised as "Potential enemy ASE-SI (svyaz s inostantsami – connection with foreigners)."

April 1944

Anna sat opposite Morozov in a small room that was his office. It was a drab, uninspiring room with only a picture of Lenin on one wall to give it any colour. Like so much of Russia she thought. It had a desk in the window which overlooked Red Square. Morozov was seated with his back to the window behind the desk. The shaft of spring sunlight coming through the window shone on her face as he looked at her and he could see the anxiety in her eyes as she attempted to answer his question. She was certainly beautiful, he thought, her long blond hair framed the high cheek bones of her face and the eyes were the bluest he'd ever seen. He saw that she swallowed hard as she answered, "Comrade, I know that I did meet the man you speak of, but that was all, I have not seen him since."

Morozov looked keenly at her, "It is good, comrade, that you have not denied this, you know that what you have done is very serious. You have collaborated with an anti-Soviet element."

Anna's eyes were downcast. Morozov was pleased to see this, he knew she would be easy to manipulate.

"What, what does it mean?" she whispered.

"It means that unless you recant, you will be charged as a potential enemy, an ASE 'svyaz s inostrantsami', which as you know means connection with foreigners, one who has any personal contacts abroad." Morozov snapped his file closed with a finality that made

Anna jump.

She looked up at him from under her eyelids, "How can I recant? You already know that I have had contact."

Morozov was silent for some moments as he stared through his steel-rimmed glasses at her.

"Under the provisions of the law I am required to hold you in detention in a camp, until further notice."

Anna felt the blood draining from her face and she had to grasp the edge of the desk to prevent herself from succumbing to the faint she felt overwhelming her. By dint of a considerable effort of will she remained conscious and returned Morozov's gaze with a boldness that surprised him.

"Is there any way out?" she whispered.

Morozov turned the pages of the file before him and was silent for some time as if the studying of it would elicit some measure of comfort for the girl before him, not that he wanted to give her any comfort, that was not his job in life. He was only there to mete out threats and punishment to all those who came before him. He looked up after what to Anna seemed an endless period.

"I have a suggestion," he pursed his thin lips. "We know that you went through a marriage ceremony to this British sailor. Because he is at the moment shore-based in Murmansk and you are able to see him, we would like you to tell us what he is working on. Give us regular reports and if they are worthwhile then we will review the sentence that is hanging over you."

There was an icy dagger that was being turned slowly inside her. Its desperate pain began to permeate her whole body as her heart raced. "We will make it possible for you to have more duties cut so that you can see him more."

Anna looked down at her hands, which she was twisting in her lap. How had this happened, she thought, how could her happiness be suddenly turned into this evil thing that was now facing her? Yet she was not surprised, the history of her family had been blighted by the Soviet system of unmitigated terror and suffering. Only a decade ago the Kruglovs had been reasonably contented farmers, 'kulaks' they were called, with a system of land usage that was as efficient as the Russian weather and custom would allow. Yet Stalin had decided that a system of land reform was needed that required the uprooting of, literally, millions of peasants and land workers into collectives. Those that were surplus to the requirements of the new vast estates were sent to places like Siberia where work was found for them in the industrial monoliths that were spawned in those frozen heartlands. In the 'so-called' efficiency of this immense relocation of labour many millions died or disappeared. So much was known intimately by the families concerned and yet had not been officially revealed. The Soviet system was highly motivated in hiding any suggestion of inefficiency within its own departments. However, Stalin, with his own mysterious agenda, deemed it worthwhile to dispose of a mass of the people that didn't fit into the current thinking of the Marxist-Leninist coterie. Anna, there-fore, was not surprised that the continuing suffering of her family as kulaks should be visited upon her. She was, however, puzzled as to what to do. Her initial shock had already been replaced by that splendid essence of fatalism that was so essential to the Russian soul and its survival. She had already leap-frogged in her imagination from being so happy in her love of Ronald to a basic survival instinct of not only life without him but even to doubt whether life itself could carry on. Such was the powerful force that informed her psyche and now brought life to her at this moment. She felt instinctively that she had to somehow buy some time and that the only way to do that in this instance was to go along with the proposal and see what happens.

She looked up at Morozov, "I will do as you say."

November 1965

He knew he had only a limited time to find what he was looking for. Sergei had left him alone for a short while to buy some groceries and he continued to search the desk. It was the last letter that he had sent to Anna that he was desperate to find. It had not been with the other one written in 1949, nor with any of the others that he had from time to time written in the forlorn hope of her being able to answer. He now knew, of course, that between the end of 1949 and the middle of 1954 she had not been in a position to tell him anything because she had been incarcerated in one of the Soviet Union's 'rehabilitation' camps. How he had felt at the time, not knowing what she was going through, he didn't want to dwell on; even now the memory of his feelings brought a hurt that he found almost impossible to quantify.

He found the letter amongst a whole heap of official documents emanating from the People's Commissariat of Internal Affairs. His Russian was still not good enough to decipher the contents of these documents but it was sufficient to discern that they were up-to-date papers apparently making Anna aware that she was still involved with them.

He tucked the letter into his coat pocket as Sergei came back.

November 1965

Humphrey Lyttleton was playing his trumpet with the Colin Peters quartet in the smoky atmosphere of the north London pub. This was the upper room of the pub and it was crowded with the appreciative fraternity of the modern jazz scene. Nina and Rachel were in the corner of the room at a small table that was covered in an assembly of beer glasses in various stages of fluid levels. The music reached a crescendo and the piece finished to the applause of the crowd. During the interval the girls were able to talk together, thus avoiding the necessity to engage in conversation with various men who were eager for their attention.

"I don't understand why Ronald should have to have a forged passport," said Nina, lighting another cigarette.

"No," said Rachel, "it makes you realise that there is something more than we can expect to understand here."

"I don't think that Witherspoon has told me all that he could tell me."

Rachel looked at Nina, "But he couldn't could he? It's obvious that there are things that Ronald is involved in that shouldn't be for general consumption."

"That's exactly what worries me," said Nina, "the more I hear of what he has got involved in the more I am concerned for him."

"He told me once," Rachel took a sip of her whisky, "that he couldn't wait to finish with his work for the Admiralty."

"When did he tell you that?" enquired Nina, looking with some surprise at her friend.

"Oh, some time when you were away," Rachel replied.

Nina noted that Rachel seemed a little hasty in her reply and if the pub's lighting had been better she would have discerned a slight blush in her cheeks.

"When was I away and he was there?"

"Yes, don't you remember? It was when you had to deliver one of your essays at short notice and you couldn't get in touch with Ronnie beforehand."

"Oh, yes," said Nina, "I remember." She also noticed Rachel's familiar use of Ronnie's name and it rang a slight alarm bell in her mind. She mentally shook herself, this is ridiculous she thought, what state had she got to, to be suspicious of her dear friend and of her lover. To cover the sudden confusion within her she asked if Rachel would like another drink and got up and went to the bar.

"A beautiful girl like you shouldn't be buying your own drinks." The voice at her side emanated from one of the musicians and she recognised the drummer. "Why don't I buy those for you?"

Nina smiled sweetly, "No thanks, I'm with my friend over there." She hastily gathered up the drinks and returned to Rachel. "I don't know why but I really don't want to get involved with anyone at the moment until I know what's happening."

Rachel demurred, "Yes, I can understand."

"But when that's going to be, I have no idea," Nina sighed.

Rachel squeezed her hand, "Perhaps it won't be long."

November 1965

Ronald Cameron stood and faced the two men who had entered the flat. One was Sergei and the other he did not recognise but thought he looked a typical grey member of the KGB.

"Comrade Cameron," said the grey official, "will you come with us please? We have some questions to ask you."

He had been expecting this but did not expect Sergei to be as relaxed as he appeared to be.

They went out of the apartment building and Ronald was ushered into the waiting black Zim limousine. It sped away and Ronald was left wondering, as he sat in the back, between the two men, how the next few hours would turn out.

April 1944

Anna and Ronald lay in bed in each other's arms, their bodies replete in their satisfaction with each other. Anna was in a turmoil. How could she tell Ronald, who meant everything to her, that she was now an official spy and was going to tell everything that was of importance in his work, to her spy masters? Yet she knew she couldn't tell him. But he would soon suspect something if she got so much time off to be with him. Also, the fact that his shore leave wouldn't go on forever would surely render her usefulness to the Department null and void. How could this situation be resolved? She had a dread that it couldn't be and that she was doomed to be cast into that vast melting point of suffering that appeared to be the lot of the people of Russia since time immemorial.

She resolved to become the stoic, to call on that immense reservoir of strength that was endemic in the Russian psyche. She would use the time available to her to enjoy what she had now and to exploit every opportunity to give her masters something that would satisfy them, but at the same time not to compromise Ronald. That sounded very good in theory, she thought, but would it and could it work in practice?

November 1965

"We have just had a communication from our embassy in Moscow," Witherspoon carried the tea cups over to a table in the corner of the canteen with Nina following behind. He put the cups down and moved a chair for her to sit down.

"It seems the Russians have let it be known that they are, at the moment, interviewing a Ronald Cameron and this Ronald Cameron answers the description of ours."

A wave of immense relief flooded through Nina's whole body.

"Oh that is such good news," she said, the delight in her face obvious as she looked at Witherspoon.

"There are, however, some worrying aspects to it."

"What are they?"

"Mainly that they seem to be accusing him of being a spy." He put his hand on Nina's arm. "That is not so bad as you may at first think," he was quick to reassure her. "They very often use this charge as leverage for some other deal that they think may give them an advantage."

"What evidence do they have?"

"As far as we know at the moment, nothing. However, that, in itself, doesn't mean much."

"You mean they could fabricate anything they liked?" Nina responded.

"Exactly so. We need, at the moment, to be circumspect about all this and see what transpires. We still don't know what he was trying to achieve anyway by leaving the main party. His brother-in-law was obviously part of the conspiracy, but whether Ronald Cameron was duped by him or being helped by him, we just don't know. There is obviously a great deal we need to find out about your friend."

"How will you find out?"

"There are various things we can do, particularly to find out exactly what he was working on and whether he was vulnerable going to Russia anyway."

"Will he be in some kind of trouble here because of what he's done?"

"Look, it's too early to talk about that or indeed worry about it. The important thing is to get him safely home and then we can sort out what needs to be sorted out."

"Mr Witherspoon," said Nina, "you have been really good to me, trying to explain what is happening, and I do really appreciate it. I just think it's so strange that the person I love should be involved in some bizarre adventure in Russia without me having any idea what he is involved in, or indeed that his previous life should be so secret that I had no intimation of it."

Witherspoon gave a slight smile, "I think that what we are living through in these times is indicative of the Cold War situation. It was different during the war, we seemed to know who the enemy was more clearly and the threat was more immediate. However, now the edges seem to be blurring rather and we are not too sure about our priorities or indeed even our loyalties."

Nina looked keenly at Witherspoon, "You know that I am reading history at London?"

"Yes," he said.

"Well, in my studies of the Russian revolution I have been amazed at the way that an apparent ideology of such magnitude can so quickly become polluted by greed and by the power-hungry, evil people who take it over," she paused as if she was embarrassed by her enthusiasm. "In other words, the system quickly became corrupted, and I don't know why more people don't see it for what it is."

Witherspoon nodded, "It's the old thing about the grass always appearing greener on the other side of the fence."

"You don't think that my Ronald has been influenced by the Russian system do you?" Nina was startled by her own question.

"I am sure," replied Witherspoon, "that if he is as you say he is, a well-balanced, gentle, intelligent man, he could not be drawn into believing the Soviet lies."

Nina smiled a rueful smile, more perhaps to herself, "I must be forgiven for saying this but perhaps that's what was thought of Burgess and Maclean at the time."

"No," said Witherspoon, "you don't need to be forgiven for that because that is a very good point. It is so difficult sometimes to believe some people are capable of doing the things they do." He took another drink of his tea, "But I am sure Ronald Cameron does not come into that category."

April 1944

Ronald sat in the basement office, which was situated in a large apartment-type building. Like a lot of Russia, at least as far as Ronald had seen, first appearances were deceptive. It looked like a domestic building from the outside but, in fact, was divided up into various offices inhabited at this particular time by agencies devoted to the prosecution of the war.

If he had thought about his situation at this present time in any logical way, he would have seen that his relationship with Anna was ambivalent in the extreme. How was it that he was able to be with her for such a lot of the time? How did she manage to get so much time off from her duties at the Soviet naval barracks? How had they been so fortunate to have the use of the apartment for so many nights together? Maybe it was the mists of passion and love that were obscuring clear thinking on his part or perhaps he didn't want to think of it at all; whatever it was, he sat in the basement of this anonymous building in the middle of Murmansk doing the work he was assigned to do with a clear heart.

The department that should have made him aware of his situation was two floors above him. It was known as the First Special Administration and was the central registry for secret police agents and "anti-Soviet elements." It kept personal files on police agents, secret employees and informers. Special "register cards" contained personal data, fingerprints, recruitment particulars and all other details connected to that person's association with the police. Informer networks continually supplied the secret police with material on all persons judged worthy of police attention. Those worthy of this attention could be so rated because of their social connection, past activities, past possessions, nationality, attitude of mind or connection with foreigners. All such persons are regarded as "potential enemies" and are labelled "ASE." (antisovetskiye elementy). "Potential enemies" were classified according to their political hue. Typical hues were:

AS (Anti-Soviet element): an overall group that encompasses people criticising the Soviet regime.
Ts (tserkovnik): an active member of a church or clergyman.
S (sektant): a member of a religious sect.
P (povstanets, rebel): a person who once took part or was in any way involved in an anti-Soviet uprising.
SI (svyaz s inostrantsami – connection with foreigners): one who has any personal contacts abroad.

Although Ronald Cameron was advised by his captain that he needed to be aware of the Soviet system of control and methods of spying on foreigners, he had largely ignored the advice and, due to his obsession for Anna, had almost forgotten it. Thus, for almost two months a special "register card" had been remarkably active in the name of Anna Kruglov.

He bent over the radio set, the earphones clamped to his head; he was listening into the mass of messages that were issuing from German-occupied Norway. He twiddled the dial trying to find the particular frequency that he was searching for. He had learnt German at school and the Navy were making use of this particular skill by giving him this shore posting. How long he was going to be able to be involved in this shore posting he didn't know, he only hoped that some way could be found for him to be with Anna for as long as possible. And what happened when he had to leave? How could he part from this girl whom he loved beyond anything that he could have imagined? The clear heart that he had at the beginning of the morning was turning into an anxious enquiry in his mind. The thought of parting from Anna made him shiver in apprehension. But it had to be faced, he knew he would not be able to bring Anna out of Russia, so what was to be done? There was the most horrendous war going on, people were being killed in their thousands every day and he was worried sick about Anna and their situation. There didn't seem any comparison somehow, his little worries were as nothing compared to the suffering going on all around him.

His attention was suddenly drawn to the sounds going on through his earphones, the frequency that he had found was manifestly the one he had been seeking.

November 1965

Nina felt wretched. As she was sitting in the lecture room listening to the tutor intoning the details of the English Civil War her heart was somewhere in Russia. She needed to be with Ronnie, wherever he was she wanted to be with him, sharing whatever dangers he was facing. She couldn't even imagine his state of mind, she could only cling to his letter and the words of love that he had written to her there. Where was he at this moment? Had he found what he was looking for there? Was his wife with him? What sort of woman was she? Did he still love her? Nina sighed a deep sigh, it was almost a groan, so much so that the man sitting beside her looked at her in a concerned way. "Are you OK?" he asked.

"Yes, I'm OK, thanks," she gave a slight smile, "too much to concentrate on." She indicated to the sheaf of notes on her lap.

"Yes, it is rather prolific isn't it?" he said. "Look, can I buy you a coffee when this is finished?"

She looked at him, he was about her age, slim and, as her mother would have said, clean cut.

She didn't see why she shouldn't, so when the lecture was over she gathered up her notes and they went together to the adjacent coffee bar.

They talked about normal things and although he was a nicely presented man, certainly much smarter than the majority of male students she knew, there was no real spark to their conversation. He ended it with an offer to take her for a drink later and, much to her surprise, she accepted.

He picked her up at the front door of her college driving a rather battered, tired looking MG sports car. Although it was November, the day was not cold and the hood was down. He drove into the West End, down Oxford Street and Regents Street, and found a parking place in Wardour Street. They went into a bar near Ley Ons, the Chinese restaurant, and sat at a corner table overlooking the street. She was surprised that their conversation was much easier than it had been earlier and she found out that he was a post-graduate doing a Phd on the influence of the English Civil War on Marxist thought of the 19th century. He was aged twenty-six, born in London and his parents were living in Cheltenham. His name was Simon Clarke and she found he had a boyish charm about him that she had failed to see earlier. They got on well and it was not long before he suggested that they go for a meal at Ley Ons nearby.

How they got onto the subject of Russia, Nina was never sure, but by the time the meal arrived she had learned about his two visits to Poland and one to the Ukraine. Whether it was the rice wine or the warmth of his personality, she wasn't sure, but she soon found herself deep into telling him about Ronald. Although the facts were straight-forward her emotions weren't and the more she talked the more she could feel that she was getting to the edge of the control she tried to have over herself. The questions he asked were gentle and not intru-sive and she felt she could trust him in the replies she was giving. Eventually he said, "Do you feel that Ronald is acting on his own behalf or that he is being led in some way?"

Nina hesitated, "Do you know, I've not thought about that before, I've assumed that he was acting on his own initiative up till now." She took another sip of her wine and looked at the man opposite as if seeing him for the first time. She leaned back in her chair and felt a curious suspicion begin to rise in her breast. But where was this suspicion coming from? Was it suspicion of Ronald and his actions or was it of Simon Clarke? Although his questions were not overtly probing she felt a reluctance to hold back and had probably revealed more than she felt she should have done. She mentally shook herself. This is silly, she thought. Why do I have a feeling that I am being interrogated?

Simon Clarke smiled, "It's not surprising that you haven't thought about it before, with a man of Ronald's experience of Russia and the Russians he would be well versed in the intrigues of that place."

"But I can't even imagine that he would be involved in any attempt to be something he's not."

Nina sensed a protective instinct rising within her.

34

Even in the subdued lighting of the Chinese restaurant, Simon Clarke noticed a blush of colour come to her cheeks. Also, he couldn't help being affected by the beauty of her face. He attempted to placate her, "I'm sure that you are right, you obviously know him far better than I do. In fact, I don't know him at all. All I know of him is what you have told me."

Nina was surprised by her reaction, she had leapt to Ronald's defence, even before there was any real justification for it.

"It's OK. I think that I feel so caught up in him that I am finding it difficult to be rational about the whole affair."

"What was the last thing that you heard about him?"

Nina was about to repeat Witherspoon's last assessment of the situation when she felt a strong reluctance to do so. "Oh, that he is somewhere in Russia, we are not quite sure where."

"Are the Foreign Office being helpful in this?"

"Yes, they are doing all they can, but it is difficult for them to find out anything definite. Besides," she ended lamely, "I don't think he wants to be found."

"Believe me," said Simon Clarke, "if the Russians want to find someone in their country, they will, pretty quickly."

Nina looked at him keenly, "You seem to know an awful lot about the Russians and the way they work."

"Yes, I suppose I do."

"Have you ever had any problems in travelling in Russia?" she asked the question more in an attempt to direct the attention away from herself than in any particular interest in the answer.

To Nina, he seemed to hesitate in his reply; perhaps it was her imagination painting an over-coloured picture but it was there, nevertheless. "No, I must admit that I haven't, although I have always had to have a guide and have never been allowed to roam anywhere they didn't want me to be."

Nina felt she needed to probe a bit further and the tingle of excitement she felt as she mentioned Ronald's name was not lost on her. "Do you think, then, that Ronald is risking quite a lot in, so far, evading being found?" She almost said "being caught", but changed it at the last moment.

"I think that whatever reason he has for going AWOL must equate with the risk involved. He must think it's worth it," he said, offering her a cigarette.

"Yes, he does, I believe that. For the time that I have known him, he doesn't do anything without a good reason." She took a cigarette and he lit it for her.

"And what do you think that reason is?"

"Well, to make contact with his wife again, I think, and to try and sort out where they go from here."

"Does that mean that his wife has made contact with him again?"

"I don't know how it has happened, but I get the impression that it was through his wife's brother that it has been possible for him to see her again."

"But if the Soviets know this, and I'm sure they do, then they will find him at her home."

"Do you think that they are that interested in him?" said Nina. "After all, he is no threat to them in any way."

"I think that the very fact that he was in Russia during the war and was involved in work that could be of interest to them, means that they will be extremely diligent in finding him. As a matter of interest, do you know what sort of work he was involved in?"

"No," said Nina, "I don't, only that it had to do with signals of some sort." She gave the answer quickly without thinking about it and then realised that Simon Clarke seemed to be taking her answer with a curiously detached air. In fact, he asked for the bill in a rather peremptory manner and, after paying, escorted her out of the restaurant without asking any more questions. She offered to pay her half of the bill but he would not countenance it, saying that she was a poor penniless student and that he was delighted to have escorted such a beautiful girl out. She felt flattered and took her seat in the two-seater sports car with a sensation of warm comfort. In fact, she had not felt like this for some time, the last time when Ronald had taken her to the ballet and they had dined at the Ritz afterwards. Then she had felt cosseted and looked after and protected all in one. It was a lovely feeling and the sudden realisation of what she was missing in Ronald hit her in a wave of sadness.

He drove her back to Kingsbury and dropped her off at her flat. She invited him in but he declined, saying that he had quite a lot of work to do before the weekend. He escorted her to the front door, squeezed her hand, smiled as she thanked him for the meal and gave a wave as he roared off down the road, disappearing into the gathering gloom of the evening.

May 1944

"You are so beautiful Anna," Ronald stroked her hair and his hand traced a pattern over her eyebrows, her nose, her cheek bones, her lips. Her hair, so silky to his touch, fell over her bare shoulders and down to her breasts. He was resting on one elbow looking into the blue limitless depths of her eyes as they lay on the bed. She suddenly looked at him, those eyes that he loved so much, seemingly clouded with doubt.

"What's wrong?"

"I have to tell you something Ronnie." Her accent made the words slow and deliberate.

"What is it?"

"It is difficult."

"Take it slowly then, there is no rush I'm sure."

"You may wonder why we are able to spend this time together, so much time." She hesitated looking deep into his face with an intensity that began to disturb him.

"I have tried not to think about it," he replied, "I just want to be with you and I can't think beyond that."

"I just want to be with you too, for always... but I know it is not possible."

"What has made you say this now," he felt an emptiness begin to inhabit the very centre of him.

She sighed, took a deep breath and began to tell him about the department of the People's Commissariat of Internal Affairs and a certain Igor Morozov. When she had finished she held him in her gaze, as if by the very intensity of it she could discern his thoughts.

"You agreed to give them information then?" he spoke softly, trying to marshal his mind into some sort of coherence.

"You must see that I had no choice," replied Anna, "they would either part us now or we would have some chance of being together if I gave them some information that would satisfy them."

"Have you given them anything yet?"

"Only where you are working and the job that you have intercepting signals."

He was silent for some moments, his head resting on her breast, feeling the even motion of her breathing and trying to come to terms with as many of the implications as he could. After what, to Anna, seemed an interminable time he said, "Perhaps there is a way round this whereby we can use it to our advantage."

She twisted her body so that she could look into his face. "How?" she said.

"What is the most important thing in our lives at the moment?" He looked intently into her eyes.

She returned his gaze, "Why, to be together, of course."

"Yes, absolutely, to be together and the only way apparently is to somehow fool the NKVD that they will get something from us only if we remain together."

"They are not fools," said Anna, "they will soon know that what we give them is not worth much."

"But not if we can give them some things that will make them think, at least it will give us some time to maybe work out where we go from here."

"But you cannot give them any real information," Anna replied, "because if you did you would become a traitor to your own people."

"I know that there is a very thin dividing line and at this moment I don't know whether it is possible to do it," he paused, "but I do know one thing, that if we don't try we shall never know if the chance we have been given would work."

November 1965

The telephone rang in the flat. Rachel answered and she called out, "Nina it's for you, it's some guy called Simon." Nina took the receiver from Rachel exchanging it for a grimace of enquiry.

"Hello, yes."

"Hello, this is Simon here. Look, I've got two tickets for the Old Vic for Monday night. Would you be interested in coming? Sorry it's short notice, but it would be great if you could."

"Um, let me have a look in the diary," Nina put the phone by her side looked at Rachel, saw the slight smile of triumph in her face and put the receiver to her ear.

"Yes, that would be lovely, thank you."

"OK, that's great, I'll pick you up from college, shall we say 6pm, perhaps. We'll have a bite to eat beforehand."

"That's great," replied Nina, "what are they doing."

"Oh, it's *King Lear*, should be good. OK, see you then, bye."

May 1944

Brian Anstruther-Plowman and Ronald Cameron walked down the main dockyard road that ended up forming a T junction with the docks. Standing on the quayside one would face due east into the Kola river which ran north–south from the Kola peninsular. As they arrived there the east wind was denying the warmth of the sun on this spring day and they shivered into their Navy duffle coats as they turned into the comparative shelter of a dockside shed.

"By what you've told me, Cameron, I don't quite know how I can help. It seems the Soviets have caught your wife between the rock and the proverbial hard place." Anstruther-Plowman looked searchingly at his companion.

"I have given you some idea of how I feel about leaving Anna and since you were a witness at our wedding I wanted you to know what the situation is now. If there is some way we can be together, then I am going to grasp it with both hands."

"But you always knew that when you married a Russian girl you would have this impossible task of taking her home."

"Yes, of course, I always knew this but I suppose I was blinkered by just wanting to make her my wife and I guess that I hoped that if we were married then the Russians would allow her to leave with me."

"Perhaps when the war is over, whenever that will be, you will be able to do that."

"The trouble is I don't think I can wait."

His companion looked at Cameron and saw the set of his face and made a mental note of the number of stress cases that he had had to deal with on these Russian convoys. As medical officer on I class destroyers, the classification of stress and the reasons for it were many and varied and it manifested itself through many different channels and resulted in a variety of illnesses. Anstruther-Plowman resolved that after the war, if he survived that is, he would endeavour to formulate his experiences into a coherent pattern of stress-related case notes and, hopefully, bring a new light into a long-neglected area of medical research. However, he realised, that didn't exactly help Ronald Cameron in his dilemma now and he turned his attention back to his companion.

He put his hand on his arm. "Things generally are difficult at the moment, you know that as well as I do, but you've got to bear in mind that there are many other things going on that could change your situation very quickly."

"Yes I realise that, of course," Cameron replied, "and I know that many other people are suffering in terrible ways and that I have no right to complain at all, but it still is very personal to me."

"Yes I know it is," Plowman responded, noting a tone of exasperation in Cameron's voice.

They walked back the way they had come, Cameron saying that he had to be back on duty soon, "I suppose I could always fabricate some stories to tell Anna to pass on to her masters," he smiled a slight, what appeared to Plowman, mischievous grin.

November 1965

"So who is this Simon?" Rachel stood with her arms akimbo, leaning against the fridge door.

"Someone from college," replied Nina, noncomitally.

"Yes but someone who knows you well enough to take you out to the theatre."

"It's no big deal," responded Nina, "we went out for a meal the other night and talked about Russia, he's been there and I wanted to know all about it."

Rachel looked at her friend and knew that she was being far too quick and easy in her reply.

"Does that mean that you are putting Ronnie on hold?"

"No, of course not," replied Nina, a little hotly, thought Rachel.

"It just means that I want to try and understand a bit more about the sort of conditions that Ronald will be experiencing." Nina noticed again Rachel's familiar use of Ronald's name and wondered.

Rachel was silent and Nina looked at her and noticed an expression on her face that she couldn't identify. They had known each other since kindergarten days and although that didn't mean they should know everything about each other, in their case it probably did. They seemed to have a sixth sense that didn't operate in normal friendships and believed they knew more about each other's psyche than they did about their own.

"It's just that I'm getting tired of waking up every morning and not knowing what Ronald is going through," Nina sighed and sat down at the kitchen table and put her head in her hands. She looked up at Rachel, "And I suppose, yes, I do want a bit of attention from a guy who is not threatening and who is here and who I can touch and talk to."

"That's good," said Rachel, " I know exactly how you feel. I felt the same when Jim and I split up. I felt so lost..." she tailed off and Nina saw her eyes filling up.

"I'm so sorry," said Nina, "I didn't realise that it affected you so much, you seemed so strong about it at the time."

"That's OK. I tried to hide it as much as I could because I knew you were going through a difficult patch with Ronnie."

"But we should know each other well enough after all this time to be able to share everything that concerns us. And the difficult patch with Ronnie was when he was talking about going away on a government contract to Norway, which would have taken him away for six months."

"I never did know how you persuaded him not to go."

"I was honest with him and told him that I couldn't understand how he could leave me for such a long time. It seems everyone I've cared for in the past has left me, including my parents when they left me stranded in a remote farmhouse when I was ten years old."

"You've never told me about that before," said Rachel, "how did that happen?"

"Oh, it was when we were on holiday in Wales. It wasn't really their fault, they thought I was with a friend in the village but I wasn't and I shut myself in the house. It would have been all right but a man came knocking on the door and when there was no answer he walked around the place trying all the doors. I was terrified and hid under the bed for hours." Nina gave a wry smile, "I guess it's made me a bit frightened of being left ever since, it's silly I know."

"No, it's not silly," replied Rachel, "it doesn't seem to matter how long ago things happen, they somehow still seem very real."

"Yes, so I was able to tell Ronald about this and he made the decision not to go, quite a commitment on his part, of course, and I made it clear that I really appreciated him doing it."

"He's quite a guy," Rachel said, almost to herself.

"Yes, he is and I don't want to lose him. Whatever I can do to bring him home I will do. But I don't know what to do, that's the frustrating part."

"When are you going to see your man in Whitehall again, Witherspoon, isn't it?"

"I am not sure, he didn't say when, I think it depends on when they hear anything that is happening, they will let me know."

November 1965

Witherspoon was getting anxious. Despite all the enquiries that he had made through his department, he was still no nearer getting to grips with the character of Ronald Cameron. He had discovered a certain amount through his girlfriend but she really seemed to be in the dark about him and certainly she didn't seem to have any idea of the work he was involved in. They had pulled apart, seemingly, his flat above the chandler's store in Poole and had found nothing that was untoward. There were details of his current work for the Admiralty but they had been obtuse in the extreme in giving any further information. In fact, the very nature of their obdurate attitude released in Witherspoon a suspicion that he was reluctant to pursue in his mind because it could lead to areas he didn't want to go into. He felt there was a curiosity here. He had never come up against such a brick wall before as that which he was experiencing in his investigation of this man. It was as if, beyond a certain point, this person ceased to exist. The only concrete thing in the whole equation was Miss Robinson. She seemed to be the only flesh and blood element that made any sense. His war record was well documented, in so far as it went, the bald facts were there. He had been involved in convoy duty up to February 1944 and had then been given a shore posting in Murmansk from then to June 1944. He was then withdrawn and his ship was involved off Normandy and in the Med until the end of the war, when he was demobbed. He seemed to disappear into the ether after that until he surfaces doing a vanishing trick in Russia.

Witherspoon pondered about the Admiralty. They were so often a difficult organisation to communicate with. Depending upon the particular area they were involved in, depended their level of response.

Russia obviously came under their difficult label. Ever since the end of the war all the resources available had been motivated towards the east. The surveillance of the Russian navy had been a paramount issue and the tracing of every Soviet ship and submarine and their movements was of vital importance. The Admiralty, quite understandably, needed all the personnel who were qualified in surveillance techniques to be on board. Witherspoon guessed that Cameron was one such individual. Witherspoon wanted to know whether he had been recruited after the war but he had been unable to find out. However, their silence on the matter spoke volumes to him.

He picked up the phone and got through to the operator, "Could you get me Commander Lyons at the Admiralty please?"

November 1965

Nina sat in the stalls at the Old Vic with Simon Clarke by her side. The cast had just finished Act III and the interval curtain came down to warm applause. They got up from their seats and went with the general crush to the bar for a drink. Simon had ordered them beforehand and they were waiting for them at an allotted place in a secluded corner of the bar.

"Well, what do you think of it so far?" said Simon, as they sipped their drinks.

"Rather gory isn't it?" replied Nina.

"That last scene, yes, I agree. When you read it, that Gloucester has his eyes put out... it presents a very different picture when you actually see it happen on stage."

"It's amazing isn't it," said Nina, "how much of the play is about the treachery that exists within families. Those who are supposed to love each other, how much they say things without actually meaning the words that they are saying. Gloucester is betrayed by his son who says terrible things about his half brother and convinces his father that his brother wants him dead."

"Yes, and Gloucester believes him," interposed Simon.

"And then we have King Lear himself believing the false flattery of his two daughters, Goneril and Regan, that they love him, and not believing his other daughter, Cordelia, when she says honestly that she loves him but without the exaggerated falseness of her sisters." Nina began to warm to her theme, "He is a weak man; but he honestly loves Cordelia more than the other two, yet he can't ignore the

43

flattery that inflates his ego."

Simon smiled, "I think you are enjoying it."

"Yes I am," Nina smiled in return, "how did you guess?"

"It's amazing though isn't it how Shakespeare was able to observe the human condition and to present it to us writ large within the framework of a play that was written to entertain." Simon was about to go on when the bell went for the start of the second half. They finished their drinks and joined the throng to go back to their seats.

When the play had ended they walked back to Waterloo station and, as they got there, Simon said, "Look it's a long way back to your place. Why don't you come back to mine and we can have a time of talking more about Lear?"

Nina was surprised about the sudden nature of the proposal and was inclined straight away to decline but she hesitated and, to her own amazement, accepted.

Simon had his own flat on Tooting Common and when they arrived he escorted her upstairs to his first-floor rooms. The accommodation consisted of a sitting room, bathroom, kitchen and bedroom. They both went into the kitchen, where Simon made a pot of coffee and they took it into the sitting room. As Nina looked around he lit the gas fire and they sat on the sofa together. She was feeling very uncertain about her presence in his flat and was wondering about the move that he was likely to make regarding her staying the night.

He leaned back into the sofa and looked at her, "I think I told you that I was studying for a Phd on the Civil War in England and the affect it had on Marxist thought. Interestingly *King Lear* brings out some points that have a relevance to the subject."

She was rather thrown by his returning to their previous discussion and for a moment she was unable to reply.

"You see," he continued, apparently not worried by her lack of reaction, "a kingdom is shared out equally, but unfairly and the corruption of men bring ruin to the original idea of fair dealing."

"How does that compare, then, to the thesis that you are preparing?" Nina responded.

"To the creation of the Soviet state you mean?"

"Yes," she said.

"Well, it's pretty obvious that the original idea of a fair society within

Russia has been desperately tainted by the activities of men who have pursued their own agendas without recourse to the theory."

"Does that mean that it has failed?"

"I think so, yes. The idea of equal shares for all is a wonderful theory, but in practice doesn't work."

"Why is that?" Nina responded, she felt she needed to keep him within the framework of this intellectual exercise to give her time to respond to the inevitable question of her staying the night.

"Why is that?" he replied, echoing her question, as if mulling it over in his mind. "Well the answers are many and varied, how long have you got?"

In a rather ostentatious way, she looked at her watch, "I think I had better be going, the last train will soon be gone."

"You can't go now," he said, looking at the clock on the mantlepiece, "I'm sorry, I didn't realise the time had gone so quickly. Look you must stay here, I can't have you travelling on your own at this time of night."

Nina looked at him, she thought ingenuously, "Where do I sleep, you only have one bed?"

"You have my bed, I shall make a bed up on this sofa."

"I don't have any night things."

"I have got various bits and pieces you can use." He smiled, she thought, a seemingly artless smile. "And before you ask, I have a sister who stays occasionally, and she keeps some things here."

"In that case," responded Nina, "I shall be happy to take you up on your kind offer, but let me have the sofa, I insist."

"If you insist then I shall accede to your request." He smiled and she began to feel at ease with him; he seemed to have a way of making her feel relaxed, and for maybe the first time since Ronald disappeared, she felt a peace settle over her.

He poured out a brandy for himself and a white wine for her and sat down again by her side. She began to notice that he moved with a grace and fluidity of style that appealed to her. She saw his spare frame not as weakness but as an aesthetic quality to be admired. As she looked at him she became surprised that she hadn't noticed these merits in him before now.

"You asked me the question why did this experiment with collective possessions not work." His statement brought her out of her reverie and she nodded and said "Yes."

"As I said before there are many and varied reasons why, but the main one is that it just doesn't fit in with human nature. Humankind is basically selfish and unless it has a compelling reason to do so will not give up what it thinks is its right."

"So why, if man is so selfish, does he keep coming up with ideas that will demand a sacrifice for others to make that in all probability will never be successful?"

"Ah, that is the sixty-four-thousand dollar question," Simon responded, "if I knew the answer to that I would earn myself an awful lot of money."

"I suppose," said Nina, "it has got something to do with something or someone, higher than man, that motivates his thinking and gives him thoughts that take him beyond his own limited thought pattern."

"God, you mean?" Simon replied.

"Yes, I suppose I do mean that."

"That, of course, takes us into a whole new realm of thinking and in a very real sense divides man into two camps, those that believe in a divine being who orders our lives, and those who don't."

"What do you believe?"

He hesitated and then looked at the clock, "I believe we ought to go to bed, it's well after one o'clock and I don't know about you but I have rather a full day tomorrow."

Nina smiled, "I think you are avoiding the question, but I agree; and I think I've got two lectures in the afternoon."

"Well, hopefully, we can repeat this again. I've really enjoyed this evening. And I'm not avoiding the question, but I think it will take us a bit more than the rest of this evening offers to answer it." He smiled as well and got up from the sofa. "Look I really think you should have my bed, I'm quite happy on the sofa, it will not be the first night I have spent on it and at least I know where all the lumps are. On new acquaintance it will take you half the night to find where they all are and the rest of the night to come to terms with them."

"Thank you," said Nina, "I've really enjoyed it too and I will enjoy your bed as well."

"OK, let me show you where all the things are then."

He took her into the bedroom and showed her the items she needed for a comfortable night and then wished her good night, holding her hand briefly and then bending forward to kiss her lightly on the cheek. She bid him good night and closed the door to the bedroom.

She found a nightdress, that presumably belonged to his sister, put it on and got into bed, snuggling down into the warmth of the double bed. She lay awake for some time, aware of the faint scent that surrounded her and mindfull of his closeness because of it. The bed was soft and it seemed to caress her and it was not necessary to have a vivid imagination for her to imagine Simon's presence. He was certainly a gentleman, she thought, he had made no move on her at all and, in fact, she began to feel slightly annoyed that he hadn't. She went to sleep with a half smile on her face, for the first time for some weeks not wondering where Ronald was.

November 1965

Witherspoon looked at the calendar on his desk. It was now three weeks since Ronald Cameron had gone missing and he felt he was really no nearer to finding out anything of real importance about the man than he had been at the beginning. He now knew that he had been found by the Russians but what they were doing to him or with him he had no idea. It seemed that he had left the main party because he wanted to make contact with his wife, maybe he had achieved that, maybe not. And why, now, had he done this? Presumably the reason given in the letter to his girlfriend, that she was ill, but how true was that? And this adventure had obviously been planned for some time, otherwise why should he go under an assumed name with a false passport? The more Witherspoon pondered the more he became confused. He had other cases to consider as well but this one kept coming to the top of his list. Was it because there was a hint of espionage in this? Yet his investigation of the other agencies that could be involved drew a blank. His enquiry of his friend Commander Lyons had also confused him. Normally open and bluff and with a genuine ability to see the absurd in most things, Lyons had appeared closed and taciturn when questioned about any possible link with Cameron. This should have sent a warning alarm to Witherspoon and to an extent it did but only to a minor degree. There were many reasons why one agency would not reveal its involvement in a particular area and Witherspoon respected that. But there was something that niggled in this example and, to his discomfort, it wouldn't let him alone.

November 1965

Ronald Cameron stood before Lavrenti Shlyapnikov and, for the first time on this trip, felt a certain apprehension. The Russian motioned him to a seat on the other side of the desk and sat down opposite him. He offered him a cigarette, took one himself, lit them both and leaned back in his chair. He gazed at the Englishman through a haze of cigarette smoke and was silent for some moments. Eventually he said, "Why did you come back?"

The question was so short and immediate that it took Cameron by surprise, despite the fact that he had steeled himself to anticipate any question.

"I... I knew that my wife was ill and I needed to see her for one last time."

"So what do we do with you now?" Shlyapnikov asked.

"Hopefully, nothing," replied Cameron, "just to let me go home."

"But we can't do that can we?" Shlyapnikov responded. "You still have too much to give to us."

"What can I give that I haven't given already?"

"That is something that I need to think about, and in the meantime you will be kept here, as our guest of course, until such time that I come to a decision." Shlyapnikov pressed a button on his intercom and spoke quickly in Russian. The door opened and two soldiers appeared who stood to attention.

Shlyapnikov addressed Ronald Cameron, "Go with these men to your quarters and we will speak again in a few days."

Ronald Cameron was escorted out of the room and down the stairs to the entrance hall. From there he was taken to a waiting car, which drove out of the Kremlin across Red Square itself and deposited him after a few minutes to the front of the Metropole Hotel. He was taken into the hotel and straight up to a room on the first floor. The room was spacious and comfortable and apart from the locking of the door behind him he felt quite at home.

November 1965

"So tell me all about him." Rachel stood with her back to the gas stove and her arms folded.

It was Tuesday evening and Nina had just returned from college. Rachel noticed that she was wearing the same clothes that she had been wearing on Monday morning and her suspicions were aroused. "You didn't come home last night did you," she said accusingly.

Nina smiled at her, "You're not my mother you know."

"What's he like," she said, ignoring the jibe, "tell me all about him."

"Nothing to tell."

"Oh come now, I wasn't born yesterday. This is only the second time that you have been out with him and then you don't come home. What am I to think?"

"You can think what you like, my love, but it was all perfectly innocent. His bed was nice and soft though." Nina smiled mischievously and took delight in Rachel's shocked expression.

"It's all right, he slept on the sofa."

Rachel heaved a sigh of relief, "What a gentleman."

"Yes, he was actually," said Nina. She proceeded to tell Rachel all about the evening and how she had really enjoyed his company.

"You know I feel so relaxed when I am with him, in so short a time as well. But at the same time I feel guilty because I'm not thinking about Ronald. I feel as though I ought to be thinking of him. I'm somehow being disloyal to him by not having him on my mind all the time."

"I'm sure Ronnie would be the first to forgive you," said Rachel.

"Do you think he would? I hope so."

"Maybe you put him too much on a pedestal, he's only human after all."

"I can't believe you said that Rachel."

"Well he is, let's be honest about him for once. Look, he strung you along well enough by not telling you he was married."

Nina looked at Rachel, "But that was because he didn't want to hurt my feelings."

"He would have hurt you much more when he began to sleep with you and you then found out. Because it would have come out at some point."

"But I'm sure he would have told me when the time was right."

"And when would that have been?"

Nina opened her mouth to say something and then stopped. She was sitting at the kitchen table with her head bent forward and with her hands twisting in her lap. Rachel thought she looked such a picture of despair that she couldn't bear it and she went over to her and put her arm around her.

"Look," she said, "don't take it so much to heart, he's only an ordinary bloke after all and they are all here to break our hearts at some point anyway. Just be grateful that he hasn't done you too much harm."

Nina began to sob and the words she was trying to say just became an unintelligible jumble of sound. Rachel knelt down beside her and tried to comfort her, she put both arms around her shoulders, which were in an uncontrollable state of emotion.

Rachel wasn't sure how long Nina was in this state but the ringing of the phone brought them both back to a sense of reality and Rachel got up off her knees and answered it. She somehow knew it was going to be Simon.

"Hello, yes, she's here, do you want to speak to her... she's in the bathroom at the moment having a shower, shall I get her to ring you back... she's got your number has she.... OK. Bye."

When Rachel put the phone back, Nina had begun to dry her eyes and had given her nose a healthy blow.

"I'm sorry I don't know what came over me but I guess it's been building up for some time and it had to come out at some stage."

"That's all right," said Rachel, "I'm sorry it was me that caused it, I didn't mean to be unkind, but just to help you to maybe see something of what's happening and the effect it is having on you."

Nina, after a decent interval, rang Simon back and she agreed to see him on Saturday night to go to the cinema. He was a member of the National Film Theatre and there was a new French film that he wanted to see *The Red Balloon*. Nina had seen it advertised and she gladly accepted.

She and Rachel cooked pasta with a meat sauce and opened a bottle of red wine and sat down in a contented state. Nina felt that a weight had been lifted from her and she looked on Rachel as being the catalyst of this contentment. Rachel was happy that her friend had somehow been able to express her feelings in the way she had and an anxiety that had persisted for some time in Rachel's heart was slightly relieved. But she knew, only slightly.

As the evening went on they both settled into the various chores that they had to do to keep the flat running in as tidy a state as possible. One of the few bones of contention that Nina was always aware of with Rachel was in the area of the washing machine. Rachel always seemed to be able to mix up their underwear to a remarkable degree and this evening seemed no different. Nina was missing a particular pair of knickers that Ronald had bought her and she knew that they had been in the wash two days ago, but they were nowhere to be seen in the fresh clean pile that she took out of the machine. She knew where they would be and she went straight to Rachel's underwear drawer. She normally didn't take such drastic action but she felt particularly aggrieved this time. She opened the drawer and begun to rummage amongst the items of clothing. There they were sure enough and as she was about to take them out she noticed a parti-cular card that had a lovely design of yellow roses on the front. Nina herself loved yellow roses and these were especially beautiful. She idly opened it, wondering who had sent this to Rachel. She recognised Ronald's handwriting immediately and the words written in the card hit her with a devastating immediacy.

"My dearest Rachel, thank you for last night, it was the most wond-erful night of my life and I now know I love you with a passion that I find so difficult to express except when I am with you. Till tomorrow, adieu. Your Ronnie, forever."

May 1944

"My beloved Anna, I think it is time for us to begin to give to your masters some information that will satisfy them." They were sitting at the table that occupied the centre of the kitchen cum living room. The room measured about fifteen foot square and was the biggest room in the apartment. They were alone in the flat, as they normally were, Anna's brother and his wife were still both working nights at the armaments factory.

"You can give them this." He pushed across a piece of paper with some diagrams and figures on it. "It's the latest wavelengths that the Germans are using for the operation of their submarines in the Barents Sea."

Anna looked at it and she gave a slight smile, "So this is our passport for staying together is it?"

"Yes, I think at least it will give us some extra time, which must be good."

Anna sighed, "Yes, it must be, but is not this information valuable to your people too?"

"Yes, of course, and we are using it to good effect, so there is no reason why it can't be used by our allies too."

"But do your people know that you are doing this?"

"No, of course not, but there is nothing that will harm my country by me giving away this information."

"Are you sure, I don't want you to get into any trouble."

"Darling," he took both her hands in his and looked into her eyes. "I can see that this troubles you, but please don't worry, I believe that this will work out. Don't ask me how but I have this feeling that all things will be good for us."

"If you are sure, then I will not worry."

He put his hands on either side of her face and held her, gazing into those wonderful eyes that promised so much of heaven. He believed he had found a paradise with her and, remembering his Sunday school days, he identified with the story of the garden of Eden, when the perfect state of grace had existed between a man and a woman. He knew he was in this state now and the promises that existed between himself and Anna would come to fruition.

November 1965

Nina sat on the edge of the bed, her hands holding the card. She continued to stare at the words, trying to find something in them that she could understand, but no understanding came. The implications seemed to be beyond her comprehension. She hadn't got to the stage of asking why or how, those questions were some way ahead. All she could cope with at the moment was, this can't be happening to me. She got to her feet and walked in a daze into the kitchen. Rachel was there, leafing through a recipe book. Nina put the card down in front of her. She saw Rachel's eyes go down to the card and immediately up to Nina's face. She saw the sudden look of panic that was in Rachel's expression. Nina continued to look at her, unable to utter a word.

"I was going to tell you... I was going to tell you." Rachel's voice rose higher as the words came out, "But I kept putting it off because of what has happened."

Nina felt empty and weak and she had to sit down, her lips moved but no words came out, her mouth felt dry and she tried to moisten her lips but no saliva was there. Rachel sat down opposite her, "I am so sorry, I would have given anything for this not to have happened between us."

Nina looked up and Rachel saw an expression in her face that she never wished to see ever again. It was one of despair mixed with a hatred that was completely alien to Nina's nature. It was as if she had been taken over by something evil, something that was out to destroy. It didn't last long, as Rachel looked it seemed to ebb and flow in intensity and then after a few more moments it had gone, leaving only such a look of sadness that it made Rachel begin to sob in sorrow. Her tears fell and her vision blurred but she saw that Nina was crying too. They put their heads together as if in mutual comfort and their tears mingled until one could not tell who's tears were who's.

November 1965

The non-proliferation treaty was signed between the two super powers of America and Russia in 1963. This was as a result of the testing of a hydrogen bomb within the confines of Russia in 1961. The bomb was of such immensity and power that the effect of it produced shock waves of realism into the most rabid of warmongers from both sides. The end of civilisation was surely staring the whole world in the face.

Witherspoon was reading a leader from one of the annual review magazines of a year ago. It was the end of a long day of frustration for him. He had been endeavouring to pursue why Ronald Cameron had done what he had done. On first acquaintance with Cameron's disappearance from the train going to Russia he had thought that he had been just another tourist who had been careless. But the more he delved into the facts of the case the more he became convinced that Cameron's actions had a definite motive behind them. More than that, he was coming to the conclusion that his actions were nefarious. But how nefarious? He seemed to have drawn a blank with the services and agencies who may have been involved. That in itself was not surprising but the manner of the blank was curious because the people he had questioned were forthright in their instant rejection of any connection with Cameron. It was as if they knew that an enquiry was taking place but that they had already been briefed not to divulge any information. He read once again the transcript of his interviews with Miss Robinson. As he turned over the second page a name seemed to leap out of the page at him, Brian Anstruther-Plowman. Not a common name, therefore it may be reasonably easy to trace, he mused. He reached for the telephone. "Can you send Barbara in please?"

A middle-aged woman came in whose rather austere appearance masked a sense of humour and joy in life that made a mockery of those who judged by appearances. "Barbara, I know you are the wizard of the records office. I would like you please to find someone for me. It may not be easy, in fact it may be darned difficult, but I know if any one can find this person it will be you."

He gave her the facts, such as they were, and told her, as it was late, that she could start in the morning. She smiled and took the relevant details and left the room. Witherspoon sighed and leaned back in his chair and lit another cigarette. The smoke, as it drifted to the ceiling, seemed to describe the will-o'-the-wisp investigation that he was embroiled in, very little substance and nothing at the end of it.

November 1965

"It was when you were away at your parents that weekend. I honestly don't know how it happened... it just did. I had just finished with Jim and I suppose I was feeling vulnerable... and Ronnie was there... supporting me." They were both sitting on the bed, Rachel sitting upright and staring into the middle distance and Nina with her head downcast, looking at her hands in her lap as they were entwined in a handkerchief.

Nina was silent and, in fact, had not said anything since she had confronted Rachel.

"He was so gentle and kind and I was crying rather a lot," Rachel continued, wanting to unburden herself as soon as she could; she had been too long keeping this secret to herself.

"He just held me and I found such comfort from that... then he began kissing me and it just went on from there..." she tailed off and glanced sideways at Nina.

"How... how do you feel about him now?" Nina spoke for the first time, hesitantly and still looking into her lap.

Rachel felt a relief that Nina had at last spoken. "I don't quite know... I think that I don't understand much about loyalty and... love, I thought I did but this has really turned me upside down."

Nina looked up, her eyes appealing to Rachel to give her the right answer. "Do you love him?"

As she asked the question Rachel knew straight away that whatever answer she gave would not comfort Nina.

"I don't think I can answer, because I don't think I know," Rachel knew it was unsatisfactory to answer like that, but she needed time to consider. Not that she hadn't thought about it to the exhaustion of her mind. Ever since it had happened she had thought of nothing else.

"Surely you must have some idea," Nina said quietly.

"If the measure of love depends on the amount of time you think about the person, then yes, I must love him..." she paused, "but honestly I am getting to the stage where the anguish that I have felt is becoming boring... because he is not here to feed the feelings, the desire for him is going." Rachel tried to touch Nina's hand but she withdrew it.

"That doesn't apply with me," Nina spoke coldly.

"Then that must mean..." Rachel tried to choose her words as carefully as she could, "that he means far more to you than he does to me." Nina gave a sigh, "But that doesn't mean that he loves me... or you."

"You mustn't think like that," Rachel reached for Nina's hand again and this time was successful, "all the time that I was with him he only talked about you."

The cold look returned to Nina's face, "Even when you were making love?"

"I didn't mean it like that," said Rachel, "but I felt in some strange way that he was completely obsessed with you."

"How could you tell?" Nina responded.

"I could tell by the way so much of our normal conversation was about you. He was worried about you."

"Why was he worried?"

"I couldn't tell why he was worried. He just seemed to be preoccupied with you. It was as if he couldn't motivate his own thoughts unless he had taken your feelings into account."

"Can you tell me if there was any particular instance of him being concerned for me?"

Rachel thought for a moment, "Yes, there was one thing that stuck in my mind."

"What was that?"

"He called you Anna."

"Anna... but that was the name of his Russian wife, why should he call me by her name?"

"Perhaps he was seeing you as her."

Nina got up from the bed, went to the dressing table and took a cigarette from the packet. She offered one to Rachel, who declined, and lit one for herself. She walked to the window and looked out, "Maybe he was worried for Anna and somehow transferred that worry to me," she spoke almost to herself and Rachel had to strain to hear the words.

"He didn't talk about Anna to me, the first I knew of her was when you told me that he'd mentioned her in the letter," said Rachel, "when he said her name it didn't mean anything to me then."

"Did he talk about his previous life at all to you?" Nina turned and looked at Rachel.

"No, not at all, except..."

"Except what?"

"Well, it may be nothing, but..." Rachel paused as if considering the implications, "I saw a photograph in his wallet, in fact, it fell out of his wallet when he was putting his coat on. He hadn't realised that he had dropped it and I picked it up for him. It was a picture of him, looking quite a bit younger, with a blond girl. In fact at first I thought it was you, but then I saw that the photo itself was showing its age, it was wrinkled and in black and white. I only had a few moments to look at it, because as I held it out to him he almost snatched it out of my hand."

"You say she looked like me."

"Yes... and in black and white her hair looked almost white and it was long like yours is now, down to your shoulders. She had the full lips, as you do, her eyebrows were particularly fine and arched, as yours are, and she had the fine cheek bones that could have been yours."

"Did she look happy?"

"Yes she did, but not just happy, somehow... serene."

"It must be why he said he loved me, because I reminded him of her."
Nina said the words slowly and deliberately as if she had become
detached from the meaning of them and that she was trying to
understand the words at the same time. Rachel sensed that Nina's
struggle was only just starting.

Nina looked down at Rachel with an intensity that startled her.
"That must be why we never made love... I believe he felt that we
would truly have been doing something very wrong. He would have
somehow imagined that she would have been standing there
watching him perform on me and knowing what he was doing. It was
as if there was a mirror in the bedroom direct to her."
Rachel was appalled.

Nina went on, "Yes... that explains so many things that I didn't understand about him. Sometimes at night, when I wanted to get close to
him, I would try and encourage him to make love to me, but he
always made an excuse of some sort and it always stopped before
anything happened. I began to think that there was something the
matter with me."

"Did he ever say what was the matter?"

"No, not really... he said things like, so many couples don't have the
intimacy of mind and soul that we have and that we were much
closer than so many others. And in a way I understood that... but at
the back of my mind I knew that what we had was not sufficient."

"Did that hurt you?"

"Yes, of course it did," Nina said crossly, "I always wanted a full relationship, almost from the beginning I needed him."

"He must have known this and the effect it was having on you."

"I don't know whether he did... I suppose it was partly my fault, we
never really talked about it... we should have done... perhaps it was
because he was that much older than me... I felt a bit inhibited by
him... he had had so much more experience of life that I felt he must
know best... and I didn't want to question his authority."

"That's a strange word to use between lovers... authority," Rachel
interposed. She continued, "I hesitate to say this Nina, but we're
talking honestly now... did you look on him more as a father figure
than a lover?"

"No, absolutely not. I yearned for him as only a lover can long for
their beloved." Nina flushed with indignation, "The very idea of that

is preposterous."

"I'm sorry I had to ask, I needed to hear you say it though."

"That's all right," said Nina, "I suppose I shouldn't be getting so heated about it but I really began to think that there was something wrong with him, physically, I mean. He kept himself in check so much when we were close together."

"But you could feel whether he was aroused or not... I suppose," Rachel hesitated.

Nina paused. "I wasn't sure, somehow he never let me get that close to him... I know that's quite an admission... but thinking about it... now you've posed the question... I didn't really know."

They were quiet for some minutes, each thinking about their own involvement with the same man. Nina broke the silence and, looking directly at Rachel, said, "I now know that there was nothing wrong with him physically."

Rachel blushed. "Yes," she answered. "I'm sorry."

November 1965

Barbara came into the office, bearing a sheaf of papers. She put them in front of her boss and left the room. Witherspoon began to read. The first page was headed by the name Brian Anstruther-Plowman and detailed his history, from his place of birth to his service in the Navy as a medical officer serving on destroyers and later on a shore posting in Brussels after the war. He was attached to NATO when that was formed and latterly was back in the UK doing time as a humble general practitioner in a practice near Poole in Dorset. He had written a number of papers which had been printed in various medical journals, chiefly on the subject of stress, particularly in reference to war-related experiences.

As Witherspoon read the details there was one word which leapt out of the page at him; that word was Poole. He reached for the phone and asked for the number of the clinic in Poole and was put straight through to the receptionist there. He enquired whether Dr Anstruther-Plowman was available and when told he was, he was put through. A measured, cultivated voice greeted him on the other end of the phone. "Doctor Anstruther-Plowman, this is Clive Witherspoon of department H at the Foreign Office. I hope you don't mind just answering a few questions about someone that you knew during the war?"

The answer was in the affirmative and Witherspoon continued, "It's a man called Ronald Cameron, I believe you were with him for a time in Russia."

"Yes."

"I'm trying to find out something about him that would help in the enquiries we are making at the moment."

"Yes, what particularly?"

"Well, he was on a recent trip to Russia and, in short, he disappeared from the main party but has been picked up by the Soviets and is being held by them as we speak."

There was silence at the other end.

"Doctor, are you there?" said Witherspoon.

"Yes, I'm here... Look, I think it might be better if we talk face to face. I'm willing to come up to see you. In fact, I'm due to give a paper in London at the end of the week. Would it be convenient if I see you on Friday?"

"Yes, of course," replied Witherspoon, "are you sure you don't mind. It would be very good of you. To be honest we are a bit worried about him and it may be that you can be of great service to us... and to him as well."

"Of course, if I can help then I would be happy to do so."

May 1944

"I'm sorry I'm late my darling," Ronald Cameron came into the apartment and immediately embraced Anna, "but we had a bit of a flap on and I had to stay to sort some things out."

She returned his kisses and said, "It is so good to see you, I need you so much."

He saw that she seemed to be upset about something, "What is it, what's the matter?"

She clung to him, "I gave the information that you told me to give to Morozov and he said they already had that and they expected better things from me."

"OK don't worry," he kissed her again and took her face in his hands; he kissed her eyes and forehead and lips. "We shall just have to give him something that he doesn't know anything about in future."

"But I am worried," her beautiful eyes looked imploringly at him, searching his face as if to convince him by her very intensity that she was serious.

"I love you and we will get through this together my beloved." He continued to hold her.

"I believe nothing can stop us from being together... look how far we have come already."

Anna sighed, "I know, but for how much longer?"

"We agreed that we must take one day at a time and enjoy that day." He took her hand and led her over to the divan, they sat down together and became entwined in each others arms.

November 1965

Nina was confused. She sat in the cinema with Simon watching The *Red Balloon* but her thoughts were far away. The emotional turmoil of a few nights ago when she had confronted Rachel seemed a long way away. It was as if she had always had this dull ache within her. How could Ronald have betrayed her so convincingly? What value could she put on his words of love now? She also had this uncomfortable feeling that if she confronted Ronald with this accusation he would rationalise it by saying something like, "What we had together was something far more important than mere sex." And if she had been with him, when he said this, he would have convinced her, she would have believed him. And she would be the one to feel guilty, because she had doubted him. Such was the hold that he had over her. Sitting in the cinema, with her mind so full of conflicting emotions she even saw Ronald as a Svengali-type figure, one who manipulated and directed according to his own will.

The film ended and they left the cinema, Simon holding her hand as they crossed the road. She felt a spasm of excitement as he held her hand and she wanted to keep holding it when he released her on the other side of the road.

November 1965

Witherspoon greeted Dr Anstruther-Plowman as he was shown into the office.

"So good of you to come," they shook hands and he was ushered to a seat. His appearance linked with his voice to a remarkable degree, Witherspoon thought, as he offered him a cigarette. He was tall and aquiline in features, and, as he took a cigarette, his hands, he noted, had long sensitive fingers.

"You were giving a paper today you said," continued Witherspoon.

"Yes, at the London Hospital."

"On what subject?"

"On stress, chiefly that caused by war."

"A fecund subject I would think," responded Witherspoon.

"Yes, it seems to be," replied the doctor

"Does this naturally lead on to the subject of Ronald Cameron?" Witherspoon asked.

"It could do, certainly, although I don't think he was a candidate for that particular ailment."

"Was he a candidate for any other?"

"Apart from seasickness, no."

"Did you see a lot of him?"

"We served on the same ship for some of the time and, of course, I did see him from time to time."

Witherspoon took a draw on his cigarette, "I suppose I really need to know about his work, as much as you can tell me, of course, but also about his marriage to the Russian girl."

"Ah, Anna, yes... a beautiful girl. They seemed very much in love, there was no doubt about that."

"But it was doomed from the start, wasn't it?"

"Well, we can never tell in life, can we? If we don't take the opportunity when it occurs we would never know if it was going to work out."

"That is true, of course, but the odds against them were pretty significant weren't they?"

"Yes they were," replied the doctor, "but certainly it didn't seem to deter them. He obtained a shore posting and they were able to stay in a small apartment rented to her brother and his wife in Murmansk itself."

"How were they married?"

"By a friendly captain of one of the freighters that we had been escorting. Ronald Cameron had met him in a bar that was frequented by sailors and struck up a friendship with him. Quite frankly I don't think it would have mattered if they hadn't got married, they would still have made a life together. They seemed to possess that great quality, not given to many of us, alas, of finding the true love of one's life, of knowing it immediately and acting on it with purpose."

"How was the marriage viewed by the Navy?"

"As far as I can ascertain, it was unofficial. The captain of Cameron's ship was a Commander Franklin and whether he was approached by Cameron or not I'm not sure. For a number of reasons Cameron didn't want me to divulge the liaison with a Russian girl and because I wasn't required to, I didn't. You must understand the conditions under which we were operating. Although naval discipline was never knowingly compromised, there were certain conditions which allowed Nelson's blind eye to be used. Franklin operated an efficient, happy ship and his allowing of the shore posting for Cameron was certainly, shall we say, fortuitous."

"Yes I see," said Witherspoon.

"Cameron was in the happy position, as radio operator, to be used ashore as part of the Navy contingent there."

"Do you know if Cameron, in view of his peculiar position with his wife, was ever tempted to, shall we say, help the Russians?"

"In what way do you mean, help?" Anstruther-Plowman responded.

"I mean, to pass on information that the Russians could use in their fight against the common enemy."

"Why do you ask that?"

"It's because of the way he has gone missing. At first I thought it was just another tourist who had been silly, but the more we have looked at Cameron's past and his involvement with Russia and the nature of his work, we are coming to conclusions that could be uncomfortable."

"I must confess, then, that I did have one conversation with him that may throw some light on this," the doctor continued. "He had found out that his wife had been directed by the Soviets to find out as much as she could about Cameron and his work. She was, apparently, under duress to find out information that could be useful to them. Under the typical Russian system she had been persuaded to comply otherwise dire circumstances would befall her or her family."

"What was his reaction to this?"

"As you can imagine, he was very troubled by it. However, he also seemed to see it as an opportunity to, maybe, use the system to his advantage."

"How do you mean?"

"Well, I shall always remember his passing remark to me."

"What was that?"

"He said that he could always fabricate some information to pass on. He said it half jokingly but I have never been sure."

Witherspoon reached for the intercom and asked for some coffee to be sent in. He leaned back in the chair and offered another cigarette to Anstruther-Plowman. "Were you aware of the work that he was doing ashore?"

"As far as I know it was an extension of the work he was doing on board ship; he was a radio operator and his business was tracing all radio messages coming out of the German-held territories. Obviously the transmissions from Norway were important, which is why there was quite a contingent of Royal Navy personnel involved in the area."

"Do you know how important the work was?"

"Very; a technician of Cameron's calibre was essential and his work was highly regarded."

"When was the last time you saw him?"

"I think it was in July' 44, he was recalled back to his ship and as far as I know he sailed back to England on the next convoy."

"Wasn't that a bit abrupt?"

"Not necessarily, we had a constant transfer of personnel, it depended on how quickly visas could be arranged with the Russians and how well we could rotate the men."

Witherspoon looked at his watch. "Look, if you have time shall we break for some lunch and continue talking over a steak sandwich?"

Anstruther-Plowman seemed happy to do so and, in fact, assured Witherspoon that his work in London was done for the day and as he was staying overnight he was at his disposal for the rest of the day. They left the building and caught a taxi to the Cheshire Cheese pub in Fleet Street.

July 1944

"My darling Anna, there is no easy way to say this," he held her close, his heart with a heavy dread paining in his chest; he had been home for about an hour trying to pluck up the courage to say some terrible words. "I have been recalled to my ship."

She continued to bury her head in his chest and he felt no discernible change in her position. He began to wonder if she had

63

heard him, when a sob broke the silence of their pain. He wasn't sure whether it came from her or from himself, such was the closeness of their sorrow.

November 1965

Over lunch Witherspoon determined to get the most out of Anstruther-Plowman. They had a robust meal of steak, done to a turn, followed by Welsh rarebit, with a Rioja and port to mellow their conversation.

"Do you know where Cameron was posted to when his ship arrived back in the UK?"

"Yes I do... but if I say to you that some of Cameron's work is classified, will you try and be a trifle circumspect with your questions?" He smiled out of the corner of his mouth as he said this and Witherspoon was not sure whether his persistence had suddenly paid off.

"You see," the doctor continued, "he was brought back because of his trade in the Navy. You must remember that the V1 flying bomb had started falling on London and every available resource was being used to counter the devastation it was causing, including the important work of radio frequency and whether jamming in some way could be used."

"May I ask how you know so much about him?"

"I was attached to Naval Intelligence during this period of the war and therefore had charge of a section that was dealing with the effective jamming of German frequencies, particularly where their U boats were concerned."

"Was Cameron's role merely passive or did he have, shall we say, a more creative job?"

"I can only say that he was at some stage brought to the Admiralty and used in a certain capacity there. You will have to draw your own conclusions."

Witherspoon took another sip of port, "What you have been telling me has certainly confirmed my feelings about Cameron and that his presence in Russia at this time is no mere coincidence."

"Yes, ever since you phoned me I have been applying my mind to this too. And when you told me that he was going to visit his wife, I have had alarm bells ringing."

"Do you know how much communication he has had with his wife over the years."

"No, I lost touch with him after the war, although for some reason that I have never been able to fathom, he sent me a postcard from Poole, about two years ago. It didn't say anything much, just commonplace things if I remember. I didn't keep the card, so I can't give you any more insight into that."

Witherspoon paid the bill and they went out into the bustle of midday Fleet Street. What he had learned from Anstruther-Plowman had certainly helped to fill in gaps in his knowledge of Cameron and he wondered if he needed to go any further. However, as he said goodbye to the doctor and put him in a taxi to take him to Paddington station, he had a distinct feeling that his association with Cameron was not at an end.

August 1944

Ronald Cameron ducked through the tunnel of sandbags that gave some measure of protection to the front of the Admiralty and went into the building. A 'doodle-bug' had just exploded not far away and the ringing of an ambulance bell heralded the arrival of help for the wounded. The dead, how many they were, were beyond medical help. Ever since he had arrived in London there had been constant emergencies with V1 rockets, fired from France, exploding indiscriminately on all parts of the capital.

The sense of a siege mentality was now prevalent everywhere and people were becoming wearily accepting of the situation. The first rocket had landed on London on 13 June at Bethnal Green. Since then they were coming over in their hundreds every day. Quite a number had been shot down by fighters and by anti-aircraft fire but far too many were still getting through.

Although he had experienced the blitz on London before he was called up, and that was bad enough, he had thought that coming back from hazardous voyages on the Russian convoys would give him some peace. He was sadly mistaken. The amount of time that he had been under fire on board ship, for nearly a year, was minimal compared to the few days that he had spent in London. Whereas there was a constant fear about something nasty about to happen on convoy duty, and for 99 per cent of the time nothing did; in London there was a constant awareness that it was highly likely that something horrible could happen. The trouble was that there was very little warning about a 'doodle-bug' attack; you heard the engine, and in so short an acquaintance he was learning to dread the sound. Whilst you heard the engine you knew you were all right, but once the engine cut out, and it was overhead, you dived to the ground, particularly so if the bomb was in cloud and you had no idea where it was. Quite a few times he had had to join complete strangers on the ground and wait for the explosion before dusting himself down, in an embarrassed fashion, and continuing on his way, rejoicing that it wasn't him this time but some other poor creature. It became a time, in a sense, when he felt guilty to have survived when others, so close, hadn't.

And thinking about feeling guilty drew him again into the situation of Anna. That he had to leave her was bad enough, the prospect of never seeing her again was even worse but it was compounded by the way they had to say goodbye. He knew it was folly at the time but he knew he had to try it. He had suggested to Anna that he would attempt to smuggle her on board one of the ships of the convoy and bring her back to England. She had, first of all, agreed but thinking about it she knew it was impossible. She knew that if she disappeared in this way her family would reap the whirlwind of the wrath of the Soviets. So their parting had an added pathos to it. He knew he had to be reconciled to the fact of this parting but knew he never could be. In some curious way he also knew that this wasn't the end of the story, how it was going to turn out, he had no idea, but there was a tiny grain of hope alive in his heart, and it was this that gave him comfort.

September 1944

"As you know our armies are racing through enemy occupied Europe, north eastwards particularly, and we have been able to overrun many of the missile launching sites," the Intelligence officer stood on the stage addressing about one hundred persons seated before him, "but there are still a few around the Hook of Holland."

Ronald Cameron was intrigued by the mixture of service personnel that were attending this meeting. There appeared to be all ages present, all ranks, of which he felt one of the lowest, and all three services represented. The official giving the briefing was young himself, under thirty certainly and, judging by his authority, of elevated rank.

"The operation going on at the moment, known as 'Market Garden', is an attempt to cross the two rivers, the Scheldt and the Rhine, in double-quick time. One of the main objectives will be to reach the Hook of Holland area before many more rockets are fired on London. You, of course, are here because you are all involved, in one way or another, with the attempt to frustrate the successful bombardment by these rockets."

Ronald Cameron knew why he was here. It was his expertise as a radio operator and as a German speaker that was allowing him to be involved in these momentous events that were unfolding. By dint of successful intelligence work and the bravery of partisan groups in occupied Europe many secrets had been revealed about the rockets that were now raining down on London. And if they hadn't found out what they had, the effect on London would have been truly appalling. The general public, of course, didn't know of the immense amount of work that had been going on behind the scenes. They were only aware of the bombs that were falling and cursed them accordingly.

His work was involved mainly in the radio transmissions that the Germans were using and the frequency that they were operating in. Having found their wavelength he then endeavoured to intercept or to distort the messages involved. Originally he was working in the maritime section but he had been transferred to the work on the rockets, as this was deemed to be the priority now. In fact, his department was trying to develop a system for the jamming of the wavelengths that were being used in the flight of the rockets. In some cases the rockets were guided along radio beams which had been preset to the target of London. If a way could be found to bend the beams then a whole new scenario would become apparent. There was so much going on within the various departments that it was sometimes difficult not to duplicate some of the work. In fact, the coordination of the work was becoming more and more vital and Cameron was sometimes frustrated by the amount of reports that had to be written to placate all the interested parties.

Because of the workload, by the end of his shift each day he was so tired he could hardly drag himself down to his bed in the basement. He shared this accommodation with ten others who were working within the same section and after three weeks he was feeling a kinship with them, although it was still only on a surface level. In another part of the same building there was a section of the Women's Royal Naval Service and there was one girl who, if he hadn't left her in Russia, he would have sworn was Anna, whom he was working alongside for a lot of the time. Her name was Shirley and after the initial shock of her appearance he began to see that there were things about her that were not at all similar to Anna. Although her physical appearance, in detail, was the same long blond hair, high cheek bones, blue eyes, her character was entirely different. She had a bubbly effervescence that permeated all her actions. He could never imagine her getting into a panic over anything, she had an unflappable composure that remained serene through all the trials and tribulations that the inhabitants of London were putting up with at this time. She had parents who lived in north London and, although she could have lived at home with them, she wanted to be on top of her work and so was billeted within the Admiralty buildings for some of the time. Because of the attraction that he naturally felt towards her he asked her out one evening and was pleased when she agreed straight away. They went to a pub just off Piccadilly Circus and sat in a corner of the crowded bar, wedged onto two bar stools. He was curiously aware of their knees touching as they talked. She was remarkably easy to talk to and he felt immediately at home with her. He was conscious of how attractive she looked in her WRNS uniform and the men around seemed to be aware also, judging by their bold glances.

"So do you have any brothers or sisters?" he asked, offering her a cigarette.

"Yes I have a brother, Alan, who is eight years older than me. He is in the Fleet Air Arm. How about you?"

"No, I am an only child; my parents also live in north London, Highgate."

"Well, mine live in Harringay, that's not far at all." She seemed excited about this and he delighted in her youthful enthusiasm.

"You were on the Russian convoys, weren't you?"

"Yes, I did two voyages and then I had a shore posting in Murmansk for a time."

"That must have been a difficult time."

"It had its moments," he said laconically. He was resolved not to tell her about any of his time there and as he said the words a dreadful pain went across his chest and for a few moments seemed to restrict his breathing. "Look, how about catching a film, they are showing *People Like Us* down the road here and if we finish our drinks sharpish we will catch the last performance."

"All right," she said, finishing up the last of her wine. As she swung her legs off the bar stool he saw a delightful glimpse of the inside of her thighs and the thought he suddenly had disturbed him greatly.

As they sat in the cinema, he realised that they were sitting in the back row. This had not been by design, but the cinema was crowded and they were shown to their seats by the usherette; the dim glow of her torch had not been enough to elucidate their position. The second feature was just starting and as with most 'B' pictures it was not too much of a problem if the first few scenes were missed. They settled into their seats and he passed her a cigarette; she took it and he lit it for her. During the film, which was a nondescript detective thriller, he was aware of her nearness and within a short time it seemed so natural to touch hands, by accident, of course. They were soon holding hands and by the time that the main feature started he had his arm around her. She didn't seem to mind and in fact, he felt, she seemed to initiate it.

The film was about girls, from different backgrounds, being called up to "do their bit" and although optimistic and patriotic it was done well and the suffering of the nation was well portrayed. They came out at the end of the performance feeling that they belonged to a nation that was determined and willing to endure unimaginable hardships in order to protect the way of life that centred, chiefly, around the family unit. A nation that professed the rule of law and freedom of the individual to express his views without fear.

"Well, what did you think of that?" he asked, as they walked hand in hand down Piccadilly.

"I thought it was nice," she said, holding his hand tightly as they crossed the road.

"I'm sorry it wasn't *People Like Us*, it must have been last week they were showing that." He enjoyed the feel of her hand in his and it surprised him that he seemed to have forgotten so quickly the missing of Anna.

"I thought *The Gentle Sex* was lovely, you couldn't have picked a nicer film for me to see."

"Yes, it was good, and I saw that it was directed by Leslie Howard – must have been his last film, he was killed shortly after that."

"Oh, was it?" she said. "I didn't notice that. There are so many bad things happening, I can't keep up with it I'm afraid."

"No, I know," he tightened his grip on her hand. "But who did you like best in the film," he said, endeavouring to lighten the mood.

"I think the girl who was very much the snooty one to start with and who comes through to seeing herself in a very different light at the end. She sees that we are all together in this war and we've all got to make the best of it."

"Yes, that's a good part she played, but I liked Lilli Palmer and Joan Greenwood, simply because I like them as actresses anyway."

They continued down Piccadilly, chatting happily together, almost oblivious to the cutting out of the engine of the V1 flying bomb overhead. It wasn't until they saw people throwing themselves on the ground that they instinctively did the same. He found that automatically he had put his body over hers as the explosion went off. They lay there for some moments before they got to their feet. They saw that they were covered in dust and debris and they began to dust each other down. The cloying smell of damp dust filled their throats and made them cough as they saw that a large hole had been blown out of one of the buildings down a side street. People were running towards the scene and they did the same as the ringing of the ambulance bell came remarkably quickly to their ears. The Civil Defence squad were quickly there too and they took over the task of trying to find out if anyone was trapped in the building. As the two of them approached they saw one man with blood pouring down his face and he was persuaded to sit on the kerb and not wander about in a daze. Shirley took out a handkerchief and held it over the wound as Cameron shouted to the ambulance man to attend. It was not long before some order had been restored and they stood up and began to move away. It was not until they did that that they both felt a weakness in their knees and they had to sit down themselves on the kerb. They both looked at each other, they were covered in dust, not only their clothes but their faces and hands and as Shirley looked at him she began to laugh. It was not a reaction that he had anticipated

and he said, "What's the matter, what's so funny?"
"It's your face, it's completely white apart from your mouth which looks as though you've been putting lipstick on." She continued to giggle and he looked at her with a bemused expression. He leaned over and kissed her on the lips. Apart from the dust she tasted very good to him. He was as surprised as she was by this action but she was not so surprised that she didn't reciprocate in full by returning his kiss.

They eventually parted and looked at each other and couldn't help smiling at their situation, he looked around at the debris strewn street, the emergency services, the medics, the general dust and confusion and he turned to her and said, "You know, when I ask a girl out, I really know how to give her a good time."

November 1965

Nina asked him up for coffee. She knew that Rachel would not be in until late so she felt confident that they wouldn't be disturbed. She had no predetermined plan about the rest of the evening, although there was something about Simon that she liked and she felt willing to pursue it to it's logical conclusion – whatever that is, she thought. As he sat there drinking his coffee and chatting about general things she couldn't help thinking about Ronald and comparing him to Simon. They were so different: their background, experience of life, attitude to the circumstances that they were in, their age, their looks. Whereas Ronald was broad in the shoulders and narrow at the hip, – a perfect figure, Nina used to think – Simon was slim and willowy but no less appealing in his own way. In colouring Ronald had light brown hair, going slightly grey at the temples with hazel eyes; Simon had black hair with grey eyes. As she thought about this critical analysis she realised, with a shock, that she was finding it difficult to remember exactly what Ronald did look like.

In their intellects they were also different. Simon had a good degree in History and was continuing with a thesis. Ronald had left school at seventeen and gone straight into the Navy, although his war experience seemed to have given him qualifications that were standing him in good stead now. In their emotions she just wasn't sure at this stage; Ronald had been passionate and romantic and moral in his refusing to compromise Nina sexually; with Simon it was too early to say. As the evening went on pleasantly enough, Nina decided to begin to play the vamp. She was wearing a short mini skirt and she made sure that as she crossed her legs Simon would not be in any doubt about her pleasure at being seen. She noticed that he seemed interested.

November 1965

They lay in each others arms, aware that their relationship had entered a new phase. Their lovemaking had been pursued with vigour on both sides and it was not until Nina heard Rachel let herself in at two thirty that she realised how quickly the time had gone. Simon was asleep, breathing deeply, his head resting on her breast. She felt at peace, completely vindicated in her own eyes at her present action. She felt no guilt, only a tremendous release of the tensions that had been pursuing her for so long. She eased herself out from under Simon's head and swung her legs onto the floor. He still slept as if dead and she padded her way out of the bedroom, pulling on a dressing gown. Rachel was in the kitchen making herself some coffee, she seemed surprised to see Nina.

"What are you doing up? I hope I didn't wake you, I tried to be quiet."

"You were quiet, I was just awake, that's all."

Nina sat down at the table, "I'll have one of those if I may," she said indicating the coffee.

She lit a cigarette and offered one to Rachel.

"I don't quite know how to tell you this, but Simon is in there," she pointed to her room.

"Oh," replied Rachel, not quite knowing what to say; she paused for a moment. "That's quick," she said.

"Yes, it does seem quick, doesn't it." Nina didn't know what to say either and they both tried to avoid each other's eye.

Nina began to toy with the spoon in her cup, "I suppose I've given up on Ronald, that's the truth of it."

Rachel came and sat at the table, "I imagine it's quite a lot to do with me."

Nina looked up, "Perhaps, although that's not the only reason... I suppose, in my heart of hearts, I didn't think it was going anywhere."

Rachel was quiet, seemingly deep in her own thoughts. Nina put her hand on Rachel's, "That does leave the field clear for you."

Rachel took her hand away, "It wasn't that sort of relationship... he was available and I took full advantage of it."

Nina was surprised at the bitter tone in her voice.

"OK," was all Nina said.

"Look, it's no big deal," Rachel continued, blowing the smoke from her cigarette over Nina's head, "we both found out about Ronnie before it was too late."

Nina looked at her, "I didn't realise you loved him so much." She spoke quietly.

Rachel stared at Nina with a shocked expression and then looked down, her eyes filling with tears, "Of course I love him, I can't think of anything else, my whole life is in suspension until I see him again." She covered her face with her hands and began to sob, her shoulders heaving in spasms of grief.

Nina got up and moved to Rachel's side of the table and put her arms around her and did her best to try and comfort her, but she could find no words to say.

September 1944

Ronald Cameron took the proffered cup of tea and smiled at Shirley's mother. "Thank you," he said, "my parents live quite near to here. It is almost like coming home."

Shirley then began to tell her mother about their evening out and the rather dramatic way it had ended. As if to emphasise the event, there was a distant throb of a V1 engine and as they kept half an ear open for the sound it stopped. There was a pause in their conversation until they heard the crump of the explosion, by the sounds of it some way to the north of them.

"This terrible war," said Shirley's mother, more to herself than to anyone else, "when is it going to end? We have had nearly five years of this constant strain."

"Yes and London has had it more than most," interposed Cameron. "I suppose we thought that when the blitz was over then that was the worst of it, but now we have these horrible weapons, when you just don't know from one moment to the next if you are going to be blown to kingdom come." Shirley thought that her mother was near to tears.

"It's the anxiety of it," said Shirley, "with these 'doodle-bugs' if you hear the engine you're OK and you just hope it keeps going and lands on someone else, it makes you selfish I suppose."

"Well," said Cameron, "our armies are pushing through Europe pretty quickly and they are overrunning these missile sites all the time, so I'm sure it won't be long before this stops." Shirley's mother looked gratefully at him, "I hope you're right. I don't know how much longer we can keep going without going out of our minds."

She smiled, Cameron thought a rather world-weary smile. "Shirley tells me you were in Russia," she refilled his tea cup and offered him another cake.

"Yes, I was on the convoys and then I had some time on the shore station in Murmansk."

"What are the Russians like?"

Cameron was never quite sure how to answer that question so he just said, "We didn't have much to do with them really, we were kept apart from them most of the time."

The conversation went on in a general vein for some time and then, at a glance from Shirley, they made their excuses and left. They caught the tube back to Charing Cross and walked along the Embankment to Whitehall. They were walking hand in hand when Shirley suddenly asked, "You don't talk much about Russia do you Ronnie?"

"There's not much to talk about, it was a job to do and we got on and did it."

"Yes but you must have had some leisure time. Was there a club that you could go to when you were off duty?"

"Yes, there was, but so much was off limits that there wasn't much of a choice. One just sat around drinking with one's mates in the same old place."

"Doesn't sound very jolly to me."

"No, it wasn't really, we just made the best of it I suppose."

Shirley turned and smiled at him, they both stopped walking and she put her hands on his shoulders, stood on tiptoe and kissed him. He was so surprised that it took a few moments before he realised the sudden delight of the moment and kissed her back.

"This is becoming a habit," he said.

"Yes it is, isn't it," she smiled, and took his hand and they continued on their walk down Whitehall.

September 1944

They got out of the train at Broadway station and as they were the only passengers to alight there they were able to use the services of the local taxi to take them the two miles to the "White Hart." It was a venerable inn situated in a quiet country lane between two small Cotswold villages. Ronald Cameron had known about it from his friend Brian Anstruther-Plowman and indeed had used his good services to book the place for him. He and Shirley had wanted to get away together, to find somewhere away from the bombing of London, to find some peace where they could talk without that sense of fore-boding that seemed to hang over them constantly in the capital. They had both obtained forty-eight-hour passes and had been planning this excursion for the past week. He signed the register as Mr and Mrs Cameron and they were shown up to their room by the homely wife of the proprietor.

"Will you be wanting a cup of tea in the morning?" she asked, noting with a benevolent eye the lack of wedding ring on the girl's finger.

"No that's OK, thank you, but we'll be down for breakfast promptly. I know from a friend how good your meals are," he said, putting the suitcase on the bed.

"Well, thank you, but it's getting more and more difficult to find the right food with this rationing."

"Yes, I know," he said and smiled, closing the door behind her. He turned to face Shirley and they fell into each others arms, hungrily kissing with an eagerness that surprised them both.

He couldn't believe the abandon with which she gave herself to him and the way that he appeared to have forgotten his past life and the trauma of Anna and entered passionately into this new relationship without any apparent regrets.

"I did have a girl in Russia." They were lying naked together, side by side, both staring up to the ceiling, both smoking the last two cigarettes of the packet bought at Paddington station.

"What was her name," said Shirley, turning her head to see his face.

"Anna," he felt embarrassed that a flicker of remorse had not surfaced within him.

"Did you love her?"

"Yes... I loved her."

"Why are you telling me?"

He looked at her, "Because I want to be honest with you; we seem to have something going for us and I want you to know what has happened in the past."

"It's only important if we believe that what we have now will have a chance of growing, and quite frankly, what with the world as it is, I don't think we can see further than the next minute." She stubbed out her cigarette with a vehemence that mirrored the despair of her words.

He was surprised at the rawness of her feelings, "But surely... what about the future?"

"I don't care about the future... it's now that matters. The future will have to take care of itself, I may not have any part in it."

"Look, I know that we are having a rough time but we've come through worse... and I believe that there is always hope."

It was her turn to look surprised, "Where do you get your optimism from? Looking around I can only see death and despair."

"But what we've just been enjoying in each other, surely that must mean something."

"Oh sure, it was our bodies enjoying the tactile brilliance of your manoeuvres, but that was as far as it went. We are lying here together now, having satisfied ourselves physically, and our bodies have nearly forgotten what it was that we were having. Where is the future in that?"

"Taking it to it's natural progression, it means the future of the human race," he grinned slightly.

She couldn't help a matching smile, "I thought you had taken precautions."

As he looked at her, and despite her apparent cold logic and completely different character, he saw Anna in her smile. He cupped his hand around her breast and began to kiss her and remembered again the immensity of the love he had for Anna.

November 1965

Simon held out his hand for Nina as she stepped down into the boat. She couldn't help noticing the feelings within herself of how she now felt about him. Since their night together she had noticed a change in his attentions towards her; it was as if he was looking into himself and trying to see what effect she was having on him. It was an analysis of himself and not of her. She found his introspection curious. She felt she should be the one being analysed. He was making himself the centre of his meditation and she wondered how long it would go on for. They were taking a river trip from Charing Cross pier to Greenwich to see the naval college and she had been looking forward to it for a week. However, although she would have anticipated her own feelings to be warm within her for him, there was something holding her back. Somehow it was a cold chill from the past that had stumbled across her emotions. However, it was a chill that hitherto she hadn't been aware she was susceptible to. And the more the day went on the more she felt she was catching the cold from this chill. At one point he put his arm around her and she felt a numbness separate them and isolate them completely. He obviously felt it as well because he said, "What's the matter?"

"Nothing," she replied, not wanting to make an issue of it at this point.

The boat was only half full, mainly occupied by foreign tourists, and they had chosen the two seats in the stern and because of this sparseness he felt able to pursue the conversation.

"Something is the matter," he said, "if we are to be together in some way we've got to be honest with each other."

"I am being honest with you, I don't know what's the matter... it's something in me, it's not you."

He looked at her face, and at the same time as admiring her skin colour and her beauty and wondering at her loveliness he also saw a set of her jaw that suggested a hardness in her that he had not seen before.

"Can I do anything to help?"

"Just try and be patient with me," she responded, "perhaps we are rushing things a bit too fast." She smiled at him, "I'm sorry, I didn't mean to put a damper on the day."

"You can't help that, I'm only sorry that you can't confide in me."

She turned and looked at him in the face, "I would confide in you if it was something I could put my finger on and identify as the problem. It's just that all the other relationships I've had in the past, when I feel that I'm getting close to someone, a barrier seems to come down and cuts me off from the one I want to get close to."

"Did that happen with Ronald Cameron?"

"Strangely, no... although my relationship with him was very different from the one I have with you."

"How different?"

She didn't answer at first and, in fact, paused for so long that he wasn't sure whether she had heard him.

Eventually she said, "We didn't sleep together."

"Oh," was all he said.

"I wanted to," she spoke so softly that he had to move closer to her because the noise of the engine was intruding on his attention to her, "but he always said that what we had together was so much more precious because it had a spiritual dimension to it that would be spoiled by the physical."

"Oh," he repeated, looking into the middle distance and not seeing. "Did you believe him?"

"Yes, I did, although I had such a mixture of emotions about it. First of all, I thought that he didn't fancy me and then I tried to convince myself that what he was saying was true. That if a relationship is based on true friendship and wanting the best for one's lover then to pollute it with a physical relationship cheapens it. Because if you think that the sex act is primarily for self-satisfaction then you are taking something away rather than giving."

"But you can't think that, can you?"

"I think that that very often is the case, certainly with a lot of guys; they go into sex with a girl purely for the self-gratification. They are not thinking of giving at all."

"Did that apply to me the other night?"

She smiled again, "No, it didn't. I wanted it just as much as you did."

"That's a relief," he said with a sigh. "I thought for one moment I was taking advantage of you."

The boat arrived at Greenwich pier and they got off with the other tourists. Despite the honesty of their conversation, Nina still could not hold his hand as they went into the museum; she felt that although there had been a bridging in their communication there was a great deal she didn't know about him, and what she didn't know worried her. Although he had told her about the facts of his life, he had told her very little about himself. He was a closed book and one where, curiously, she didn't feel inclined to turn the pages.

September 1944

It was a fine autumn day in the Cotswolds and they strode out happily, content in the knowledge that they had in each other. The country-side, with it's rolling hills and ancient cottages, seemed to epitomise the essential nature of England. Its tranquility, its beauty, the apparent unchanging character of the solidity of its structure. They both felt at one with the environment, and the sun, with it's gentle late-summer warmth, gave them an extreme sense of general well-being. It was also the difference between this countryside and the harrowing experience of living and working in London. There was a healing presence here that, if it could be bottled, would be worth a fortune.

He put his arm around her as they walked. "Do you know, you are a strange mixture. You are very beautiful and your outward nature is very bubbly and up front but underneath you have this hard pragmatic logic that seems at odds with the outside of you."

"Perhaps it's a form of protection," she said, "you can only get so far and then my defences come into play and you can't get any further."

"Has anyone?"

"Not as far as I know they haven't."

"Will the real Shirley George stand up please, I want to find out what she's really like." He appeared to joke but she knew the intent was there.

"You probably wouldn't want to know, you would lose all interest in me."

"I doubt it, what I've seen so far makes me want to see more and more of you."

"Judging by last night, I can assure you you have seen every little part of me."

He smiled in grateful memory of that and said, "Do you remember the film the other night, *The Gentle Sex*, and the mixture of girls that were portrayed?"

"Yes, of course."

"Well, it got me thinking about the complex mix that makes up a human being, both men and women. But I think that the mix is more recognisable in women, it is more in the open. Therefore, it is that much more intriguing. Men very rarely show their emotions anyway."

"Yes," she answered, wondering where this was going.

"It is what, to me, makes women so fascinating. In the film, if you remember, there were seven girls, all with entirely different characters, one was closed in and cold, one open and friendly, one compassionate, one shy and homesick, one northern and coarse, another intensely feminine and graceful. For the purposes of the film they each had to display a particular trait.

However, what to me was fascinating was that each girl had a little bit of all the other characteristics rolled into her. Therefore each girl could possibly display and emphasise one trait more strongly than any of the others."

"Yes, I'm still with you," she replied.

"So, in short, if I say that a girl, let's take you my darling, is bubbly and open, that doesn't mean that she can't also be closed and cold at times. It depends on the balance; 90 per cent of the time a girl can be bubbly and open and she is defined by others in that light. In a sense it doesn't matter about the other 10 per cent, we can almost dismiss it as an aberration."

"But that means," she interposed, "that if a person is 55 per cent good and correspondingly 45 per cent bad the judgement on that person must be good."

"Is that a question or a statement?"

"It's a statement, you can shoot me down if you wish."

"I suppose it depends on how brilliant that 55 per cent is, and does the brilliance and attractiveness more than outshine the rest."

"Do you think it does with me?" she asked.

He knew she was being provocative and the half smile on her face proclaimed it.

"If you're fishing for compliments then you have one coming. I think you are gorgeous and beautiful and vivacious for 99 per cent of the time and therefore, in my eyes, utterly adorable."

"Ah, but is that just your prejudiced view of me and is it only 1 per cent that you don't like?"

"I didn't say anyway that I didn't like the 1 per cent, only that there must be something in you that is not utterly adorable... but I haven't found it yet."

She smiled again, this time in full acknowledgement of his compliment.

They had some refreshment in a little tea shop in the high street

of Bourton on the Water. There were some other customers in there
and they waited for a few minutes before a table was cleared for them
by the window. They sat down and ordered a pot of tea for two. There
was also a rare treat, some cake; it turned out to be carrot cake,
which, despite the ingredients, turned out to be rather nice.

She looked at him over her tea cup, "This is really so good... to be
out of London and in this wonderful place... I can hardly believe it."
She squeezed his hand and her eyes shone with that blue
transparency that he was coming to love so much.

"It is good isn't it, and it is so good to be here with you." He spoke,
meaning the words but longing to have been able to say them to
Anna.

November 1965

Lavrenti Shlyapnikov and Ronald Cameron sat in the lounge of the
Metropole Hotel with coffee cups set before them. The Russian
didn't believe in leading into conversations by subtle means and started
straight away with his intent, "So now your wife is dead, you will no
longer help us."

Cameron, already well versed in the Russian way, replied, "It depends
on the terms that are available."

"We can talk about terms when I know your will in this."

"I am willing to carry on with what I can do, but I need some
incentive to make it worthwile."

"We can arrange a package for you that, I am sure, will satisfy you."

Cameron nodded in agreement, "First, can I ask you some questions?"

"If I can answer them I will do so."

"You will recall that I first began giving you information during the
war when I had to leave my wife here. When the war ended, in order
to keep my wife out of harm, I was obliged to continue."

"Yes, this is so."

"I was assured that she would be able to continue with her work in
Moscow, but in 1949 she was suddenly shipped off to the detention
camp in the Ukraine and she remained there until 1954, despite me
coming over in 1951 to see what could be done for her."

"By you coming here then, when Stalin was still alive, you nearly
made it worse for her." The Russian took another cigarette out of a
silver case and offered one to Cameron, "You obviously did not

understand the system we were under then. It was only through our strenuous efforts that we were able to keep her alive."

Cameron attempted to hide his disbelief in this statement, "But it was in your interest to keep her alive because you had this hold over me."

The Russian took a long draw on his cigarette, "In Russia, my friend, there is nothing that is obvious. There were certain elements that wanted all traitors to be, shall we say, subject to the law and Anna Kruglov was one of the candidates for this."

"So you were able to preserve her... then I am grateful for that," Cameron's bitterness was hidden in his carefully chosen words.

"I know that the regular letters that you arranged for her to send to me was the only indication I had that she was still alive and her carefully chosen words in those letters were equally carefully vetted by you," Cameron continued.

"That was the arrangement that you insisted upon," said Shlyapnikov.

"Yes," replied Cameron, "I know I could not have gained anything better, but when she was freed under a general amnesty in 1954 why was she kept in the Ukraine for so long before she came back to Moscow?"

"She was working on a special project."

"What was that?"

"I cannot tell you what it was."

"Where was it?"

The Russian hesitated and studied his fingernails, he then made a slow survey of the immediate surroundings and of others who could have been in earshot. Having satisfied himself that they were isolated from anyone overhearing he said, "It was a town on the River Pripet, it was a place called Chernobyl."

November 1965

They returned from the maritime museum and went up to Nina's flat. It was still the afternoon and Rachel would not be back from work for at least three hours, so Nina knew she had some time to try to talk to Simon about her feelings in more congenial surroundings. He seemed to know what she wanted, "What is it about Ronald Cameron that makes him different from others?"

She sat down beside him on the sofa and poured out the tea, "It is so difficult to say, but I guess you know he is the reason why I'm feeling detached somehow. Until what happens to him is resolved I can't move on in any real sense."

He smiled at her and took a sip of his tea, "I realise that. I only hope it won't take too long."

"So do I, I have tried to delve into myself and find out what it is that makes him so special in my eyes, but I cannot see what it is. From the first time that I met him he became special to me. It was as if it wasn't the first time I had met him, but of course it was; we had a link somehow and we carried on where we had left off. As soon as he came into the room that day it was as if I recognised him... that's it," she sat bolt upright, as if stung by an invisible force, "I haven't seen it like that before... I recognised him... it was as if there was an essential part of me that belonged in him and correspondingly an essential part of him that belonged in me."

"That makes me seem a bit inadequate," Simon responded.

Nina put her hand on his, "No, don't think like that, just different."

"But how can I compete against such opposition?"

"It's not a competition."

"But when we are together I feel that there is a great deal of you that is not with me at all."

"I'm sorry that you feel like that. I have tried not to do that, but I'm only trying to be honest with you and explain how I feel." Nina got up from the sofa and began to walk up and down the room, at the end of the third pacing she turned and said, "Perhaps I could have some time on my own, I'm sorry that I can't explain any more than I have, but I just need some space to think things out."

Simon got up and went over to her and placed his hands on her shoulders, "Look, don't worry, I'll go; I'll give you a ring tomorrow to see how you are." He kissed her lightly on the forehead, collected his coat from the hook on the door and let himself out. The relief that Nina felt when he had gone was immense and she sat down on the sofa, closed her eyes and tried to come to terms with her thoughts. She was not aware of how long she was in this state but she was still there when Rachel came in.

"Hello, are you all right?" She went into her bedroom without waiting for an answer and began to call through the door, "Met a great guy today, he came into the bank to deposit five thousand pounds; he said he would like to take me out to the Ritz or some-where." She came back into the sitting room having changed into jeans and a sweater and saw that Nina was still sitting on the sofa. "You all right?" she repeated.

Nina looked up, "Yes I think so, went out with Simon today and we came back here and I started talking about Ronald and how I felt about him and I guess he couldn't take it and I said I needed space and he left."

"That's a quick synopsis I'm sure," said Rachel, "now tell me what really happened."

November 1965

Simon Clarke arrived back at his flat, went to the wardrobe in his bedroom, took down the suitcase from the top and put it down on the bed. He pulled up a chair and opened the case. Inside was revealed the radio set, complete with earphones and a long aerial, which he proceeded to unravel and drape up over the frame of the window, making sure that he had already drawn the curtains. He sat down on the chair, put on the earphones and began to turn the knobs on the dial, when he was satisfied that he had found the right wavelength, he started to tap the morse code key. After fifteen minutes he finished and packed away in the reverse order and put the suitcase back on top of the wardrobe.

October 1944

Ronald Cameron and Brian Anstruther-Plowman were seated together in the main hall of Victoria station. They sat side by side both staring at the main notice board which proclaimed the departures of trains to the south coast. Neither of them was interested in the trains as they spoke to each other.

"When were you approached by this individual, Cameron?"

"Last Thursday, as I was walking down Whitehall, he came up behind me and slipped this letter into my hand." He handed Anstruther-Plowman a letter, "It's from Anna."

Cameron stared straight ahead as his companion was reading, when he appeared to have finished he looked at him. "What do you think?"

"She says she's in trouble if you don't help."

"Yes and she infers that if I can't do what I was doing before, then

they are going to cart her away to some detention camp of some sort."
Anstruther-Plowman looked at his friend, "What exactly were you doing before?"

"You remember the conversation we had on the dockside at Murmansk, when I said that maybe I would be forced to give the Soviets some innocuous information, well that's exactly what I did."

"I see and did that satisfy them?"

"It appeared to, for a time that is, and then they started putting pressure on her to produce more in-depth sources... I couldn't do that, of course."

"I'm glad to hear it," said Anstruther-Plowman laconically.

Cameron, sensing his companions displeasure, said, "They are our allies after all, it's not that I was doing anything wrong."

"That's a very thin dividing line I would say and one I would hesitate to analyse before a board of the Admiralty."

"What are you going to do?"

Anstruther-Plowman pursed his lips and Cameron saw that he was putting his friend under pressure to accommodate the situation.

"You must leave it with me at this juncture, but what I also want to know is who was the individual who approached you?"

"It seems he was from the Russian embassy and had been trying to find an opportunity to make contact with me for some time."

"That's interesting... this could work to our advantage, in the long run, that is. Meanwhile write a reply to Anna, telling her that things are under review, but don't be specific. You presumably have arranged to see this official again?"

"Yes, when I have a reply ready to send he will arrange the onshipment of it."

"Good, you have a phone number do you?"

"Yes, I do."

Anstruther-Plowman got up, "OK, that's good, you'd better have this back," he handed Cameron the letter. They both went off in opposite directions, leaving the busy station behind and not noticing the individual who had been watching them for some time follow Cameron out of the concourse.

November 1965

Nina had made a special effort to make Simon a nice meal for dinner that night. They had lasagne and salad and a bottle of red wine that she had bought that evening on her way home from the college. He was in a good mood, she thought, in view of her brushing him off the other day; although she had not found him varying in mood very often, he seemed to have an even temper about most things. They were halfway through the lasagne when he said, "Have you heard any more from Ronald Cameron?"

She was surprised that he kept mentioning him the way he did, so she replied, "No, why? I don't expect to for some time. Whether he is in a position to send a letter I don't know and I'm not at all sure whether the Russian postal system is up to it."

"Have you heard any more from your Foreign office chap?"

"He phoned me up the other day to say that they think he is being held in Moscow for the Russian authorities to make further investigations."

"It seems strange to me, knowing something about the Russian mind, that they just don't send him back, he must be an embarrassment to them." He took another sip of wine and filled Nina's glass up.

"I wish they would," she said, "I'm not sure how I can live normally with this uncertainty hanging over me."

"Have you any idea what he was working on when he went?"

"That's a funny question, how am I expected to know that?"

"Well I guess he told you most things that were affecting him and I just wondered whether he mentioned something about his work."

"I just know that he had this ship's chandler's business in Poole and that he did various bits of work on government contracts now and again."

"Did he seem worried at all about his work?"

"This is a bit of an interrogation isn't it?" Nina smiled, trying to hide her slight annoyance at what seemed an intrusion into a part of her life that she had considered, until now, just between her and Ronald.

"I'm sorry, I didn't mean it to be, it's just that I'm trying to help you face the various possibilities that might exist about him."

"What possibilities could you be talking about?"

"Well, for one, in view of his history with his wife, he could be passing information to the Russians."

"That's terrible," expostulated Nina, "he wouldn't do anything like that."

"You just don't know the sorts of pressures that could have been put upon him," he replied, "they could have been blackmailing him in some way."

"How?"

"By forcing him to pass on certain things, because if he didn't then his wife or her family could be taken away."

"That's a terrible situation to be in," she said, "and so lonely too, you can't tell anyone what you are doing."

"Not even your nearest and dearest." She thought he said this more in the form of a question than as a statement, but maybe she was mistaken.

"What other possibilities are there?"

He thought for a moment, "It could be he's just being naive, he just wanted to see his wife and couldn't think of any other way to do it or, for reasons we have no inkling of, he wanted to go and live in Russia."

"He is definitely not a naive person, but he may just have wanted to see his wife, as he said in his letter to me. And I cannot imagine that he would want to live in Russia."

"People act in curious ways from a multitude of reasons."

"I know, but I think the more you know someone the more you are able to understand why they act in a certain way and I believe that I know Ronald and that he would try and act in as honourable a way as possible."

"The more I go on in life the more I realise that human beings seem to act irrationally without any plan or much logic, despite believing that you know them," he said.

"I can't go along with that," responded Nina, "when you know someone as well as you know yourself, you are able to second guess their actions and know why they do things."

"But how well do you know yourself, how perfidious is your own heart? My old school motto was 'Man know Thyself', which I thought was silly at the time, but the older I've got the more sense I can see it has."

"That makes for a very cynical approach to life," said Nina, as she refilled the wine glasses.

"No, a realistic one, and it also prevents you from getting too hurt sometimes."

They finished their meal and decided to go out to the local cinema, which was only a few hundred yards along the high street.

They saw a film called *Make me an Offer*, starring the Australian actor Peter Finch; it was about an antique dealer who finds an extremely valuable Grecian vase and because of his knowledge of the subject is able to purchase it at a knock-down price. His life's dream is realised when he looks at it and knows that it is his at last.

"That's a great state to be in, isn't it?" Simon said as they came out. "To know that your life's dream has been achieved and that you can look at it and rejoice over it."

"Yes isn't it, I wonder if that will ever happen to me?"

He looked at her in mock horror, "Do you mean to say, young lady, that you haven't found your life's dream in me?"

She giggled and tried to tickle him under the arms as they ran along the street back to the flat. He reciprocated and chased her up the outside stairs to the front door. By the time they got back inside they were both out of breath and fell somehow into each others arms. She found it remarkably easy then to fall into bed with him.

Nina got up as the dawn began to show its early light through the curtains. She went into the bathroom to have a shower before Rachel needed to get up. Simon stirred in the bed as he felt Nina leave his side. He sat up as he heard her go into the bathroom, he switched on the bedside light and opened the drawer in the cabinet beside the bed. He knew that was the obvious place that she would keep intimate letters and a quick search revealed a bundle of envelopes. He quickly found what he was looking for, made a mental note of what it was and replaced the letters in the same way that he had found them. When she came back she found him in the same position that he was in when she left; she bent over to kiss him and he responded sleepily.

"I must get up," he said, "but not before we have said good morning properly." He pulled her down onto the bed and proceeded to take off her dressing gown. There was no way she could resist him in her present mood and she succumbed to him in as pliant a way as was necessary to please him.

October 1944

In the Soviet embassy, M Gousev, the ambassador, noted the list of individuals who were willing to be of assistance to the Russian war effort. This was not the official list of how much Great Britain had helped in the sending of supplies by the means of convoys and of the vast amount of war materials sent; this was the unofficial list of persons who, for one reason or another, had sympathetic leanings towards his country. He was disappointed at the low numbers, he had expected more to want to be involved but maybe the numbers would increase the more the Russian successes in the field became apparent. British people would appreciate, he was sure, the more they saw that the Soviet system was the one dominant creed to overcome the world, how they would want to join and share in the joys of communism.

He noticed one name, a Ronald Cameron, who, apparently, had a wife in Russia and who was willing to cooperate. He saw that the official in the embassy M. Filippov was the "rukovodstvo agentom", in other words the "agent running." He was the operational officer who would ensure that Cameron, as the agent, carried out his operational assignments.

The ambassador rang through on his intercom for Filippov to come to see him. Within a few minutes Filippov arrived and was gestured to a seat on the other side of the desk.

"As the operational officer responsible for Cameron," Gousev patted the file in front of him, "you will be 'obucheniye agenta', and as such you will be involved in the training of Cameron; you will instruct him in specialist knowledge regarding all practical abilities and skills that he is likely to need for carrying out intelligence assignments."

"Yes comrade ambassador, I understand."

"You will probably find that in order to get the correct information back to the department in the mother country it would be best to use the photographic services that are available."

"Do you mean for me to use the micro dot technique, comrade ambassador?"

"You can if you think it advisable. I will leave it to you. Whatever activities you are involved in you will be under diplomatic cover – 'diplomaticheskoye prikrytiye'."

"Thank you, I shall be starting as soon as Cameron makes contact with me again."

"You are sure that he is a 'kandidat na verbovku', a candidate for recruitment? Have you ensured that he is reliable and has the necessary ability to carry out assignments and ensured that there is a basis for making the recruitment and circumstances which will make it possible to carry it out clandestinely?"

"I am sure that he is a good candidate for recruitment. The fact that he has a Russian wife will make it that much easier to have the necessary hold over him," Filippov was relieved that his first agent in this country was such easy material to work with. All his training had centred on the need to make sure of the reliability of the agent you would be running and he felt that this man, Cameron, would not give him any trouble in that department. Filippov had been anxious that his first tour abroad, in the prestigious posting of Great Britain, would get off to a good start, and in this agent he believed he had that.

November 1965

"I am so happy that you seem to be getting on so well with Simon," Rachel was at the stove cooking some cauliflower and making some cheese sauce; she was busy stirring the cheese sauce in the saucepan as she spoke to Nina. "He seems a nice guy."

"Yes he is, we seem to be getting on pretty well."

"So I noticed, you seem to be sharing a few breakfasts with him now." Nina smiled, "I hope we are not disturbing you too much?"

"No, all I seem to take to bed with me at the moment is a good book." She suddenly realised that maybe that wasn't the most tactful of statements to make in view of her previous altercation with Nina. She, however, didn't seem to notice.

"But it's strange you know, the more I have to do with Simon the more I think about Ronald. And it's a curious thing that Simon keeps talking about Ronald, I don't know why."

"Perhaps he sees him as a rival and wants to find out exactly how you feel," Rachel responded, relieved that Nina had not noticed her insensitive remark.

"Do you think so? I hadn't thought about that."

"I think that it is a distinct possibility."

Rachel noticed that Nina had put on her thoughtful look, the sort of look she reserved for her more demanding essays, "Do you know, there is something that is bothering me about the conversation that we had yesterday before we went to the cinema."

"Yes, what is that?" Rachel responded.

"The trouble is I can't think what it is, but it was when he said it first of all, and I suppose I was enjoying looking at his face at the time and didn't take in the full implication of what he said. What was it...?"

"If you stop thinking about it and talk about something else it very often comes to you."

Rachel began to pour the cheese sauce over the cauliflower and Nina laid the table with plates and cutlery. "Shall we have some wine, we had some left over from last night?"

"Yes, let's," replied Rachel.

They began to eat their meal and were enjoying the relaxation of the moment when Nina suddenly put down her fork, a look of disbelief and shock on her face, "I have remembered what it was that Simon said that puzzled me."

"What is it?"

"We were talking about Ronald and then he suddenly said 'in view of his history with his wife', and I thought, what a strange word to use, 'history', because of my reading of history as a subject I didn't think it fitted in there. But it isn't the word that's the problem, it's the fact he mentioned Ronald's wife and history together."

"So what's so strange about that?"

"The trouble is I don't know, but there is something troubling me. Simon seems to know a great deal about the Russian system."

"But he's an erudite guy," said Rachel, "and at the moment he's writing a paper on Marxism, isn't he?"

"Yes, I know all that, and maybe I'm just being paranoid, I don't know. Perhaps I just can't believe that such a seemingly gorgeous guy has fallen into my lap, so to speak."

"You deserve something good to happen to you, don't be so suspicious, just enjoy what it is that the gods are giving you at this time and be grateful." Rachel seemed to sum up her own philosophy of life in one sentence and Nina smiled and resolved that maybe she was being too sensitive about a conversation that wasn't of great significance. Nevertheless, although her experience of life was limited, she was beginning to trust an inbred instinct of her psyche that told her when things were not right. And she had that feeling now.

November 1965

Simon Clarke drove his open-top MG sports car fast down the winding Dorset road. There was very little other traffic around and he indulged his love of speed and the feel of the car to the full. The morning was fine and dry but the sharp nip in the air presaged the end of autumn and the beginning of the season he least liked in England. By lunch time he had pulled up at Poole railway station and parked in the station car park. He pulled the tonneau cover over the car and fastened it down. He then went to the taxi rank, gave the address to the driver in the front cab and climbed into the back. After about ten minutes the taxi pulled up in the harbour area outside a warehouse. He got out, paid the driver and looked around him. The warehouse in question had a painted sign above the double doors proclaiming 'Cameron Ship's Chandlers'. He noticed that there was a small door to the side which said 'office'. It had a yale lock which, after looking around him, he opened with the help of a master key.

He went inside, closing the door behind him. He switched on the light, which flickered on, through a neon tube, after a few seconds. He looked around him. There was the usual scene of an office in a healthy state of efficient untidiness. He started in as methodical a way as possible, the box files on the top shelf, then working his way down through the filing cabinet. He grunted in satisfaction once or twice, making notes in his notebook as he did so.

After three hours, during which he was only conscious of the passing time by the rather insistent tick of the replica ship's clock above the door, he straightened up, looked at the clock and took out of his pocket a small camera. He then proceeded to take pictures of various documents that he had laid on the desk. When he had finished he placed the documents back in the files from which he had taken them, put them at the angles that he remembered they had been at and with a final look around the room, opened the door, turned off the light and let himself out. He walked along the quay, admiring the variety of marine craft that were in the harbour. As he was in no hurry he walked, following the signs to the station and arrived at his car in time to see the five o'clock train to London pulling out of the station. He undid the tonneau cover on the car, slid behind the wheel and drove slowly out of the car park, taking a minor road inland. As he got out of the speed limit he began to use the performance of the car and was soon ten miles out of the town when he recognised the pub sign that he was looking for. He pulled off the road and into the car park by the side of the building. He got out of the car and went in the front door. The bar was just opening; he ordered a pint of bitter and enquired if there were any rooms for the night. He booked a room and also made a reservation for a meal that evening. As he looked around the bar he saw one other man come in who was carrying a newspaper, he put the paper in front of him and ordered a drink, Simon looked idly at the headline, it said, "Wilson government expels another Russian diplomat."

As Simon went down to dinner and viewed the other diners in the restaurant he took a perverse pleasure in the knowledge of his own secret life that these others would not have the slightest inkling of. Ever since he was a boy, growing up in urban Manchester, he had always valued secrets. He supposed it stemmed from the secret that he kept from his mother that his father was having an illicit affair with a girl from his work. His father had found out that Simon had seen them together and he swore him to secrecy, never to divulge this to his mother. Simon had kept the oath and had been greatly rewarded by it from his father, who had given him increased pocket money whenever he needed it. This had produced in Simon the knowledge, early learned, that blackmail and secrets went hand in hand and would be of great use in later life if handled correctly. As he sat, enjoying his meal, he thought of the development of this skill ever since.

It had been greatly helped at university when he had joined an anti-capitalist league and had entered into all the multitudinous nefarious dealings of the far left in England. It was the time of the intense debates raging about the purity of the Soviet system and how much better it was than the outmoded Western capitalist corruption that kept the working people under the thumb of the evil bosses. He easily identified with the extreme Marxist/Leninist dream of world domination. Going hand in hand with this was the caution that must be evident if he was to be useful to the cause. He was soon recruited by an agent who saw the immense promise that Simon would have if he was correctly directed in the communist pattern. Since then he had been used in a number of ways and, as with his father, he had been well rewarded. He thought with intense satisfaction about the assignment that he had currently. Not only was he trying to find out as much as he could about an "illegal" agent but he was also able to indulge to the full his delight in the seduction of the agent's girl-friend. He dwelt for a moment on the gorgeous girl that appeared to be completely smitten by him. What pleasure he had been able to indulge in with her. How much she appeared to desire him, to answer his every whim sexually. He took another drink of beer and had a sudden need to see her again. He resolved to phone her as soon as he got back to London. His mind also went back to the day when he had been asked to swear the oath to the Party and the excited pleasure it gave him to pronounce the oath; it was almost the same sense of excitement as his liaison with Nina. He recited it again in his mind, he had a prodigious memory and had no difficulty in its remembrance,

> Deeply valuing the trust placed upon me by the Party and the fatherland, and imbued with a sense of intense gratitude for the decision to send me to the sharp edge of the struggle for the interest of my people... as a worthy son of the homeland, I would rather perish than betray the secrets entrusted to me or put into the hand of the adversary materials which could cause political harm to the interests of the State. With every heart-beat, with every day that passes, I swear to serve the Party, the homeland, and the Soviet people.

It was a far cry from his upbringing and the nominal allegiance he had felt to his country of birth; he was committed to the ideals of Marx and fully identified with the way it had been pursued in Russia, the way the experiment in social revolution had succeeded. He felt immensely satisfied with his own intellect and the way he had been able to see, when so many others hadn't, the obvious accomplish-ments of communism in the world. The New World order would soon take over the world, to its inestimable benefit, and he was one of the valiant soldiers in this war they were truly winning.

He finished his meal and decided to drive back into Poole to see what night life there was available. The girl that he picked up was only interested in the money he paid her and not in his devout Marxist beliefs, which he forgot to tell her about.

October 1944

Ronald Cameron got out of the train at Manor House tube station and made his way to Wightman Road. The day was quiet and he had a sense of peace within him as he walked up Green Lanes and Endymion Road to arrive at the southern end of Wightman Road at just before eight o'clock in the morning. The fact that he felt so peaceful came as a surprise to him; certainly his activity that morning didn't suggest it. He was on a clandestine mission to deposit material into a DLB (dead letter box) and he was only too aware that this would not be looked on favourably by his masters at the Admiralty. However, the sun was shining in that late autumn way of hazy golden light that seemed to lay a blessing on everything it touched. The trees down the side of the road were turning their leaves towards the light and reflected and absorbed the sun's colour. As he walked up Wightman Road he soon came to number 40, his DLB. He walked up to the letter box and pushed the envelope through the flap. As he did so, at the very moment that the letter hit the floor on the other side of the door, there was a whooshing stunning crack that seemed to hit him in the very centre of himself. His next conscious awareness was looking up from the ground and seeing the leaves on the trees being blown up into the air, together with various materials which looked like gate posts and sparkling pieces of glass which caught and reflected the sun's rays. Within milliseconds this was all over and an immediate silence settled over the street as the glass particles and debris settled down on him.

He looked up; the sky was an azure blue and it looked so beautiful as he gradually became aware that he ought to try and get to his feet. He managed it by dint of holding onto the front door of number 40 and hauling himself up. As he did so the door opened and an ashen-faced woman looked out. She looked at him and then down the street and began to babble in an incomprehensible language that was completely alien to him. He looked down the street and then was aware that where there had been houses a few hundred yards away there was now nothing except a smoking mess of debris. He walked shakily out into the road and began to walk towards where the bomb

95

had exploded. Others were doing the same; in the time that it took for a confused handful of people to gather, bells were heard which presaged the arrival of the Civil Defence corps. They and the ARP warden soon went into a well-rehearsed drill, that they had wearily repeated too many times for them to remember or to want to remember, and took control of the situation.

One bystander, too confused to know what he was doing, began to light a cigarette; the resulting cursing from the warden to put it out because of the possibility of a fractured gas main reduced the smoker to a shaking crumpled figure in the road. Cameron went over to him and put his arm around him, the man continued to shake and whether he was aware of Cameron or not he gave no sign.

The salvage team continued in their unhappy task of trying to see if there were any survivors and, whilst Cameron was there, brought out what he at first thought was a doll – a baby's body, crumpled and torn; the body of the mother was found shortly after.

He wandered away some time after that, realising that his presence there would not benefit the dead and was of little use to the living either. He walked without purpose for some time until he found himself at another station on the Northern line. He caught a glimpse of himself in a mirror, as he bought a ticket and did not recognise the image that he saw there. The gaunt, dusty, dishevelled figure bore no relation to the confident, smartly uniformed sailor that had set out on the outward journey. It was with a sense of shock that he took a seat in the tube train and as the train rumbled through the darkness of the tunnels and he could see his reflection in the blackened window, tears began to course down his face. He could not stop them, nor did he care to; he had at last joined the suffering of Londoners in their torment and these tears were his badge of office.

November 1965

Nina sat opposite Witherspoon in the comparative quiet of his office. She had decided to go and have another talk with him, partly because she needed to know if there had been any other information about Ronald and partly because she somehow felt nearer to Ronald by being with Witherspoon. She could rationalise this by the obvious communication that she was having with him but also by his kindly feelings towards her and the way he showed it. She had lost her own father at the end of the war when she was only three months old. Because of this she felt the need for a father figure at certain times in her life and somehow Witherspoon was filling this gap now. Nina was sure he was unaware of this and if he had been aware she was sure it would have embarrassed him profoundly. To add to her confusion on this matter her mother, had told her that she had been adopted as soon as she had been born, so she had this additional curiosity of knowing that perhaps her biological mother was still alive. She had, obviously, thought about this at various stages in her life, sometimes more than others. She was also aware that maybe her attitude to men had been circumspect at times and that perhaps she had chosen men friends who had a certain maturity about them that appealed to her. All this she fully acknowledged where her relationship with Ronald was concerned.

However, as she sat opposite Witherspoon at this moment she detached all these reflections from her mind to listen to the latest that he was telling her.

"I am so pleased that you got in touch with me again as you did because I was about to ring you to tell you to come to see me."

"Why, have you got some news?" She found her eagerness hard to conceal.

"Yes, good news, Ronald Cameron is coming home."

"Oh, that's wonderful," she clasped her hands together in a spontaneous gesture of joy.

"Yes, the Russians are releasing him, and he is being flown home tomorrow." He smiled broadly in response to the obvious joy that he was giving to this beautiful girl.

"He is being met at Heathrow and we shall bring him back here to debrief him. I am sure that it won't take long as a process and, hopefully, you will see him some time tomorrow."

"Oh, thank you so much," Nina felt so overcome that, despite her efforts to prevent them, the tears began to fall down her face. Witherspoon leaned forward and offered her a tissue from a box in front of him. He had made special provision for just such an eventuality and had asked Barbara to provide the necessary materials. She gratefully made use of the offer, "I'm sorry... silly of me," she said, her hands shaking with the delighted emotion that was now filling her.

"So, if you want to, ring me tomorrow in the afternoon and I will then be able to tell you when he will have finished with us."

He rose from his chair and held out his hand. She took it gratefully and for longer than convention allowed. "Thank you so much for all your help to me in this, I really am so grateful to you." On impulse she leaned forward and gave him a kiss on the cheek. He felt the slight dampness of her tear-stained face and had the distinct impression that he would be extremely sorry if he didn't see this girl again.

October 1944

Number 65, Wightman Road, Harringay, London, had just been bombed by a V2 rocket. It and six houses either side were now rubble-strewn holes in the ground. There were grotesque evidences of the carnage that had been visited on the site; a bed, leaning in a drunken fashion out of what was left of the first floor, a kitchen sink complete with dishes from breakfast, remarkably unbroken, lying in what had been the front garden, a pile of nappies fluttering in the fresh breeze of the autumn morning. A haze of smoke still issuing from the scorched debris and that unmistakable smell of damp, burnt plaster hung around the civil defence workers as they completed their job, the hopeless task of finding any more survivors.

The "agent-soderzhatel konspirativnoy kvartiry," an agent keeper of a clandestine apartment, picked his way carefully over the rubble-covered road, his stomach churning in the evidence of this sudden terror death that had been visited in his road. He had been out of the house for only half an hour, and although his house was some way up the street it could so easily have been his that had been hit. He hoped his wife was all right and he hurried as fast as his careful steps would allow. He soon saw her outside talking to neighbours and went to her in a grateful embrace. He had been expecting a package that had to be processed and he feared that this bomb may have prevented this from happening. When he got indoors he saw the item that he hoped for in the letter box and he took it immediately into the room that he used for photography. By a system of delicate exposures he was able to reduce the particular document down to a size that enabled the information on the paper to be fitted onto the size of a pinhead. This relevant dot he now transferred onto an innocent letter that would be sent to the department that would process it accordingly. His work satisfactorily done he went and had some lunch with his wife and their talk was of the neighbours that they had lost that morning and of their hatred of the system that had provoked such an outrage.

November 1965

Nina could not sleep that night, at least it seemed like it, perhaps she did, but the ever present image of Ronald was constantly before her. She could not imagine how she would feel when she saw him again, what should she say, what words could possibly convey the feelings that she had. She was up before dawn, anxious for the day to start. She showered and in her bath towel went back to her room to decide what clothes to wear. This took some time, dismissing first this and then the other outfit. By the time she had decided on a black skirt, not too short she thought, and a baby blue roll-neck jersey, Rachel was up and knocking on her door with a cup of tea.

"Do you think long boots or shoes with black tights?"

"Shoes I think," said Rachel, "you have nice legs, you need to show them."

"What about the rest of the outfit?" Nina asked, showing her the skirt and jersey.

"I think, black jersey, with your blond hair it goes so well with black, particularly if you wear it down."

"Thank you, I think you're right... but it's so difficult, I'm in such a tizzy."

"Look, he will just be overjoyed to see you, whatever you wear."

"I hope so."

"Why do you doubt it?"

"Oh, I don't know, perhaps it's because I've learnt so much about him in these past weeks, he almost seems another person... a stranger."

"But you've not found out much more about him have you, you are only imagining that you know things about him?" Nina sat down on the bed. She looked at Rachel, "I've found out about him and you."

"Yes I know, but do you think you've found out things about yourself too?"

"You mean Simon?"

"Yes."

"I suppose so, but I've been thinking about him quite a lot. He came in just when I felt so deserted, maybe he took advantage of me and my vulnerable state. But that doesn't mean that I didn't want him, I did. He is kind and considerate and I just wanted a hug now and again and he was there for me."

"Where does that leave Ronald now, will he understand about Simon?" Rachel felt brutal saying it in such a way but she knew Nina needed to hear it.

"I don't know... I really don't know. I suppose that's what is really bothering me. I should have been prepared to wait for him and I haven't."

Rachel put her arm around her friend, "Look, you let me read that letter that he sent to you and it was full of love, and that was written after he had been with me. So I don't think that there is any question of him not wanting you and still loving you in the same way. Just give him some space and let him relax with you again and see what happens." Nina would never know what an effort that was for Rachel to say those words, it was the bitterest of harvests of Rachel's time with Ronald, a time that had a dream-like quality but had now become a nightmare.

Nina smiled at her and gave her a hug, "thank you, I shall dress now, have some breakfast and then give them a ring to see what's happening," she smiled once more at Rachel and hugged her again, "I love you," she said.

Rachel left her and went into the bathroom, whilst she was showering she wept tears of anguish, frustration and love.

November 1965

Witherspoon left them alone in his office. Nina looked at Ronald and went to him and took both his hands in hers. She gazed into his eyes and saw there a hurt that she had never seen before.

"My darling," was all she could whisper. He smiled that slight smile that she loved, which started at the corner of the mouth and went straight to the eyes. He put his arms around her and pressed his face close to hers. His skin felt the moisture of her tears.

"It's all right my beloved... it's all right, I'm home now."

She searched his face eagerly, "Yes it will be all right, won't it?" He sensed the passion in the words and the need, like a child, not to be alone again.

He stroked her head and kissed her eyes and told her he loved her. She felt complete comfort and satisfaction as they held each other and she knew that all the doubts and fears were now dispersed.

October 1944

"Where did you go today?" Shirley was in the bath and Ronald was kneeling on the floor, leaning over and bathing her back. The statutory requirement of the maximum water depth of five inches in the bath was, as Shirley said, barely adequate to cover her embarrassment, but as Ronald would use the same water after her, in order to conserve vital supplies, she didn't want to complain.

"I had to deliver something in Harringay and whilst I was there Herr Shichulgruber dropped one of his special deliveries."

"What were you delivering?"

"You know better than to ask me in wartime what I was doing."

"Yes, I suppose so." She flicked some water at him and for the next ten minutes they enjoyed a display of water sports that didn't do much good to the lino on the floor.

They were using Brian Anstruther-Plowman's flat in South Kensington; he was away for a few nights and they were able to relish the luxury of being alone and together. Fortunately, their duties coincided for these few days and they were able to travel to work with each other and back again.

Whilst Ronald was having his bath Shirley began to make some supper. She considered her corned beef hash superior to most other people's and she had developed a particular relish that went well with the rather predictable dish. She mused that there are only a certain number of ways that corned beef could be served and she felt she had developed all of them.

She was in a bath robe as she was cooking and as she heard Ronald come into the kitchen she was just about to say that he'd better not get any ideas whilst she was at the stove, when an enormous explosion rocked the building. The glass shattered in the windows and despite the adhesive tape on the glass, it went everywhere. A part of the ceiling came down in the hall, just where, a few seconds previously, Ronald had passed underneath. Neither of them had any opportunity to drop to the floor, they just stood there looking at each other. Again, the silence and then the shocked reaction.

"Bloody hell," expostulated Ronald.

"I couldn't have put it better myself," said Shirley.

They both went to the shattered window in the kitchen and looked out. The second-floor flat overlooked a central garden and on the other side they saw that the rocket, with its ton of explosive, had landed on the block of flats that was parallel to the one they were in. Shirley looked at Ronald and for the first time noticed that there was blood coming down his face from his forehead. She went over to him, took out a handkerchief and began to mop at his brow.

"We'd better go over to see if there is anything we can do," he said, "are you all right?"

"Yes, I'm OK. The glass must have missed me."

They made their way down the stairs and out into the square. She had quickly put an overcoat over her bath robe and they both remembered to put on shoes. The scene that greeted them was, unfortunately, a familiar one; the flames, the smoke, the acrid smell of a mixture of ingredients that they didn't dare to analyse, the confused shouting, the ringing of bells, the indiscriminate piles of debris, the utter devastation of chaos and eventually the Civil Defence team endeavouring to bring some order out of the madness. "We can't do any good here," he said, "you're shivering." He put his arm around her and they walked slowly back to the flat.

As they went through the front door Shirley started to cry, "I'm sorry... I didn't mean to... it's just this constant bloody business... when's it going to end?" She sat on the sofa and continued a quiet sobbing weeping. He continued to put his arms around her, as her shoulders shook, not in a violent way but, he thought, as if there was a gentle engine ticking over inside her.

November 1965

They went back to Kingsbury together. Their journey on the tube was quiet, only talking about generalities and trying to avoid a conversation that would provoke an intensity that they both knew they couldn't cope with at this stage. However, when they closed the door behind them in the flat they felt the imminence of that talk that both their psyches knew was inevitable.

"Did you find your wife?" Nina asked the question that above all others she needed to know the answer.

"Yes, I found her... and I was with her when she died."

"Oh," she was at a loss to know what else to say, but there was something inside her that went snap, as if in relief or tension, she wasn't sure.

They held each other then, each wanting something vital from the other, but not quite knowing the true nature of the thing they desired. They kissed and the emotion generated produced an awareness of how much they needed to be physically open to each other's needs. Nina led him into the bedroom and they responded frantically to their inevitable coupling. Their nakedness was a natural essence of this and Nina was swept away into a dream-like trance of wonder, only for it to be suddenly abated as Ronald stopped before the fulfilment of what their bodies were eager for.

She looked at him and saw in his eyes that same look of hurt that she had noticed when she had first seen him a few hours ago.

"What's the matter?"

"I don't know... it's not you... it's something in me." He broke away from her then and sat on the edge of the bed.

She put her hand on his back, "You must tell me... is it something I'm not doing?"

He turned to look at her, "It really is not you... it's just..."

"Yes," she was suddenly aware of her nakedness and a terrible vulnerability and, curiously, a sense that she knew this was going to happen.

"There is something in me that is stopping me from doing this to you."

"You make it sound as if you are doing me harm."

"That's the trouble, that is exactly what I feel would happen if this went the full course."

Whatever he was saying she could not understand it and she tried to arouse him again, but he swept her hand away, almost roughly.

"Please try and understand me," he said, "I know it's so difficult... I barely understand myself at this moment... so I don't know how you can."

He got up off the bed and put on his shirt and trousers and sat down on the bed again. "I feel terrible," he said softly.

Nina pulled the sheet up over her nakedness, "How do you think I feel?"

He turned to look at her again and the look in his face displayed a measure of despair that shocked her deeply.

"You are the most beautiful girl I have ever known, and I want to make love to you more than anything else in the world; I would give anything within my power to make you happy at this moment but," he shrugged, "I can't."

"But why?"

"Something is stopping me."

"What?"

"I don't know... if I did I would do something about it."

She then said something that she regretted it deeply as soon as she said it, "You didn't feel like this when you made love to Rachel."

The impact of the remark showed in the shock on his face, and to Nina's discomfort, because she loved him so much, he literally hung his head in shame. He was silent for some moments and then said softly, "I'm so sorry."

She put out her hand to touch him on the arm and as she did so, her eyes filled with tears. He moved his hand to hold hers and without looking at her face sunk his head on her breast and began to sob. She had never imagined how much sorrow could be expressed so quickly. The convulsions of his body shook the bed as she held him tightly to herself. How long this manifestation of grief took she had no idea, except she never thought it was going to end. Eventually it began to subside and she stroked his head and she was conscious of two things, particularly: one, the moisture of his tears had soaked the sheet over her and she felt the wetness on her breasts and, two, a deep peace seemed to pervade the whole room. She felt it deep in her heart and as he lifted his head off her, she saw it in his eyes.

October 1944

As Ronald Cameron looked over the table at Shirley he began to wonder why he hadn't met this girl before. If he had, his enterprise in Russia would not have ended in the sad way that it had. If he had, Anna would still be without care and her life would not be as complicated as it was now. But that is not true, he thought, when he linked Anna's name with the word, care: it seemed in Russia everyone had a problem of some sort or another. There was no carefree life in that benighted land, as far as he could see. His involvement with Anna had given both of them an experience of love that they would not have experienced if they hadn't met each other. In so far as he believed in such things, it was as if their meeting was a destiny that had to happen. But why had it happened? What good had come of it? He had had to leave her in the grip of a system that exploited human beings in a savage and subhuman way. If there was a measure of good that could equal out the bad in life, maybe the goodness that they experienced in their love was going to alleviate someone else's suffering. It certainly didn't alleviate his and Anna's suffering now. He felt so miserable when he thought of her. The joy that he knew in her company was wonderful but it had been more than taken away by the end result.

When he first got back from Russia, having to leave his beloved there, he didn't know how he was going to live through each day. He became a robot, living through a hell of despair that no amount of involvement in anything else could take away. However, curiously, as he surveyed the beauty of Shirley, he realised, with a shock, that he wasn't thinking much about Anna at all. In fact, he was almost disgusted with himself. How long had he been home now? Four months was it? The experience of Shirley had taken over his desire for Anna. Maybe it was because she was present and available and their enjoyment of each other was mutual, but what did that say for the loyalty and faithfulness of man, and of him particularly?

Therefore, he knew that he had to be honest with this girl, with whom he realised he was falling in love.

He took her hand. "My darling Shirley, I think I need to tell you something that has been on my heart ever since we started going out."

"That sounds awfully serious," she said, squeezing his hand in return.

"I love you."

"That sounds a good start, I love you too."

"But that's not what I wanted to say at this point, you are trying to distract me. What you need to know is that the girl I knew in Russia was very special to me."

"I know that my sweetheart," she replied, "but you are going to tell me, aren't you, how special?"

"Yes, you see... " his mouth suddenly felt very dry, he knew a lot depended on him doing this properly, but how properly do you tell the girl you are in love with that you are already married?

He knew there was no proper way.

"We were married... by a sea captain... in Murmansk."

"Oh," she said.

He didn't know what reaction to expect and whatever she said would have not surprised him. He looked at her, she appeared calm and beautiful as she looked at him.

"Where does that leave me?" she asked.

"Where do you want it to leave you? I still feel the same about you. I love you and I want to be with you." He was more surprised by his own words than her question.

She let go of his hand, "It must be up to you... if you are still married... how can our relationship... " she tailed off.

"How can our relationship...develop?" he finished her sentence for her.

"Yes," she said.

"I have anguished long and hard about this," he studied his hands which were clasped together, as if in prayer, his fingers digging into the flesh with the intensity of his feelings. "None of us know whether we are going to survive another day... the way things are... each day... is... precious." He lifted his head to look at her, "I only know that you bring me a joy and lift me out of the dread of the danger of another day in London. Maybe I am being selfish, but this is how I feel. If I lost you... " he shrugged.

"So you want to carry on with me?" Shirley took his hand again. "It's really up to you and how you feel about your wife and maybe how she would feel if she knew about us."

"This may sound strange, to hear me say this, but I believe the nature of the love we shared was such that Anna would understand. I believe that I would understand if she found someone else." He again found it curious that when he mentioned Anna's name, a thrill of excitement shot through him. "We had such a complete cut off that there is no way I can reach her, or she can reach me, and therefore the relationship is dead. So really, it's not so much if I want to carry on with you but if you want to carry on with me. I'm no great catch... in fact I'm no catch at all... I would want to marry you... if I was free to do so... but you will have to take me as I am, with no prospects, I'm afraid."

"You would want to marry me?"

106

"Yes, of course, I would marry you tomorrow, that is, if you would have me."

"Yes, I would have you, Ronald Cameron, in the absence of any decent fellow, that is." Shirley held both his hands across the table and he could see by the twinkle in her eyes that she meant it. She got up and came round the table to him and he moved himself for her to sit on his knee. They kissed and then she said, "I guess then if you have proposed to me, and I have accepted, I had better make a special pre-nuptial feast for us tonight."

"No," he said, lifting her up and carrying her into the bedroom, "I think I shall treat you to a night at the Ritz, I have some cash saved up and we will blow it all on something special. But before that... I have something I need to do to you."

November 1965

Simon Clarke was home in his flat on Tooting Common. In the bathroom, which he had made into an occasional dark room, he undid the back of the camera and took out the film. He proceeded to develop it and when it was done he studied the documents revealed there. At various stages he referred to other papers that he had hidden amongst his essays on the Civil War. The resulting study took most of the afternoon, but after about four hours he straightened up at his desk, got up and went to his bedroom. He took down the suitcase from the top of the wardrobe, opened it and revealed the radio set. He extracted the aerial and wound it over the top of the window frame. He looked at his watch, put on the earphones and began to turn the dial to find the frequency he needed. He transmitted the message; it was short and he knew, to the point, "Cameron genuine."

November 1965

Ronald Cameron sat in the waiting room, passing time until the previous patient finished. He picked up a local newspaper and idly scanned the front page. There, halfway down the middle column, was his name. It was a report about him being missing in Russia. It said that he had disappeared whilst on a train to Moscow. There were no more relevant details, only that the Foreign Office were making all necessary enquiries. The newspaper was dated two weeks previously. As the doctor was now ready to see him, he took the paper in with him and put it down in front of Brian Anstruther-Plowman.

The two men greeted each other. "So good to see you and that you are OK." The doctor gestured him to a chair, "No problems getting back?"

"No, it was all right," Cameron pointed to the newspaper, "I see we made the news."

"Yes, but no harm done, I don't think. But you must tell me all the relevant details."

As he told him the series of events that his trip incurred, the doctor made notes, looking up occasionally in interest as a particular point came up that was relevant. When he had finished he leaned back in his chair. "Tell me more about this," he studied his notes, "Lavrenti Shlyapnikov, what sort of man is he?"

"Typical KGB, appears to be solid and unemotional, but, I think has a streak of, what shall we say, humanity, lurking quite close to the surface. Therefore could be vulnerable to various suggestions on our part."

"Do you think he told you anything that he didn't want to tell you?"

"Certainly I got the impression that things changed drastically when Stalin died and there was quite a trade off amongst the various factions within the Politburo. There was apparently a drastic jostling for position to find out, particularly, how the secret police were going to fare."

"How is the situation now, do you think?"

"Well it's very interesting, that's if you can stand back and view it from a distance. You see among the many problems that Stalin left his successors, one of the most urgent was how the secret police were fitting into the Soviet system."

"And how do they fit?"

"The secret police were essential for the preservation of the whole Soviet system, of course, both for the Party dictatorship internally and for the consolidation and expansion of its power abroad. Because of that the secret police are powerful enough to challenge the Party itself."

"So what does that mean for the whole structure of the system?" Anstruther-Plowman poured out a gin and tonic for himself and for Cameron.

"There is another problem that is part of this jigsaw, because the controls that the secret police have over every part of Russian society, stifles initiative and hampers progress; any attempt to modify the system encourages an upsurge of opposition to the dictatorship. We've seen this in the East German uprising in June 1953, the Vorkuta strike of summer 1953, the Poznan riots of July 1956 and, of course, the Hungarian uprising in 1956."

"But what, do you think, will happen next, what will it mean to us in the West?"

"I don't think it will make a lot of difference. It is their internal purges that will bring to power different people at different times, but basically we have to sit it out and hope that the whole system will self-destruct at some stage."

"How long is that going to take, one wonders."

"I suppose it depends on how heavy a hand is imposed on the structure and who comes to the top of the heap. There has been so much blood-letting to 'purify' the system, they say to 'return to revolutionary legality', that it beggars belief that it has lasted this long. The more the outside world sees that Soviet communism is an empty, corrupt system the sooner it will collapse. But, of course, they are past masters at hiding the truth and, in fact, would not see the truth themselves even if it was the proverbial hand in front of the face."

Anstruther-Plowman leaned forward in his chair, "It is good, is it not, that Anna is well out of it and will not be troubled by the system any more."

"Yes, indeed, along with millions of others, of course," Cameron replied, "but it makes one wonder how many more are going to be 'liquidated' or 'disappear' before the system crumbles.'

"Incidentally," he continued, "Shlyapnikov mentioned that Anna was involved on a special project in a place called Chernobyl, do you have any information about the place and what they are involved in there?"

"Chernobyl, no I don't know the place, but I will find out about it, as much as we can, of course, and let you know."

November 1965

Nina dialled Simon's number and when he picked up the phone to answer she seemed to hear a faint echo or click before he spoke.

"Simon, I have to tell you that Ronnie has come back from Russia and that, obviously, I won't be able to come out with you on Saturday." There was a significant silence on the other end.

"Oh, OK," he said eventually, "perhaps we can make it another time?" Nina paused briefly, "No, I don't think so, I think it's best if we perhaps don't do that."

"Why Nina? Look, I feel very deeply about you, and I don't want to lose you like this. Does this mean that what you are trying to say is that it's over between us?"

"I think it's best," she replied, sensing a tenseness in his speech and feeling it in herself too.

"I can't give you up," she heard him say, noticing an anger creeping in to his voice.

She felt an anger in herself as she answered, "Well, I'm sorry you'll just have to."

Again, a silence on the other end, this time prolonged, until she thought the line had gone dead; and she was just about to put the phone down when he said, "I'm sorry too because I can't give you up and that's final." This time the anger had been replaced by an icy deadness that so surprised her that she could not believe she was talking to the man she had grown fond of and whom she had taken to her bed with such abandon and pleasure.

Before she could say anything, he continued and what he said completely shattered any illusions she had that her life might be returning to a normal level.

"I must tell you, Nina, that if you persist in doing this to me then I shall be obliged to tell your Ronald Cameron that we have slept together, and I leave it to you to work out what that would do to your relationship with him. And what is more, I have information on him that, if it became known to the authorities, would finish him in this country. So I leave the decision to you, unless you continue with our relationship – and that means all that we have done before continuing – then I shall finish Ronald Cameron for good."

She could not believe what she was hearing, a numbness covered her and absorbed every one of her organs, "I'm sorry, what did you just say? I can't believe you just said that."

"You know what I've been saying well enough; your precious Ronald is a traitor to his country and I will expose him if necessary."

"A traitor, what do you mean? I have no idea what you are talking about."

"I know he has been giving information to the Russians. Of course, if you can find out what information he is giving, then I won't be so hard on you, I won't denounce him and I won't tell him about us."

"How do you know he has been giving information... how do you know these things?"

"I know because I make it my business to know. Anyway that is not for you to worry about, it is sufficient for you to know what I tell you is true."

Nina had to sit down, she was perspiring profusely and her legs were trembling.

"I realise this has been a shock for you," he appeared to have a tone of conciliation and curiously, she seemed to take heart in this.

"What about," he continued, "we meet up after you've had a little time to think this over and maybe you will have a clearer mind about this?"

She was almost past coherent thought at this point, but she found herself saying a tentative, "Yes, where?"

"I will pick you up on Saturday, in the morning, about nine, at the flat."

"OK," was all she was able to say.

"And don't worry," he continued, "I'm sure you will understand why I am doing this. It's because I love you so much that I can't bear for you to be involved with someone like him and destroy yourself. I know what is best for you, my darling."

Nina was absolutely appalled at what she had just experienced. It felt as though her whole life was suddenly shattered, destroyed, empty. Simon seemed to have revealed all the nastiness that was in her. All her apparent goodness was going to be exposed as a sham. She had been shown to be a whore and a whore of the worst kind. And she was trapped, trapped in the worst possible way. She had no way out. If she told Ronald, she showed herself to be a manipulative, sexual predator, promiscuous and self-seeking. He would have no more to do with her and would rightly cast her away. But if she didn't tell him she would be entering into a whole new realm of duplicity of the worst kind. Disloyalty, unfaithfulness and lies would be her new way of life. Her whole being would become tarnished irreversibly. And she would become linked to Simon, irretrievably. With his hold over her she would be his captive; open to every one of his whims, and to his vices, whatever they were; and she was horrified at the thought of what he might expose her to. He could be into all sorts of devious sexual manipulations and destroy her in mind, body and spirit. She would become his plaything, with no protection and no hope. So could her only hope be with Ronald? Could she tell him about the worst part of herself? Could she trust that declaration of love that he had made to her in that letter? Could that carry her through this most turbulent of times? And if she told him it also meant she was endangering him to the threat of this exposure that Simon was talking about. What did that mean and what proof did Simon have? Could it be, and she recoiled from this thought, that he was a traitor to his country? Such a thought was monstrous and she dismissed it utterly. She must confide in someone. She thought of Rachel.

"I don't know what to do, I am completely at a loss," she was talking to Rachel as they were sitting in the kitchen of their flat in Kingsbury. Rachel had never seen Nina in such a state before: her face was drawn and grey, as if she hadn't slept the previous night, which indeed she hadn't; her eyes, which were normally alive with light and beauty, were dull and moribund; and her silky corn-coloured hair was dry and stringy, although she had tied it back in an attempt at tidiness. However, above all was the attitude of her body, which had assumed a listlessness akin to atrophy. All her movements were slow and devoid of that vibrancy that she had always displayed, and that Rachel had always envied. It was as if she was attending her own funeral and was reluctant to get there.

Rachel poured out another mug of tea and handed it to her, "You can't be held by Simon in this way, it's terrible."
"What choice do I have? If I refuse him he will tell Ronald."
"But what's to stop you making up some story about what Ronald is supposedly telling the Russians."
"That's impossible, I don't know enough about espionage to even make up a story that would sound at all plausible."
Rachel was silent and she studied the inside of her tea mug, as if to find inspiration there. Nina sighed a deep, tired sigh, drained her

tea mug, leant forward and put the mug on the table. Even these simple movements were executed in such a despairing way that Rachel felt deep concern for her friend.

"Perhaps then, the only solution is," Rachel hesitated momentarily, "for you to tell everything to Ronald, and that way you will be free of Simon and maybe, just maybe, will find out a new dimension to Ronald's love for you."

Nina realised at that moment that she had not told Rachel about Ronald and herself when they had been reunited and how difficult it had become when they were about to make love.

Somehow she wanted to keep that to herself. It had been such an intimate aspect of their new relationship that she had needed to keep the memory of it shielded in her own heart. There were so many complexities in Ronald's character that she had a feeling that she was only scratching the surface of who and what he was. Maybe, when confronted with this revelation of Simon, he would not act in any conventional way but would be able to liberate her in a way that she couldn't imagine. After all, he was a man with vast experience of life and perhaps would be able to see new ways to combat this evil that confronted them both.

Nina looked at Rachel and gave a smile of gratitude, "Yes, do you know, I think you may have the answer there. I think you are right, it is the only thing to do." She grasped Rachel's hand and held it.

"Thank you for being a true friend, I honestly don't know what I would have done without being able to tell you. You brought sanity into this when I was in a complete fog."

Rachel squeezed her hand, "You know we both have a reason for being able to understand Ronald."

"Yes I know," Nina replied and extraordinarily she felt no jealousy towards Rachel. Her emotions had been through such a turmoil since she had discovered about Rachel and Ronald that it almost seemed of little significance.

November 1965

Nina looked at Ronald's face, it was in profile and the strong features were set in concentration. They were in the audience at the Old Vic for a performance of *The Merchant of Venice*. Although he was obviously enjoying the interplay of the characters, she was finding it increasingly difficult to get into the mood of the play. Her mind seemed completely absorbed by her need to tell him about Simon and about herself; she could not take any other distraction into focus. She had planned to tell him tonight before she had to see Simon in the morning, but the more she thought about it the more she became distraught at the prospect of the confrontation. How could she tell the man she truly loved that he had been cuckolded and that the man responsible would not give her up because he had such a hold over her that if she refused to go with him he would destroy all that she cherished? It seemed so simple when she and Rachel had come to the decision, but in the cold light of reality the implications were horrendous.

The play finished and they left the theatre with the main throng of people. They had decided that Ronald should stay at the Kingsbury flat that night before going back to Poole the next day. As Nina opened the door of the flat she was intensely grateful that Rachel had said she would not be in that night. She had found a new boyfriend who was more than accommodating in letting Rachel stay with him; in fact, in more normal times Nina would have cautioned Rachel about this infatuation, but she had not the energy left to focus on anything other than her own situation.

"Coffee?" she asked as she turned on the lights in the sitting room and switched on the electric fire, for the nights were getting more chilly.

"Yes please," he answered, opening a packet of cigarettes and offering her one. She declined and he went to sit by the fire as she went into the kitchen to boil the kettle.

"It was a good play, wasn't it," he called out, "I enjoyed it very much."

She was about to reply when she realised that they had already discussed it on the way home on the tube. It was another one of those curious little memory slips that she had noticed he had become prone to ever since he had returned; or perhaps it was her imagination, perhaps she was being affected by her own stretched nerves.

She brought the coffee mugs into the sitting room, smiled at him and gave him a mug. He smiled in return, took a sip of the liquid and said, "Look, Nina my darling, I've been anguishing long and hard about the other night and how my behaviour must have seemed so... bizarre," he took her hand and the look in his eyes told Nina his true concern.

"It's just... I suppose... getting over the death of Anna and trying to come to terms with all that has happened... it just threw me."

She felt nonplussed; she had been all geared up to begin to tell him what she was going through and he had pre-empted her. She was silent, chiefly because she couldn't think of anything to say.

"I want, so much, for us to be together in every possible way, but at the moment I am so confused about a number of things, that I have to sort it out in my own way first." He continued, and grasped her hand, "Please try and understand... I know it must be difficult for you... but I love you so much and I want so much for this to work out for us."

She squeezed his hand, "I'm trying to understand," she smiled at him, "I love you too and I also want desperately for this to work out, but I also have a problem which needs your understanding."

"OK, what is that."

"It's not going to be easy," she took her hand from his and felt more isolated now than she had ever felt in her life, "in fact, you say you have anguished long and hard, well I have too. But it's nothing to do with what happened the other night, it's something entirely different."

"Whatever it is my darling, I am listening."

She felt a great weight on her chest and she suddenly experienced a difficulty in breathing.

"When you were away," she looked down at her lap, she could not look into his face, "I felt so lonely... and sad, I wanted, so desperately, to be able to help you in some way... but there was no way I could be of any help to you... your letter... when it arrived... was such a joy to me... it said all those things that I longed to hear from you." She looked up suddenly into his eyes and smiled, "And I knew then that somehow... I don't know how... but everything would turn out all right."

"And it has, hasn't it?" he interposed.

If she could have ended there and drawn a line and not gone on with this torture, she would have rejoiced, but she knew she had started and there was no end to it until she had completely unburdened herself.

"No, it hasn't finished yet," she touched his hand with her fingers, but wouldn't get hold of it.

"Because I felt so lonely... I became friendly with a guy from the college." She looked quickly at him, and she saw that sudden hurt in his eyes.

"Yes," he said slowly, as if knowing a revelation was coming that he didn't want to hear.

She looked down at her lap again, "We slept together." She almost whispered the words, but knew that he had heard because of the prolonged silence that followed.

November 1944

The clarinetist was coming to the end of his solo and as the music from the quartet reached a crescendo Ronald Cameron and Shirley sat enthralled by the exuberance of the atmosphere. They were enjoying a night out in a north London pub whose upper room was crowded with similarly enthused jazz lovers. When the piece finished he was just about to go to the bar to get some more drinks and, in fact, had risen to his feet, when the ceiling fell in. It seemed to him such a ridiculously severe climax to the piece of music; it took him some seconds to realise what had actually happened. It was one of those fleeting out of body thought experiences that was completely out of context. The fact that the V2 rocket had landed just four hundred yards from the pub front door was the main reason why the ceiling had come down and the occupants of the building were now severely aware of it.

The ensuing mayhem was wearily predictable. Ronald Cameron was aware that he was face down on the floor with, what seemed to be a heavy weight on his back. Dust was choking his throat and was filling his lungs with a detritus of burning vapour. He tried desperately with all his might to move his arm to try and find Shirley, but to no avail. His voice was drowned by all the other voices trying to find help or companions. Apart from the inability to get to his feet he felt no pain and if there was any panic in his system it became nullified as he lost consciousness.

November 1965

Ronald Cameron sat in the corner seat of the train carriage surveying his fellow passengers. They seemed a cross-mix of humanity, all absorbed in the complexities of their own lives, all seemingly oblivious to him; completely unaware of the confusions that existed within his own mind. But how could they be aware? He comforted himself in the thought that human beings were so constructed that their inmost thoughts were completely invisible to the outside world. If they hadn't been, the rampaging chaos of his own mind at this juncture would have surely terrified his companions.

He went back to those memories of last night, in fact he'd never left them, they were there hanging in his mind, like tapestries in a medieval cathedral. And like those decorations, they had a life of their own, they were there as an immense, immovable backcloth to his life. His life was now incomplete without them. Nina and her revelations had changed his life irrevocably.

First of all, she had confessed to an infidelity, which had surprised him but was not life destroying. Then had come the character of the man who had seduced her; and that had changed the whole nature of the situation. Ronald Cameron had now been forced back into a state of defence, he was no longer in charge, there were pressures on him that, if he didn't handle them correctly, would bring about the destruction of so much that he had worked for for so long. Yet he felt a strong sense of "déjà vu", he had been here before. His thoughts went back twenty-one years to the wonder of Anna, how much he loved her, how much all his yearnings were centred on that beautiful girl, and how much the revelation of the Soviet system had threatened to destroy them both. Yet they had managed, for a time, to delay the inevitable. By dint of imagination and subterfuge they had fooled the controllers and they had managed to forge a short, but glorious, time together. It was only ended because the separations of war had intruded. Would something similar be possible now? Yet conditions were very different now, it was a Cold War and the enemies were different. The enemy revealed this time was shown to be just as evil and just as tenacious as the previous one but its demands were more subtle, more devious. He knew he had been playing a very dangerous game, trying to balance what he knew to be right for his country and yet endeavouring to keep the devouring, poisoning and all-consuming system from destroying what he loved in Russia.

So how could he deal with this new situation? He knew that he loved Nina; and he loved her with a passion that was similar to his love for Anna, but it was different. He knew, only too well, that it was possible to love more than one woman at a time, and before Anna died that was the case for him. He saw such a similarity in both women, not only physically but also mentally and in their spirit, they were curiously united. Now, it was as if Nina had taken over the role, the baton had been passed to her. She seemed to be the two girls rolled into one. Somehow, the situation that he and Nina found themselves in was curiously predictable. Was it something within himself that was a magnet not only for the girls but for the tenacity of the predicaments that attached themselves to him? Was he doomed to be the catalyst of such scenarios? He mentally shook himself; this meandering amongst the daisy meadows of reflection was not working out the particular problem that now faced him. What were the priorities? He needed Nina and he wanted her to be happy. Whether she was going to be happy with him was a question for the future. He hoped so with all his heart and he intended to see to it that she knew this. So how could they get this Simon off their backs? What was his agenda? That he appeared to be in with some sort of inside knowledge was obvious. Where had this knowledge come from? It could only be from two possible sources. If it wasn't from the British side, MI5 or MI6, then the only other source would be the enemy, he must be a Soviet agent. Yet if he was a Soviet agent he was taking a terrible risk. He must know that to reveal himself in this way would leave him open to exposure. So perhaps he had his own secret agenda, perhaps he had become so besotted with Nina that he was willing to risk a great deal. Ronald Cameron smiled grimly to himself, maybe the KGB were being hoisted by their own petard. The honey pot that they had used so successfully against Western agents and the blackmail that ensued was, maybe, in this case, to be their weakness. There was no doubt that this Simon was risking everything in order to satisfy his obsession with Nina. As the train pulled into Poole station Ronald Cameron was resolved and settled in his mind as to what he had to do next.

November 1944

He occupied the end bed in the ward. There were eight beds in two rows facing each other. He knew, from the nurses, that all the patients occupying the beds were casualties of the bombing of the pub. Their injuries were severe in some cases and he seemed to be the most fortunate in that he had only sustained minor injuries to his ribs and lacerations to his face. As soon as he had regained conscious-ness he had asked about Shirley and after an agonising wait whilst the nurse went to enquire, he learned, to his immense relief, that she was less affected than him.

It was the next day, after he had found this out, that she came into the ward. He saw her lovely face before she noticed him and it delighted his heart as he saw the recognition in her expression as she saw him. She came, half running, down the ward and almost threw herself into his arms. He winced slightly as the pressure of her embrace made him aware of his bruises. She noticed his expression and apologised with a childlike vulnerability that made him aware of how much he loved her. They talked then for some time until the sister came to tell them that he had better rest.

"I will come and see you tomorrow my darling," she said as she took her leave of him. He kissed her eyes and her mouth and they held hands until, getting up, she moved away from him. As she walked back, out of the ward, she kept turning round until, finally, she went out of the door with a final smile and a wave.

He learned, the next day, that he could be allowed to leave that day if he wanted to. She came to collect him and they both left the hospital by way of a taxi to Shirley's mother's home. They had both been given sick leave and her mother insisted that she was the only one who was qualified to look after them. They both succumbed gratefully and with undisguised pleasure to her ministrations. It was there, a few days later, that they learned that he had been posted abroad. His job at the Admiralty had finished and he was to join his ship in a week's time.

November 1965

Brian Anstruther-Plowman listened with an expression that was as close to astonishment as he could muster. At least Ronald Cameron thought that he revealed such as he told him of the events surrounding Nina.

"What I would like to know is where is this Simon Clarke coming from? I would hesitate to consider that he is one of ours."

"Quite," replied his companion.

"Can you find out for me? Because until I know I will not know how to proceed."

Anstruther-Plowman considered for a moment, "He must think you to be genuine, in other words, a spy for the Soviets, therefore he can't be working for us otherwise he would know your true nature. And if he knows that you are giving information to the Russians he could only have one way of knowing." He flipped open a file in front of him and began to scan the page, "According to the numbers and names down here, of the staff at the Russian embassy, and we know of the majority who are 'legals' that is, agents who are working to gain information from various sources. I would say that he is an 'illegal', set up by the Russians to run an agent in this country."

"How can we be sure?"

"We will make enquiries, discreetly, of course, and find out about this man. Interestingly, whatever task he has had there is no doubt that by coming out into the open, in the way he has, he has blown his cover for good, and that will not please the Soviets one little bit."

November 1944

"How am I going to manage without you?" Shirley asked the question as she and Ronald Cameron were walking home from the cinema. In four days' time he was due to join his ship and they had both studiously avoided asking the one question to which, they knew, there was no answer.

He turned and looked at her, "I don't know and equally I don't know how I am going to do without you."

They linked arms and continued walking along the street. "Maybe it will all be over soon," she said, "and we can all get back to a life without the threat of death around the next corner."

"Let's hope so, my beloved," he answered, his words a reflection of the hope he was not sure of.

"Shall we try and get away to that place in the Cotswolds that we were at in September?" she asked, her face turning to him in anticipation. "It was so lovely and it would mean such a lot to us."

He smiled at her, "Yes let's try. I'm sure I can borrow some money. We must take the opportunity if we can."

They walked back to Shirley's mother's house and had a bedtime drink with her mother. They told her of their plans and she insisted on giving them the money for it. He made it clear that it would only be a loan and that he would pay it back when he could. They said good night to each other outside Shirley's bedroom and he went to his room with a lighter heart than when he had woken in the morning.

November 1944

The morning sun was shining through the floral curtains as they lay in bed, his arms around her and her head resting on his chest. It was the last day of their three days in the old coaching inn in the Cotswolds. The ancient building was set at a crossroads of two country lanes, about three miles outside the village of Bourton on the Water. The rolling green hills seemed to enfold the inn within a comforting tapestry of safety and calm. They had both felt the peace of the place, it had inhabited them with it's presence and endowed them with a serenity that a few days ago they could not have imagined possible. They were no longer afraid to voice their worst fears to each other and, indeed, in doing so had found a liberation within themselves that they sensed was truly remarkable.

"I wonder if we will ever be as happy again?" Shirley murmured.

"I wonder," he said, "but whatever happens I want you to know that I have found a happiness with you that I didn't think was possible." He knew he truly believed his own words but the memory of Anna suddenly presented itself and he realised, with a shock, that he had said exactly the same words to her, what was it, no more than four months ago. Why should the memory of Anna suddenly be so startlingly before him? The girl in his arms now was amazingly similar to her physically, yet they were so different in personality. What was Anna doing now? How was she coping with the conditions of war and the imposition of a system that seemed so alien to reasonable civilised behaviour? Was the information that he was giving to the Soviets sufficient to keep her in safety? He had loved her with a passion that, he found, was very difficult to imagine as he lay with this other beautiful girl in a very different set of circumstances and in a very different location. How do you judge passion with any reliable yardstick? It must depend upon circumstances and environment and the chemistry between two people.

His reverie was interrupted by Shirley, "You will write to me, won't you? I know it will be difficult my darling... but I will write every day." She looked up at him with that innocent vulnerability that he found so disturbingly attractive.

"Yes, of course, my beloved, as soon as I get the opportunity, I will be sending you my thoughts and trying to express to you how I feel about you and how much I will be missing you."

"Where will you be going?" She knew there was no answer to that one, but with her job at the Admiralty she was in the best position to know, possibly, before he did.

"Wherever it is, you will know that I shall be thinking about you," he kissed her head and buried his face in the luxurious sweet smell of her hair.

They spent most of the day in bed, only getting up to go to supper in the bar. He discovered that in the cellar of the pub they had left a few bottles of champagne and, counting up the money left over from the rail fares and the accommodation, he decided to use the little that was left to buy a half bottle of 1939 Moet. They enjoyed it with a shepherd's pie that was on the menu. They drank a toast to Shirley's mother.

"Without her we would not have been able to be here," he said and they clinked glasses and linked arms and drank to each other, looking into each others eyes and vowing eternal love.

November 1965

"Simon Clarke was recruited at university and appears to be one of those dedicated 'fellow travellers' who is used as an 'illegal' agent, who runs other agents. In the KGB parlance he is part of what they call an 'illegal residency' a 'nelegalnaya rezidentura'." Brian Anstruther-Plowman was relaying this information to Ronald Cameron in the plain but comfortable surroundings of his consulting room.

"So, what shall we do about him?"

"I think we should run with him for a while," replied the doctor, "let him realise that Nina will not go along with him and that he will be obliged to expose you."

"He may not, of course," replied Cameron, "it may be a gigantic bluff on his part. After all, he would not wish to blow his cover in this way."

"But it would not necessarily blow his cover, he could report you to whoever he considers to be the relevant authority anonymously."

"Yes, but, if he exposes me it means the Soviets have lost me as an informer and it will not take them long to know who it was that shopped me."

"Apparently that's a risk he's willing to take," replied Anstruther-Plowman. "It seems his infatuation with Nina will be his undoing."

"I guess he won't be the first man to discover how weak we men are when it comes to women," he smiled grimly in remembrance.

"There is, of course, a rather more serious issue here," Cameron's companion went on, "how this will effect the information that we are giving the Soviets. At the moment they appear to be accepting as genuine what you are channelling through to them and because of that we can see that they are being led on a wild goose chase... it will be a shame if that has to stop."

"But it doesn't have to stop," said Cameron, "we can arrange an investigation into my activities and I can be cleared officially. Rather like what happened to Philby."

Anstruther-Plowman smiled slightly, "And that way, when you are cleared, your information to them will appear that much more, how shall we say, genuine."

"Exactly," Cameron responded, "and we shall have, hopefully, got rid of another spy, particularly in a way that does not rebound on us. The Soviets will have to clear up their own mess, believing it to be their own agent to be in error."

"You have not met this Simon Clarke yet?"

"No, and it would probably be a good idea if I didn't. Nina is due to meet him on Saturday to talk over their previous conversation and to tell him of her decision."

"It would be good then if we put her under a protective surveillance and follow her to the rendezvous," Anstruther-Plowman made a note on his file, "we need to know the physical identity of Simon Clarke."

"Thank you, yes, I need to know too that she will be safe, I don't like the sound of this man and the threats that he seems to be capable of. After all, when she says to him face to face that she doesn't want any more to do with him, how is he going to react? It would be far better for her to say this over the phone, it would be much safer for her anyway."

"For her, yes, I agree," responded Anstruther-Plowman, "but we need to see this man and although she could prevaricate, I believe he could force an answer out of her. She is a girl of some spirit, I believe, and would not hesitate to give her mind if her ire was up."

"She is, as you say, a girl of some spirit," replied Cameron, "and I believe she is willing to take the risk if it means that this man is brought to some form of justice."

"That's why we must have a surveillance team involved, we can't afford anything to go wrong. He appears to be someone who is unpredictable, and because of that doesn't act according to normal rules."

"I will go back to London now," Cameron replied, "and give her our thoughts and hopefully she will be happy with the arrangements."

"Yes, and I will organise the team." Anstruther-Plowman stood up and held out his hand to his companion, "Don't worry, this seems an opportunity for us to get one back on the Soviets, that is if we think ahead of their next move."

November 1965

Simon Clarke arrived promptly at nine o'clock on Saturday morning at the Kingsbury flat. Unbeknown to him his arrival was also noted by the milkman, who, for the first time, had an assistant who was less interested in the milk deliveries and more in the visitor to number 23. Nina opened the door to Simon's ring on the bell. He tried to kiss her on the lips but she averted her face and he was left with the option of her cheek. She ushered him in and they went into the sitting room and sat down together on the sofa. If he was reading her body language he would not have needed to ask the question, but he did. "Have you come to a decision about what we talked about?"

"Yes," she replied.

"Well, what is it to be?"

She turned to face him on the sofa and looked full into his eyes. She expected to see hostility there but saw instead an expression of wounded innocence, which had always fascinated her and, despite her determination not to allow it to, was attracting her now. "I was very hurt by your forceful attitude and you gave me an ultimatum, which is not nice."

"I'm sorry," he said; he looked at her so mournfully that she had to resist a strong urge to throw herself into his arms and beg forgiveness herself.

He looked down at the floor, as if embarrassed, "I was so desperate not to lose you that I said some stupid things."

She was instantly getting the feeling that if she wasn't very careful she would be drawn again into the subtlety of the net that he was drawing around her.

"But how could you threaten me like that?" she made a great effort to confront the romantic emotion that was rising within her. The look of his face, which she had seen with longing when he had been making love to her, again appealed to her in ways she tried not to contemplate.

He looked again at her with those clear grey eyes that spoke to her of love and compassion, "I must have been mad, I honestly don't know what came over me. It was just the thought of you with someone else... and after all we were coming to mean to each other...", he tailed off with a gesture of his hands that spoke of hopelessness.

She was now so confused that the clarity of her thinking was nonexistent. She thought of Ronald, who, if he knew her thoughts, she was sure would have shared her confusion.

"But you must understand," she said, " that Ronald has come back and you must realise what he means to me. What we did together... was a mistake."

"Is that all it meant to you?" he spoke quietly, almost whispering the words.

"No... I mean," she blushed in her confusion, "I needed you at the time... probably more than you'll ever know... but now... it's different."

"So I can just be discarded, is that it?"

Nina noticed a hint of bitterness creeping in to his voice. "No," she said, "I didn't mean it like that, it's just... I love Ronald."

"And you don't love me, is that it?"

"I don't feel the same way about you that I do about him." She was beginning to feel pressured and vulnerable.

"How do you think I feel?" he stared straight at her as if challenging her to read his heart. She hesitated momentarily, "I don't know."

She saw that he was clenching his jaw and his face became set as if in granite, he was wringing his hands as he spoke, "I know that I can't live without you, I have become completely obsessed with you... you fill every one of my waking moments... I can't get you out of my mind... not that I want to," he smiled briefly, she thought, as if a warm spring wind had suddenly blown across freezing snow.

"I don't know what I should do if I lost you," he continued, "I love you more than I thought it would be possible to love anyone."

Nina became transfixed by this declaration. There was a part of her that felt a macabre thrill, as if hypnotised by a swaying cobra, but it was more than overwhelmed by a feeling of revulsion, not at the statement itself but in the way it was pronounced. She felt horrified by an implied threat woven amongst the words of love.

She looked at him, trying to sum up what to say and, having said it, what effect it would have. "So... if you can't have me..." she spoke slowly, as if reluctant to complete the sentence, "what are you going to do?"

He looked at her, his eyes now ice cold, he spoke deliberately, "I have already had you and what I have had... I keep."

December 1944

The destroyer was pitching into the turbulent waters of the Bay of Biscay. She was about twenty miles out in the bay on the northwest corner of Spain. She was part of a flotilla of destroyers protecting a convoy bound for Malta. The sea was creaming over the bows of the ship as she dipped into the troughs and Ronald, in the radio room, had to steady himself on the console as the ship bucked up onto the next crest. The Germans had installed a transmitting station near Lugo in northwest Spain, which would transmit a fan of beams out into the Atlantic and over the Bay of Biscay. There was a similar station near Brest in France which would provide a cross-pattern of beams by which an aircraft, ship or U boat could determine its position. The Royal Navy was making use of the same arrangement by using their own receiver to intercept the beams and thus provide their navigating officers with a simple method of location, not only of their own ships but of the enemies as well.

Ronald Cameron had been seconded to the Signals Section of the Directorate of Naval Intelligence, NID9, and his presence on this convoy was to monitor the beams and the tracing of U boats in this part of the Atlantic. By using the developed receivers on board ship he was able to listen in to the signals being transmitted to the wolf pack of submarines active in the area. His earphones picked up a strong signal and he adjusted the configuration on the dial to locate the receiving vessel. She was about two miles distant and, judging by the clarity of the reception, she was on the surface. He immediately notified the bridge and he heard the order for Action Stations follow within the next minute. Such was the veracity of the equipment he was using he was able to follow the attack by the destroyer and to hear the signals being sent out by the U boat. It seemed she was on the surface due to some problem and when the Royal Navy ship arrived she didn't dive but stayed on the surface and proceeded to use her deck armament. The subsequent engagement was short and predictable and the U boat was dispatched to the sea bed. The survivors were picked up by a naval pinnace from another ship.

November 1965

Simon Clarke left, leaving a bewildered and distraught Nina. Of all the possible scenarios that she had envisaged this was the most unlikely one to have surfaced. Yet she should have foreseen it. But what puzzled her more than anything was, if she wasn't willing, how could he possibly maintain a hold over her? He had resorted to threats of blackmail before and how he was going to destroy Ronald, but he hadn't alluded to it this time. Had he forgotten or was it just an empty bluff? He could not take her by force, or rather he could try but it would be a short-lived campaign. Perhaps he was hoping that by holding the threat to Ronald over her head he could maintain this hold over her. Of course, as soon as his threat became reality he knew he would lose her, he would have no hold over her then.

So she knew he was on a knife edge, he had worked so hard to try and keep hold of her, he had used all the armaments in his battery to keep her. Perversely she felt a sneaking admiration for him, the fact that he was willing to hazard so much to keep her; it filled her with thoughts that she knew she shouldn't be thinking.

She phoned Ronald as soon as she had collected her thoughts sufficiently and told him the outcome of the meeting. To her surprise he didn't seem all that concerned. He was intrigued by Simon's eventual statement to her and asked her how she felt about it.

"I am very confused, at the end he seemed so different from the beginning," she said, "I mean to say that, he was... well... loving at one point... and when he left I felt a shiver of... yes... fear."

"Are you all right?" Ronald sounded concerned. "Shall I come over?"

"No, it's OK. I'll be fine."

"I'm staying at the club tonight, I've got to meet some bigwig from the Admiralty early in the morning so I need to be here."

"It's OK, really, darling," she repeated, although she desperately needed a hug she refused to show it in her voice and in her words.

As she put the phone down Rachel came in and, in her normal bouncy way, asked how she was. She received the reply with a flood of tears and an urgent embrace.

December 1944

The torpedo struck Ronald Cameron's destroyer at two o'clock in the morning. It hit amidships just below the radio room and demolished the complete cabin. Earnie Watts was killed outright, struck by the section of floor as it yielded to the forces below it. Ronald Cameron, who had just ended his watch, was blown through the door and into the steel wall opposite. He lost consciousness as the water flooded through the breached hull but came to as the icy sea submerged his body. His next moments were a confused jumble of trying to swim as if within the confines of a sardine can, he kept hitting hard objects, and his breathing, such as it was, came in tortured gasps. After what seemed an endless succession of buffeting and submerging, he bobbed up to the surface and attempted to swim in the stinking oil of the freezing sea. After a time, he didn't know how long, he no longer felt cold and began to imagine that he was floating on a cloud of incredible softness. He remembered no more until, gasping with the intensity of the pain that seemed to inhabit every part of his body, he lay spreadeagled on a sandy beach in northern Spain.

December 1965

To his intense annoyance Ronald Cameron was not able to see Nina the next day. It was the first day of December and he was involved in a whole series of meetings with various individuals who needed his advice on assorted matters relating to the latest signals technology. She decided to work from home, she had an essay to write and she found some measure of relief in being able to submerge herself in the technicalities of the Hundred Years War. She was still full of emotion, the legacy of Simon's visit, and was still trying to work out her feelings about him. That she hated him, she was willing to admit, certainly that was her foremost emotion after he had left. However, that hot passion had now died down and more and more she was noticing that another feeling was creeping in. And this was the feeling that was now disturbing her. For she now found that the very intense emotion that he had displayed and the obvious strength of feeling that he had was beginning to inhabit her. Where she should have disliked all that he stood for and denigrated those qualities that she thought he previously had possessed, she was beginning to recognise that, perhaps, she had misjudged him.

Although she hated herself for it, she could not resist the images of him coming through her confused mind; the vigorous nature of his lovemaking; the soft gentleness of his consideration towards her when she was upset; his patience when he didn't understand her; these disturbing images of him begun to influence and dilute her previous convictions.

She was interrupted in her deliberations by the phone ringing, she picked it up, it was Simon.
Her heart seemed to do a double patter as she heard his voice, "Hello, are you all right? Look I'm so sorry about yesterday... it was really bad of me to say those things to you."
She, literally, was speechless, she couldn't even murmur a "hello."
"Hello, are you there?" he went on. "Look, it's difficult talking over the phone, can we see each other, can I take you out to a meal and perhaps a show, and we can try and forget the past few days?"

Nina attempted to collect her thoughts, she said, "It's difficult to suddenly forget, perhaps we should give it a bit more time."
"If that's what you want, of course, I'll leave it to you to decide...I just wanted to apologise and let you know that I am so sorry if I have hurt you."
She rang off then, her thoughts a jumble of conflicting emotions.

December 1944

Shirley, as a cipher clerk, was just collating the mass of information that had been received that morning into an orderly file, when one of the other Wrens made an exclamation that caught her attention. "We've lost three more destroyers, two H class and one I class, on the Malta convoy."
Shirley went over to see what their names were and she knew,

because it was one of those mornings, that the I class destroyer would be Ronald's. She was not incorrect, it was his.

Despite her premonition, her heart seemed to freeze inside her.

"Do we have the casualty lists yet?" Her mouth was as dry as dust and her companion knew by the quiet urgency of her request, that it was more than idle curiosity.

"No, not yet," she glanced quickly at Shirley and noted the strained concentration on her face.

"Is it Ronnie's?"

"Yes," was all she could say.

The morning dragged by, the minutes on the ship's clock above her head seemed to take ten times as long as normal. At midday some casualty lists came out and she scanned them rapidly but his name was not there, she then read them again, in case she had missed the vital words.

She lost count of the number of times she read the list, and by the end of the day she could have repeated all the names on the list by heart. But all to no avail, his name was not there.

"Of course, it's not an exhaustive list," the CPO told her, "there are many times when a man has been picked up and the ship concerned has not registered the name as it should have done."

But whatever anyone said, she knew, with a deep-down certainty, that his name would not be amongst the list of survivors. She went home that evening and told her mother and they both comforted each other as best they could. Her mother knew her daughter well enough to know that whatever words of solace she was able to utter, her daughter would see it as false optimism.

December 1965

Ronald Cameron could tell as soon as he saw Nina, that she had changed. She no longer had that hard attitude of resistance to Simon Clarke. There was a remoteness to her, a detachment, that he'd never seen before. She was no longer the open-hearted, joyful girl that he had loved ever since he had known her. She was closed up to him.

"So he turned up and you had this conversation, and he didn't threaten you?"

"No, he was really quite nice," she found she had difficulty looking him in the eyes.

"And so you have finished with him, for good?"

She didn't like the way the conversation was going or, she felt, the brusque way that he was asking the questions. "I think so," she replied.

"You think so... forgive me, but didn't he threaten you the other day?" She had never seen him exasperated before and she thought he was going to lose his temper. "And didn't he reveal that he was going to blackmail you through me and shop me to the authorities?"

"Yes, he did," she knew this was going to be difficult and she felt so miserable about hurting Ronald, but she knew that she had to be honest, and looking at him at this moment she knew, also, with a shock, that she no longer loved him as she used to.

"But I believe he has changed... I saw something in him that I hadn't seen before... he was really sorry for hurting me."

Ronald Cameron sat back in the chair and couldn't believe what he was hearing. He knew he was losing this girl, probably had already lost her, and he felt something vital slipping away from him, yet he couldn't do anything about it.

She saw how much she had hurt him and her heart was needing to give him some solace, "I need some time to think this out, I don't know what to do." She touched his hand, as if the very touch would channel the sorrow that she felt away from him.

"What will time do for you?" The statement seemed as sorrowful as the tone in which it was said.

She shrugged and looked at the floor, "I don't know," was the whispered reply.

"OK," he shrugged also, seemingly resigned to the inevitable.

She glanced quickly at him, and had the memory of him sobbing his heart out on her breasts when he had aborted their lovemaking. He looked just as sad now. His sadness seemed to reach out and absorb her and her sorrow and become one vast sea of stricken emotion. She took both his hands in hers, "I'm sorry," she whispered.

"I am too," he said, his face a bleak mirror of his feelings.

He looked up, "Will you ring me, when you can and tell me what conclusions you have come to?" She gave a half smile to him, "Of course."

December 1944

The two Spanish fishermen found Ronald Cameron's almost lifeless body the next morning. As they knelt over him and turned him over he groaned and vomited. They picked him up and trundled him back to their village on the cart they used for carrying their catch. One of them took him into his house and his wife proceeded to minister to his needs by nourishment of warm soup and tending to the various abrasions that covered his body. Despite his ordeal he seemed to recover quickly. By the end of a week he was walking about the village conversing with as many people who wanted to talk to him. His Spanish was as good as his German so he was able to find out where he was and how far it was from Madrid. After thanking profusely the family who had looked after him and promising to inform the British embassy how well they had looked after him, he arranged to have a seat on the next lorry that was taking fish to Corunna. There, he made contact with the British chargéd affaires, who was only too happy to escort him, by train, to the embassy in Madrid. Once there, the processing of his details for on carriage to England was arranged and also the transport of himself on the next *Liberator* flight. Before that happened he had two days in Madrid, and in wandering about the city he was able to confront the ghosts of his recent past. Not that he had to conjure them up, they appeared of their own volition, parading themselves like soldiers on a march. Some he recognised as old friends, others were strangers to him.

The sweetest ghosts were Anna and Shirley and he dwelt on the aspect of them with a mixture of sadness and joy. It seemed such a long time ago that he was with Anna. How was she? What was the war doing to her? What was her relationship with Morozov now that she was relying on his despatches from London to keep her safe? What was Morozov's department of The Peoples Commissariat of Internal Affairs making of the information that he was sending them? And what of the situation now? How would Anna fare if he was not able to keep sending secret despatches to Moscow? Would it make it impossible for her to avoid the stigma that the Party would put upon her as an ASE-SI potential enemy (connection with foreigners)?

He heaved a sigh of remorse, that he had brought such heartache on such a beautiful creature. Yet what choice did he have? How could you choose who you were going to fall in love with? When, and if, you were smitten, what risks do you take to keep that love alive? Without love, he knew now, life was barely worth living. Having once tasted such joy the thought of life without it filled him with despair. Yet the important thing was that the experience of love was so profound and immense in its effects, that, even if it was lost, the legacy of it remains and stimulates forever. He thought about Shirley and the apparent ease with which he had found love with her. Yet it was easy because he had first found Anna. Anna had shown him the true magic of love and that sense of awe had carried over to Shirley. Anna had opened his eyes, never to be shut again. His sigh of remorse turned into one of relief as he pursued these thoughts and he knew he had been given a unique insight into a world that was, in a sense, secret, but was open to everyone.

He knew, of course, that the mechanics of his life were by no means simple; he had a wife, but she was no longer within his compass and the conventions of the world would deny him any attachment to the girl he was now with. How could he reconcile this situation? He wanted to do what was right, but what was right in a world that had gone mad? What did it matter what he did when most of the world was immersed in such evil that it beggared belief. He knew, of course, that it was not as simple as that. Each person was responsible for his own actions, otherwise there was no order, and life would be reduced to a chaotic state. But that brought personal morality into the equation and the system of belief that each person must find for himself. He had been taken to Sunday school as a child and maybe the example that he had been shown there – of a special man's life and sacrifice; allied to a God who was demonstrating, not only that He had created the world, but that those he had created were precious and special, born of a love that was impossible to break – could inform his life too. He certainly knew the power of love in his life, could God's love be the same?

He was shaken out of his reverie by the thought of Shirley and the need to let her know that he was all right. Because she was not his next of kin the Navy would not be aware that information should be passed to her. Hopefully her position at the Admiralty would allow her to see the lists of survivors and she would soon know that he was alive. Even if he wrote to her now he would arrive before the letter. He consoled himself with that thought and learned only later that it would be a poor consolation.

December 1965

Three days later Ronald Cameron answered the phone. It was Nina. "I have thought so long, I haven't slept... and I still can't see what to do... the more I think the more I seem to get confused." Her confusion came through in her voice.

He knew he should be concerned about her but the thought of their last conversation and the way she had seemingly denied him had hurt him more than he wished to show her. So he had gone for his old defence mechanism, he had begun to shut her off from his feelings. As soon as he sensed that she was beginning to exclude him a wall of indifference began to be built within him. Not that he wanted this to happen, he didn't, but in order to protect himself he had to do this, otherwise he knew that something vital within himself would be destroyed. He felt it was similar to the watertight doors in a ship, if the structure is compromised, then the defences must come into play.

"I don't think I can help," was all he could say.

"I don't want to hurt you Ronald... that's the last thing I want to do." It's too late for that, was what he wanted to say, but he bit back the words before they could do harm, "I know you don't," was all he could utter; however, he was waiting for the "but."

"But, I just can't get Simon out of my mind."

So far, he thought, she was being predictable and saying all the things she needed to say to end a relationship but, with a shock, he realised how cynical he was becoming. He loved this girl, a few days ago she was the most precious and lovely thing in his world and now his attitude to her was absolutely abominable. How could his feelings change so quickly? He was blaming her but how much was he to blame for the whole situation? Did she sense something in him that was detached from her? Did the problem that he had about their physical consummation begin to put doubts in her mind? There was something about a mote in someone else's eye and a beam in his own that seemed to come to mind.

"I know it is difficult," he said, "but I just can't help you, you have to work this out in your own way."

"I know," she paused, and then went on, hesitantly, "you know that I love you... and will always love you... no matter what happens."

This was the statement that he'd always feared; he had prepared himself to lose her and now here she was offering a way back, but a way that was full of agony and pain of the worst kind.

"I know," his voice thickened, "and I will always love you."

December 1944

The *Liberator* landed at Mildenhall in Suffolk, with Ronald Cameron on board, and he was driven straight down to Plymouth, where his new ship awaited him. After being debriefed he went on board the ship, which was another I class destroyer with the latest radar and radio equipment fitted. However, before he went to the ship he was able to make a phone call, from the dockside, to the Admiralty, to the department where Shirley worked.

The operator put him through to the section he wanted, but Shirley was not there. After some enquiries he got through to one of her friends. There was a significant pause when she realised who it was, "Ronald Cameron... yes... I'm sorry... um," she was hesitating and he somehow was reluctant to hear what she was going to say.

"She was at home last night... and there was a raid, well it was actually a V2," she hesitated again, "look, it's so difficult."

"Is she badly hurt?" he whispered the words because he knew she needed some help.

"The information we have is that the house was demolished and that two bodies have been brought out... our section leader made enquiries... when she didn't report for duty," she tailed off and the leaden weight that had closed around his heart finally reached his knees and he buckled under the pressure and slumped against the wall of the phone box.

December 1965

Simon Clarke was reviewing the situation. It was some days since he had spoken to Nina and, although he had been pursuing his work at college he had also been maintaining contact with his controller. He had been trying to follow up a contact at the college to see if he was sympathetic to the Soviet cause and had been encouraged by the response so far. Therefore the situation with Nina had taken, in his mind, a secondary place. Whereas with Nina it had assumed gigantic proportions in her thinking and had taken over all her nervous energy, with Simon it was only a comparatively small issue. An intriguing issue, of course, and he dwelt on the possible excitement of it with pleasure, but, nevertheless, a minor one.

She rang him just after she had spoken to Ronald and again she heard that slight click and a change in tone as the phone was answered.

"Simon, this is Nina," she still wasn't sure how much he recognised her voice. "I've been thinking so much about us and wonder whether we could meet up and, maybe, talk some more."

"Yes, of course," his heart gave a curious surge of anticipation and he knew that he had her now. There was no going back, where she was concerned, he had landed her and she was his to do whatever he liked with.

Ever since he had been recruited by the KGB as an "agent-nelegal vneshney razvekdi" (an illegal agent of KGB external intelligence), he had become obsessed by the idea of the control he could have over other peoples lives. The official definition by the KGB of the status that he had been accorded was,

> A specially trained, reliable and experienced agent of external Intelligence who might be a Soviet citizen, a foreigner or a stateless person, who cooperates on an ideological and polit-ical basis and who settles temporarily in a target country or a third country with documents reflecting the new particulars attributed to him for the purposes of carrying out intelligence tasks.

The money that he was receiving for this work was regular and, in some cases, generous. He tried to convince himself that his work was purely ideological; that he identified completely with the Soviet cause and that the money was hardly necessary, but he had to acknowledge, in his occasional honest moments, that he would work for the highest bidder, no matter what system it avowed.

It seemed so easy, in England at the moment, to be involved in espionage. In the society in which he worked the student organisa-tions were hotbeds of potential recruits to the "great cause". The development of leftist cabals were all around and the tradition of free speech, which the English system of democracy insisted upon, was conducive to the growth of these groups.

It seemed also that, provided he was careful, he could use the knowledge that he had about certain people, such as, Ronald Cameron, to good effect. The hold that he now had over Nina was an amazing bonus, he experienced again that thrill of excitement when he thought of her and looked forward to the next meeting, when he would be able to consolidate this hold.

He had been speaking to her whilst he had been thinking these things, "I can't see you until next Saturday," he found himself saying; he wanted to keep her nervously energised whilst she waited for him, and he thought she would be that much more eager to see him then. "Oh, all right then," she replied, and he delighted in the disappointment in her voice. "If you can't see me until then I suppose I will have to wait patiently."

"Yes, but I promise we will have a good time then," he said, mentally working out where was the best place to put her into the right mood. "Look, I'll pick you up from the flat at about, shall we say, eleven and, depending on the weather, we have a few alternatives to choose from."

"Yes, OK," she replied, "I'll look forward to that."

"I love you," he said.

She hesitated momentarily, "You too," She put the phone down and was annoyed at the thrill that ran through her body.

May 1945

Ronald Cameron was dancing around the statue of Queen Victoria with a girl he had only just met. They were outside the railings of Buckingham Palace and they were waiting for the re-appearance of the King and Queen and possibly Winston Churchill to come and be greeted by the multitude of rejoicing people, who were celebrating the end of the war in Europe. He had been in London most of the day and he and thousands of other servicemen and women were sharing the unrestrained joy of this moment with Londoners and whoever else was in the city on this momentous day.

Earlier in the morning he had gone to the house in Harringay, or rather the bomb site that was where the house once stood, and reflected on Shirley and all that she had meant to him. Over the last two years he had seemingly become inured to all the tragedies that he had witnessed. The Russian convoys, the leaving of Anna, his time in London and the bombing assaults on the capital; the sinking of his ship and his miraculous survival; the news of the death of Shirley; all these events had taken their toll by wearing away at the sensitive heart of himself. And the true core of him had been replaced by a harder accretion of indifference. It was, of course, a wall of defence to save him from further hurt and he knew that, but as he stood at the site of Shirley's last physical awareness, he was surprised that he didn't feel anything. He tried to summon up some tenderness of emotion but nothing came, only a slight annoyance at himself for surviving when so many others hadn't.

During the long day, which was full of embracing strangers and being bought drinks that he didn't really want, he and most of the population gravitated to Piccadilly Circus and The Mall. Here he found himself dancing with the girl and, after a number of extra visits to pubs, found the girl amenable to a more intimate examination. Even the close emotional encounter with her didn't release any tenderness that he could recognise, only a vigorous, rough taking of something that was being offered.

He awoke in the morning next to her. As he looked at her sleeping form he found it hard to believe that he had thought that she was the girl of his dreams. He had a dim awareness that he had said that to her. As he quietly got out of bed he hoped she didn't remember.

December 1965

Simon Clarke arrived promptly at eleven, driving his MG sports car with the hood up in deference to the rather inclement weather of this early winter day. She had been waiting for a good half an hour, looking anxiously out of the window and trying to avoid the concentrated stare of Rachel.

"I honestly don't know how you can be tolerating Simon like this," she said unable to keep silent any longer.

Nina pretended to only half hear her as she continued to look out of the window, "Um, what's that?"

"I said... oh, it doesn't matter, you won't listen to me anyway."

Nina turned to face Rachel, "We are only going out to talk about the situation." She turned back to the window.

"You've already made your mind up, I don't see why you are trying to deceive yourself as well."

"He's here," said Nina moving quickly across the room to the door, "I'll be back... oh some time," she wanted to go down to meet him to avoid him coming up and being confronted by Rachel.

"Yes, don't keep him waiting," Rachel managed to riposte before the front door was slammed behind Nina's retreating figure. "He might get the wrong impression," she tailed off, knowing she wasn't heard. She went to the window just in time to see Nina climb into the low-slung sports car. She muttered a prayer, not quite knowing why.

December 1965

Rachel was doing all those chores around the flat that needed to be done at least once a week, when she heard the ring on the door bell. It was Ronald Cameron.

"I'm afraid she's not in," she said as she ushered him in. She embraced him and she felt he held onto her rather longer than the greeting required.

"I somehow thought she wouldn't be," he answered and hesitated.

"Would you like a coffee? I am just about ready for a break," she bustled into the kitchen before he had a chance to answer, and switched on the kettle. She had the feeling that he wanted to talk and she experienced a warmth towards him that had a curious, unsettling effect within her.

"She went out with Simon earlier this morning."

"Oh," was all he said as he sat unbidden on one of the kitchen chairs. Rachel looked at him and noticed his unnatural pallor and the dark shading under his eyes.

He looked up at her and smiled, she thought, a weary smile. "I've got to expect that I suppose."

"Did she talk to you about what she was going to do?" Rachel asked, handing him a mug of coffee.

"Yes, she did, but... I don't know... I thought she was going to decide, how shall we say, in a rather different way." He sipped his coffee.

"For what it's worth," Rachel said, "I think she's crazy."

"It's good of you to say that, but... there are a lot of factors to be taken into account, which... you, maybe, are not aware of." Cameron smiled at her, "and maybe you are prejudiced, a little bit."

Rachel, to her intense annoyance, blushed. "Yes I suppose I am," she dropped her gaze and made a study of the kitchen floor.

Cameron reached across and took her hand, "We mean something to each other, my dearest Rachel, and I value you and your friendship more than you will know."

Somehow, to Rachel, at this moment, friendship wasn't what she was interested in. She looked at him, "you know that we were more than friends," she whispered.

He smiled again, and this time he was smiling with his eyes as well, "I know we were, but I feel as though I treated you badly. I took advantage of you."

"My dear Ronnie," and this time the boldness of this dark-eyed, curly-haired girl took over, "you can take advantage of me any time you like."

"Do you know I came over today half hoping that Nina wouldn't be here and that I would be able to see you," he continued to hold her hand, "maybe, partly, to put you in the picture and also, I guess, to be with you."

This conversation was beginning to please her heart and she squeezed his hand in response.

"The situation is not as clear cut as you imagine. I don't know how much you know or how much you know about this guy Simon?"

"Not a lot, only that I have been suspicious about him from the start, he seemed far too smooth for me."

"Do you know about the Russian connection?"

"Yes, I know about your wife and that is the reason why Simon thinks he has some hold over you."

"Also where Nina is concerned," he continued, "I have a suspicion that she may be attempting to protect me by agreeing to be with him, so that he isn't tempted to shop me."

Rachel drew her hand through the tangle of curls that cascaded around her forehead, "I don't know, she seemed very eager to see him this morning," she somehow didn't want to raise his hopes, for reasons that were not entirely altruistic. She despaired at her nature, that even at this difficult time for him she was taking away the crumbs of comfort that he needed.

"Do you mind me asking," she went on, "how much are you involved with the Russians... I mean, is there some reason that Simon could have in believing he is right?"

Ronald Cameron looked across the table at this pretty girl and realised that the answer he gave should be very carefully chosen. "There are at least two answers I could give you, both have an element of the truth about them. You must understand that during the war the Russians were our allies and consequently any help we could give them was important. I was able to come to an arrangement to help them in a certain way, in return for them allowing me a concession, where my wife was concerned." He took out a packet of cigarettes and offered one to her. She took one and he lit it for her and also for himself. "After the war, the situation became rather different. They became our enemies and therefore any communication with them had to be looked at in, shall we say, a rather more circumspect way."

"So if Simon knows something about this," she had the feeling that she was reaching the limits of how much she could probe, " he could justifiably make things awkward?"

"Even if he knows a very little, which I suspect is the case, yes, he could make things awkward, as you say."

"How do you think he has this knowledge, where did he get it from?" Cameron shrugged, "at the moment I don't know."

"Are you trying to find out about him, I mean, is there a way of finding out?"

"My dearest Rachel, there are always ways to find out about people, no one is a closed book."

Rachel stubbed out her cigarette in the ash tray and put both her hands under her chin and looked at him with that winsome smile, that he was trying so hard to resist, and said, "and what have you found out about me?"

He smiled, and with relief she saw that his grey pallor had gone and been replaced by a suffusion of pink. "I'm still working on it," he said, "you are more complicated than I at first thought."

December 1965

Ronald Cameron was staring at the report by a journalist by the name of Edward Crankshaw, who wrote in a periodical in 1948 about the plight of Soviet women being sent to a labour camp. Edward Crankshaw was a journalist with a singularly resilient character. In 1947 he became the Moscow correspondent for the *Observer* newspaper. He became their Russian and East European expert and became a thorn in the flesh of the Kremlin, with his withering attacks on their system. They attempted to vilify him by various means, including blackmail through trying to exploit his sexual liaisons. He was not intimidated and continued to write the truth as he saw it. He was globally syndicated through the *Observer*'s Foreign News Service, the *New York Times Sunday Magazine* and lectures and broadcasts. He wrote in 1951, "There is only one group of people in the world today, which is actively and deliberately... committed to the downfall of our society: the group of Russians who form the government of the Soviet Union."

During the Second World War he had served with the British Military Mission in Russia and, whilst serving with the mission he had lived with two girls – the artist T.S.Andreyevskaya and her friend E.S. Rosinevich. In 1948 they were both arrested, forced to confess that they were British spies and sent to a labour camp. Crankshaw was not intimidated despite this, however, he wrote an account and this was what Cameron was now reading. He had read it before, in 1951, when it had first come to his attention and it was this that largely motivated him to attempt to make contact with Anna in that year by going to Russia as part of a cultural exchange. His trip, of course, was abortive and the reading again of the account brought back the sweet agony of Anna.

'Another thing you become aware of in the north, and which dominates your ideas, is forced labour in its many different forms. As you sit at breakfast in your hotel you hear the dreadful sound of a woman wailing, half hysterically, in the street outside. And looking out you see thirty or forty women and girls being marched along the frozen street by guards with fixed bayonets, each woman with a small bundle. You do not know where they are going; but you know they are being marched away against their will, that the call came suddenly and roughly, and that behind them they are leaving homes which are, as it were, still warm, while they trudge through the snow with nothing but their bundles.'

He thought of Anna and what she went through. Whatever

complicity he had in her punishment, purely because of her association with him, he was unable to do anything about it. She had been
put into a labour camp in 1949, when the information that he was
sending was deemed to be polluted by inaccuracies and he appeared
to be no longer of use. This happened at the time when the MGB
(the future KGB) and the GRU (Soviet military intelligence) were
temporarily combined into the Committee of Information. This
amalgamation disintegrated in 1951/2 and the MGB resumed its
traditional rivalry with the GRU. Because the information that
Cameron was supplying was largely military in essence the GRU
insisted on handling it, however the MGB didn't agree and an
internecine dispute developed. Neither organisation knew, of course,
that his information was deliberately inaccurate. Although they had
the opportunity to double check some of the details, others were so
closely intricate that it took some time to work out whether it was
genuine. There was confusion for some time about this within the
core of the organisation. Whatever the reason, Anna was sent to a
labour camp until such time that pressure could be put again on
Cameron to be accommodating.

He wasn't aware, at the time, of what was going on behind the
scenes, he only knew that the correspondence with Anna had dried
up. His operational officer who was "running" him informed him
that there was a "difficulty" with Anna and, after a time which was
fraught with anxiety, told him what had transpired.

That she was released in 1954 was owed to two factors: the first
and foremost was a general amnesty and reassessment after the death
of Stalin in 1953; the second was the pressure that was again put
upon him to supply information in order to keep Anna away from a
camp. Her letters to him at this time, written in micro dot, were full
of gratitude to him for keeping her safe, or what passed for safe,
within such a system.

It was at about this time that Cameron, through the kind offices
of Brian Anstruther-Plowman, was asked to join the SIS (Secret
Intelligence Service), Section IX. This section had a special responsibility to study past records of Soviet and communist activity with a
remit for the "collection and interpretation of information concer-
ning Soviet and communist espionage and subversion in all parts of
the world outside British territory". It was through this that he

became involved in one of the most remarkable Western intelligence operations, up to this time, in the Cold War. The plan was for the construction of a secret 500-metre underground tunnel from West to East Berlin, built to intercept landlines running between the Soviet military and the intelligence headquarters in Karlshorst, east of the city. The tunnel became operational in May 1955.

The codename for this operation was GOLD and Cameron was posted to the location a month later. His job was the monitoring of all communications and he was employed there until the tunnel was discovered "accidentally" by the KGB in April 1956. They had, in fact, been aware of the tunnel since it was first discussed by the SIS and CIA. They had been tipped off by the double agent George Blake, who, at a meeting with his controller, had handed over a copy of the minutes of the SIS/CIA conference that had first discussed the possibility of a tunnel. The KGB, however, did not dare to interfere with the tunnel's construction or the initial operations for fear of compromising their star spy, who had established himself as one of their most important British agents.

George Blake had joined the SIS in 1944, after a time in the Dutch Resistance and then serving in the Royal Navy. He was recruited by the KGB a short time after the dismissal of Philby by the SIS in June 1951. Blake had been born in Rotterdam to a naturalised British father (by origin a Sephardic Jew from Constantinople) and a Dutch mother.

Despite the tunnel being in operation for less than a year, GOLD had yielded over 50,000 reels of magnetic tape recording intercepted Soviet and East German communications. In fact, Cameron was employed for over two years helping to process all the intercepts, such was the prodigious output from the operation.

Although it would have been possible for the Soviets to corrupt the communications, there was not much evidence that they did, and a large amount of vital material was found out about the new improved nuclear capability of the Soviet airforce in East Germany; a new fleet of bombers and a new fighter division in Poland; new airforce installations in the USSR, GDR and Poland; the organisation of the Baltic Fleet; and organisation and personnel of the Soviet atomic energy programme. These, amongst other revelations, made the whole enterprise a considerable success.

Whilst musing about these things Cameron looked around his

office and, as he surveyed his desk, he realised there was something missing. After some moments he knew what it was, it was the photo of Nina, it was no longer there in the silver frame, which had been positioned opposite to the one of Anna. It didn't take long for his thoughts to pursue a logical path and he got up from his chair and went straight to the filing cabinet. Before opening the top drawer he released the switch mechanism that operated the small camera that was concealed within the back of the cabinet. Although everything appeared in order he knew that someone had been searching through the files. In fact, it was too much in order, that was what alerted him. He had devised a simple system whereby he always put one file out of sequence, knowing that anyone who was trained would assume that all the files were in correct order and put them back in the way they should be. There, however, was his one test file, back where it shouldn't be. He took the camera out of its location and went into the dark room, opened it and processed the photos. It showed a man in his mid-twenties, with a lean clean-cut face; he was facing the camera and his hands were reaching into the files.

"Gotcha," Cameron exclaimed. He went to the phone and dialled the Kingsbury flat.

"Hi, Rachel, are you in tomorrow, I've got something I must show you."

December 1965

They sat at the corner table in the magnificent dining room of the Ritz Hotel in Piccadily. As Nina looked around, every table seemed to be occupied and there was a general buzz of contented diners enjoying their lunch. She looked again at Simon Clarke, he seemed so self-assured in such sumptuous surroundings and she wondered again at the wealth that he displayed whenever he took her out. This in such stark contrast to the normal student who had taken her out in the past.

He glanced at her, his grey eyes searching the beauty of her face, "Are you content with me then?"

She gave a slight smile, "I am content with what I see here," she paused, "and I am content with what I see in you too."

December 1965

Ronald Cameron ran up the outside stairs to the Kingsbury flat and rang the bell. He was instantly refreshed when he saw the pretty face of Rachel peep around the opening door, the dark, bouncy ringlets of her hair proclaiming a life of their own. She stepped back to let him in and instantly embraced him, his lips found hers and their brief urgent kiss proclaimed more than a friendship between them. "How lovely to see you again, so soon," she said, taking his hand and leading him into the kitchen. She switched on the kettle and turned to face him, leaning against the work surface. She was wearing a pair of rather tight jeans, which emphasised the slimness of her body, and a loose turtle-necked pink sweater. He thought she looked fresh and neat as if newly picked from a daffodil field.

She poured out the coffee and they took their mugs into the sitting room where the gas fire was providing a welcoming warmth. They sat down together on the sofa and Cameron was more disturbed than he felt he should be by the proximity of this girl. The remembrance of their closeness in the recent past came back to him with a renewed vigour.

"Well what is it you have come to show me?" she asked provocatively, smiling encouragingly.

"It's this," he said, bringing an envelope out of his pocket. He took out the photograph and showed it to her, "Do you recognise this man?"

Rachel took it and said immediately, "Why yes, it's Simon."

"I thought it would be," replied Cameron, "that's how he knows about me."

"Where did you get the photo from?"

"It's a long story my love, and I won't bore you with it now, suffice it to say that this Simon Clarke is rather more formidable than we thought."

"Are you able to do anything about him then?"

He paused, he didn't want to tell this girl too much for fear of her becoming involved in something that may get her out of her depth, and he felt very protective of her at this moment.

"I'm sure we can do something about him, at some stage. The important thing, of course is, that we don't allow Nina to get too embroiled with this guy."

"How are we going to stop her?"

"At this moment, I'm not sure. He obviously has a hold over her and it will take some clever work on our part to ease them apart." He hesitated, "Did she come home last night?"

"Yes, she came home last night but not the night before. She said that he had taken her to dine at the Ritz. She said that she doesn't know where he gets his money from to take her to all these expensive places. But wherever it is she seems happy to accept it."

"Um, that's interesting," Cameron mused, and thought, but didn't say, I bet I know where he is getting his money from. Instead he said, "Unfortunately, the more she sees of him the more difficult it will become to convince her that he is not right for her. He has got to make some horrendous mistake for her to be convinced."

"Do you still have feelings for her?" Rachel asked, half fearing the answer.

"Yes, of course," he replied, but feeling the hesitancy with which she asked the question, he tempered it with, "but not in the same way that I did before."

"How do you feel about her now?" Rachel knew that the opportunity to ask him would not happen again in the same way and she resolved to know about her own part in this.

Cameron looked at her and also knew that his answers in the next few minutes would be important to her and possibly to him.

"I must be honest with you," he hesitated again, not sure at all where he was going in this, "I was convinced at one stage that Nina was, to me, the embodiment of Anna and that she somehow represented that vital something that I had lost. Because of that I pursued Nina and felt such a love for her that I found so difficult to express. In fact, I couldn't express it in a physical way at all, which surprised me immensely." He looked at Rachel and he could see that she was hanging on to every word as if her life depended on it.

"I know you girls are very close, maybe she told you about what we were going through?"

Rachel was so absorbed by his words that she couldn't answer at first, "Er, yes she told me a certain amount." She was reluctant to let him know how much she knew at this point.

"Well, what I'm trying to say, in a very poor manner, is that when it came for us to, shall we say, consummate our relationship, I couldn't do it."

"Oh," was all she said.

"And I really don't know why, something seemed to stop me," he shrugged and Rachel saw a look of desperation flicker across his eyes.

"Anyway," he seemed to recover from this brief reverie and looked at her, "I'm sure you don't want to hear all this, what is important is that the love that I have for her now is on another level. It's... almost like a father–daughter relationship. But I don't know if she looks on it like that, certainly she has now excluded me as a lover, in the truest sense, that is."

Rachel reached across and took his hand, he smiled briefly and squeezed her hand in return. She didn't need to say anything; what had been so close in her heart and what she longed for was being fulfilled.

December 1965

Simon Clarke eased himself out of bed and left Nina sleeping peacefully. He moved silently across the bedroom floor to the writing desk that was under the window. There was sufficient light for him to see what he wanted to see. He let the flap of the desk down and began shuffling through the papers that were there. Not being satisfied, he closed the flap and opened the top drawer. There he found the passport holder; he took out the passport and closed the drawer. He went across to his clothes, which were lying on the floor where he had left them after taking them off in such a hurry, found his trousers and put the documents in the pocket. He looked across at the bed. He could tell by her measured breathing that she would not wake for some time and opened the door carefully. He went across to Rachel's room and stood outside for some moments. He turned the handle, opened the door slowly and peered inside. He listened for her breathing and saw the inert shape under the bedclothes. He crossed the floor to where he knew she kept her papers. After a quick look through the three drawers he couldn't find what he wanted, so he went to the wardrobe and opened the door to the compartment where she kept her sweaters and underwear. A quick feel of the underwear brought his hand to the shape of the passport. He took it out, closed the door and, after a swift glance at the still undisturbed bed, went out of the room, closing the door silently behind him.

Nina was still breathing peacefully as he put the passport into his trouser pocket, and slipped back into bed. She murmured sleepily as he put his arm around her and began to kiss her neck.

148

December 1965

Brian Anstruther-Plowman and Ronald Cameron were walking together in Regents Park. The roar of London traffic was subdued by the trees and the spaces of the parkland. They walked in a close companionable way, neither looking to right or left, and with their eyes mainly on the ground. They talked quietly and unless a listener was beside them they could not be overheard.

"Your controller at the embassy, do you think he is aware of Simon Clarke?"

Cameron considered the question, "I don't know, but it is something I need to ask him."

"What is his name?"

"His codename is Ozerov, but I'm almost sure his name is Oshchenko. He's the legal agent at the embassy."

"So if he is the legal agent," said Anstruther-Plowman, "is it possible that Simon Clarke is an illegal?"

"If he is, then that must mean they are in competition with each other."

"We know that the KGB's responsibility for diplomatic and other civilian traffic is very often in conflict with the GRU's military mandate and we don't know if this is the problem here. Perhaps Clarke is dancing to the GRU's tune and Ozerov to the KGB." Anstruther-Plowman replied.

"If that is the case, then, maybe, we have an opportunity to drive a wedge between the two and cause some interesting diversions," said Cameron.

"I think we need to be careful," cautioned Anstruther-Plowman, "we don't want to throw too much light on the information that is being given by us."

"I know that, but I just feel that this is an opportunity to get back at Clarke," Cameron looked at his friend, "maybe I'm taking this a little too personally, but I really want to get this guy out of the situation that he is in with Nina. If we force his hand we can get rid of him quite easily."

"And how do you envisage getting rid of him?"

"It would be easy for me to drop a hint to Ozerov that my cover is at risk through the stupid actions of Clarke," Cameron shrugged, "and let the Soviets deal with him."

"It would certainly be an interesting scenario; it would also give us an idea as to how the Russians view their illegals." Anstruther-Plowman responded.

"Shall I do that then?"

"I would like to find out more about Clarke," said his friend, "particularly how many converts he has managed to recruit at university, and who they are. Maybe there is a vast spawning ground around him. He seems to be a persuasive fellow."

"Because Nina is attending the same campus it would be ideal if she could be persuaded to make some enquiries on our behalf," Cameron hesitated, "but I think at the moment any suggestion on my part would be looked upon as prejudiced."

"Yes I agree, she would certainly see it as an attempt by you to sully his good name in her eyes."

"I don't think he can do any wrong, as far as she is concerned anyway," Cameron continued.

"Would her flatmate be any good? What is her name, Rebecca?"

"No, Rachel," he was fearing this, that she would be dragged, unwittingly, into a world that was alien and hostile and he determined that it shouldn't happen. He continued, "It would be very difficult to explain to her what we were trying to do without telling her what I am involved in. And even if she understood it I doubt she could persuade Nina to identify with it as well anyway Nina would not want to go behind Clarke's back and try and find out what he had been involved in. No, forgive me but I think that is a non-starter."

"OK, I can see that you feel strongly about it." Anstruther-Plowman was intrigued by this passionate outburst.

"Yes I do, I have a feeling that we don't need to involve more people than we have to."

"In that case," continued Anstruther-Plowman, "we will get someone from SIS to investigate at the university and see what they come up with."

"And I will not mention anything to Ozerov yet, until such time as we know more about Clarke's activities," Cameron replied.

"As a matter of interest," his companion responded, "what are you working on at the moment?"

"I'm doing some work for a defence electronics firm in Feltham, as a test engineer."

"What does that involve?"

Cameron continued, "I'm in the quality control section, and at the moment we are testing radar fuses for a new bomb."

"What are you passing on to the Russians?"

"Well, the detonator for the fuse operates on a radio frequency and there is plenty of opportunity to mess about with the radio frequency that would activate the detonator."

"Is this an attempt to corrupt their intelligence, because of the damage that was done before?" Anstruther-Plowman enquired.

"Yes it is; as you remember, the security was breached by a double agent and the information on the bomb was revealed to the Soviets. I have the job of convincing them that a lot of the information they had before was false."

"So you think this is confusing them?"

"Well, let's say that it is not making it any easier for them."

"Incidentally, now that they no longer have any hold over you, because of your wife's death, how are you convincing them that you are now helping them, shall we say, altruistically?"

Cameron smiled, "I'm now doing it for money, and they are believing me."

January 1966

Simon Clarke walked into the college with the two other students. One was a girl called Angela and the other a young man named Roy. After cultivating their friendships for some time, he began to raise the issue of Russia and what their views were. He used the technique of being devil's advocate and abusing the Soviet system until he felt it was time to play his main card. They both appeared convinced of the purity of the first worker/peasant state and they were beginning to berate him for his reactionary views. It seemed such a fail-safe system and he had used it many times. He then drew them in and put before them the untold advantages of belonging to a state that would reward them greatly for their commitment to its aims. He stressed that it was a long haul before they would see the destruction of the capitalist state but he reassured them that they would experience prestige and honour given to them by the communist ideology that was manifestly at the heart of their lives.

He had cultivated Angela rather more devotedly than he had Roy, basically because he could not resist the challenge of another sexual

151

conquest. He achieved his purpose one night after they had been drinking in a bar, he took her home to his flat in Tooting and she didn't need much persuading to stay the night. His only reservation was that he had to tell Nina that he was working on his thesis and, in the middle of his passion with Angela, he had the strange sense that Nina knew what he was doing. He quickly dismissed the thought from his mind as he renewed his energy in the girl on the bed.

April 1958

Ronald Cameron's work, decrypting the Soviet communications that were intercepted by the SIS in the tunnel dug between West and East Berlin, was coming to an end. He had spent nearly two years immersed in a plethora of morse code signals and German-and Russian-language messages; any help he could give to Anna was sparse and meagre. He received no communications from her in all the time he was in Germany, chiefly because his controller in London lost contact with him. This was deliberate on Cameron's part, as the work he was doing in Berlin had to come into a different category of espionage. However, when his posting finished in Berlin he was advised to return to his ship's chandlery business in Poole and keep a low profile.

It was there, towards the end of the month, when the spring flowers were displaying their glory to enhance the beauty of the English countryside, that Shirley walked through the open door. As he looked up and saw a woman with blond hair, he did a quick male assessment of the rest of her attributes and noted with satisfaction that she was worth a second look. On this second look, as she smiled at him, a chimera of memory glanced through his mind, and then recognition took over. But it was not recognition with any anchor to it, because what he was recognising had no basis of fact. He had dismissed this memory from his mind because it was too painful to bear. He sat in his chair for some moments before he could utter a word and then all he could say was "Shirley?"

His tone of voice must have had a large element of incredulity about it because she came across the room with that lithe grace that always fascinated him, and was instantly her in his mind. He rose from the chair and she took his hand and looked into his eyes with the blue intensity of her own.

"How on earth?" He began.

She put her finger over his lips, "there is so much to say, and I'm in danger of saying too much too quickly."

"But..." was all he could interpose.

"You must let me speak first, I've had three weeks to work out what I want to say, and I am desperate to tell you." Shirley's face was flushed with the immediacy of the moment.

He took her by the hand, led her to the armchair and he wheeled his desk chair alongside it. They both sat and looked at each other.

"Start at the beginning then," he said, at last starting to recover some composure.

"I was in the house when the bomb hit and I was knocked out but I only had superficial injuries. My mother, God bless her, was in the bedroom showing a neighbour a dress she had just made up and they had no chance. I was getting something from under the stairs, I can't for the life of me remember what it was, but obviously that's what saved me."

"But when I enquired at the Admiralty they said that two bodies had been brought out, and I naturally assumed that because, you were staying at your mother's, you were one of them. They obviously thought that too, because, as you hadn't reported for duty that morning..." he tailed off.

"Yes, I know, and when I reported back at work after a week's incapacity leave, I had already had the news of your ship being torpedoed and you weren't on the list of survivors, so I had already assumed the worst before I was injured."

"When I got back, after my landing on a beach in Spain half dead, and enquired about you, I couldn't follow it up because I was immediately posted to my next ship." Cameron took her hands and they looked at each other in amazement.

"It seems we both assumed too much," he shook his head in a gesture of astonishment, "I can't believe this, it's impossible."

"We have to believe it," she leaned forward and kissed the scar on his cheek, "that's something new about you, what other scars do you have?"

"Quite a few," he answered, "but it's been, what, nearly fourteen years, where have you been in that time, and why have you found me now?"

She smiled the gentle smile that reminded him of so much of their days and nights together.

"At the end of the war I met a guy who had been in the RAF. and, in short, we got married and went out to Southern Rhodesia. He was Rhodesian; we farmed tobacco, he took over from his father."

"So what are you doing here now?"

"He got shot down during the Battle of Britain, and got burned, and the burns he suffered needed some more treatment, and we have come over together. He is in the burns unit in East Grinstead. And I have taken the opportunity to look up some old friends here."

"That still doesn't explain what you are doing here in my obscure office in Dorset."

"No, it doesn't; in short, I made contact with a friend of mine at the Admiralty, and in the course of conversation your name came up and she told me, almost in passing, that you had survived the sinking."

Cameron shook his head, not for the first time this morning, "So how did you find me?"

"I made enquiries through various friends and I eventually discovered, two days ago, that you were here. I didn't want to phone because, well, for obvious reasons, I wanted to see you as soon as I could."

"And how is your life in Africa, you always wanted to travel, as I remember?"

"It is so different, we have about ten thousand acres of plantation, and of course the climate..." she tailed off.

"I'm so glad it's worked out for you," he said, "when I thought I'd lost you... it was the worst moment of my life."

She squeezed his hand, "It is so wonderful to see you again, it's a miracle."

He looked at her in the way she found so disturbing in the past, "I loved you so much," he said his voice thickening with the emotion.

"And I loved you too, you know that," she suddenly seemed to take notice of what she was saying and tried to change the mood. "Do you know, I have two children, both boys, one is ten and the other eight."

"Oh, that's great," he replied, feeling at the same time a twinge of regret but not quite sure why.

She suddenly looked down at her hands, still holding his. "Ronnie," she said, and looked up at him as if asking his permission to speak, "there is something that I have to tell you."

He saw the blue eyes clouding over with apprehension and hastened to reassure her, "What is it, it can't be that bad, surely."

"It's not that it's bad, it's just... oh I've gone over this speech over and over, and I thought I was word perfect... there's no easy way to say this."

He took her by the shoulders, leaned forward and kissed her on the mouth, she responded almost immediately and for some moments they were locked in an embrace that they both realised they had been deprived off for so long, and needed so desperately.

When they disengaged they looked at each other and smiled, "I've been wanting to do that ever since you walked in," he said.

"And I've been waiting for you to do it," she responded.

"So what is it you have to tell me, is it easier now?"

"Yes, thank you, it's amazing what a kiss can do. Well, when I was in hospital, after the bomb, I discovered," she paused again, but only momentarily, "I discovered that I was pregnant."

He leaned back in his chair and the look on his face told her all she wanted to know.

"Pregnant, so what did..." he couldn't finish the sentence because she again put her finger on his mouth.

"I was so happy, I had my suspicions, but this was confirmation. It meant that in a very real sense I hadn't lost you, you were here present in my body."

"Darling," he spoke softly and couldn't say any more.

"The baby was born in August '45. It was a girl."

"A girl... so what happened to her?"

"I had my confinement with my aunt in Sussex, and it was at a time when things were difficult for a single mother." She tailed off and looked away from him and he could see that her eyes were filled with tears.

"I know that life is always difficult for single mothers," he said gently, caressing her hands.

"After the birth I got so depressed, and no matter how much my aunt cared for me, I could see no hope for the future." He took out a handkerchief and began to use it to dry the tears that were flowing down her cheeks. She attempted a smile and took the handkerchief from him.

"After three months, I was still no better. My aunt had some very good friends nearby, who were married and who couldn't have children, so after a lot of heart-searching... I gave the baby to them for them to adopt." She finished in a rush, as if to end the agony as quickly as possible.

He found the tears in his own eyes the response to her sorrow.

"I promised that I would never make contact with her, until such time that she knew about me and wanted to meet me," she shrugged. "So far that hasn't happened."

"Do you know anything about her, how she is getting on?" Cameron asked.

"I deliberately haven't made any enquiries... it would be too painful to do so, because if I found out about her I would need to get involved... and I can't."

"Does your aunt know about them and where they are?"

"I haven't asked," she responded abruptly, and he had the feeling that he was coming to the end of these revelations because of the pain she was absorbing.

He knelt beside her and put his arms around her shoulders and she put her head on his breast and began to weep. He was not surprised by the immensity of her emotions or the time it took to exhaust them. He was reminded of that time in October 1944 when they had both experienced the nearness of obliteration, when a V2 had exploded across the square to where they were. She had responded then in the same way and he remembered the feeling of holding her until her sobbing, the way a gentle engine ticks over, had subsided.

January 1966

The pub was crowded, it was lunch time and Ronald Cameron and Brian Anstruther-Plowman were seated at a corner table in the smoke-filled saloon bar. The pub was only a short walk from Cameron's chandlery and they had agreed to meet there to discuss the latest circumstances regarding Operation Stigma, the code name given to cover Simon Clarke.

"We have an operative who has made contact, and he has come up with some interesting information." Anstruther-Plowman took a sip of his beer.

"Good," responded Cameron.

"Yes, he and a female companion, also an agent, have been recruited by Clarke. At the moment he is obviously acting as an 'agentrazrabotchik', a cultivation agent, and is endeavouring to reel them in."

"There is no mistake about this?"

"No, none at all, but it is one thing knowing this and an entirely different thing to prove anything against him."

"Have we been able to find out anything about his previous life?" Cameron enquired.

"We know he was recruited at university, in fact his controller then is under surveillance now and we hope to possibly recruit him as a double."

"Is there any hope that we could turn Clarke?"

"Judging by his rather passionate views about the purity of the Soviet system, I doubt it. Although if he is accepting generous funds from the Russians, he might be persuaded to take a better offer from us."

"But would he be any use to us?" Cameron asked.

"He could possibly be of value, certainly where his knowledge of agents operating in this country is concerned and also the structure of the espionage system used by the Russians here."

"Of course," said Cameron, "there is always the opportunity we have to let his name slip to the Soviets, that we are on to him, and they will have no choice but to exfiltrate him."

"That will obviously help you in your need to extricate Nina from his grasp," responded Anstruther-Plowman.

"Yes, I would consider that as a considerable bonus."

"There is also one other thing that our agents told us about Clarke, in fact it was the girl who divulged this."

Cameron leaned forward, the better to hear the soft tones of his companion in the noise of the bar, "Yes, what was that?"

"He slept with her, apparently he had no compunction in having sex with her, there was no suggestion from him that he had a steady girlfriend."

"Well, I guess that doesn't come as any surprise," said Cameron.

"No, but, it could help you in your efforts to make her see what sort of a man she is involved with."

"Do you mean that I could somehow let it slip that he is sleeping with someone else?"

"Yes, however not you directly; maybe you could let her friend Rachel know and she could drop a few hints to her."

"Yes, I certainly wouldn't do it myself, she would know that I was

trying to blacken his worth in her eyes, for obvious reasons. I wonder if it would work," Cameron mused, "it seems obvious to us mere males, but women have a rather different attitude to certain things. It may be that it would make him more appealing in her eyes."
"There is always that, of course," agreed his companion.
"However, it's worth a try, because if we are going to tip the Russians off, and they bring him out, at least she will not be too unhappy about it."

May 1944

He had considered all the options or at least he thought he had. He was absolutely convinced that he wanted to do the most harm he could possibly do to the communist system that held sway in Russia. Before he first landed on its benighted shores, he considered that the war against Germany was the foremost task of the allies. And Russia, although signing a non aggression pact with Germany five years ago, was now involved in the most bitter fight for survival against its former ally. Both Britain and America knew that Russia was absorbing so much of the punishment that would have been unleashed on them. That's why aid in remarkable quantities was being given to the Soviets at this time. He knew all this profoundly and that he was also risking his life by his presence on the convoys but hearing from Anna about her family and the way they had been persecuted under Stalin caused him to reconsider his feelings.

A few days after his fiftieth birthday, Stalin unleashed a campaign of terror against the kulaks (rich peasants). His plans to revolutionise industry had foundered because of shortage of grain and he determined to speed up the process by forcing peasants (muzhiks) into collective farms and to get rid of the kulaks, whom he considered to be parasites on the body politic of communism. They were portrayed as reactionary agricultural bourgeoisie, intent on choking communism to death by famine It was true that they had taken advantage of Lenin's New Economic Policy in 1921 by selling their surplus grain on the open market instead of to the state, and by feeding the grain to their animals because they could get a better price for the animals than they would for grain, but that was no reason for the extremes of Stalin's paranoia. Because of this they were decreed to be class enemies and their persecution would terrify the lesser peasants into joining collectives. Their land was confiscated and Stalin declared war on his own people. In the first two months of 1930 approximately a million kulaks were stripped of their possessions and uprooted from their farms. In the next three years over three million were deported and most of these perished. Cameron knew that these figures were only approximate, but he learned from Anna of the extreme hardship that she, as an eight-year-old, and her family had to undergo. Her grandparents did not survive, also both her aunts and uncles perished. Very little of this seemed to be known in the West; if it was, it was rationalised by the dictum that in order to build the great experiment in social engineering, the Worker's State, the kulaks had to be destroyed. The great communist experiment had many apologists.

Anna had preserved a statement written by a witness to this great 'experiment', and one night she read it to him, "Trainloads of deported peasants left for the icy North, the forests, the steppes, the deserts. There were whole populations, denuded of everything; the old folk starved to death in mid-journey, newborn babies were buried on the banks of the road side, and each wilderness had its crop of little crosses of boughs or white wood."

She looked up at him and gave a half smile, "It was like that... only worse," she said, "I do not understand how so much suffering has to be endured because of one man."

He held her hand, "But is it just one man? There must be many others who go along with him and seem quite happy to inflict their own perverted lusts on others."

"Yes," she said, "there are many others, but maybe they do it because if they didn't they would become the next to be persecuted." Anna looked at him and he had never seen an expression like the one she now portrayed, it was a mixture of sorrow and sadness and extreme resignation. "Perhaps," she continued, "you think you are going through difficult times in England, and I'm sure you are, but you are fighting against a common enemy; here in Russia we not only fight against that, but also against ourselves, we are tearing ourselves apart."

January 1966
Cameron had taken Rachel out to the National Film Theatre. They had seen a reissue of a Brigitte Bardot film called *And God Created Woman* and were walking back across Waterloo Bridge to have a meal

in the Strand. He began to sound her out about Nina and whether she had seen any changes in her recently.

"I think she is becoming more and more preoccupied with Simon, she doesn't seem to have time for any other thoughts but him. She even seems to be neglecting her college work. There are some days when I am sure she hasn't been to lectures and her work at home is non-existent."

"Is she at home much... at night I mean?" Cameron said.

"No, that's what worries me, apart from the fact of it being lonely, I do miss her company very much."

"She, presumably must be staying at his place then?" Cameron continued.

"I imagine so," said Rachel.

"I have found out some more about him, particularly, that he is seeing another girl."

He had taken her hand as they were crossing the Strand and she turned to face him as they reached the centre island, there was considerable surprise in her face. "Another girl?"

"Yes, don't ask me how I know," he smiled, and suddenly he wanted to kiss her very much, which he resisted, instead they ran across the other half of the road where there was a gap in the traffic.

"But how do you know," she giggled as they reached the safety of the pavement.

"Look you," he took her by the shoulders and pretended to be severe with her, although his grin belied the intent, he leaned forward and kissed her, "there are some things little girls shouldn't know."

She continued to be coquettish, "But I'm not a little girl," she smiled, "and you should know that more than anyone."

"OK, you win," he laughed, "I'm very pleased I know that too... but you must believe me my darling, when I say that it really is best if you don't know, just trust me; one day I promise I'll tell you."

"Oh, all right, I'll be good... but just for now, don't think that I will forget."

"I'm sure you won't," he replied, pleased that the girl he was falling in love with was also sensible.

"But let's be sensible," he said attempting to get to the serious point of his dialogue, "there is something that you can do for me."

"Oh, yes please, I would love to," she again gave a suggestive smile and he sighed with delighted frustration at this girl who was bringing new life to his jaded psyche.

"You really are impossible," he put his arm around her and kissed her on the forehead, "but I am seriously worried about Nina. I think it's terribly important that she is parted from Clarke. I have discovered that he is not a nice man, and I don't just mean his philandering. There is something that he is involved in which throws a whole new light on him." He looked at her, "and don't ask me what it is because I can't tell you at the moment, but believe me, I will tell you when it's OK to do so."

"Sounds intriguing," she said, adopting a serious tone.

"It's also important because I know she is going to be hurt, in a big way, if she is not eased away from this guy soon."

Rachel looked up at Cameron as they arrived at the door of the restaurant, she saw the expression on his face and knew his intent was serious. They got seated in the restaurant, at a corner table overlooking the street, and ordered the meal.

"So, really what do you want me to do?" She held his hand across the table and smiled gently at him.

"I think, if you have the opportunity, obviously, to try to tell her that he has been seen with another girl, and see how she takes it."

"Well I can tell you now, she won't take it very well, I know I wouldn't, and I don't think any girl would," Rachel responded.

"I know she won't, but there are degrees of not taking things well, and it's by seeing how affected she is we can, maybe, determine her feelings."

Rachel looked unsure, "Ronnie you are a darling, but I think your knowledge of women and how they think is, maybe, a bit, how shall we say, simplistic."

He looked amazed, "Do you mean to say that women are not predictable?"

She laughed at his mockery. "The same as men aren't," she said.

"But seriously," she continued, "she will want to know how I came by this information, so what do I tell her?"

"Maybe you could say that you saw them in the street somewhere, and that they looked as if they were more than friendly."

"Yes, OK that might work, it would certainly unsettle her, I know it would me."

"That's all I ask for, at the moment, that is." He poured out some more wine and they clinked glasses together.

"What sort of time scale do we have for this to be done?"

"As soon as possible really," he answered. He knew his regular meeting with Ozerov was organised for two weeks' time.

"I will try and make contact with her," Rachel responded, "although I can't guarantee anything."

"That's all I ask for," he smiled, "I really appreciate whatever you can do."

"You forget," she said, "that I have as much interest in her as you do, and I want to see her restored to that fun-loving girl she used to be."

"I know you do, I forget, I suppose, that you have known her far longer than I have."

"From primary school days, yes, I almost look on her as being the sister I never had."

January 1966

Ronald Cameron sat down at his desk and began to write. It was some weeks since he had written and Shirley needed to know what was going on. It was eight years since she had suddenly turned up and revealed such amazing news to him, not only about the fact of her being alive but also about the daughter that they had together. In all the events of his life so far, that event was the most wonderful and the most exciting. The more he thought of it the more incredible it seemed. Yet he knew it was only half the story, there was so much more that would be revealed, he felt sure.

Shirley had gone back to Rhodesia with her husband after his treatment had finished. He had met him and liked him immediately, so much so, in fact, that he had an open invitation to visit them in Africa. As far as he was aware Shirley had not told her husband about him and what they had meant to each other but he was sure that being an intelligent guy, considering the conditions of war, he would put two and two together and understand. That's why he knew he would never take up their invitation to visit. But he knew that he had to write and keep up a regular correspondence. She had written as soon as she arrived back in Rhodesia and they had written and received letters from each other ever since. They were warm, intimate, missives and they expressed to each other something of the emotions they had shared, more than twenty years ago, in conditions that were a world away from their present situations. There was no doubt that he still loved her. He had told her about Nina and Rachel, and about his visit to Russia. He was able to express to her how he had felt about the death of Anna, and he believed she was the only one who would understand. By explaining to her about these things something was released within himself and this release was enabling him to come to terms with his present condition. Yet he realised she was more than a mother confessor. By the very reason that they had shared so much together, they, had as it were, a ticket of admission to each other's psyche. The very fact that she was so many thousands of miles away also meant that she was not physically available to him. Apart from the fact of her being married, he knew that if she was with him, present in body, he would, very quickly, become involved with her again. And, because of Rachel, that would not be a good idea.

As far as he could, he told her about Simon Clarke and the effect his presence was having on Nina. She had asked him, in her previous letter, how that was making him feel regarding his own feelings about Nina and he had been able to tell her about the problem that suddenly presented itself when he had come back from Russia and she had been so overjoyed to be with him again.

I suddenly felt so inadequate because I couldn't experience with her what we so obviously wanted from each other. I couldn't understand it and still can't. It's as if a complete block has been put on our relationship and I am sure that's the reason why she has chosen to go off with Clarke. In a very real sense I feel guilty about letting her down. I suppose because of what's happened between Nina and myself my feelings for her have inevitably changed, although I still have a deep love for her, but it has changed, there is no doubt about that.
Which is why it is so lovely about Rachel, I must seem some sort of a cad flitting from one girl to another! I should be getting too old for this sort of thing!'

He carried on writing about mundane issues, asking about the health of her boys and whether tobacco farming was worth all the effort and he signed off with his usual seven kisses, which was the secret sign they had for the eternal nature of their love.

January 1966

Rachel was in her room when she heard the key in the front door and the door open. She went out into the hall and met Nina coming in. She mentally rejoiced when she saw that she was on her own.

"My lovely Nina," she exclaimed, as she did her usual bounce up to her and embraced her.

Nina received the exuberance of the greeting with a smile and a kiss. "How are you? I haven't seen you in such a long time," Rachel was determined to make her feel wanted and at home as much as possible.

"I'm OK," Nina replied, "tired, but I guess a good night's sleep will cure that."

"Why haven't you been sleeping?" said Rachel, then realised what she had said, blushed and said, "Silly question, probably."

"Well it hasn't all been that," Nina responded, slightly amused at her friends discomfiture, "we have been to the theatre and shopping and the other weekend we flew up to Scotland and spent a heavenly time in a castle there."

Rachel was not prepared for this, she sensed Nina's excitement at the whirlwind time that he was giving her and guessed that her own attempt to put some realism into her romance would not be very fruitful or well received.

"Sounds great," she responded, her heart sinking.

"Yes it is, and I've just come back to pick up some essential clothes and I'm afraid I'm going off again."

"Why, where are you going?"

"He says that it's silly for me to keep coming home here, when I could stay with him and we could travel to college together in the mornings," Nina glanced sideways at Rachel, trying to gauge her reaction to this news.

"Oh," said Rachel, "I shall miss you terribly."

"I'm sorry," Nina replied, "but I really love him and it would be wonderful to be with him all the time."

"Perhaps," Rachel realised that this would be the last opportunity for her to tell Nina what she needed to say, "perhaps, then, I have to say something to you that is difficult for me to say, but I must, even though it may effect our friendship."

Nina looked concerned, "I'm sure nothing could harm what we feel for each other."

"Wait until you hear what I have to say," Rachel continued.

Nina sat down at the kitchen table and looked hesitantly at her friend.

"Shall I make a coffee?" Rachel went to the kettle, filled it with water and switched it on.

She turned to face Nina, "Simon has been seen with another girl." She spoke softly and gently.

Nina looked blankly at her, "So, he's allowed to be friendly with anyone he meets, surely."

Rachel swallowed hard, "It's just that he was seen being, shall we say, more than friendly."

"Who saw him?" Nina demanded.

This was the question Rachel dreaded because she hadn't quite worked out how she would answer it. "It's someone you don't know, but who knows me and also knows you by association."

"That's not good enough," expostulated Nina, "I must know who it is who is casting such lies."

Rachel could see the suffusion of pink that was spreading over the fair skin of Nina's complexion, denoting the rising of her passion. "Surely it doesn't matter who it is," Rachel responded.

"Of course it does," said Nina sharply, "it matters a great deal, it could be someone who has a grudge against Simon, or me even."

"I can assure you it isn't." Rachel recognised the predictable way this conversation had to go and steeled herself to see it through.

Nina looked at her friend and her expression had a purpose and a hardness to it that spoke to Rachel of a threatened tragic cutting off of the vital spark of love that they had hitherto enjoyed.

"It could even be you," Nina almost seemed to spit the words, "because you are jealous of the happiness that I have found in Simon?"

"I can assure you it's not me," her mouth was dry, "I was as shocked as you obviously are."

"Until I know who it is who has spread this horrible rumour, and heard it from their own lips, I won't begin to believe it," Nina responded.

"All right," said Rachel, "I'll have a word with this person, and if they are willing, I will arrange a meeting. But I just want you to know how sorry I am to have to be the bearer of this news. It is the most difficult thing to have to say to..." she hesitated momentarily, "to someone you love so much," she finished softly.

Nina looked down at her hands, "I'm sorry too, you mean a great deal to me and I wouldn't want anything to come between us, but this is horrible to hear." She looked up, "you must appreciate that."

"Of course I do," Rachel reached over and touched her friend's hand. "I would prefer to do harm to myself than hurt you in any way, but I just had to tell you, I want you to be happy."

"But I am happy now, I've never been so happy," responded Nina, taking Rachel's hand, but only briefly. "He's all that I ever imagined a partner to be, gentle, loving, caring, and I want to be with him, for always."

Rachel's heart sunk, and not for the first time. "All right then, I know how you feel," she shrugged, "and I will try and get this person to tell you what they saw."

February 1966
Ronald Cameron was writing again to Shirley.

I feel as though we need, or at least I feel the need, to try and find our daughter! The thought has been growing in me in the last few months particularly. I don't know why, it's just the feeling that it will be terribly important for us to attempt this. Whether we will be successful I don't know, but I think we have to try. If you agree, perhaps you would let me know the address of your aunt. She seems to be the best place to start. I have never met her so it may be a good idea if you write to her first and let her know the situation. I also don't know if you are in regular communication with her. Perhaps a Christmas card once a year is regular! Anyway darling, I hope you agree and that it doesn't open too many old wounds to do so. Also I have this ongoing problem with Nina. Rachel was able to tell her about Simon being seen with another girl, but of course she wasn't able to accept it and needed to meet the person who had seen them together. Of course it's not as easy as that. I heard it from a third person and so we can't satisfy her on that point. Anyway she is, at the moment, living with him, which is not at all satisfactory! She seems to be completely besotted by him, talk about Svengali, he had nothing on this guy!

Whether you have any ideas about the situation I would be

very grateful for your wise insight into it. I hope this letter is not too much of a shock to you i.e. our daughter, but I really do think action is needed. As Churchill was wont to say to his subordinates, ACTION THIS DAY! I love you xxxxxxx

February 1966

Ever since Rachel had confronted her about Simon, Nina had in the back of her mind the thought of what she had said. It threatened to undermine all her actions regarding him, although it had not been proved and the evidence was nonexistent, she still had that trace element of doubt lurking in her mind. If she had been capable, she would have cursed Rachel for what she had said to disturb her so much. She had hesitated to confront him, knowing that it would only bring dissension and high emotion, which she hated above all things. They had settled into a routine of daily life in the sense of going into college together, seeing something of each other during the day and going home to his flat in the evening. The evenings were involved with a certain amount of shopping, for her cooking sometimes when she felt like it, but more often than not, going to a restaurant, locally or in the West End. They saw shows, went to the cinema and sometimes attended parties given by mutual friends. She was always amazed at the amount of money that he seemed to have available for all this entertainment. She occasionally mentioned it to him, but he always passed it off with a comment about a rich aunt, or something similar. Anyway, in regard to money she was always quite happy to accept it and not worry, unduly, about where it came from.

The person who had apparently seen Simon and a girl was not forthcoming; although Rachel had said that she would bring the person to see her, they had not materialised. She wondered who it could have been – perhaps it wasn't anybody, perhaps it was just an attempt by Rachel to put doubts into her mind. Rachel was jealous of her, she was sure of that, the fact that Rachel had slept with Ronald and he was still only interested in her was evidence of that.

However, maybe she would ask Simon one day about it and see what he had to say, she was sure he would have an innocent explanation.

February 1966

Ronald Cameron met Ozerov in the National Gallery. They sat down together on one of the centre seats overlooking a section of the School of Dutch painting. As if discussing the finer points of the artist's work Cameron started to tell him of Simon Clarke. The Russian listened with the stolid attention that he had come to expect of him, not showing any emotion, only a slight flicker of the eyes when he was told of the blackmail threat. He got up and left after five minutes but Cameron stayed a little longer, got up and wandered around the gallery for another half an hour and then went out into the freezing wind that was blowing around Trafalgar Square.

February 1966
Cameron opened the letter from Shirley, he read,

'Dearest Ronnie,
I thought long and hard about the contents of your last letter. I must admit it was a bit of a shock and although I suppose it was only a matter of time before we initiated something like this, all the same I was unprepared. Yes, I do correspond with my aunt and, yes, mainly at Christmas! In short I think you are right and that we should make some enquiries of her. Whether she will agree that we are doing the right thing I don't know. But she is a kind person and I think if I write to her and tell her our true feelings she will give us the information we need. I will give her your address so that she can write to you if she wants to.
Regarding Nina, I think you have a real problem there, and basically the main problem is you!
I don't mean that in any negative way, only that you are in the way of her sorting this out for herself. She is trying to prove something to you and although she probably doesn't see you at the moment, you are there standing in the wings, a bit like the ghost at the feast! She feels as though she is living under a microscope and if she fails in this relationship, she will hear you saying, I told you so! Not that you would ever be so cruel to do that my dear Ronnie, but that's how she would feel. So treat her gently, she is obviously a lovely girl and needs to be treated with care and concern. Rachel sounds lovely too! You really are a very lucky guy to be surrounded by beautiful women!

The letter went on detailing something of the trials and delights of living in Rhodesia, particularly by the problems brought on by the illegal declaration of independence by the Rhodesian Prime Minister, Ian Smith, and ended with a cautionary note about how she would try to tell her husband that he had a step-daughter. Cameron filed the letter away, with all the others, with a reverence befitting a holy object.

February 1966

Nina collected her books together as the lecture finished. The lecture room was crowded with history students eager to put their newfound knowledge into the essay that was pressing so painfully into their consciences. They bustled out in a motley array of disorder and Nina looked around for Simon. She had tried to find him earlier, but he was not to be seen then, but suddenly she saw him, or rather she saw the girl first. She was tall and elegant, almost model material, she thought, and she was paying an unnatural amount of attention to Simon. And, so Nina thought, he was not averse to the closeness of her body to him. There was a general crush of people going out of the door, but she was aware that the contact of their bodies was not accidental. She followed them down the corridor, some handful of people separating them, and she was almost embarrassed as she noticed the intimacy of their touching. If she had been a casual observer she would automatically have assumed that they were about to take the first opportunity they had to get a more minute inspection of each other. She felt sickened by the spectacle and it was with a distinct reluctance that she found herself following them along various corridors until they came to a door. She stopped at the corner before the door and to her astonishment saw Simon take a key out of his pocket and proceed to open the door. They both went in and shut the door behind them. She went up to the door and saw that it was marked Science Lab 2. As she went past she heard a key turn in the lock.

She, somehow, made her way back to the library, where she attempted to find books that she was suddenly not interested in. How could he do this to her? Who was this girl? Why was he with her? Wasn't she, Nina, enough for him? How could she confront him? These thoughts whirled around her brain to the exclusion of everything else. She felt numb and sick, not the least because she remembered Rachel and what she had warned her about. She felt guilty and used, because she had given all of herself and it had been thrown back in her face.

He was waiting for her in the car park as usual; she got into the car and turned her face away as he attempted to kiss her.

"What's wrong?" he said, looking with concern at her.

She turned to face him, "who was that girl I saw you with in the lecture hall?"

"Oh, Angela, yes, just met her, she's a first year... nice girl, but a bit tall."

"Her height didn't seem to worry you when you went into the science lab together," Nina's tone was cold and she stared intently at him.

She saw that, to give him his due, he went noticeably pale, but that was all.

"Yes we did. She wanted the notes on a particular experiment that had been conducted in the eighteenth century, the original manuscript had been kept in the lab, and it was part of the history project that she is involved in." She had to admire the ease of his circumlocution and it told her more about the deviousness of his character than he, perhaps, wanted to show.

"Which is why you had to lock the door I suppose."

"Look, what is this third degree you are giving me?" his face flushed, and in some strange way she was pleased that his control was not absolute.

She stared straight ahead through the windscreen, "you have made me so unhappy." She said it quietly and matter of factly, "and if you don't mind, will you take me back to my flat? I don't think I want to carry on with our relationship."

"I can't believe that you are saying this," he said, "nothing happened with this girl, I've only just met her, why would I want to get involved with anyone else when I've got you?"

"You tell me why," she responded.

He turned to face her, "I love you, you mean everything to me, without you I am nothing."

"These are just words, they don't mean anything," she remained icily aloof. "Now please take me home or, if you won't, I'll get the train."

He was silent for some moments and then he turned the key in

the ignition and started the engine. They drove in silence as he nego-
tiated the traffic around Marble Arch and up the Edgeware Road. His
driving was erratic and she began to fear that he would provoke an
accident before they arrived in Kingsbury. However, they arrived
without incident and the silence was broken as he turned the engine
off outside the door. He turned and looked at her, "I honestly don't
know what you think I've done, but whatever it is, I am truly sorry if
I have hurt you in any way."
She gave him a long, hard stare, "you really believe that don't you, and
that really is the worrying thing, that you delude yourself in this way."

His hands were still around the steering wheel and she noticed his
knuckles turning white in the intensity of his emotion, "I have no
choice, then, but to tell you why I have been friendly with this girl.
What I am about to tell you is in strictest confidence and I would be
in terrible trouble if this got out." She began to wonder how he was
going to talk his way out of this and she almost felt like an outsider, a
non-participant, as she waited for his explanation. She was not
prepared for what transpired.
"In short, I am an agent for the British government and this girl is,
believe it or not, a Russian spy. She has been put onto the campus by
the KGB to recruit those students who are interested in communism
and who are disallusioned by the democratic system we enjoy here. I
have been given the job of finding who these students are and what
effect she is having." He smiled grimly at her and shrugged, "I also
need to find out who her controller is, that is the resident in the UK
who tells her where to go and what area she is to work in."

She sat back in the car seat completely amazed; of all the explana-
tions she had imagined he would try, this was, she thought, the most
implausible.
"I am pretending to go along with her and make her believe that I
am interested," he continued.
Nina attempted to recover her composure, "But why do you have to
be so friendly with her?"
"It's all part of my cover, I have to appear that I am not only interested in what she is and what she stands for but am not averse to
being friendly with her as well." He took his hand off the wheel and
placed it on hers, "what I have told you is absolutely secret, if you
blow my cover I shall be in big trouble, believe me. I shouldn't have

told you, but you mean so much to me that even if it means that I am in danger, it's worth it if I don't lose you."

"So what you are saying is, you are doing this for England!"

"I know it sounds incredible, but yes."

Nina tried to hide the sense of amazement that she felt, she couldn't believe that she would ever have been the recipient of such nonsense. She removed her hand from under his, "It's you that is incredible, you cannot expect me to believe such a story."

What was equally amazing to her now was that he looked crestfallen, as if the fact that she wouldn't believe him had never occurred to him. She put her hand on the door lever, but he caught hold of her arm, "remember what we agreed, if you are with me no harm will befall Cameron; if you leave me now then I shall be obliged to remind you that I have the means to destroy him."

It was not so much the words, although they were terrible enough, it was the way he said them that finally convinced her that she had to rid herself of the evil of this man. There was no passion in the way he spoke, in fact it was the lack of passion that frightened her, it was as if an automaton was speaking, with no blood in his veins only icy water, no heart that felt compassion, only cold calculation that measured pragmatism.

She brushed his hand away, opened the car door, got out and slammed the door shut. She ran up the stairs to the front door of the flat, fumbled in her handbag, found the key, opened the door and went in. Rachel met her in the hall and she fell sobbing into her arms.

February 1966

Ronald Cameron was making the final calculations to the series of graphs that were in front of him on his desk. He was in his office in Poole and the work that was absorbing him was the final draft to the radio frequency for the detonator for the free-fall nuclear bomb. However, he was also being distracted by the news that he was hearing from Moscow.

During the, twenty years plus that he had been involved in Russia, Cameron had, naturally, made his mind up regarding which side he was on. In that time he had made the acquaintance of two authors, Andrei Sinyavski and Yuli Daniel. They had been arrested by the KGB in September 1965. Their "crime" was that they had published anti-

Soviet literature. Not that it was published in Russia, that would have been impossible, but it had been published in the West, initially in Paris in 1959. Sinyavski's manuscript was entitled *The Trial Begins* (*Sud Idyot*). According to the Soviet agent in Paris, it had reached France from Moscow, being smuggled out by means undiscovered at the time. His friend Daniel had manuscripts smuggled out afterwards, being published, also in Paris, in 1961.

Their trial was taking place whilst Cameron was working at his desk in Poole. Though many Soviet writers had been persecuted for unorthodox opinions before, Sinyavski and Daniel were the first to be put on trial purely for what they had written. The trial was officially a public one, although only those with official passes were allowed in. As Cameron had read in the *New York Herald Tribune*, the "full rights" granted by the court to both defendants was a farce; "These rights included the right to be laughed at by a hand-picked audience of 70 persons... and the right to have only the prosecution side of the case reported in some detail to those who cannot claim access to the 'open' trial because they have no passes." The whole thing was a typical stage-managed show trial and Cameron knew what the result would be despite any spirited defence that the writers could put up.

The phone rang, it was Brian Anstruther-Plowman, "Have you seen the *Herald Tribune* today?"
"Yes I've got it here, I've just read about the trial. What do you think they will get?"
"Probably five to seven years, depends on how much they antagonise the judges."
"You never told me how difficult it was getting the material out," said Cameron.
"It wasn't difficult, only a bit nerve-wracking at the time, if I remember correctly."
"Can we meet up some time?" said Cameron. "I've got some more info about Clarke and I would like to talk it over with you. I've got to go up to London soon, can we meet up there?'
"OK, I'll take the car," replied Cameron, "will Friday be all right?"
"Let's look in the diary... yes that's fine, do you want to pick me up at the surgery?"
"Yes, OK, about nine?"
"Yes, thanks, see you then, bye."

February 1966

The Mk II Jaguar drove powerfully through the Dorset countryside as Cameron gave it the benefit of his skills. He had picked Anstruther-Plowman up at the prescribed hour and they settled down to a companionable time together, as befitted two men who had known each other through many vicissitudes of time.

"I heard from our resident in Moscow yesterday that our writers have been sentenced." Anstruther-Plowman looked across at Cameron to see his reaction.

"Oh, yes, what was it."

"Sinyavski got seven years and Daniel five, both in labour camps."

"It's crazy," responded Cameron, "things don't get any better there."

"I made a copy of what the state prosecutor said in his so-called, judgement." Anstruther-Plowman pulled a sheet of paper from his pocket, "Shall I read it to you?"

"Yes please," said Cameron as he pulled out and overtook a slow moving lorry.

"He started by saying, 'They pour mud on whatever is most holy, most pure, love, friendship, motherhood. Their women are either monsters or bitches. Their men are debauched.' Very melodramatic I must say and then he went on about their most serious crime, 'ideological subversion'. 'The social danger of their work, of what they have done, is particularly acute at this time, when ideological warfare is being stepped up, when the entire propaganda machine of international reaction, connected as it is with the intelligence services, is being brought into play to contaminate our youth with the poison of nihilism, to get its tentacles into our intellectual circles by hook or by crook." He folded the paper up and stuffed it back in his pocket, "Typical isn't it?"

"Yes, I am afraid so," replied Cameron. "Thanks for reading that, but when you analyse what he said, what on earth does it mean?"

"I'll tell you what it means," replied his companion, "they are running scared. They must realise that the structure of their society is so shaky that it is threatened by two writers who happen to write the truth as they see it. It means that they can't trust their people to make up their own minds for fear the whole ramshackle place falls around their ears."

"Yes, that's it, isn't it?" replied Cameron, "and I heard the other day

174

that they are attempting to muzzle Solzhenitsyn; apparently they have discovered and confiscated manuscripts that he'd left in the safe keeping of a friend."

"Yes, it's funny about Solzhenitsyn," responded Anstruther-Plowman, "his *One Day in the Life of Ivan Denisovich* was personally blessed by Krushchev when it was published in 1962. But now they are fearing further revelations from him that may not be to their taste."

"And, changing the subject slightly," said Cameron, "there have been some interesting developments regarding Clarke. It appears that he has blown his chances with Nina. She saw him with this other girl, that we were talking about. She confronted him with it and she has walked out on him. But his Parthian shot to her was that if she doesn't reconsider then he will be obliged to shop me."

"Did you see Ozerov to tell him about Clarke?"

"Yes, I did. It will be interesting to see what they do about him."

"Well, they obviously don't want one of their prize contacts to be compromised, as you will be if he does what he threatens," said Anstruther-Plowman.

"I think their only course of action will be to exfiltrate him as soon as possible," he drove smoothly into a garage to fill up with petrol; the attendant came out from his booth as soon as he had stopped.

"You know it's curious that Clarke, who is obviously a seasoned professional at the espionage game, should hazard so much over this apparent obsession with this girl."

Cameron turned to his friend, "I don't think I like Nina being just described as 'this girl'. You've never met her, have you Brian?"

"No, I must confess I haven't had the pleasure, you have kept her very closely confined."

"I think that if you knew her you would not dismiss her so lightly," as he said the words he felt a pang of something within him begin to come alive.

He paid for the petrol and they proceeded on their journey, eventually reaching the west of London by midday.

"How about lunch at my club," Anstruther-Plowman said, "there is a parking place for me so we can use that?"

Cameron acquiesced, grateful for the suggestion as he headed down the Cromwell Road, past the Victoria and Albert Museum and eventually into the clubland of Piccadilly. He parked where he was instructed and they got out and stretched their limbs.

They went into the bar and ordered drinks. As they settled into the deep leather armchairs they perused the day's menu and decided on some grilled lamb chops.

"Why are you needed in London today, Brian?"

"I have a meeting at the Admiralty this afternoon. How about you?"

"I have to pass on something for Ozerov via a DLB, and I shall take the opportunity to see Rachel and maybe Nina."

"What a pleasant life you have, old boy," said Anstruther-Plowman, taking a sip of his sherry.

Cameron smiled, "It's been hard won I can assure you, it may look as though I am surrounded by pleasures galore, but I am like the proverbial swan, serene on the surface but a heck of a lot of activity going on underneath."

Every citizen of the USSR. is bound by law to act as a political informer under articles 58-1c, 58-1d and 58-12 of the Criminal Code of the RSFSR, which prescribe imprisonment for terms of six months to ten years for failure to report "treason" or a "counter-revolutionary crime".

Political informing is officially regarded in the USSR. as a noble deed, and informers are hailed as heroes. A typical case was that of Pavlik Morozov, a boy of whom the Soviet press made a hero for denouncing his parents.

February 1966

It was towards evening and Cameron was let into the flat by Rachel. She flew into his arms and she embraced him with an intensity that nearly overwhelmed him. Her smile of welcome was a refreshment of spirit to him and she took him by the hand and led him into the sitting room.

"It is so good to see you again," she said, her words only a faint reflection of how she really felt.

"And you too, my beloved Rachel," he took her hand, put it to his lips and kissed it. "There is a big gap in my life when you are not with me."

She beamed a beatific smile, took his hand and put it to her lips. She couldn't say anything, her happiness felt complete.

They looked at each other in silence, both lost in the joy of the moment. Eventually he spoke, "how have you been? When we talked on the phone you said that it was difficult with Nina."

"Yes, she has been moping about the place, I've never seen her so depressed, there doesn't seem to be anything I can say, or do, that will break her out of it."

"Does she talk about it at all?"

"No, that's the difficult part, if she did I'm sure she would begin to see the state that's she's in."

There was a noise at the door, of a key being put in the lock, and Nina walked in, her arms full of books. Cameron got up and went to her. She looked at him with surprise, put down the books and greeted him with a kiss on the cheek.

"Ronnie, what a surprise, what are you doing here?"

He gave a quick glance to Rachel, "I was passing and I wanted to see how you were, and Rachel, of course."

"Well, I'm sure she is all right and I think I am."

"Are you really? I realise that it's been a bit difficult for you."

Nina looked at him, her beautiful face a mask of indifference, "do you realise that? I honestly don't think you have any idea."

She gave him a look of cold calculation and went out of the room. He turned to Rachel and gave her a half smile of understanding, "I see what you mean, she is really hurting."

"Yes she is and she won't let me anywhere near her," she replied.

"Did she tell you what happened when she confronted Clarke, did he deny it or give any excuse?"

"When she first came home she was very emotional, and she told me quite a lot about it, but since then she has completely closed up. Apparently he came up with the most bizarre of reasons."

"And what was that?"

"He said he was working for the British government and he was being employed to find out who was involved in espionage activities in the university. He said that the girl he had made contact with was endeavouring to recruit on the campus those interested in communism."

"Well, that is interesting," said Cameron, "one can't help admiring his nerve."

"But how do you think he thought he was going to get away with it, with a story like that? Rachel asked. "He either is a very quick thinker or he had prepared his story beforehand."

"What puzzles me," said Cameron, "is why he would risk losing the prize of Nina for a fling of dubious value."

"I've heard of these female spies," Rachel responded, "and the way they prey on guys by using sex to find out various things."

"Greatly exaggerated, I'm sure," said Cameron, "anyway what secrets did Clarke have that she wanted to find out about?"

"Do you think she could be employed by the Russians?"

Cameron smiled, "I should think it's very unlikely. No, I think it's all a figment of Clarke's vivid imagination."

"It's a great pity that Nina had to get involved with a man like that, he's hurt her so much."

"Yes," Cameron mused, "I think there must be something more to this guy than just a desperate need to bed as many girls as possible. Look at the way he threatened me if she didn't go along with him. It's not just the normal reaction of a jilted lover, after all there are plenty of girls around who would accommodate him without any angst on his part."

"He obviously saw something in her that he wants," Rachel replied.

"We both know that she is special," said Cameron, smiling at her as he ran the tips of his fingers down the side of her face, "just as you are very special, my darling."

Rachel persuaded him to stay the night, although, because Nina was there, he was reluctant to do so. However, she went to bed early without speaking to them again, so he found it impossible to say no to Rachel, such was the need they had for each other.

The Foreign Administration (Inostrannoye upravleniye):

Every modern government has a system of intelligence by which it seeks to learn facts about other countries. But the Soviet government has approached the problems of intelligence in a manner entirely different from other nations. In accordance with the ultimate objective of the Soviet rulers – forcible communisation of the whole world – Soviet intelligence has been made a powerful weapon in the cold and hot war against the non-Soviet world. It is aggressive, ever watchful and untrammelled by any moral scruples or economic limitations. It has a keen interest in all countries of the world and in all aspects of life within each country. Every scrap of information about the enemy world is valuable. Any method of obtaining it may be justified by the results.

February 1966

Brian Anstruther-Plowman and Ronald Cameron were seated on the end of the row of seats in the middle of the room. The room was in one of the buildings in Whitehall. They were listening to a civil service mandarin who was talking about an up-to-date reassessment of the Soviet system of espionage now prevailing in the United Kingdom.

Depending on a given country's importance from the Soviet point of view and the importance of the objective or problem being attacked, there may be two, three, four and even, in special cases, five independently directed networks of agents. In addition there are independent, parallel networks of neighbour organs, that is, intelligence organs of different departments. For example, the Foreign Administration of the KGB has a series of its own networks. At the same time, the Intelligence Administration of the General Staff operates parallel networks.

An agent network consists of a number of residences (rezidentury), headed by residents. A group of residences may be headed by a senior resident, but not necessarily. Residents and senior residents maintain direct contact among themselves only in rare instances. Only very rarely do some of them have direct contact with the operational points. As a rule, their contact is maintained through contact agents, secret meeting places (tainiky) and mail drops. Only in rare and particularly urgent cases is it effected through strictly conspiratorial personal meetings.

Residents must meet personally with their agents, but they too use secret meeting places and mail drops, Agents of a residence are supposed not to know each other.

In general, every contact, joint action and transmission of documents is organised in such a way that if one agent is uncovered, all or part of the residence is not exposed, even in the event that an arrested agent turns traitor.

At this point Anstruther-Plowman and Cameron glanced at each other and made relevant notes on their pads. The speaker went on,

If a resident is uncovered and the entire residence is exposed, the contact agent, the senior resident and, even more, the higher echelon must not be exposed. If a contact agent is exposed, the residents or other links in the agent organisation must not be. Although great importance is attached to the use of conspiratorial methods, in practice there are almost always violations of the rules which may lead to disaster for the network.

Espionage agents are usually part of the residence, but in some cases they work outside it. They have direct contact either with a senior resident or with an operational point or centre. These, of course, are the most important and reliable agents, but even with them contact is usually maintained through contact agents or by other means, for the most part without personal meetings. Sometimes, however, using strict conspiratorial precautions, a reliable agent is secretly summoned for a meeting with a leading officer of Soviet intelligence, somewhere in neutral territory or even in an area under Soviet influence.

A group of espionage agents is known as an "active" or "reserve" group, depending on the extent of its functioning. An active group can be transformed into a reserve group for an extended period, while a reserve group may become active for a long period or for a limited assignment. A reserve group may be specially sent to a foreign country or may be recruited there and spend several years without going into action, while it seeks to achieve political respectability, perhaps even by engaging in anti-Soviet or anti-Communist activity.

When the speaker finished, Anstruther-Plowman and Cameron got up and left with the rest of the audience. When they emerged into Whitehall, a scattering of snow was swirling across the road. They hailed a taxi and were taken the short distance to Anstruther-Plowman's club in Piccadilly. When they were comfortably ensconced in the main sitting room, they ordered drinks and perused the menu for the day's lunch.

"According to the information we've just heard, Clarke is not under diplomatic cover and, maybe, is being run by a network unknown to Ozerov," Cameron said, as he lit a cigarette.

"It would be interesting," responded his companion, "if you could elicit from Ozerov what control the embassy has over Clarke."

"Of course, he may be operating in an entirely independent way in this particular case. He is using blackmail, not to get useful information, but to satisfy his own desires," said Cameron, "and that will not please whatever agency network he is being run by."

"Exactly," responded Anstruther-Plowman, "and that will give us the opportunity to, hopefully, drive a wedge between networks."

"Or, at least, to confuse them sufficiently to identify more of their agents, and in that respect, I wonder if Clarke is for turning," Cameron mused.

"Or, if he is worth turning?" Anstruther-Plowman gestured to a waiter and ordered their choice of lunch.

"He certainly seems to be a loose cannon," said Cameron, "and loose cannons are always dangerous to whatever organisation they belong to."

February 1966

Rachel handed the letter to him, "This came for you yesterday," she said, "when you weren't with me," she pouted deliberately to make the point of her dissatisfaction with him. He had just arrived, in the afternoon, after his lunch with Anstruther-Plowman; she greeted him, with enthusiasm. He adored the pretended annoyance that she teased him with and kissed her on the end of her nose. He recognised Shirley's writing on the envelope and went into the sitting room to read it, appreciating Rachel's sensitivity in leaving him to it. It read,

Dearest Ronnie,

First of all I had to explain to my aunt, who you were! She thought you were dead! The last time I was with her was when I gave my baby away! Although I had been in correspondence with her from Africa, she hadn't seen me and for some reason I hadn't told her about you and the fact that you had survived the war. I suppose it was always painful for me to even mention those times with her and a great part of me wanted to forget. Anyway, I have now told her all about us and how we want to try and find our daughter. I have had a reply from her and it was rather guarded. She said she would have to think about it and if she was able to mention it to the family concerned. It has always been the understanding that if our daughter didn't want to meet her natural parents then that would have to be respected. She doesn't know yet if they have even told her that she is adopted but, of course, she profoundly hopes they have. She will be twenty-one in August this year, and I imagine it would be a terrible shock at this late stage in her life to be told that her parents, who have brought her up, are not her natural mother and father.

Anyway, that is the situation at the moment; and I will tell you more, if and when, there are developments. I hope you didn't mind me sending to the address in London. I have a feeling that you are there, more than in Poole at this time! I hope you have been able to tell Rachel about me, I am sure she would understand, particularly, if she loves you as much as you hope she does.

The letter ended with the usual endearments, which he almost took for granted until he realised the rather unusual nature of their relationship and the way they had been given back to each other in such an amazing way. She had appended a PS. "I tried to tell Bill, my husband, if you remember him! But I couldn't, the time didn't seem right (When will it ever be?) xxxxxxx."

He folded up the pages, put them in the envelope and placed them in the breast pocket of his jacket. He got up to find Rachel in the kitchen, went up to her and put his arm around her shoulders. "Darling, can I tell you something," he said.

"You can tell me you love me, if you like," she said, inclining her face up to his to be kissed.

He happily complied and then said, "The letter that I have just had is from a previous girl friend."

"Oh, yes," she replied, looking enquiringly at him.

"Come and sit down," he took her by the hand and they went into the sitting room and they sat side by side on the sofa, their knees touching. He held both her hands and smiled gently at her.

"She was a girlfriend from rather a long time ago, during the last year of the war."

Rachel gave a half smile, "you don't have to explain, you know."

"I want to," he replied, "you mean so much to me and I don't really want to keep any secrets from you. We were very much in love but, as you know, I had a wife in Russia and because of that we couldn't get married. But the love we had we found impossible to deny. In short, she became pregnant, but at about the time that she knew this, I had been posted missing and she assumed I was dead. When I, eventually got back to England I tried to find her but due to a misunderstanding, which, incidentally, happened quite a lot during those times, I thought she was dead. Anyway, it eventually transpired that she wasn't; I only discovered this eight years ago, we met again and found out the truth. She got married at the end of the war and moved with her husband to Rhodesia."

"It must have been terrible for you both," said Rachel, her eyes filling up.

He shrugged, "they were the times we were living in and we somehow accepted what was happening and got on with making the best of it."

"I love you," said Rachel.

"And I love you too," he replied, "more than I can say."

"But you said that she had become pregnant, what happened to the baby?" Rachel asked.

"Well, that's the point; the reason why we are communicating so much at the moment is that the baby was adopted and we feel it is right to find out where she is and, maybe, make contact with her... it was a girl, by the way."

"Knowing you I'm not surprised," said Rachel.

February 1966

Simon Clarke was sitting on the bed with the short wave radio set suitcase open before him.

He was deliberating what to tell Centre about his recent findings. He knew that it was risky sending any message, therefore they were always kept to a minimum and only for vital information, but he was desperate to somehow expiate the pain he was feeling and he felt that to do that only extreme measures would do. He had to hit out at the one person he considered to be responsible for the anger and anguish that he was feeling now. He looked at his watch and switched on the set. He put the headphones on and adjusted the dials to link into the wavelength that he needed. He tapped out the message, "Cameron no longer reliable, has been turned by SIS – repeat –no longer reliable – do not trust anymore info – repeat – do not trust anymore info." He signed off with his codename (Silas) and switched off the set.

February 1966

Shirley's aunt was not at all like her sister. She was short, some would unkindly say dumpy, and she had dark hair, permed to distraction, whereas her sister, Shirley's mother, had been tall and willowy with fair hair, naturally wavy. She walked up the path of the suburban villa that fronted this detached house in Wimbledon and rang the door bell. As befitted someone in her mid-sixties, she did not relish having to wait for a door to be opened for her, and she was relieved when, within a short interval, the door obligingly opened. Standing there was a woman of very similar stature to Shirley's aunt and she greeted her caller with undisguised pleasure.

"How good to see you Mildred, please come in." She ushered her in and they entered the front sitting room where tea had been laid on the dining room table.

"How good to see you too, Win," answered Mildred, "it's been some time since we last met."

"Yes, when was it, about two years ago? When we saw that exhibition at the V&A wasn't it?"

"Yes, that's right," replied Mildred. They continued talking about ordinary things, the things that make life bearable, and then Mildred said, "can we talk about your daughter?"

"Yes," said Win, hesitantly, "what about her?"

Shirley's aunt then told her all the relevant details about her niece and the rediscovered father of her child and that because they had found each other again they wanted to make contact with their daughter.

Win listened with an increasing apprehension and when Mildred had finished said, "I understand their need to see her, I really do, but... it must depend on our daughter of course, and whether she wants to see them."

"Of course it does," replied Mildred, "and it would be entirely wrong to do otherwise. I suppose," she continued, "that she knows she's adopted?"

"Yes, she does, we told her when she was thirteen, in 1958."

"Did that effect her in any way, do you think?" Mildred asked.

"No, I don't think so," said Win, "in fact, she went out of her way to say that she was only interested in us, because she felt we were her true mum and dad. And for a thirteen-year-old to say that we thought was lovely."

"Yes it is," replied Mildred, "whenever I've seen her I've thought what a lovely girl she is. And I'm not surprised; you have brought her up so beautifully and loved her, that's the most important thing, and she knows she is loved."

Mildred put down her tea cup and looked at Win, "may I ask you a question?"

"I think I know what you are going to say," interposed Win, "would we be able to ask her whether she wants to meet her real mother and father?"

"Yes, that is what I was going to ask you."

"I will, of course, talk to Arthur about it, but I am sure that we would feel it right that she should be given the choice, yes." Win smiled at her friend.

Mildred leaned back in her chair, "that is a relief, I've anguished long and hard about this and been trying to pluck up the courage to talk to you about it."

"It's been difficult for you, I'm sure," said Win, "we obviously want to do the best for everybody concerned. When was the last time you saw Shirley?"

"Not since she went to Africa, after the war, she went straight out and married out there. She has kept in regular correspondence. But I think it's always been difficult for her because whenever she communicated with me it reminded her of a traumatic time in her life. In fact, she said so the other day, when she first told me about the decision to find their daughter."

"She certainly went through incredibly hard times, poor girl," responded Win.

"During the war, we all did, of course," said Mildred, "although some more than others."

"Yes, it's amazing we kept our sanity at all," answered Win.

"Some of us didn't," said Mildred.

"It would be good to meet Shirley, although obviously if we do meet, it will not be the easiest of coming togethers," Win smiled, "but I am sure it will work out."

"If it happens," replied Mildred, "it will be very interesting, I'm sure."

March 1966

Vladimir Mikhailovich Oshchenko (codenamed Ozerov) was walking down Balham High Street on his way from the tube station to Tooting Common. He was thinking deeply about the interview that he had had with the Ambassador. He had been informed about a Simon Clarke (codenamed Silas) who was an illegal agent operated by an agency that could be the GRU (Soviet military intelligence), but could also be another agency that neither of them were aware of. Cameron (codenamed Mariner) had told him of Silas but it had also now come to the attention of Centre and they were considerably exercised by new information they had received from another source. His mission, this beautiful spring morning, was to find out as much as he could about Silas. He had already followed him around the campus of his college, posing as a visiting lecturer, with documents provided by Centre purporting to show him as an academic from Moscow, and had seen his method of approach to other students. He had discovered his address, by dint of contact with the college porter, and he was on his way to it now.

Although Ozerov was operating under diplomatic cover, out of the residency, he knew that Silas, as an illegal agent, had much more flexibility of operation and was not under the possible scrutiny of the British SIS, as the legals, without doubt, were.

He arrived at the address given to him by the porter and after ringing the bell, as a precaution, he easily unlocked the door and went in. There appeared to be two bedrooms, and judging by the clothes in the drawers and the wardrobes, one was used by a girl. The other at the front, had men's clothes and a double bed, and he soon found evidence, in the drawers of a dressing table – letters with Simon Clarke's name on the envelope. It didn't take long to find the short wave wireless set in the suitcase on the top of the wardrobe and inside, also, the code book with contact numbers. He made a copy of the relevant details that he required and he also found a letter from the girl that Mariner had mentioned, who was involved with Silas and, judging by the content of the letter, more than obsessed with him.

After half an hour taking notes and then making sure that he had put everything back where it should be, Ozerov left. He walked back to Balham tube station, taking his time and being casually deliberate in the way he didn't pursue the straight way back, but went up side turnings and doubling back to the main road. He didn't consider that there was much of a possibility of him being followed on this particular assignment, but experience in a number of foreign stations had made him wary and cautious. He took a leisurely lunch in a café near Waterloo station before heading back to the embassy, making doubly sure that he didn't recognise anyone behind or in front of him that he had noticed before.

He got back to the embassy and began to check the various files that would indicate where Clarke came from and who was running him. The original information about him had come from Soviet military intelligence and he pursued his enquiries with them. They were adamant that Clarke had been infiltrating into an area that was of a sensitive nature and they didn't want to divulge any more information about him. Ozerov had another meeting with the Ambassador and because the KGB were running Mariner, they did not want his work with them to be put at hazard by the maverick efforts of a rogue operator, for such was the way they viewed Clarke. Therefore, they determined to exfiltrate Clarke despite the GRU (military intelligence). But how to do it?

March 1966

Simon Clarke was feeling uneasy. Since the altercation with Nina he had been trying desperately to find some way back into her affections. But, even to his warped imaginings, he could find no easy course to limit the damage that had been done. He cursed Angela, without the utter weakness of his sexual control he would have been able to resist the opportunity that she gave him to seduce her. Now he knew he was in trouble with the Centre. The agent who had been running him was aware that the KGB were making noises regarding the suitability of Silas. Something or someone had told the legals that there was an operator who was running counter to their perceived view of things. He knew he had stirred up a hornet's nest by even mentioning the possibility that pressure was being put on Cameron. So, he thought, that must put Cameron pretty high on the calibre list of KGB favourites. They would not want him to rock the boat to unsettle Cameron in any way. However, he was now determined to carry out his threat to Nina. She would have to be taught a lesson she would not forget. If he couldn't hurt Cameron then he would take it out on her. If he couldn't have her, then he was damned sure no one else would. He resolved to pit all his intellectual resources into the plan to destroy her, but in such a way that blame could be placed elsewhere. But before her demise he would take full advantage of the sovereign delights of her feminine nature, he was sure of that.

March 1966

Rachel was already busy at the stove when Nina got back to the flat from college. She was producing one of her specialist shepherd's pies and without turning round called out to her, "hope you're not going out tonight, I think I've made more than I meant to."

"No, I'm not going out," she replied. "Who would I go out with?"

Rachel turned, held out her hand to grasp her and said, "try not to let that swine spoil the rest of your life."

Nina shrugged, "he's already done that. And it looks as though he's going to spoil Ronald's too."

"Look, Ronald can look after himself," Rachel protested. "Don't worry about him, and knowing him as we do I'm sure he has a plan to counter this man."

"I saw him today," said Nina.

"Who, Ronald?"

"No, Simon Clarke. He was going to one of the lectures... I avoided him."

"Did he see you?"

"No, I don't think so... I really feel as though I don't want to see him ever again."

"I shouldn't think you do," replied Rachel.

"In fact I really hate him, I never thought that I would feel like that about anyone, but he has produced in me such a reaction that I can't stand the sight of him."

"It's not surprising," said Rachel, "when you consider what he has done to you and the way he has threatened you, you would have to be a saint not to feel as you do."

"I feel sickened by the very thought of him," Nina continued, "I don't know how I could have been taken in by him so easily, I am so gullible."

"By the sounds of it you are not the first to have succumbed to his so-called charms," said Rachel. "But it's not that surprising, after all, you were very unhappy when Ronnie was in Russia. You didn't know what was happening to him, or why he was there, and you were vulnerable to the next apparently nice guy who came along. Don't blame yourself for what other people do to you."

Nina sat down at the kitchen table and gave a weary smile to her friend, "I know you are right, it's just I feel I could have done things a little differently and not been so eager to please him in the way he wanted pleasing. I gave myself so easily and all of myself too."

"You won't be the first girl to say that," Rachel riposted, "and you certainly won't be the last."

"But it's strange you know," replied Nina, "I know that you will probably be cross with me for saying this but I do feel a bit sorry for him."

Rachel came away from the cooker and came and sat next to her at the table, "you can't honestly mean that, after how he has treated you and threatened you."

"But his actions have always been good to me, he made me feel alive again and when we were together, it was always good... it was only... finding out that he was seeing another girl..." she tailed off.

"That, on it's own, must be sufficient reason to say goodbye to him, surely," said Rachel, "and then, on top of that, he threatens you and Ronald, how can you say you feel sorry for him?"

"Oh, I don't know," Nina shook her head in exasperation. "It's just that I, maybe, encouraged him too much into thinking that I was committed to him, irrespective of how he treated me."

"You mean you are blaming yourself and feeling guilty because you gave him all of yourself and he didn't reciprocate, so it's your fault?" Rachel was nearly despairing of her friend.

Nina had the temerity to blush, "I know it sounds crazy to say that, and, in a way, hearing myself say it, it does sound weird."

"It not only sounds weird but, to my mind, it shows how much he has brainwashed you. And, don't forget, you have been able to see, before it was too late, the nasty side of him. For that you should be grateful." Rachel took Nina's hand and held it.

"Yes, I know I should," responded Nina.

"Look, let's go out tonight, just the two of us, we'll go to the cinema, after we've had the shepherd's pie, and have a few drinks and try and forget the likes of Simon Clarke," Rachel was determined to shake her out of her mood of despondency and she made a deliberate attempt to sound more jocular than she felt.

"OK, let's," Nina replied, "and thank you for helping me, even though I don't understand it yet, I suppose I must have made the right decision, but what really worries me, is," she hesitated and Rachel looked at her enquiringly, "what is going to happen to Ronald."

"I told you, he can look after himself," Rachel replied.

Nina looked doubtful, "you weren't there when he made those threats against Ronald, it was really that he had such a vindictive expression on his face, that it makes me shudder just to think of it."

"He didn't give you any idea what his threats were, I suppose?" Rachel said.

"No, except that he would ruin him, something about Ronald being involved in an affair that would discredit him in some way."

"He must be pretty sure if he is going to make threats like that," replied Rachel.

"He certainly gave the impression that it was not an empty threat."

"I wonder what it could be?" Rachel replied. "I can't imagine Ronnie doing anything that would attract blackmail."

"No, I can't either," replied Nina, "but he has been involved in government work, perhaps it is something to do with that. I know that when I first met him, at the party at my parent's house, he was looking for some funding for a particular project that he was working on."

"You never told me why he was at the party?" Rachel enquired.

"Well my father is a banker and he was invited because he was doing some scheme with my father. I know money was involved somewhere," Nina replied.

"That all sounds very respectable anyway," said Rachel, dishing out the shepherd's pie onto two separate plates.

"If my father was in it then it is respectable," Nina poured out the wine from the bottle that they had started yesterday.

"Is there any other clue that you can think of that would give us an idea of what Simon is up to?" Rachel asked.

"Well there is this preposterous story that he told me as to why he had got involved with this girl."

"And what was that?" Rachel said, taking a sip of wine.

"He said he was a British secret agent, trying to find any communists on the campus, and it was because of that that he became entangled with this girl. He suspected that she was endeavouring to recruit spies for the KGB, or whatever the Russian spies call themselves."

Rachel laughed outright, "you are joking?"

"Sadly, I'm not, that's exactly what he told me," Nina smiled in return.

"He must be mad if he expected you to believe that," Rachel riposted.

"I believe he did expect me to accept it and, in a way, that's the sad part. He looked absolutely devastated when I obviously didn't. Did he think I was that naive to take in a cock and bull story like that?"

"OK," replied Rachel, "let's assume, for the moment, that his story is true and that he really was on a mission to find some secret from this girl, does that make him any better in your eyes?"

"Absolutely not," said Nina, "there must be other ways to get information than having to compromise relationships in this way. I understand that, if he is working in some espionage department for the government, he couldn't tell me about it, but there are ways of warning someone you, supposedly, love."

"I don't think it works like that," said Rachel.

March 1966

Simon Clarke picked up the phone, the voice on the other end said, "Silas, this is Pimpernel, you have to leave on code 'Ubezhishche'." The phone went dead. He stood there for some moments, his heart racing, the blood pressuring in his head. For some unaccountable reason he looked out of the window, expecting to see, he knew not what. He looked at the phone, still in his hand, and then placed it carefully back on it's stand. His mind was turning cartwheels, "Ubezhishche", that means "refuge", he remembered the definition, "Clandestine intelligence premises in a target country, which are intended as a temporary hiding place for an illegal or agent pursued by the judicial or counter-intelligence agencies of a target country." What to do first, what to pack? Then the training clicked in. He went to the wardrobe and took the radio set down from the top. He hauled out the soft bag from under the bed, which contained his emergency supplies, put on his jacket, checked that his keys were in the pocket, stepped to the door, took one last look around and went out, closing the door behind him. He ran down the stairs and out of the front door. His car was parked a few yards from the front of the house, he went to it, threw his luggage in and, as he glanced quickly around, eased himself into the driving seat, started the engine, selected first gear and roared off down the road, the exhaust echoing back from the row of terrace houses in the street.

March 1966

Ozerov was sitting in the third room of the National Portrait Gallery on one of the centre seats when Cameron joined him. There was no one else in the room so Cameron did not feel obliged to saunter around before he sat beside the Russian.

"We cannot find Silas, he is not attending the college and he has not been seen at his flat for some days," Ozerov glanced briefly towards him.

Some weeks ago that news would have pleased Cameron's heart mightily, but hearing it today an ominous trickle of apprehension entered his consciousness.

"Did he know you were going to exfiltrate him?"

"No," said Ozerov.

"I will make enquiries my end, but it will be better for him if you take him and not us," Cameron replied.

"And better for you too?" Ozerov queried.

"And you too, I guess," responded Cameron.

"Yes, we both have good reasons for him to come to Moscow." Ozerov rose to depart, "I will leave it to you to contact me then, if you have any more news."

March 1966

"Are we going to pull in Clarke?" Ronald Cameron was talking to Brian Anstruther-Plowman as they waited in the car for Tower Bridge to close. It had just been opened to allow a medium-sized cargo ship full of bananas to go to it's wharf alongside London Bridge.

"I think we may run him a little longer," replied his companion, "and see how much further he takes us in making contact with others we don't know about yet."

"Because I have the feeling that if we leave it too long he will be taken by the other side first," Cameron looked at his passenger.

"You said that they couldn't find him the other day."

"No, they couldn't, but why doesn't that give me much comfort?" Cameron put the Jaguar into first gear and they moved off from the bridge.

"I don't think you need to worry," replied Anstruther-Plowman, "his cover has been blown and whatever he does will now be compromised."

"I think what worries me mainly is the fact that he is running around loose, and in view of the threats that he has made, particularly to Nina, I would feel that much happier if he was off the scene entirely." Cameron accelerated the car along Leadenhall Street towards the Bank of England.

"I can understand that, but I think he has an idea that he has to lie low, perhaps he has been tipped off," Anstruther-Plowman responded.

"By whom, one wonders," said Cameron.

"It could be the agent who is running him; that would be the most likely scenario. I doubt he has second sight in his nature."

"Where would he go to ground?" Cameron asked.

"There are safe houses, refuges all over the place, he could be anywhere."

"How could he support himself?"

Anstruther-Plowman smiled slightly, "in their refuges they are well stocked with all the means of life, enough to keep body and soul together for a considerable time. And, depending on the brief he has been given, they may think it desirable to move him completely away from where he has been, to somewhere entirely different. They would issue him with another set of false papers and he could be set up in another part of the country or indeed in another country altogether. Where he will end up depends on what sort of cover he is given."

March 1966

Simon Clarke had found the key and the directions to the "Ubezhishche", the refuge, from the dead letter box that was located behind Clapham Common tube station, in a wall which contained a niche with a loose brick concealing a small wooden box. The directions gave a route to the refuge, which was ten miles to the north of a town in mid-Wales. He read the instructions as he was parked at the back of the tube station. He looked at his watch, it was midday, he studied the road map again, it was over two hundred miles to his destination. If he started now, he reckoned he could get there in about five hours. He drove out into Clapham High Street and headed north, crossing the River Thames at Westminster Bridge, making his way, in increasing traffic, to Hammersmith. From there he picked up the A40 trunk road, which headed due west to Wales. As the volume of traffic diminished he began to use the performance of the MG sports car to begin to eat up the miles and within just over three hours he was near the Welsh border at Ross on Wye. He left the A40 there and headed north on the A49 to Hereford. He kept driving despite increasing fatigue, wanting to put as many miles as possible between himself and London, as soon as was possible. From Hereford he made his way to Llandrindod Wells, the town indicated in his instructions. His weariness made him stop at a pub on the outskirts of the town, where he had a pork pie and a pint of beer. He looked again at the directions north from the town. It indicated leaving the town by the Newtown road for five miles and then taking a white unsurfaced road on the left, signposted Bwich-y-sarnau. When he arrived at the junction, the low-slung sports car did not take kindly to the rough track and he had to drive slowly and carefully to negotiate the many hazardous potholes that littered the way. He had been driving into the hills for some time when he eventually came to the refuge (the Ubezhishche). It was a small, stone-built cottage, a few hundred yards from the main track. It nestled into the hills surrounding it with an almost pre-historic aspect to it. Attached to the building was a wooden shed, which, on inspection, was just about large enough to hide the MG. This he did before attempting to enter the cottage. When he entered he discovered it to be one large room downstairs, with a bedroom and bathroom upstairs. The kitchen area occupied one corner of the main room and an armchair and settee were placed around the large fire place. Opposite the fireplace was a large picture window. In front of the window were placed a dining table and four chairs. The window looked out onto the hills at the rear and he had an immediate thought that wireless reception was not going to be great from the cottage. Perhaps, he thought, Centre, or whoever chose this place as a refuge, considered that to be of secondary importance to the greater need of a safe hiding place for the occupant.

He quickly familiarised himself with the utility details of the building, including the essential immersion heater - which he switched on as soon as he found it, his need for a shower being paramount - and the well-stocked fridge, which included copious amounts of canned beer. He drank two whilst he waited for the water to heat up. The larder contained enough food for at least two weeks and he chose a tin of beans and spaghetti and some cheese for his first meal. After a shower and whilst he waited for his food to heat up, he wandered outside in the gathering dusk and pondered the day's events. When he had got up this morning, he had no inkling that he would have been chased, or so it felt, out of the centre of his operations in London and into a rural backwater such as now surrounded him. He wondered about the agent who had alerted him and what he had discovered that demanded such a precipitate exit for himself. Nevertheless he was grateful to him and thought again about the organisation that had such a comprehensive back-up system that allowed them to be so vigilant on his behalf.

March 1966

After two days he was beginning to wonder what he was doing there. The immediate excitement of flight and possible discovery was now relegated to his memory and he began temporising on why he had obeyed so instantly. There were so many things that he needed to sort out amongst his new contacts in London and he felt he was very close to being able to reveal a particular individual as being a double agent. But he needed more proof and he sensed that a few more enquiries near the source would have revealed that. Because of that he felt frustrated, but over and above these things he knew what was creating in him a barrier to any constructive thought. That barrier was Nina. As the days went on the thought of her and what she meant to him absorbed his entire nature. She was with him in every action he took, everything he did had her standing beside him, he had only to reach out and she would take his hand and provide those delights of herself to him, without reservation. But she was not there, and no matter how much he tried to wrench her out of his mind to convince himself that she wasn't there, she came gliding back with that exquisite sense of perfume that intoxicated the very fibre of his being. By the third day he knew what he had to do.

March 1966

Simon Clarke had first been contacted by Igor Vitalyevich Voytetsky (codenamed Paul) three years ago. He was an illegal agent who had first come to Britain in January 1963, marrying another illegal, Yulia Ivanovna Gorankova, in Dover Register Office. They had then, jointly, embarked on a full-time career as illegals working for Soviet sabotage and intelligence groups (diversionnye razvedyvatelnye gruppy) or DRGs. A year ago he had made contact again with him and Voytetsky had selected him to be one of a group of agents specialising in sabotage operations. Voytetsky had travelled around Britain selecting various sites that could be used as landing areas in the event of war breaking out. He also identified suitable bases for 'resistance movements' for the use of local cells of communists. These involved the preparation of large dead drops for sabotage equipment. One such cache of arms and equipment was not more than a mile from the cottage that Clarke was presently occupying.

Clarke knew that the department that was identified as organising sabotage and intelligence groups from Moscow was the Thirteenth Department, but it had been reorganised last year as Department V. He determined to contact them direct and with that in mind went outside to the shed, where his car was, removed the wireless set and brought it back into the cottage. He set it up in the bedroom, the highest area of the building, and attempted to transmit. The set was completely dead, there was absolutely no response or sign of energy in it. He looked out of the window, the landscape appeared as dead and lifeless as the radio, in fact he had seen no evidence of any other human being since his arrival. So he carried the suitcase out of the cottage and up to the top of the hill at the back.

The result was the same, no response. He surveyed the landscape in a 360 degree compass and came to the extraordinary conclusion that he was alone in the world. There was absolutely no one else out there.

He went back in. He knew, from Voytetsky, that all refuges would have secret instructions detailing the place and the surrounding area and he suddenly remembered that the instructions to get to this place had had, a PS at the bottom. He hadn't taken much notice of it, at the time, being more occupied in arriving here successfully. He found the note again in the glove pocket of the car. After the route it had a cryptic - "Both Your Houses - Philip Gibbs."

He went to the book case, where there was the normal assortment of dog-eared paperbacks and tired-looking hardbacks. On the second shelf was a small hardback book with a red cloth cover: *Both Your Houses*, by Philip Gibbs.

He took it out and opened it. Taped inside the front cover was a folded sheet of paper. He prized it off and unfolded it. It read,

A BR-3U radio transmitter no. 609072-9126 has been placed in a waterproof package in the Bwlch-y-sarnau cache on 15 April 1964. This cache is located as follows. Take the path from the back door of the dwelling, heading in a northwest direction. Follow the path for about 800 metres until you come to a fork where there are two paths, continue along the path to the right which begins 10 metres from four large stones on the main path. These two paths go round either side of a hillock. After following the right hand path for about 100 metres from the point where it branches off, you will come to a large white stone on the left. Turn left there and go up the hill for about 10 metres. On the hill and on its slopes there are holes, as if trees have been uprooted. Among all these holes there is a group of four which are side by side. The cache in which the load is secreted is a square hole which is next to another large hole of irregular shape like the figure eight. At the bottom of the hole a chamber has been dug in the direction of the fork in the paths and it is in this that the trunk with the two-way radio has been placed. It is covered with earth and stones to a depth of 55-60cm. After the case was covered with 25 cm of earth a first marker was placed; two lengths of green wire have been put across the spot diagonally; the case was then covered with another 50 cm of earth, when a yellow wire was placed diagonally across the spot; this was then covered with a 55-60cm layer of earth. The overall depth of the cache is 1 metre. WARNING - The case container has an explosive device which is made live by means of the MOLNIYA (Lightning) explosive device.

Appendix1; Instructions for disarming the MOLNIYA (Lightning) Explosive Device.

1. When digging out the container from the earth, take care not to strike the handle by chance. Dig until the upper surface of the container with the handle comes to light; remove the board and the plywood which cover the container.

2. The handle must only be turned and the container tilted and taken out of the hole after the explosive device has been disarmed.

3. In order to disarm the device, one must have a pocket torch battery of not less than 3.5 volts. Attach two wires of 30-50 cm length to the battery, with sharp probes at the end (a nail or a needle).

4. Without taking the container out of the cache, place one of the battery contacts on the body of the container, and the other on the left lock fitting, assuming that the lid of the container faces the operator. The contact points must be applied after scratching the paintwork on the body of the container and on the lock fitting.

5. When contact is made with the battery, a 'click' should be heard inside the container; this indicates that the explosive device has been disarmed. If there is no 'click', check the contact points again and repeat the operation to disarm the

device.

6. If, when the operation is repeated, there is still no "click", it is forbidden to take the container out of the cache and the cache must be filled in.

To open the container and remove the electric detonators from the two-way radio; remove the padlocks and lift the lid of the container with the key, which is inside the container. Unscrew the four screws and remove the metal casing under which the two-way radio is located in the ALIOT packaging. Cut each of the wires which connect the container with the ALIOT packaging and remove the package from the container.

Simon Clarke read the instructions with a peculiar sense of detachment. He had read them before on a training course but had not imagined a scenario when he would have to use them for himself.

Whether it was the sparseness of the landscape outside the cottage, or the reading of the instructions for the cache, or the sense of complete isolation that he felt, but he had a strange feeling that maybe there had been a general alert from Centre to all agents that there was an emergency brewing. He reflected on the sudden call that he had had, to flee to a refuge without any explanation. And once having got here, to be out of touch completely with the outside world. Perhaps the balloon had gone up and the Cold War had, at last, become a Hot one. There was only one way to find out, he surmised, and that was to find the radio and try and make contact.

March 1966

He recognised the familiar handwriting on the airmail envelope. He slit along the line and unfolded the sheet. He read,

Dearest Ronnie,

I have had a letter from Aunt Mildred, she says that OUR DAUGHTER... wants to meet her mother and father! Isn't that great news? It seems that she went to see her friend who adopted her, who I met once, of course, although I don't remember much about it, and she has said that she talked about it to our daughter and after some hesitation, she has agreed!

So, my plan is to come over at the end of the month, probably the 30th, and we could then arrange a date for us to meet her. Won't that be amazing! Although it will not be easy, I suspect.

By the way I have at last told Bill. Curiously it was not that difficult. We were talking about the war one day, and how difficult things were and how it was a miracle we all survived as we did. And it suddenly came out. He said that he had had an affair with a girl who was in the Women's Land Army, when he was recuperating from his injuries, after he was shot down and they nearly got engaged. So it seemed natural somehow to tell him about us and that we had a daughter. He took it very well and somehow seemed chuffed to be the step-father of a girl!

I wonder how it will all work out? It's very exciting really, I suppose, but I can't help thinking that there are some emotional times ahead! Particularly where girls are involved! Are you sure you want to pursue this to its logical conclusion? Only joking, of course, I know that you were the chief mover of this in the first place.

So, all being well, I will fly over on the 30th. I will let you know flight times etc. and it will be wonderful to see you again, in fact I can't wait. All my love, your Shirley. xxxxxxx
PS Have written to Aunt M to tell her.

March 1966

He found a spade in the shed and with the directions in his hand followed the path from the rear of the cottage up the hill at the back. He had no difficulty in finding the site of the cache, the instructions being so explicit. His intention was only an initial survey. He wanted to see if it was there and also how difficult it would be to find again. Also at this particular point he didn't have a torch battery, so the opening of the container would not be possible.

He found the irregular-shaped hole easily enough, the figure eight being recognisable. He began to probe the square hole beside it. After about a half spade depth he came across a yellow wire, he set that aside, and further scraping came to the two green wires, he set those aside too. He soon had the container revealed and he carefully brushed the loose soil away from the sides so that the whole container was evident.

By the side of it he found a parcel wrapped up in a waterproof cloth. He took it out and delicately eased away the cloth to reveal a pistol. He recognised it as a 7.65 calibre Mauser, with cartridge clip and twenty-one live rounds of ammunition. With a distinct twinge of satisfaction he wrapped it up again and put it in his jacket pocket. He got up from where he had been kneeling and looked around at the surrounding countryside. He was not surprised to see no other living being around and proceeded to fill the hole in, taking care to put the wires back at approximately the same levels they were at before. He finished the filling in and, with a final survey of the site, made sure that any loose earth was brushed away from the site of the hole. He walked back down the hill, turning around at the bottom to satisfy himself that any casual observer would not notice anything amiss.

He approached the cottage, conscious of the weight of the pistol nudging his side and also the plans being formulated in his mind.

March 1966

This land of such dear souls, this dear, dear land,
Dear for her reputation through the world,
Is now leas'd out,- I die pronouncing it,-
Like to a tenement, or pelting farm:
England, bound in with the triumphant sea,
Whose rocky shore beats back the envious siege
Of watery Neptune, is now bound in with shame,
With inky blots, and rotten parchment bonds:
That England, that was wont to conquer others,
Hath made a shameful conquest of itself.
Ah! Would the scandal vanish with my life,
How happy then were my ensuing death.

Brian Anstruther-Plowman, and a woman that Cameron had not met before, himself and Rachel were occupying the four centre seats of row F in the Old Vic theatre for a performance of Shakespeare's Richard II. They were settled happily in their seats, enjoying the actors' interpretation of the play. As Act II started with John of Gaunt's dying speech, Ronald Cameron felt a sudden release of energy within him that was almost a physical slap. How much this speech summed up, he thought, what was going wrong within England at this time. He looked around him, surreptitiously, as if to see similar revelations to those around him. He was disappointed that he didn't. Could he be the only one to realise?

At the interval, as they were in the bar, he broached the subject to the others. They looked at him as if trying to understand what he was attempting to get across but not quite making it.

He gave a metaphorical shrug and as the bell went for the second half they processed in with the rest of the audience. However, the impact of John of Gaunt's speech continued to haunt him for the rest of the evening and, like a terrier with a rat, his mind refused to give him any quarter. And there was something important in a corner of his brain that hung there unspoken and unreleased. He determined to pursue it until it revealed itself.

March 1966

He met Shirley at the airport and they went straight down to Sussex, to her aunt's, where she would be staying for the duration of her visit. "I think I will feel a bit strange meeting her," said Cameron, as they drove down the A23 towards Brighton.

"You shouldn't," replied Shirley, "she's very kind, and she really only wants to help."

"It's just, I suppose," he said, "that she has seen and met my daughter before I even knew I had one."

Shirley put her hand on his knee, as a measure of comfort, "darling, I know that must be difficult for you."

"You know, it's amazing, life is so extraordinary," he responded, "who could have imagined this scenario. Here we are, two lives that were torn apart twenty years ago, being together again, going to meet our child, whom we haven't seen in all that time, and expecting we know not what."

"I think we are expecting something good to come of it," said Shirley, "otherwise we wouldn't be doing it, would we?"

"I suppose not," he said.

He drove the Jaguar into the small cul-de-sac and into the drive of Aunt Mildred's bungalow. She came out to meet them, the small dumpy woman that Cameron had envisaged, and greeted them with a hesitancy, that he also expected. Shirley and her aunt embraced, not with familiarity, but with the reserve expected of relatives who haven't been physically close for some years.

"This is Ronnie," Shirley introduced Cameron with a shyness that he hadn't expected.

He took the proffered hand and noticed a warmth of glance that immediately set him at ease.

She ushered them into the modest front room, where tea was already laid on the small round table in the window.

"It is lovely to meet you at last," she said to Cameron, pouring out the tea from a highly decorated tea pot.

"And you too," he responded, "I've heard such a lot about you from Shirley."

"All good, I hope," she said smiling.

"Oh, indeed," he said, "you have been very important to her... and, it seems, to me too."

"It's a strange story, isn't it?" she said, offering around the cake tray.

"Yes," replied Shirley, "I still find it difficult to believe how it all happened. But thanks to you we've been brought through to this time when we can have a chance of making things a bit more right than they were."

"Yes," replied her aunt, "I still don't know, of course, how your daughter will respond to you or indeed how her adopted parents will view you."

"No, of course not," said Shirley, she glanced across at Cameron, "we are just so grateful to you for arranging a meeting at all, that's more than we could hope for."

"Do you know much about her, our daughter I mean?" Cameron interjected.

"I have met her, once or twice, she is really very beautiful, both in nature and looks."

Cameron grinned, "must take after her mother then."

Aunt Mildred smiled also, "yes, indeed she does, there is no doubting that they are mother and daughter."

"What is she doing now, work I mean?" Cameron asked.

"She is at university, London, I think."

"And we haven't even asked what her name is," said Shirley, "I was in such a state at the time that I didn't even think of a name for her...' she tailed off and Cameron held her hand as he sensed the emotion in her question.

"Her name, yes, of course, how silly of me, that I have not told you, her name is Nina."

March 1966

Simon Clarke was at a garage in Llandrindod Wells. He was arranging the exchange of his MG sports car for a rather more sedate Ford Cortina saloon. As the Ford was only a year old and the MG rather more so, money needed to change hands too. However, he was satisfied with the transaction because the new car gave him the priceless gift of anonymity. He finished the deal and proceeded to transfer his effects from one car to the other. He thanked the salesman, filled up with petrol, drove out of the forecourt and took the road east out of the town.

He knew that by going back to London he was risking a great deal, but he only intended to be there a short time and he believed that what he had to do could be accomplished quickly.

He reached London within five hours and drove straight to the address in Kingsbury that he knew so well. It was Saturday evening and he knew he would be lucky if she was in; she might not be. He was at the stage now, although he was only dimly aware of it, that he was operating on instinct, without much thought to the consequences. He parked and went up to the front door of the flat. There was a light on in the hall, which he could see through the glass of the door. He could hear, faintly, the sound of music. He rang the door bell.

"Have you forgotten your key again?" Rachel sang out as she opened the door. She stood there momentarily, staring at the sight of Simon, a split second before she slammed the door shut. She was a fraction of a second too late, the door hit his foot and he stepped through the opening before she could do anything else. He moved swiftly into the hall and shut the door behind him.

"Where is she?" he demanded.

Rachel, not a girl to panic easily, leaned back onto the wall and said, "Who?"

"You know who, Nina, of course."

She could discern, by the flush of his complexion and the high pitch of his voice, that he was not at a stage to be put off easily.

"She's not here... in fact I don't think she's coming home tonight."

"You're lying, you are expecting her, any moment." His hand moved to the comforting weight in his pocket and his fingers closed over the gun.

Her eyes followed the movement and she suddenly had the feeling that she was not in control any more.

"Look, I don't know what you want," she said, attempting to placate him, "but if you give me the telephone number of where you are staying, I will get her to ring you."

"I'm not staying anywhere," he replied, "apart from here, that is."

"Look, if you don't go I'll have to ring the police."

"I don't think so." He put his hand in his jacket pocket and drew out the Mauser pistol and pointed it at her.

She tried to hide the rising tide of terror that threatened to over-whelm her. "I... I've just made some supper... why don't you share it with me. I'm sure we can sort this out. There's no need to upset yourself." Her words were a tumbling mirror of her confusion.

"No," he said, "I'm staying here, with you, until she comes home."

"Wha... what are you going to do then?"

"We'll have to see, shan't we?" he retorted.

"Look, Simon, why don't you put the gun down? I'm not going to do anything. I guess it's Nina you want to talk to."

He suddenly brushed past her and pulled her into the sitting room. He pushed her down onto one of the armchairs and went over to the window and looked out. He pulled the curtains and turned back to face her.

"I don't have to tell you what I'm going to do," he said, "it's between Nina and me."

"I don't think she wants any more to do with you," Rachel answered.

"I think she will, when she hears what I have to offer her."

"She already knows what you have to offer," Rachel responded, "she hates you." She sensed she was taking a risk in exacerbating his wrath, but she had the feeling that if she didn't, he would feel more in control and therefore more dangerous.

She was surprised when he smiled, "you know what they say, hate is very close to love. I believe she loves me still. It was only a lovers' tiff that we had. When I explain to her that I was under pressure at the time, she will understand."

"I don't think so," responded Rachel, the shaking of her limbs beginning to subside. She was amazed that he seemed to switch, in his mood, from heated to ice cold, within seconds. As if he genuinely believed the words that he was saying and took solace from them.

"You don't know what we had together," he continued, "it was truly a meeting of souls and, of course, bodies."

She felt sickened by the leer he gave in pronouncing the last word.

"Yes, I know she still loves me, but even if she has been brainwashed into thinking she doesn't, I will soon have her with me again and will be able to convince her otherwise."

"Why, where are you going to take her?" Rachel's sickness was persisting.

"Far away from here I can assure you..." his words tailed off as a key was heard turning in the front door.

Rachel was suddenly energised, she leapt up and began to run to the door, but he was too quick for her intention and cut her off.

"Nina, don't come..." his hand closed over her mouth and muffled any further words that she may have tried to utter.

Nina's voice came from the hall, "Rachel, it's only me."

Simon Clarke pushed Rachel out into the hall, with the pistol to her head. Nina was confronted by this sudden vision of terror and shrank back onto the closed door.

"Now don't do anything stupid, either of you, and you won't get hurt," he said, gesturing with the gun, "now get inside Nina, and keep quiet, both of you."

March 1966

Shirley and her aunt and Ronald Cameron had made an appointment to meet Nina at her adopted parent's home in Wimbledon on the last day of March. As they were driving up there that morning Cameron began to ponder on the extraordinary events that were now shaping their lives. He remembered, of course, the party that he had attended, where he had first met Nina. That was in Wimbledon and he had been a guest of Arthur Robinson, who was the banker, who would, hopefully, provide some much needed finance for the navigation equipment that he was developing.

Nina had seemed like a vision of the past, her beauty, a mirror of Shirley, the girl of his heart, who, he thought, was taken from him, but, instead, became unattainable. And of Anna, the first girl of his heart, who was soon to be no more. Nina was, to him, the rebirth of his dreams. Yet, not of his dreams, his realities. She was the re-establishment of all that he'd ever wanted in life. That perfect helpmeet and partner that every man desires, but so few attain. And the more he knew her, the more she seemed to be the embodiment of those desires.

When he had first heard the name of his daughter, he knew absolutely, without doubt, that she was his Nina. The girl that he felt such a desire for, but he was unable to consummate their love, because of something inside him that refused to allow him to do so. He now knew what that something was.

And Shirley, how did she feel? Her emotions must be on a roller coaster as well. But, maybe, more straightforward. She had just given her baby away and had had no more contact, until now. Yet their daughter was now bringing them back together. Shirley, whom he thought he'd lost forever, came back, literally, from the dead. Yet the offering of herself back to him was not forthcoming, because she was given elsewhere to someone else. Would the physical evidence of their daughter be a spark to rekindle what he and Shirley had together before? He feared the answer to that question, because into the equation came Rachel. How would she view the curiosity of her life-long friend, being the daughter of her lover? He had to smile silently to himself.

But he was brought up short by the real implication of this imminent meeting and without doubt the most important and profound. What sort of a shock would this give to Nina. He had been so full of his own feelings, and how he would be affected by it, but what about her? He could not begin to imagine how she would feel. The man that she had looked upon as her lover, possibly potential husband, was now her father!

Such a scenario was barely imaginable. Was it too late to back out, to save Nina this trauma? But how could he back away now? It was too late. Too late to tell Shirley about the depth of relationship that he and Nina had experienced. She could have understood it if Nina had been just a girlfriend, but not now. There was something distinctly unsavoury about it and he needed to keep some modicum of dignity about himself. But was it even too late for dignity? Would that be lost too? Again he shook the mental cobwebs of self away, it was Nina who was important, not him and his dignity.

A sensitive young girl, on the threshold of all the delights that a free life has to offer, suddenly confronted with the unseemly evidence of what the reality of life could bring. But, of course, it could be worse, far worse, he and Nina could have become physical lovers. Such a thought made him sick in his spirit and he felt eternally grateful to whatever had prevented such a catastrophe.

He continued to muse as he drove through the traffic into Wimbledon. The closer he got the more intense his nervousness became. He could not remember such agitation, even during the war, there was nothing to compare with this. By the time they drew up outside the Wimbledon house, which he now recognised, he was quite ready to turn round again and forget all about trying to meddle in things that should, quite obviously, be left completely alone.

Arthur and Win Robinson remembered him, particularly the impression that he had made on Nina. They could not believe that it was him. They had to sit down to take in the realisation of the situation. Arthur Robinson kept repeating, "I don't believe it... this is incredible, how could it be you", until his wife interjected, "Oh stop it, Arthur, you will give Ronald a complex!"

They had expected Nina to be home by now, she had said, apparently, that she would be there in time and they kept apologising for her.

"I don't know what's kept her," said Win, "Arthur, will you ring the flat whilst I prepare the lunch, and see if she's left yet?"

He picked up the phone and dialled the number, "It's ringing," he said.

March 1966

Rachel heard the phone ringing through a haze of other buzzings in her head. The tights that were holding her wrists and ankles together were biting into her and the scarf around her mouth was threatening to restrict her breathing. She had lost consciousness when Simon first tied her hands and feet, whether through fainting or not she wasn't sure, but she had the impression that he had placed something over her mouth before the scarf. It was now daylight and she realised that she must have been unconscious throughout the night. Where was Nina, what had happened to her? Rachel was lying on the sofa, and she looked around as well as she could. There was no one else in the room. She decided to try to get to her feet and despite the restraint she managed to. Where to go from here. The phone had by now stopped ringing, so she began to hop into the kitchen with the idea of finding something to release the bonds on her wrists. She suddenly remembered the broken tile on the work surface that they had been meaning to get repaired. It was on the edge and they had both been taking care that they didn't cut themselves on it. She managed to make her way to it and because her wrists were tied behind her back she had to turn and feel the tile with her fingers. Having located it she began sawing away at the sharp edge. She hadn't realised until now how strong tights were and it was some minutes before she felt the immense relief of the slackening of the restraint.

They fell away. It took some moments of massage of her wrists before the full feeling came back to her fingers. She undid the scarf, sat down with her back to the kitchen cupboard and undid her ankles. She sat there for some minutes endeavouring to clarify her mind. As the implications of what Simon had done began to crystalise she knew the first thing would be to ring Nina's home. She thought of the police but hesitated because of the peculiar nature of what had happened. She got through straight away and Arthur Robinson answered. He remained calm as she told him about the previous evening and that Nina was no longer there.

"I am really afraid," she said, "shall I ring the police now?"

"Yes, and then ring me straight back, will you?"

The others noticed the pallor of his face as he came back into the drawing room.

"Nina has disappeared," he said.

It was as if a mental grenade had exploded amongst them. Their shocked expressions a measure of their individual concern. For Ronald Cameron, it was all his worst nightmares coming true in an instant. His need to be with Rachel and to comfort her was paramount but he had to temper his anxiety with the needs of Arthur and Win. The shrill ring of the phone concentrated their collective anxieties. Arthur picked it up again and was silent as he listened. He appeared to be ending the call when Cameron intimated that he wanted to talk to Rachel.

"Hello darling, it's me, Ronnie. Look, I know you don't expect me to be here...", he paused as her excited response prevented, for some moments, further explanation.

"I know. I've got a lot to tell you and I wish I had time at this moment to explain, but you'll just have to trust me. Look, I need to know straight away about Clarke, you said that he had come to the flat," he paused as she repeated what she had told Arthur.

"You say he had a gun?" The hearers collectively were silent.

"Have you told the police that?"

"Are they coming round to the flat?"

"Look, darling, I shall come straight up there to be with you and then we can decide what to do."

"OK, darling, I'll be with you very shortly." He put the phone down and turned to the others.

"It seems that Nina has been kidnapped."

"You seemed to know of the man who has done this?" Win said.

"Yes, I do know of him," Cameron replied. "He actually is someone that Nina was going out with, and she had finished with him."

"It doesn't look as though he took no for an answer," said Shirley.

"This is all very confusing," Win sat down, and Mildred put her arm around her and looked up at Cameron. "Do you have any idea where he would have taken her?"

"Not at the moment, no, which is why I must go up to the flat and talk to Rachel to see if there any more clues as to her whereabouts."

"Can I come with you?" said Shirley.

"Yes, of course, I think I need you there too," Cameron smiled at her and he could see an easing of the tension within her.

"Is it something we need to leave to the police?" Arthur interjected.

"I think they will need our input," responded Cameron.

"I will stay here and keep Win and Arthur company," said Mildred.

"That would be good dear," Win took her hand, "I think we need to talk over a few things together."

Cameron and Shirley took their leave, with assurances that they would let them know as soon as possible when they had any more news. He drove as quickly as the traffic and the law allowed and arrived at the Kingsbury flat within an hour of leaving Wimbledon.

Rachel saw them arrive and ran out to them. Cameron met her halfway up the stairs and they embraced amidst the flood of tears that had suddenly been released within her.

"I'm so glad to see you. Oh, it's so wonderful that you are here," she said, letting him dab her face with his handkerchief.

Shirley had stayed at the foot of the stairs in deference to their need for each other, but he looked around and gestured her to come up.

"This is Rachel, Shirley and Rachel this is Shirley," he had his arms around both of them as he introduced them and the two girls held hands as a token of the intimacy that they knew they shared in him. They smiled at each other and knew it would be good between them.

"Have the police arrived yet?" he had his arm around her as they went into the flat.

"Yes, they left about half an hour ago."

"Were you able to give them a description of Clarke?"

"Yes, and I told them the sort of car that he drove, although I never did know the number."

"He's had a good start, of course, and he could be anywhere in the country, or even abroad in this time." Cameron responded.

"Do we know if she had a passport?" Shirley said.

"Yes, she did," replied Rachel, "although I'm not quite sure where she kept it."

"Let's look in her desk and see," said Cameron.

After a time looking in all the obvious places there was no sign of it and they surmised that out of the country was a possibility.

"I think we need to let the police know, so they can at least check the ports." Cameron picked up the phone and dialled the number.

March 1966

"So she doesn't know you're her dad?" Rachel said, as she sat with Shirley on the sofa with Cameron sitting in the armchair opposite.

"No, she doesn't," he replied, "and that's going to come an awful shock as well."

"You can say that again," she said, "with bells on."

He smiled, "And how do you feel about that revelation?"

"My darling, it doesn't really effect me, does it?"

"No, I suppose not, it's just I thought you might feel a bit awkward about it."

"I'll get used to it," she smiled in response, reached across and took his hand. He squeezed it in reply, but let it go in deference to Shirley's presence.

"But we need to concentrate on Nina and where she is now. He clearly is a psychotic with malign tendencies and he has obviously taken her somewhere as a captive. Not for any blackmail purposes, we would have heard by now, but just in a perverted way to keep her for himself." He looked across at Rachel, "did he say anything that would give us a clue as to where he has taken her?"

She shook her head, "no, I really have been thinking hard about all that happened, but after he had tied me up, I lost consciousness and when I woke up... well you know the rest."

"What was Nina doing whilst you were being tied up, surely she wasn't just standing there?"

"He threatened to shoot me if she tried anything, she was obviously so convinced that she didn't do anything, she seemed frozen in fear."

"Where did he get the tights for you to be tied up?"

"He told Nina to get them, he had to shout at her; I seem to remember, she was like a frightened rabbit and it was only his shouting that seemed to get her out of her trance."

"Then she brought them back, what happened then?"

"Well, as I said, he tied me up with them."

"Did she just stand there then, watching?"

"As far as I could see, yes. You've got to remember, that I was having these things done to me, I wasn't exactly concentrating on her."

"No, I know sweetheart, it's just that there must be some clue somewhere which will tell us where he has taken her." Cameron suppressed the frustration he was feeling because he knew Rachel could not take much more of this interrogation.

He picked up the phone and rang the Robinsons in Wimbledon. "No news yet, but it's early days," he said, "at least we know it's not blackmail. If it was he would know that you are in a position to pay whatever was asked."

He paused whilst the person on the other end asked something.

"In a way, yes," he answered, "but I don't think he would harm her physically, he obviously wants her for himself."

"I shall make enquiries, I have some contacts this end who may be able to help," he answered to another question and then rang off.

He turned to the girls, "shall I take you, Shirley back to Sussex via Wimbledon to pick up your aunt?"

"Yes, perhaps that is best," she answered.

"May I come too," said Rachel, "I don't want to stay here on my own."

"Yes, I was going to suggest that," replied Cameron, "I don't want you on your own anyway."

She smiled a gentle, shy smile that went right to the centre of his being and touched a vital part of himself, which he thought had been long submerged by the accretions of life.

April 1966

Ozerov was as definite and honest as any KGB agent could be in the limited atmosphere of their faith.

"We have no idea where Silas is, as far as we are concerned he has disappeared off the face of the earth."

Cameron had met him again at their prearranged place in the National Gallery.

"Do you not have safe houses, refuges, where you can put those who need to disappear for a while?"

The Russian looked quizzically at him, "you know we do, but our agency has not got him."

"Could some other organisation have exfiltrated him, that you don't know about?" Cameron knew the answer before it was uttered.

"No," was the brief reply.

"Then if we haven't got him, which I'm almost sure is the case, he's acting entirely alone, which is strange in view of his previously being run by a controller."

Ozerov looked at him, in itself a bold gesture for an undercover obsessive, "have you considered that someone is controlling him that neither you nor I know about?"

April 1966

"It was two days after we were at the Old Vic that Nina was snatched." Cameron was talking to Brian Anstruther-Plowman as they walked through St James's Park. He was briefing him on the latest news about the activities of Simon Clarke.

"And do you know the extraordinary thing is that Nina is my daughter."

Anstuther-Plowman's incredulous expression made nonsense of his normal patrician bearing and unflappable nature.

"Your daughter, how can that be?"

Cameron appraised him of all the recent revelations and in the retelling seemed to bring home to himself how bizarre it appeared.

He, also, had never seen his friend so exercised in the astonishment he showed. However, although he seemed to take in all that Cameron was telling him, he felt, that there was a strange absorption in his attitude that Cameron could not quite understand. It was as if there was a huge block stopping his normal thought processes.

Cameron decided to change the subject to try to bring his friend back to the problem in hand.

"So what shall we do about Clarke?"

"Clarke," Anstruther-Plowman said the name as if he'd just heard it for the first time, "yes, what shall we do?" He said abstractedly, looking at Cameron as though he was seeing him for the first time too.

"I'm really getting very little help from the police," Cameron continued, "not that I expected to, of course, they have very little to go on."

"No, I don't suppose they have," Anstruther-Plowman answered in a manner that didn't, seemingly, require his mind to be engaged.

Cameron looked hard at his companion, "I know that you have a lot on your mind, most of the time, but I would appreciate if you could apply yourself a little bit more to this matter than you appear to be doing."

Anstruther-Plowman seemed to shake himself mentally, "I'm sorry, yes, I do have rather a lot on my mind at the moment, but that's no excuse for neglecting you. Yes, what do we do about Clarke. I must confess, old chap, that at the moment I don't have much of an idea."

Cameron continued, "I know that this is mainly my problem, Nina is very special to me and means more to me than to anyone else. I don't care about Clarke, he can go to hell as far as I am concerned, and probably will, but I care desperately about her and I want her out of the danger of this man as quickly as possible."

His companion looked suitably abashed, "yes I know you do, I can only imagine what you are going through. But I can only make enquiries my end and see if there is anything going on in the rather nefarious dealings of our trade."

"If money is needed," said Cameron, "I am sure we can always find it. Someone must know something and money has an amazing way of oiling the passageways of memory."

"Leave it with me," Anstruther-Plowman replied, "there are quite a few individuals who will delve into the rather darker areas of life and find something out that we hadn't even imagined possible."

"Thank you," said Cameron, "meanwhile I think I will make more enquiries into the university side of Clarke's life and see if there are any who know more about him than he, maybe, would have wanted them to know."

April 1966

Cameron met Angela in the refectory of the college the morning after seeing Anstruther-Plowman. It had not taken him long to find out the girl who Simon Clarke had been particularly interested in. Clarke was, apparently, the chosen guy by many of the girl students, who had personally experienced his attentions and envied the next girl who would benefit. There, apparently, was no jealousy between the females of the college about him. They enjoyed the brief fling and knew that he would soon go on to another. He was one of those favoured male escorts who was desired for the attention that they would give the recipient but who was known to have a limited attention span. Cameron had only to show his photograph around the campus that morning for the result to be achieved.

Angela was intrigued by the research that had gone on to find her and equally so by the interest in Simon Clarke. She was only too happy to tell of her activities with him but was reluctant to divulge anything that might be of use to Cameron.

She was tall and elegant, not scruffy student material at all, thought Cameron as he sat drinking coffee with her. Her brown hair was long and silky, her eyebrows perfectly arched and her skin flawlessly textured. If he wasn't as committed as he was, he would have been extremely tempted to pursue this acquaintance with her. However, he dismissed such thoughts from his mind as he tried to concentrate on what she knew about Clarke, or at least, what she knew that would be of relevance to him.

"When was the last time you saw him?" he asked, offering her a cigarette.

She took one and he lit it for her, "about a week ago," she replied, exhaling the smoke elegantly.

"Was he trying to interest you in the communist system?"

"Yes he was," she said, "but I wasn't really interested. My boyfriend

215

was more interested than I was."

"Forgive me for asking this," said Cameron, "but wasn't your boyfriend aware that Clarke was more interested in you than perhaps he should have been?"

"Possibly," she answered, "but we have a grown-up arrangement, if he goes off with some other girl for a short time, I don't worry him with petty jealousy."

Cameron had the distinct impression that such was her attraction, her boyfriend made the best of a bad job because he needed her more than she him.

"Oh, here is Roy now," she said waving to a man walking towards their table.

Cameron saw that he was medium of stature, dark and with a sharp, almost ferret-like countenance. Cameron had the fleeting thought that he looked more like a minder than an escort of one of the more desirable creatures of the planet. Cameron stood up as he came to the table and Angela introduced him. He shook Cameron's hand with a disinterested, taciturn countenance.

"Darling," she said, "Mr Cameron has been asking questions about Simon Clarke."

"Oh yes, and what does he want to know?" her boyfriend avoided looking at Cameron and kept his eyes on her. Both the men sat down and although Cameron was looking at Roy, there was no reciprocal arrangement.

"I wanted to know if Angela," he inclined his head towards the girl, "knew anything about his whereabouts. He's disappeared, you see."

For the first time Roy met his gaze, "Oh, really," was all he said.

"Yes, you see it's terribly important that we find him. I'll let you both into a secret," Cameron leaned towards them both in a conspiratorial fashion, "I represent a law firm, it seems that he has inherited quite a legacy and for some reason, known only to himself, he has not left a forwarding address. Therefore we can't let him know the good news."

Roy still did not look impressed but Cameron noticed that Angela's flawless complexion took on a more suffused glow.

"I really didn't see him very often," interposed Angela, "so I can't see how I can help you."

Cameron knew that she had now shut down and that he wouldn't get any more from her, now that her boyfriend was present.

"If you do think of anything that could be of any help in finding him I would be most grateful if you could give me a call on this number." Cameron took out his wallet and produced a card and gave it to the girl. He noticed that Roy glanced at the card, possibly, so Cameron thought, to see if there was any devious message written on it. He knew then something of the extent of his jealousy, towards any man who would have the temerity to pass a note to his girlfriend. He wondered, then, about how he had contained his feelings about a man who had obviously taken up so much of the time and passion of his girl. She obviously relished the power that she had over men in general and one in particular. Cameron said goodbye and left them at their table. He glanced back as he reached the door of the canteen and he couldn't help noticing that Roy was absorbed in Angela, looking intently into her face, whilst she was looking after his own disappearing figure, with more than passing interest. He was certain that he hadn't heard the last of Angela.

April 1966

He arrived at the Kingsbury flat that evening to be greeted by the adoring figure of Rachel, brandishing a piece of paper. After the normal passionate embrace she assumed the air of the hurt and bewildered female, "and who is this Angela who is ringing you at all hours, desperate for your ministrations?" She stood with her arms akimbo, looking anger personified, apart from the give away, slight, smile on her face.

"Oh, has she rung already," exclaimed Cameron, "that's jolly quick."

"You were expecting her then, were you?" She was trying so hard to be fierce but she couldn't quite convince him.

He chucked her under the chin and gave her a light kiss on her lips. "That's the trouble being so exciting to all females - I can only give them my phone number to two at a time."

"Apart from the fact that it is my phone number, I would begin to believe that statement," she said, giving him the piece of paper.

He went to the phone and dialled the number, when she answered, the voice, devoid of her looks, sounded even more alluring than when he was sitting opposite her.

"Mr Cameron, how nice to hear you again," she said.

217

"You have something for me?" Cameron answered.

"I have, well, I think it will be helpful, it's strange really. Look I will be honest with you, I was more than just a friend to Simon."

"I rather thought you were," he responded.

"It's just that we got pretty close," she continued, "and perhaps I led him on a bit, about wanting to be part of the great Soviet experiment, that is. In short, he wanted to marry me."

"Oh, I'm surprised, he didn't seem the marrying type." For the first time in days, Cameron felt a slight glimmer of a breakthrough.

"Well, I was surprised as well," she said, "but I was flattered also."

"Forgive me for saying this," Cameron said, "but how did your boyfriend take this?"

"Oh, he didn't know, of course, although it was difficult sometimes to make excuses not to see him."

"I bet it was," Cameron responded.

"Anyway, the point I'm trying to make is, he said to me once that I could have his car, his MG, if he ever got rid of it."

"That was before he asked you to marry him, I suppose?"

"Yes, that's right, and I thought he'd forgotten about it, but yesterday...", she hesitated, "I got this note through the post from a garage in Wales, of all places."

"Who was the note from?" Cameron's pulse quickened noticeably.

"It was from a guy who owns this garage, and he said that he'd got an MG for sale and would I be interested. He said the person who had sold it to him wanted me to know and to have first refusal on it."

"Where in Wales was this from?" Cameron reached for a pencil and paper.

"It's an address in Llandrindod Wells," she gave the full address and he scribbled it down, conscious of Rachel watching him.

"Well, that is most helpful Angela, hopefully we will be able to trace him from that."

"If you do," she said, "tell him that I was surprised that he left me without telling me anything."

"Yes, I will certainly," replied Cameron, "and I am most grateful to you for all your help."

"That's OK," she said, "and any time you are at the college, I would love to treat you to one of their special jam doughnuts in the canteen."

He smiled at the possible scenario, said goodbye to her and put the phone down.

He looked at Rachel, who was watching him with a half-amused expression, "Well, that sounds encouraging, it seems the car has turned up in the middle of Wales."

"What, the MG?" Rachel responded.

"Yes and it means we have a lead, at last."

"What are you going to do?"

"I think we obviously need to go over to the garage in Wales and see if we can trace him from there. I will let Brian know and see if we can go together."

April 1966

Nina felt no pain. She seemed to be drifting in and out of consciousness as she lay on the bed. She had lost the sense of time. As she looked at the ceiling of the room she was in, she tried to summon up the feeling of why she was there, and when she had arrived. She could come to no definite conclusion on either point. She could have been there for months for all she knew. And the figure of Simon manifested itself to her in all manner of ways. One moment he was sharply in focus, standing over her, at other times, a shadowy obscure configuration dimly in the shadows. She seemed to be lying down most of the time, although there were memories of standing and walking. For most of the time she felt no fear, no apprehension, although there were recollections of him being very close to her and doing things to her that she had no control over. She knew that they lay together for a lot of the time, he seemed to be physically close to her and curiously, she felt a comfort in this closeness.

As to why she was here, she had no intimation, but it did not bother her in the slightest, it seemed to be the natural state to be found in. Anyway she had no choice in the matter, she was here, doing the things she was doing, or rather, having things done to her, that were not at all unnatural.

There was bright sunlight coming through the thin curtains of the bedroom. She had to screw her eyes up to see. Curiously she seemed to be aware of being able to see more clearly and, at the same time, of a dull ache behind her eyes. She looked around the room and noticed, seemingly, for the first time, the large floral design of the wallpaper. The only other furniture, in the room, apart from the bed, was a washstand under the window. She was lying on the bed alone and she shivered involuntarily, as if missing the closeness of another body.

She suddenly felt afraid. The house was silent and motionless. She made a decision to get up off the bed. She realised she was naked and looked around for something to put around her. There were no clothes so she wrapped the bedsheet around her shoulders. She went to the window and felt dizzy as she looked out on the barren hills surrounding the house. She decided to go downstairs. The sheet was too voluminous to negotiate the stairs, so she discarded it and went down. The room was unoccupied. It had light coming in the large picture window and she noticed, seemingly for the first time, the table and chairs by the window and opposite, the sofa and armchairs by the fireplace.

She saw some clothes draped over the back of the sofa. She went to them and began to dress, becoming dimly aware that they were hers and that when she had last put them on they were fresh and pressed but now were creased and stained. Her underwear, she couldn't find but the thought didn't distress her too much.

It was at that moment that Simon Clarke opened the front door and came in. He was carrying a suitcase and seemed visibly shocked when he saw her.

"How are you?" he said. "I've been really worried about you, are you feeling better?"

She looked at him, as if seeing him for the first time.

"Simon," was all she could say.

"Yes, it's me darling," he replied.

"How... how did I get here?"

"We came here on holiday, a few days off out of London, don't you remember?"

"No," she replied, "I don't."

"Yes, and when we got here you came down with some flu-like bug," he came over to her and put his arms around her. He looked into her eyes, "are you feeling better?"

"I suppose so," she said, not wanting his arms around her but not having the energy to shake him off.

"What is this place?" she asked, glancing around the room.

"It's a holiday cottage, in Scotland," he replied.
She sat down on the sofa, her knees suddenly feeling weak. "Did I want to come away with you?" she spoke quietly, not looking at him. He sat down beside her, "of course you did, don't you remember? We talked about it for some time."
"No, I don't remember," she replied.
"Let me make you a cup of tea and I'll do some toast, you sit quietly there and take it easy."

He went to the kitchen area and busied himself with the kettle and teapot. She sat in the corner of the sofa and heard him make some toast and spread it with some butter. He brought it over to her and poured out the tea. She sipped it and, after a few minutes, began to feel drowsy; as he was talking she dropped into a sleep inhabited with dreams of incredible colour and violence.

April 1966

"Yes, I'll come with you, certainly," Brian Anstruther-Plowman was speaking on the phone to Cameron, "who else are you taking with you?"
"Rachel wants to come and Shirley," he replied.
"Then I think we had better take two cars, particularly as I think we need some back-up, just in case. I will probably bring a man from Special Branch with me." Anstruther-Plowman put the phone down and pondered the conversation well into the night.

The next morning he rang Cameron. "Look, I don't know whether we are going off on a wild goose chase here. It would probably be better if we ring the garage and try to find out what address was given for the new car that he undoubtedly has."
"I've already done that," replied Cameron. "It's a Ford Cortina, and I've got the registration number, and he gave the address in Tooting, London."
"So we're not that much further forward are we?"
"Except that he obviously is in that neck of the woods, otherwise he would not have used a dealer in mid Wales," replied Cameron.
"But there is no point in us rushing down there in the vain hope of finding him, the proverbial needle comes to mind," responded Anstruther-Plowman.
"Well, you can do what you like, but the need to find Nina is para-

mount to me and if there is a chance of her being in that area, then I believe I can find her." He felt needled by the suggestion that he should hang fire.

"I fully understand how you must be feeling, old boy, but we must be sensible about it," Anstruther-Plowman replied.

Cameron doubted whether he did know how he was feeling, "why should I be sensible about it?" he responded. "Look where being sensible has got me so far in this case."

His friend realised that emotions were now prevailing, "all right, you go down there and see what good you can do, but let me know as soon as you know something yourself, OK?"

April 1966

The three of them started off the next morning. The sun was shining as they left London and their spirits were lifted by the sight of the spring flowers and the scudding of the white clouds across the sky. His mood, however, was pensive. Was this a wild goose chase? Was there any chance that they would find Nina? And if they did find her what state would she be in? The police had been alerted to the number of Clarke's car and had been informed not to apprehend but, if found, to hold a watching brief.

They made good progress down the A40 and by lunch time had reached Ross on Wye. They dined in a pub in the town and enjoyed the aspect of each other and the easy conversation that flowed between them. Cameron scrutinised the two women. He loved them both, but the dimension of love was different in both of them. In one there was history as well as love, a history that was marked by joy and tragedy, by intense sadness and incredible rebirth. In the other there was newness and freshness and excitement and hope for the future. He thought himself, at this moment, to be the most fortunate of men. And there was the other dimension of love, embodied in the one they were all three endeavouring to find. And the one they were trying to find was encountered by him, first as a lover and then a daughter. Could there be a more curious yet desperate search? She was the bridge between them all, without her they were still islands, isolated and lonely, with her they became united as one purpose.

And yet there was still one more, the one who had started it all, the one who was now no more. She must be the fulcrum of them all.

She had started him on this odyssey, this search. Without her they would not be here now. She had revealed to him the vision of what love was and is. Anna was no longer with him, yet the spirit of what she was, lived within him, enlivened him, opened his eyes to the true nature of herself and of himself. Their love had been born amidst the turmoil of war and tragedy and their permanence together was doomed from the start. Yet love, seemingly, needs only a brief moment to burst into life. And once becoming alive never diminishes, never dies. It may change, it may alter in its aspect, but it is always there, always sustaining, always life-giving. And it changes people; once it touches you, you will never be the same. He had never been the same since that moment on board ship in Murmansk. How could such a powerful force as love be so invisible, yet so penetrating and so selective? Why had he been picked? Why had Anna? Was there that something in them that attracted this force? That magnet that drew in this life-giving sustenance. Yet it had also given him the pattern; once he had seen Anna and the beauty she displayed, he needed others just like her in aspect. It could be said that Rachel was not of the type of Nordic beauty that the three others were, yet she inhabited the same psyche, the same amazing capacity to absorb beauty and to exude it at the same time. She was able to translate, to take in and to breathe out that same beauty of love that the others lived in.

His reverie ended as the meal did. He paid the bill as he heard the delighted chatter of the girls coming back from the rest room. They went on their way, heading towards Llandrindod Wells. They found the garage without too much trouble and the proprietor in his office. After the preliminary conversation, Cameron asked if he knew of where Clarke had been staying.

"No, he didn't say," was the taciturn reply.

Cameron decided to change tack, "I am interested in the MG, could I see it." He explained that he may be interested in buying it for the girl in London. The proprietor became less taciturn where he could see that there was a possibility of money to be made and he showed them round to the back of the garage, where the MG was parked. The red bodywork was spattered with mud, it was caked under the wheel arches and the wire wheels were coated in it.

"Where has it been to get so filthy?" exclaimed Rachel.

"We've had a bit of rain in the last few days," the reply came, "this sort of mud you get by being up in the hills."

Cameron made a pretence of studying the condition of the car. "The last owner must have gone over some pretty wild tracks to get it in this condition."

"Yes, he said that he was staying up north towards Newtown way," said the proprietor.

"Oh, when did he say that?" Cameron tried to sound unconcerned.

"He had to go back for something for the car that he didn't have on him and said that it wouldn't take him long. He was back within the hour."

"I'd like to know something about the history of the car," said Cameron, "I wonder if I can get in touch with him and ask him some questions."

"Well, he said that he wasn't on the phone where he was, so the only way is to find out would be to talk to him face to face, like."

Cameron went to his car and took out the map book, he brought it back and showed it to the proprietor. "Where would you say he could be?"

The man looked at the map and pointed with his finger. "I reckon it could be up that white road towards Bwlch-y-sarnau, there are one or two small cottages up there. That's about the right distance for him to have done a return journey in the time."

Cameron took the map book from him, "that's most helpful, thank you. If I find him and get some information on the car, I'll come back to you and maybe we could have a road test."

The man grunted and nodded his head, as if to say he'd heard that before and nothing comes of it.

They took their leave of him and headed out on the road north to Newtown.

April 1966

Simon Clarke had set up the radio transmitter in the bedroom. He had left Nina drugged on the sofa, he knew she would be out of consciousness for some time. He began transmitting, paused, and then took notes as he listened to the reply. There was one particular passage that he asked to be repeated. When he had finished he packed the radio back in the case and put it into the wardrobe. He went downstairs and studied the recumbent form of the girl. Her blond hair was lying half over her face and her limbs were in that form of abandonment that particularly appealed to him. He was just about to manifest his imagination into reality with her, when he knew he had to make plans about their future together.

There was no general emergency, Centre had assured him that it was his controller who had pulled him out for specific reasons. His controller (codename Pimpernel) had then transmitted some information, the import of which caused him to ask for confirmation, such was its impact on him.

This new information certainly exercised his mind. It threw a whole new slant on the situation. By now, he knew, Ronald Boyd Cameron would be trying his utmost to find him. He would be using all the resources at his disposal. There could be no question of a half-hearted measure. He knew that much about him. His investigations into Cameron's operations were enough for him to know that. But Cameron confused him. There was a time when he was convinced that he was a genuine illegal agent, working towards the successful fulfilment of the overthrow of the Western system, but, latterly, he wasn't sure. However, he was more and more convinced that, whatever motive was at his core, he was unreliable, and was almost certainly a double agent. And the more dangerous because of that. He didn't know how much time he had to formulate plans. He knew he couldn't stay where he was for much longer, sooner or later the grapevine of intelligence would seek him out, which side, he was not sure.

He knew both sides would have their reasons to curtail his movements. Yet he had been useful to his masters in Moscow; some of the intelligence that he had passed on had been of first-class material. He was sure that they would protect him when the time came for the show down, which he was convinced was coming. But sometimes their motives were obscure, even he would acknowledge that. Perhaps he wasn't as confident as he should be. He had to trust the system, though, didn't he? He had staked his whole thinking towards the ultimate victory of the first worker-peasant state in history. They would take care of their foot soldiers, surely. No, he didn't have anything to worry on that score. But he still had a lingering, nagging, doubt in his mind that things were not going to work out in the way that he wanted. It was all the fault of this girl, of course; if it hadn't been for her he would be in line for the Order of the Red Star and possibly a pension and, maybe, even granted Soviet citizenship. He began to wonder why he had become so infatuated by her. Of late she had become too compliant, too negative, too much like all the other girls that eventually passed through his memory. She was no longer the vibrant, exciting woman that had first attracted him. He had been willing to sacrifice everything to possess her and she had thrown it back in his face. What could he do now to redeem the situation? Perhaps she still had some value, of course. Whilst he still had her he could use her as a bargaining tool to get himself out of the situation that she had caused.

He continued to think on these matters as he heard a moan from the sofa. She was beginning to wake up. He looked across at her. She was certainly very attractive; even in the state she was in, he could still feel the stirrings of desire. She opened her eyes and looked across the room at him. It took her some moments to focus on his form and when she did, was that a look of disgust that flitted across her face? He wasn't sure, but it was a possibility. He went over to her and sat down beside her, "how are you feeling now, my darling?"

She blinked uncertainly as if not recognising his voice.

"I, don't... know," she replied, smoothing her hand over her face.

"I've got something to tell you," he said, holding her hand, "it may help you to recover."

"What is it?"

"Ronald Cameron is your father." He stated it baldly, wanting to shock her.

She looked at him blankly, as if she hadn't heard and was waiting for him to say something.

"Oh," she said.

If he was expecting a greater reaction, he was sadly disappointed.

"Don't you understand what I've said," he took her by the shoulder and began to shake her, as though to wake her up.

"My father is Ronald Cameron," she said in a monotone voice.

He looked at her in the way some people look at an idiot child, not being sure how to communicate and fearing that they can't deal with the result.

"My father is Ronald Cameron," she repeated.

He shook his head in exasperation. This was not having the effect he desired. He had anticipated disbelief, perhaps anger, even sorrow, but not this. Her brain seemed to be disconnected from her emotions entirely. He got up and went outside, he needed to think.

April 1966

Ronald Cameron guided the low-slung saloon over the rutted and potholed track. The mud was prolific and sticky, evidence of recent spring rain, and after about fifteen minutes he began to wonder when they would come to any habitation. He need not have worried because around the next bend was a cottage nestling amongst a background of low hills.

Simon Clarke had seen the car coming up the track before the occupants of the car had seen him. As he looked, he wondered whether it was meant for him, or for the handful of other houses in the village of Bwlch-y-sarnau, some miles further on. It stopped at the junction of the tracks which led to the cottage. He saw three people get out, one man and two women. One of the women he recognised, it was Rachel. His heart gave a leap of anticipated action and he ran inside and up the stairs to where he had put the pistol. He checked that it had a loaded clip and put the pistol into his pocket. He came down the stairs two at a time and glanced across at Nina, she was still on the sofa, staring into the empty fireplace. He looked through the glass of the front door and saw the three coming down the path towards him.

April 1966

Brian Anstruther-Plowman had spent the night in a hotel in Llandrindod Wells. He had anticipated Cameron finding the refuge and, indeed, he had checked with the proprietor of the garage that afternoon to discover that they were on their way there. He stopped his car about half a mile from the cottage and walked the rest of the way. As the refuge came in sight he halted. It was all quiet and looking at it, it appeared deserted.

He walked up to the front door, he listened, he could hear voices coming from inside. "So you are Ronald Cameron." He recognised the voice of Silas. There were other voices, female, that he didn't recognise; they were more high pitched and excited. He didn't want to risk looking through the front door window, so he crept around the back of the cottage and peered through a corner of the large picture window.

He could see the back view of Silas, and facing him were the frightened faces of two women and Cameron. Why they were frightened soon became evident, when Silas moved slightly and Anstruther-Plowman could see that he was pointing a gun at them. His quick glance also showed him the crouching figure of another woman on a sofa. She appeared to be only partly interested in the proceedings in the room.

To Anstruther-Plowman it was clear that Silas had not heeded the advice given to him and was playing his own game, which was strictly against the orders that the Centre had insisted upon. He then heard the voice of Cameron. "I suggest you put the gun down Clarke, your argument is with me. Let the women go and I will do whatever you want."

"You don't understand, do you?" replied Clarke. "I need Nina, she has to go with me."

"It's too late for that," said Cameron, "there is no way that you can leave with her. Within minutes this place is going to be surrounded by police."

There was the sound of a swift movement from inside the cottage and a shout, Ansruther-Plowman was not sure from whom. He looked quickly inside and saw that Silas had the girl that had been on the sofa by the arm and was walking backwards towards the door, with the body of the girl in front of him. He had the pistol pointing at her head.

Anstruther-Plowman acted quickly. He ran round to the front of the cottage and was just in time to catch Clarke as he backed out of the door with the girl still in front of him. Because he was not expecting anyone there, he was taken completely by surprise as Anstruther-Plowman came up behind him and calmly took hold of his wrist, twisted it and took the gun from him.

Cameron was there immediately and held Clarke with a vice-like grip that had him grimacing in pain.

"Well done, Brian," said Cameron. "How did you get here and how did you know he was here?"

"I'll tell you later," was all the explanation he got as they led Clarke back into the cottage and sat him down in a chair. Anstruther-

Plowman stood over him with the pistol as Cameron put his arms around a weeping Nina. Rachel stood back in deference to Shirley, who stroked her daughter's face for the first time in twenty years.

April 1966

"Manevrirovaniye agentami."* He said it cooly and softly to Clarke as he stood over him. Cameron, embracing Nina, did not hear it, neither did Shirley but Rachel heard it and looked with puzzlement at Anstruther-Plowman.

Clarke, with his head downcast, suddenly looked up at him. Astonishment was written all over his face as he seemed to understand what had been said.

Cameron handed over the comforting of Nina to Shirley and came to stand with Anstruther-Plowman over the crestfallen agent. Clarke looked from one to the other as if deciding in which lay his salvation. Before he could speak Anstruther-Plowman said, "According to the powers invested in me I arrest you for the forceful abduction of Nina Robinson and anything you say will be taken down and used in evidence against you."
Cameron looked at his friend with a certain amount of surprise. He had expected the police to have arrived by now and was imagining that the official arrest would have been done by them.
And where was the man from Special Branch, that Anstruther-Plowman had said he would bring?
There were one or two elements that Cameron was unsettled about and he was just about to question Anstruther-Plowman about

---

* Manevriroyaniye angentami: redeployments of agents.

'Timely redeployment of agents from one sector of counter-intelligence work to another in order to make more effective use of them in resolving problems.

Depending on the area of operational activity this may involve:

1. Redeploying agents who are in contact with an operational officer, within the area in which he is conducting counter-intelligence activity.

2. Redeployiong agents between various sections or areas of work within a KGB branch.

3. Redeployiong agents between various independent branches of the KGB (between local branches of the KGB or KGB Directorate, between local branches of the KGB and KGB Special Departments, or between Special Departments).

them when there was a cry from Nina. He turned round and he saw that she was sobbing in great convulsive shakes of her whole body in Shirley's arms. He went over to them. Shirley looked at him, "she asked if it was true that you are her father."

"How, on earth did she know, she hadn't been told by Arthur or Win, or anyone else," he expostulated.

"I don't know, she didn't say."

"What did you say?"

"I said yes," responded Shirley, "I was so surprised, that I had to straight away."

They both held Nina as her body responded to the emotion of this reality. They took her to the sofa and sat down either side of her, their hands stroking her back as her head was buried in her hands. They were thus so occupied that they didn't notice Anstruther-Plowman talking quietly and softly to Clarke, although Rachel saw it and thought idly that they looked like old friends musing over old times.

After what seemed an age, Nina's sobbing gradually subsided and she lifted her tear-stained face to blink thankfully at her two comforters. Rachel went to find a towel and came back with a damp flannel with which she proceeded to gently wipe her friend's face. This was the first time she had an opportunity to minister to her and she felt curiously thankful. Nina smiled gratefully and took the flannel from her when she felt she had finished. She wanted to wait until she had, because she too felt her need.

"Thank you," said Nina, squeezing the hands of all three of them. She looked directly at Cameron and smiled at him. He saw it as the most wonderful smile he had ever received.

"Hi, Dad," she whispered softly as the tears came again into her eyes. He set his face not to crumple into the tears that he knew were very close to the surface, but as he looked into the face that he loved so much, he could no longer hold them back.

The tears of gratitude that flowed down his face that day were evidence of a form of release and relief that had been a long time coming in his life. He felt the catharsis of the moment healing so many of the unspoken terrors and hurts that he had been through. He smiled at her through his tears and when, after a while, they subsided he knew there was one other essential thing she should know. He placed her hand into Shirley's hand and looked, first at Nina and then at Shirley.

"This is also the time to introduce you to your mother."

He left them then to pursue their mutual wonder at this revelation and the sharing of how it had come about. He knew there was so much memory travelling to be done that he could catch up when there was time.

He went over to where Anstruther-Plowman and Clarke were seated. Ansruther-Plowman had pulled up a chair and was seated opposite Clarke, looking at him, face to face, a few feet apart. Cameron had the impression that they had suddenly ceased to talk and he had the distinct feeling that he was, somehow, intruding.

"What shall we do with him now?" Cameron addressed Anstruther-Plowman.

"I think we should take him back to London to face charges," Anstruther-Plowman replied, "and I will advise Special Branch that we have him."

Cameron looked at Clarke and the thought of all that he had put Nina through came to the surface. He felt he wanted to throttle the man. Not only was he an agent of Soviet Russia, with all that implied in the communist takeover of the Western world, but his personal agenda and morality of using people for his own ends, summed up the fuller motive of the system he served. "The ends justifying the means" was writ large in his psyche.

However, he knew that his own personal vengeance would not achieve anything but a temporary relief and appalling consequences. He looked at his watch, "It's getting late now, we can either sleep here tonight, which won't be very good for the girls, or we can make our way to either Newtown or Llandrindod Wells, and find some accomodation there."

"I think you are right," replied Anstruther-Plowman, "in which case we can use the facilities of the local police station for our miscreant here." He gestured towards Clarke, who, thought Cameron, appeared remarkably calm at the prospect.

Anstruther-Plowman made a quick search of the cottage, whilst Cameron kept Clarke under surveillance, and came back with the radio transmitter and some documents. "We will take these with us but we'll have the place turned over later."

231

Rachel drove Anstruther-Plowman back for his car; they returned within ten minutes and the two cars started back down the track. The girls and Cameron in his, and Anstruther-Plowman with Clarke as his passenger. To make sure that Clarke did not abscond, they tied his feet and hands together with some rope found in the garage.

They decided to head for Llandrindod Wells as the hotel that Ansruther-Plowman had used was apparently likely to have rooms. They went first to the police station, where the police were, naturally, suspicious until they were assured, after a phone call to London, that the people before them were bona fide. They locked Clarke up in one of the cells and the others went off to the hotel and managed to book three rooms. Cameron shared with Rachel, Shirley with her newfound daughter another and Anstruther-Plowman had the single room.

They met in the dining room for an evening meal. As Cameron glanced around the table he was not surprised to notice how tired they all looked.

"We have come a long way today," he said, "and not just in miles."

"Do you know," said Cameron, "that Lenin never invisaged a police force after the Revolution?"

Anstruther-Plowman looked at him with some amusement, "why do you suddenly mention that?"

"I've just obtained a copy of his The State and Revolution and he, apparently, never saw the possibility of mass opposition to a revolution carried out in the name of the people."

As Cameron said this he heard a choking sob, he looked across the table and saw that Nina had her hands over her face and was just getting to her feet. He, closely followed by Shirley, got up and put his arms around her. They escorted her out of the dining room and into a small sitting room, that was empty. They tried to comfort her as best they could. She attempted to say something but her words were hidden by the crying. Eventually she became more lucid and said, "I'm sorry, it's just I find it so difficult to take in all that has been happening." She looked at Cameron, "I can't get used to the idea that you are now my dad and I used to call you Ronnie." Her tear-stained face was turned up towards him.

She turned to Shirley, "It's different with you, because I never knew you and was getting used to the idea of a meeting with my real mother

232

and father. Although, I felt it could be difficult, I felt I had control of the situation because it was my own choice."

Shirley smiled, "We understand sweetheart."

Cameron took both her hands and faced her, "look, my darling Nina, what we both meant to each other is not lost... it's just, I suppose, now in a different department of our lives. We can move on from that. I thought I had lost you for good," he smiled, "or for bad, if you like... but we have been given back to each other. We both understand," here he put an arm around Shirley, "that what you are going through is very difficult. It would have been difficult enough without the complication of Clarke, but we know it's a double shock to have to go through all that you have suffered, and then to have the trauma of meeting your parents for the first time."

Nina smiled at them both, her eyes glistening with tears.

"And we want you to understand," he continued, "that we are not taking you away from Arthur and Win. In a sense they are your true parents because they brought you up. You owe just about everything to them."

"Thank you," Nina whispered, "Shirley told me something of what you both went through and I can barely comprehend how you survived at all. I think it's a miracle that we are here now having this conversation."

Cameron grinned, "yes, I know I can hardly believe it. But we must take care of you now. In a very real way I feel guilty that you had to experience someone like Clarke. If it hadn't been for me and the things I was involved in, you would not have met him in the way you did."

"I don't really understand what you mean," said Nina, "he was at college and I met him, it was nothing to do with you."

"There are things that I will explain at a later date," replied Cameron, "but suffice it to say that the pressure he put on you was mainly because of me."

"Oh, OK," she said, nodding.

They went back into the dining room, where Rachel and Anstruther-Plowman were still seated with a bottle of wine in front of them. They joined them at the table and ordered the meal. The five of them, although weary from the day's exertions, enjoyed the relief of the achievement of the day and all seemed relaxed enough to expand on their feelings.

"I think as soon as we get back to London," said Cameron, "and after we have delivered Clarke to the authorities, we need to give his flat a really good going over."

Anstruther-Plowman looked sceptical, "perhaps we shouldn't put too much emphasis on his worth to the Russians, my considered opinion of him is that he is a very minor cog in their machine."

"You talked to him quite a lot, didn't you Brian," said Rachel, whose familiar use of his name was not lost on Cameron.

"He actually has given us some very interesting information," responded Anstruther-Plowman.

"What is that?" Cameron asked.

"It's something about George Blake."

"He's in the Scrubs, isn't he?" Cameron responded.

"Who's George Blake?" Shirley asked.

"He was sentenced in 1961 for spying for Russia." Cameron answered.

"Yes, he's in Wormwood Scrubs, but it seems, according to Clarke anyway, that there is a plot to spring him out of jail." Anstruther-Plowman pursed his lips.

"Is this an attempt by him to do some horse trading with us?" Cameron asked.

"Probably," said Anstruther-Plowman.

"The sooner we get him back to London the better," responded Cameron.

"I agree," said Shirley, "he gives me the creeps."

Cameron noticed that Nina only shook her head vaguely in agreement, as if not entirely sure.

"Yes," said Anstruther-Plowman, "if we collect him early in the morning, we should be back by early afternoon. I suggest that I take him in my car and you follow in yours with the three girls. I believe he will be all right with me; he won't try anything because he thinks that he can make a deal with us."

"Perhaps some handcuffs from the police would be a suitable restraint for him," said Cameron.

"We could try that, yes," said Anstruther-Plowman.

April 1966

They collected Clarke from the police station at 8am. The police had had notification from London to do all that was necessary for the secure passage of the prisoner. To these ends they handcuffed Clarke, giving the key to Anstruther-Plowman. He was escorted to the car and placed in the rear seat with the doors locked from the outside. A constable was detailed to accompany the prisoner but Anstruther-Plowman was insistent that it was not necessary as their journey would be fast and it would not be necessary to stop. The police did not need much convincing because of their manpower shortage and within a short time they were ready for the journey to London.

They drove out of the town just after 9am, Cameron, in the Jaguar, following Anstruther-Plowman in his rather more sedate Alvis Silver Lady saloon.

Cameron was never quite sure what had transpired during the conversation that Anstruther-Plowman was having with Clarke in the car, but after about half an hour, Anstruther-Plowman gave a slowing down signal and they stopped by the side of the road. He got out of the Alvis and walked back to the car behind. Cameron was surprised that he had left Clarke in the car but Anstruther-Plowman seemed unconcerned as he came up to the driver's door.

"He doesn't seem very well. I've left him sleeping and...," he tailed off as he heard his car being put into gear and he turned round just in time to see it roar off down the road.

"What the..." his other words, if there were any, were lost in the frantic crunch of the Jaguar gearbox as Cameron slammed the throttle down and the car leapt forward in furious pursuit.

The three women remained stoically silent as the car responded to the urgent touch of the driver. The Jaguar showed its racing heritage and very shortly was in sight of the Alvis. The road was twisty and narrow but Cameron was soon just behind, almost hanging onto its back bumper. Shirley, in the front passenger seat, was extremely conscious of the nearness of the edge of the road, for they were still in the hills and the drop down her side of the car was precipitous. She murmured in a matter of fact way that there was very little road on her side and if Cameron had had time he would have noticed the whiteness of the girls faces in the back. Both cars were swaying and rocking to the force of the bends and the gradients and just as Cameron was deciding that he ought to slow down slightly in order to give Clarke some leaway, the Alvis did one hop and slide too many. The front nearside wheel went off the edge of the tarmac and the rear wheel followed. The driver didn't have room to correct the resultant slide and the car was doomed as it slid off of the road and down the steep, rock strewn hillside. It remained on its wheels for a remarkably long time as it gathered speed, going down backwards. Cameron had a glimpse of Clarke's face as the car disappeared from sight, it was a face of stark terror as it stared back at him.

Cameron stopped the Jaguar as quickly as he could and the four of them tumbled out and stood at the edge looking over. They couldn't see the bottom because a ridge hid it from view. However, they heard the sound of a large heavy object as it hit and bounced and they could use their imagination as the sound stopped and, momentarily, there was silence, followed very shortly afterwards by the crunching, muted explosion. They smelled, rather than saw, at first, the smoke, as it drifted in a leisurely fashion up towards them.

They looked at each other in horror, Nina particularly, Cameron thought, with an expression of haunted nakedness, as if all her sins were suddenly exposed to the light. Cameron went cautiously down the hillside until he came to the ridge. He stopped and peered over. He could just make out the front section of the car, on its back with the wheels still spinning. The flames were beginning to consume the whole of the wreck and, although it must have been, he judged, three hundred feet down, he could still discern and appreciate the elegant shape of its chassis; he thought, inconsequentially, of the dreadful waste of such a fine car.

He came back to the women, who were hesitatingly coming down to meet him.

"It is difficult to see, but it is a complete wreck. I can't see any more, but I can't imagine how he could have survived." He put his arm around Nina, knowing that she needed as much comfort as she could get.

"We had better get the emergency services here as soon as we can," Shirley responded, looking nervously over the edge.

"And also make contact with Brian," said Cameron, "he must be wondering what's happening."

They went back to the car. Cameron turned it round, not easy because of the narrowness of the road, and they drove, rather more sedately, back the way they had come. He stopped when he saw Anstruther-Plowman by the side of the road, sitting on the grass verge, about where they had left him.

He listened, grim faced, as Cameron recounted the events of the last half an hour. He climbed into the front seat of the car, whilst the three girls squeezed onto the rear seat and they carried on their journey back to the police station in the town.

To say that the police were surprised when they heard the story would be the understatement of the decade, but they quickly put into motion the mustering of the mountain rescue team that would locate the crash scene.

Two police cars followed the Jaguar back to the site of the accident, with the rescue team in their Land Rover turning up very shortly afterwards.

After assessing the situation they quickly organised the laying out of ropes and, with the Land Rover as a stable platform, they belayed the ropes and threw them over the edge. Two men went over first, but after some minutes hauled themselves back. The ropes were not long enough to reach the wreck and so they detached one from the vehicle and took it down with them on their second descent. Where the rope ended they anchored the other one securely by hammering in a spike and thus were able to reach the wrecked and still burning vehicle. The others waited anxiously at the top, not knowing what was going on, whilst an ambulance arrived and another police car.

"I can't imagine how he did that," muttered Anstruther-Plowman, "he was soundly asleep when I got out of the car."

"And had you taken off the handcuffs?" Cameron asked.

"No, I hadn't," Anstruther-Plowman answered.

"No wonder he found the car difficult to control," Cameron answered drily.

Their conversation was interrupted by the appearance of one of the rescue team who had climbed down to the wreck. They saw him shaking his head in answer to a question, and they went over to him just in time to hear him say, "we couldn't find anyone there."

"What no sign?" Cameron expostulated.

"But we saw him go over," Shirley said, as if that was sufficient evidence.

"That's impossible," Rachel added.

"I can only say what I saw, or rather, didn't see," responded the man, not normally having his evidence questioned, and finding it rather irksome to be so interrogated.

At that moment the other rescue team member appeared above the ridge and hauled himself up the rope towards them.

"No, there is no one in the wreck," he answered to their query, as he came up to them.

"Is it possible that the fire was of such ferocity that it destroyed all evidence of him?" Anstruther-Plowman asked.

"No," said the first man, "it's still smouldering, and there would be charred remains if he was still in there."

Cameron, with his arms around Nina, felt her shudder. He had hoped that this whole episode would have ended the menace of Clarke, but it seemed that it was not to be and that he was premature in his hopes.

May 1966

"Nina told me that Clarke had told her that I was her father. How did he know?" Cameron posed the question to Anstruther-Plowman. They were seated in the rather austere surroundings of a corridor in one of the Foreign Office buildings in Whitehall. They had both been interviewed by the relevant departments that were interested in Simon Clarke and his activities. Their debriefing had centred on how much they had known him and whether they were aware of the extent of his work. The Welsh police were, apparently, satisfied with their enquiries into the accident, although the way he was able to drive off whilst still handcuffed puzzled them somewhat. They were still instigating a search for Clarke and had every confidence that he couldn't have got far in his condition. Although it was now a week since the incident and nothing had been forthcoming about his whereabouts.

The SIS had searched Clarke's flat in Tooting and come up with some remarkable finds. A powerful high-speed transmitter used for communications with the Centre and a short wave radio used for receiving messages from Moscow on high frequency bands, both hidden in a cavity beneath the sitting room floor; one-time cipher pads hidden in flashlights and a cigarette lighter; a micro dot reader concealed in a box of face powder; equipment for micro dot construction; a cookery jar containing magnetic iron oxide used for printing high-speed morse messages on to tape; thousands of pounds, dollars and traveller's cheques; and seven passports. They also, much to Cameron's disquiet, discovered scores of pornographic photos of various girls, some including Nina. The SIS officer, responsible for the search, passed the photos of Nina over to Cameron, including the negatives, on the understanding that they would not be produced as evidence and that he should destroy them forthwith. This Cameron did, thankful that his friendship with this officer had yielded true dividends.

"I haven't the faintest idea, old boy, how Clarke would have known that you were Nina's father," answered Anstruther-Plowman.

"When you come to think of it," Cameron continued, "who else knew? There was Arthur and Win, of course, and Mildred, and Rachel, that's all... oh and you, of course."

"What do we know about Arthur Robinson?" Anstruther-Plowman asked.

"Surely you're not suspecting him?" Cameron was incredulous.

"You and I know that in the game we are in no one is above suspicion," Anstruther-Plowman answered.

"No, I know, but there are limits. He is her father, or the one who deserves to be called her father, and he would not put her in peril. He's an honest banker, he wouldn't have anything to do with the Soviets or the communist system," Cameron was adamant.

"It wouldn't be the first time and it certainly won't be the last, that an individual has fooled the authorities like that," Anstruther-Plowman smiled grimly.

"I can't believe that you're even suggesting such a thing Brian, there are limits, even in our twisted imaginations," Cameron did not smile in return.

"We'll see," said Anstruther-Plowman, "I'll have him checked out."

"You may as well run a check on me whilst you are about it, it's just as ludicrous."

"What makes you think we haven't done that already?" Anstruther-Plowman issued an urbane patrician smile.

"This is getting ridiculous, Brian. And you are also laying a giant smoke screen. Whoever did tell Clarke about me and Nina, it's only a handful of people who knew. And the more I think about it the more I hesitate to even conjecture who it might be, because if I am right the implications are unthinkable."

May 1966

Shirley had moved in with her daughter Nina and with Rachel into the Kingsbury flat. She had left Aunt Mildred in Sussex on the understanding that she would go down to see her before she left for Rhodesia. She enjoyed the time with the girls far more than she thought she ought to. There was something wonderfully warming being with them. Even though Nina was still suffering from the recent trauma, both Shirley and Rachel could discern a gradual improvement in her condition day by day. They found that they could share more and more of their mutual love for each other. Nina was the catalyst and she seemed to bring out in them a longing to give to each other in a way that none of them had ever experienced before. That Ronald Cameron was the one thing they shared was not voiced between them although it was a tacit agreement within their individual psyches that this was so. They had each received from him a measure of love that was special and unique to only them. And it was an experience that contained no jealousy whatsoever.

There was only one subject that they seemed studiously to avoid, and that was Simon Clarke.

He was taboo, although he lurked, unseen, behind all their thought patterns.

One evening, ten days after the incident and the rescue of Nina, Cameron was at the flat on his normal evening visit and he appeared to be more animated than usual.

"I guess you realise," he said as they all sat down for supper, "that it's no secret, and I won't be contravening the Official Secrets Act, that Simon Clarke was a Russian spy. It's all over the papers tomorrow, principally because the journalists have got hold of the human interest story about Nina being kidnapped." He held Nina's hand and smiled at her, encouragingly.

"I don't know how they found out," he shrugged, "but that's the British press for you. Anyway it may mean more Russian diplomats being expelled from this country and then they will expel some of ours, typical tit for tat, I'm afraid."

"Will they mention about him not being found?" Shirley asked.

"Probably," answered Cameron, "you know the press, they will make a drama if they can."

Nina visibly shivered. "The sooner we can forget about him the better."

"I agree," interposed Rachel, "but what about Brian? I can't get over the way he seemed to know Clarke."

"There's something you ought to know about Brian; he's got his fingers into lots of pies in the past," Cameron responded. "But he is intensely loyal and a true patriot. He has an intimate knowledge of the Soviet system and the way the Russians think."

"But it's strange that Clarke should know about you and Nina and your relationship," said Shirley, "when only a few of us knew."

"What, my love, are you suggesting?"

"I don't think I'm suggesting anything," she answered, "except that someone must have tipped Clarke off, and," she looked around at the three of them, "I'm pretty certain it wasn't us."

"So am I," said Cameron.

"Rachel and I couldn't have," Shirley continued, "so that just leaves you and who you told."

"Well, you know that the only person was Brian and I refuse to even imagine that it was him. I would consider myself more guilty than him. I would trust him with the most intimate of things knowing that he would never divulge, unless he was told he could." Cameron sounded more adamant than, perhaps, he felt."

"Perhaps he didn't think it was all that vital as information and he may have let it slip to a confederate in a passing comment in conversation," Shirley answered.

"If you knew Brian as I do, you would know that he is not a person to ever make a passing comment without thinking about it beforehand," Cameron responded.

"So what conclusion do we come to?" Rachel shrugged.

"There must be something going on that we don't know about," said Cameron, "there may be a very simple explanation to this. Something that I haven't thought of."

May 1966

Ozerov met Cameron in the National Gallery in the third room, as arranged. After a brief conversation, during which Cameron thought that Ozerov was rather more nervous than usual, he uttered a phrase that confirmed why he had made this appointment.

"There is an agent, codenamed Pimpernel, who knows all about Silas."

"You have my full attention," Cameron replied, his pulse making that little surge that was usually the precursor to something unusual.

"I have been talking to him and he is going to tell me what the situation is."

"Pimpernel has been running him?" Cameron asked.

"Yes," the Russian replied.

Cameron knew better than to ask how he had found this out. The convolutions of the legal residency working out of the Russian embassy were near to impossible to work out by a mere outsider. And the illegal agents floating about the country, not attached to any base, were, literally, a law unto themselves. Cameron guessed that Clarke would have been an illegal, and being an illegal he had much greater freedom of action within the society that they were trying to infiltrate and subvert.

Cameron pondered whether Pimpernel was an illegal or if he was a legal operating within the framework of the embassy. Of course Pimpernel may not even be Russian, he could be any nationality who had been recruited to the cause. Cameron's thoughts turned to Kim Philby, who had finally defected and gone to live in Russia in 1963. How many more, he wondered, were still working in Britain, buried deep into the society they were desperately trying to destroy. They represented a canker, eating away at the healthy growth of democracy and freedom. He looked at Ozerov and saw the heaviness of his Slavic features and imagined the obduracy of his Soviet nature, stilted and stunted within the confines of the communist system. He looked through eyes that were coloured to reject all the good that was obvious to those who lived within the freedom that he despised.

He thought again of John of Gaunt's speech in Shakespeare's Richard II, about England being beset with "inky blots and rotten parchment bonds," and that she has made a "shameful conquest of itself." Was this conquest to come about by the subversive acts of others because we were not vigilant enough to parry the "slings and arrows of outrageous fortune?" Were we now too weak in our moral responses to counter the evil effects of a more persistent faith?

The answers were left hanging in the air as Ozerov got up from his seat and sauntered out of the gallery.

Cameron was left sitting, staring at a rather gruesome painting of the crucifixion of Christ by an Italian artist of the sixteenth century. The image was one that seemed curiously relevant to the tortured state of a lot of England's institutions at this moment. Had we left the example that Christianity had given us as a nation too far behind? Many sacrifices had been made in the past to buy us what we enjoyed now; were we selling our birthright too cheaply by forgetting this?

He left too, pondering the emotion of the moment.

May 1966

The report from the Welsh police came through three days later. A man had been found wandering over the hills in a dreadful state of confusion. He answered the description of Simon Clarke and he was discovered about twenty miles from the crash scene. He apparently had suffered minor contusions and some broken ribs and was at present in the hospital in Aberystwyth. Cameron and Anstruther-Plowman decided to go down to see if it really was him and if possible interview him along with the local police.

They travelled in Cameron's Jaguar and arrived there the next day. They booked into a hotel in the town, made contact with the police, who had been advised they were coming, and went on to the hospital.

Simon Clarke was lying in a private ward, with a police guard outside the door. He appeared unresponsive when they spoke to him and there was a bandage around his head which, according to the doctor, covered a wound on his temple. After some minutes, without any significant awareness from him of them being there, Cameron went outside to talk to the doctor.

"He has been like that since he was brought in here," the doctor responded to his question.

"Is it the head wound that is the problem?" Cameron asked.

"No, apparently not, it is superficial and would not cause the confusion that he appears to be suffering from."

"Would there be any other reason why he should be acting in this way?"

"General trauma is obviously the first choice, I would say," the doctor answered, "but after a few days, if he hasn't improved I think we should be thinking about a brain scan to see if there is a tangible reason for his condition."

"Can that be done here?" Cameron asked.

"No, we will have to transfer him to Cardiff, they have the facilities there."

"We will ring in the morning and see if there is any change in his condition," said Anstruther-Plowman, as he joined Cameron, outside the room. "By the way, I am in general practice and I therefore have more than a passing interest in this patient."

They shook hands as they left and went back to their hotel for an evening meal.

When they rang the hospital the next morning they were informed that Clarke had manifested convulsions during the night and that, hopefully, they were stabilising the situation. They went over straight away.

"We have heavily sedated him and it looks as though it is working, the spasms appear to have stopped for the moment." The doctor informed them as they came into the main ward.

"However, I think it advisable that we send him to Cardiff, to have cranial tests and whatever they think is necessary," The doctor continued.

"Is he going there now?" Cameron asked.

"Yes, straight away."

"Can we follow the ambulance?" Anstruther-Plowman enquired.

"You can if you wish, but it will take some time to get the results of the tests," the doctor said. "It would surely be better if you ring up the hospital in Cardiff, in a few days' time, and see the results of the tests then."

This they agreed to do and went back to their hotel to formulate their plans.

Over lunch they decided to go back to the cottage where they had discovered Clarke with Nina and make a further search of the place. As far as they knew the police had had a cursory look around, but they were not sure if they would have been looking for the same things that would interest them. They phoned the police station in Llandrindod Wells, and made sure that the place was still available to them, and drove over there in the afternoon.

May 1966

The warm spring sunshine was colouring the soft hills around the cottage as they drove down the track to the front door. The unlocked door opened and they went in, Cameron noticing particularly an indefinable sense of depression in the place, as if a monstrous crime had taken root or been planned here. They set about a systematic search, starting with the furniture and progressing to all available hiding places. Along with various items of clothing they discovered documents relating to the two-way radio and communication to Moscow Centre. Also the route to the cottage from Clapham, which included a note about Philip Gibbs' book, *Both Your Houses*. Anstruther-Plowman found it in a bookcase and the instructions inside about the cache near the cottage.

They followed the path and the directions to the cache. The disturbed earth told them the location, and they began to cautiously dig the soft soil with the shovel found in the shed. They were not sure whether the site had been booby-trapped again. However, after going down to the prescribed depth they didn't find anything apart from a waterproof sheet, apparently discarded after the item had been taken. They guessed that the two-way radio, found in Clarke's possession, was the item taken. After further examination of the cottage they found what, almost certainly, were additional items from the cache, being a cipher machine and radio antenna and accessories. They surmised that the 7.65 calibre Mauser pistol that Clarke had was also a product of the cache.

After some hours there and being satisfied they had found all they needed, they packed all the relevant items into the car and drove back to Aberystwyth.

May 1966

Two days later they drove over to Cardiff, to the general hospital, after receiving news that tests on Clarke had revealed interesting developments. They were met by a senior consultant who took them into a side room.

"We took an X-ray of the skull, after injecting Myodil into the ventricles of the brain. We found no abnormality in their shape or size," he said, addressing his remarks, particularly, to Anstruther-Plowman, recognising his credentials beforehand.

"However, we followed this up with an angiography."

"What does that involve?" Cameron enquired, not wanting to be a mere bystander.

"A radio-opaque dye is injected into the carotid artery and an X-ray of the skull is then taken." The doctor continued, "the dye outlines the blood vessels and may show up an aneurysm."

"Did it, in this case?" Anstruther-Plowman asked.

"No, interestingly not."

"So you then considered an electro-encephalogram?" Anstruther-Plowman asked.

"Yes, indeed we did. As you may know," The doctor turned to Cameron, "this involves the measuring of the electrical waves given off by the brain. We attach electrodes to the skull and measure in graph form."

"What did you find?" Anstruther-Plowman asked.

"That there are areas of the brain that are definitely moribund." The doctor paused as if to give added emphasis to the statement.

"But how could this be caused?" Cameron asked. "You said that there was no obvious damage to the skull by the wound."

"That's true, there is no external trauma that could have caused this."

"So where do you go from here?" Cameron enquired.

"We shall do extensive toxicology tests to see what poisons, if any, have been responsible."

"How long will that take?" Cameron asked.

"Well, there are routine procedures such as examination of urine and blood pressure, blood urea estimation and the Wassermann test, so that won't take long, but we need a few days."

"Perhaps we need to go back to London now," said Anstruther-Plowman, "and get back to you in a few days time."

"That probably would be best," replied the doctor.

They went down to the car park and got into the Jaguar. As Cameron guided the car onto the road for London he asked Ansruther-Plowman what the Wassermann test was.

"It's the test for syphilis," he answered.

May 1966

Cameron took Shirley, Rachel and Nina down to Wimbledon in order to familiarise Arthur and Win with the latest developments. It was the first time that Nina had seen them since being rescued, having spent two weeks having hospital tests and generally coming to terms with what had happened. It was felt that she needed time to overcome the trauma before she saw them. They understood, as always, only wanting to be sensitive towards her.

That the time with them was emotional was to be expected and after a period of tears and tactile embraces, they began to talk about the recent past and the possibilities of the future.

"It's extraordinary, you know," said Cameron, "that if you, Arthur, hadn't invited me to your party two years ago none of us would be here together now."

"That's true, you wouldn't have met Nina then, but probably you would have one day, if you wanted to meet your daughter at some stage," Arthur responded.

"And you wouldn't have met me," Rachel riposted quickly.

"We may have met some time in the future," said Shirley, "but not like this. We couldn't have planned this, and it has taken an apparent tragedy to bring us together with such strong ties."

"I would think that these ties will never be broken either," interposed Win.

"I don't want to be overly sentimental at this point," said Cameron, "but somehow this experience of ours is a microcosm of the greater picture of our nation. Particularly as evidenced by the last war, 'our finest hour' as Churchill put it. We experience strength and purpose when things are truly difficult. It somehow produces the true fibre of what we are made of."

"I agree," said Arthur, "but we are a diffident bunch, we don't like to put it into words, it embarrasses us too much."

"You know, it's very interesting," Nina was sitting on the sofa between Win and Shirley, "I have been studying the mythology of England, up to last month anyway, particularly of King Arthur," she smiled at Arthur, "and the way the stories of the myths of England have been always there."

"I agree," said Cameron, "I believe the myths of a nation are very important too."

"They are persistent," continued Nina, "and in a way, it doesn't matter whether the myths are true or not."

"Again, I agree," he smiled at her across the room, relishing the charm of her personality.

"Why don't you think it matters whether they are true or not?" Arthur interposed.

"Because what is important for a nation is the yearning within its very heart. And the story of King Arthur is that of a courageous, Christian knight, who, with a band of brothers having an equal sentiment, set-out to right wrongs and behave honourably towards the weak and dispossessed." She had the sparkle in her eyes that Cameron had longed to see again.

"And I believe," said Cameron, "that occasionally we, as a nation, have operated in those high ideals."

"Yes, I must agree, that is true," Arthur said, "unfortunately not often enough."

"We can always do better," Cameron replied, "particularly at this time in our history, there is so much going on that King Arthur would not agree with at all."

"What had you in mind?" Arthur enquired.

"Oh, there is the mindset that tells us to take the easy course. Also, I fear, there are too many people in high places who are trading into an alien faith because they believe that, intellectually, it is right, although they would not want to live in that faith at all. It would inter-fere terribly with the comfortable lives they are living here."

"You mean people like Philby?" Arthur responded.

"Yes, I do, and unfortunately there are others who are lurking within our society too ready to want to destroy it."

"So, it's like putting your money where your mouth is," commented Rachel.

"Exactly so," responded Cameron, "if these individuals are so in love with the communist system, why don't they go and live there, and do us all a favour, by doing so."

"Well Philby has, and Burgess and Maclean, of course," said Arthur.

"Only because they had been uncovered here and really there was no other choice for them."

"But it seems that those three particularly, recruited whilst still at Cambridge, followed a true ideology," replied Arthur, "they really believed that they were saving the world by putting Russia on a par with the West and therefore preventing the USA from dominating the world."

"Seemingly so," said Cameron, "although from what I have heard, the Soviet system, and living under it, is not entirely to their liking."

"But how do you know where to draw the line," Shirley interjected, "if you give secrets to the Russians, how do you know how much to give them before they become the real threat to peace. I am sure that America doesn't want to take over the world. But what I hear is that the Soviet system is just about that. They want their ideology to spread throughout the world, so that everyone will have to live under communism."

Nina gave an involuntary shiver. "What a horrid thought," she said.

"Yes, it is a horrid thought," responded Arthur, "that is why anyone who is discovered to be a spy and is a traitor to his country, should, I believe, have the book thrown at him. To me it is treachery, pure and simple."

"People do that sort of thing for a variety of reasons," said Cameron, "it's not as simple and clear cut as you make it sound."

"To me it is," replied Arthur.

"OK, let me give you a possible scenario," Cameron responded, "what would you do if you were in a situation where, by reason of your job, shall we say, you had information that the enemy knew would be invaluable to him. And in order to get that information, the enemy takes measures to blackmail you into giving them what they want. Would you succumb to blackmail?"

"No, absolutely not," Arthur replied.

"Not under any circumstances?" said Cameron. Shirley noticed that he had a slight smile on his face as he posed the question and he heard Arthur's repeated denial.

"What about if the threat was not just to you but to someone that you loved. If you weren't willing to accede to their threats then they would put at risk that person?" Cameron continued.

"It depends what you mean by, at risk," Arthur responded.

"Well it's simple really. If I come to you and say, if you don't give me what I want, I will kill the one you love, would you then think twice and then betray your country?" Cameron asked.

"I think it is up to you, as an individual, not to put yourself in that position to start with," Arthur responded.

Cameron laughed. "Oh, come off it Arthur, you are dodging the issue. Many people have been put in that position, unwittingly, not knowing that they would be at such a risk. And they have been landed in it and, quite frankly, the only way out would be suicide."

"I think you are painting an extreme picture," said Arthur.

"I can assure you it is not an extreme picture. I could give you many examples where this has happened." Cameron knew he had to be careful as he noticed that they were all looking at him in a certain way and he realised that the passion that he was feeling was showing.

"Well, you probably know more than me," Arthur ended lamely.

"Yes, probably," Cameron answered.

May 1966

Cameron took the phone call at the Kingsbury flat three days later. It was Anstruther-Plowman. "I have just phoned the consultant at the hospital."

"Oh, yes, what did he say?" he answered, smiling at Rachel, whom he could see through the open bedroom door as she lay in bed.

His smile faded as he listened to his friend on the other end of the phone.

"He says that he has done the tests and that they can't say for sure but it seems that a drug of some sort have compromised his system. They can't at this stage identify the drug." Anstruther-Plowman continued, "he seems to be fading rather fast though."

"Can he say how long he could last?" Cameron asked.

"No, not at the moment."

"When could the drugs have been administered?" Cameron said.

"He didn't say, but, of course, it depends on the poison used, some have a much more gradual effect than others. He could have taken it himself; after all there was no one else who could have given it to him," Anstruther-Plowman answered.

Cameron thought that, to Anstruther-Plowman's credit, he didn't seem to consider himself to be included in that possibility.

"It's curious, you know," said Cameron, "he didn't seem the type to end his own life in this way."

"You can never tell with people," answered Anstruther-Plowman. "In my long time as a medical man, I have been constantly surprised by the variety of ways that individuals will hide their feelings and their emotions. The most apparently stable can do things that are completely out of character."

"Yes, I suppose so," Cameron admitted, "so is that the end of Simon Clarke?"

"It seems that it is very near the end. And I suppose we must be grateful that by going this way, it has avoided embarrassment all round. If, and when, he dies, it will just mean the post-mortem and, hopefully, no other inquiry."

Cameron couldn't help noticing that Anstruther-Plowman seemed to be relishing the premature demise of Clarke. He went back to join Rachel in bed, wondering if his own feelings were as transparent.

May 1966

Colin Witherspoon stood up as Ronald Cameron was ushered into his office.

"Good to see you again," he said, as they shook hands.

He gestured him to a seat on the other side of the desk, sat down and opened a file in front of him. Without any preamble he said, "I have to tell you that a Russian by the name of Nikolai Oshchenko, who you may know as Ozerov, has recently walked into our main office and declared an interest in being turned."

Cameron looked back at Witherspoon as if he had just asked him whether he wanted a cup of tea or not. Witherspoon could not tell what effect his words had had.

"He has told us already some very interesting things, particularly about individuals, British nationals, who are working for the Russians."

Cameron remained stony faced.

"Along with a list of names, there are two who are of particular interest." Witherspoon paused as if to give dramatic effect to his words, which, knowing his temperament, was the wrong analysis. "The two go under the codenames of 'Mariner' and 'Pimpernel'."

Cameron met Witherspoon's gaze, "you know that I am 'Mariner', of course."

"I do now," said Witherspoon, "I know also that you were recruited by the Russians during the war and that you became a double agent, working for us, in 1951."

"Ozerov never knew this, of course," responded Cameron, "which, as you can imagine, was very useful to me, from time to time."

"Yes," replied Witherspoon, "however, it is the identity of 'Pimpernel' that, I think, you will find of interest."

"I think I know who it is, but I need confirmation."

Witherspoon handed him a piece of paper and watched him closely as he opened it and read the name. He could discern no change in expression on his face, only someone close enough would have noticed the flicker of passion in his eyes.

" 'Pimpernel' did the reverse of you, if I may put it like that, that person became an agent for us during the war and was later turned by the Soviets and became a double agent, for them, in the late 1940s." Witherspoon turned over a page in his file, "we have that person under surveillance now and, as far as I know, he has no idea that Ozerov has turned. Therefore, does not suspect anything."

Cameron looked up, "Why have you told me?"

"Because you are very close to this person and out of deference to you we have decided to give you the opportunity to confront them, and to bring them in." Witherspoon smiled a half smile, "It's rather unorthodox, I admit. If you don't want to do it, we will understand."

Cameron stood up, "No, I will do it, and... thank you."

Although he said the words, the profound impact of his confirmation of the identity of Pimpernel had frozen his wits and his thinking. He held out his hand, Witherspoon rose and they shook hands.

"Thank you too, and how is Miss Robinson, by the way, a lovely girl, as I remember?"

Cameron smiled, "It's a long story, I'm afraid, and it will have to wait for another time, but at the end of it all she is now fine. But you will have to hear it from me, you probably wouldn't believe it otherwise."

May 1966

Cameron went straight down to Wimbledon. As it was a Saturday he knew that Arthur would be in, but, nevertheless, he had phoned to say he was coming. Arthur met him at the door and they both went into his study.

May 1966

To say that Cameron was shocked by the revelation of the identity of Pimpernel would be understating to a remarkable degree. He knew that Witherspoon was right, he was the only one who could confront this person, their lives had become so intertwined, it was going to be necessary to do delicate surgery to separate them.

Yet separate they must, one will go one way and the other, in another direction entirely.

May 1966

It was late on Sunday night when Cameron rang the doorbell of Brian Anstruther-Plowman's flat. It was the same flat that he and Shirley had borrowed for a few precious nights over twenty years ago when the V2 rockets were raining down on London. It was a flat full of memories for him and it added to the extreme mixture of emotions that he was now feeling.

He wanted to find some answers and he knew this was the only place to find them.

Brian Anstruther-Plowman opened the door; despite the lateness of the hour, he did not seem surprised to see him.

"Come on in, I've been expecting you," he said.

"Why?" Cameron said, as he was shown into the sitting room.

"Call it sixth sense," he replied.

He went to the drinks cabinet, "a whisky?"

"Yes, please, but a small one, I'm driving."

They settled down, one on the sofa and the other in the armchair, facing each other.

"What drug did you use to disable Clarke?" Cameron asked quietly, looking into his glass.

He glanced up, Anstruther-Plowman showed no change in his expression.

"Ricin was the main constituent," he said calmly, taking a sip of his whisky.

"Why did you do it?" Cameron responded.

"Why did I poison Clarke or why did I become a Russian agent?" Anstruther-Plowman asked so casually that Cameron was momentarily taken aback.

"Well, both I suppose."

"We'd better start at the beginning," responded Anstruther-Plowman. "As you know, I was a medical officer with the rank of lieutenant commander. And I served with you on the Arctic convoys." He got up from his seat and went to the drinks cabinet again. He turned to Cameron, "as this is likely to be a long night, would you like another whisky?"

"Yes please," said Cameron, handing him his glass.

He was not surprised at Anstruther-Plowman's demeanor. His urbane manner had not deserted him and his thin ascetic face showed no more emotion than if he had been ordering a fish supper. He poured out the drinks and came back to his armchair.

"I'd better start before that. I took my medical degree at Cambridge and found I was mixing with the likes of Kim Philby, Guy Burgess and Donald Maclean. I joined the Communist Party and also more esoteric ones like the Apostles, which was a teetotal intellectual discussion forum and the Pitt Club, which was entirely different, being socially exclusive and heavy drinking. It was a wild time at Cambridge then, you've got to remember that it was when there was great resi-stance to the upsurge of fascism and an intellectual acceptance of the ideological dominance of international communism. The Russian system of the ideal worker/peasant state was on the lips of any self-respecting thinker then. It was going to be the salvation of mankind, the Utopia of all our dreams. And we were going to be in the vanguard."

"So you were drawn into this?" Cameron interposed.

"Very much so," replied Anstruther-Plowman, "I became very friendly with Guy Burgess at Trinity College; he was an amazing character, in fact still is, as far as I know. He introduced me to an equally amazing man by the name of Arnold Deutsch, an Austrian Jew, a brilliant academic who was awarded the degree of PhD with distinction in chemistry whilst he was still only twenty-four. He was an illegal Soviet agent and he was one of those characters who looked at you as if nothing existed that was more important in life than you and talking to you at that moment... and he also had a marvellous sense of humour. He didn't tell me at that point that he was recruiting me as a Soviet agent but that I should break all contact with the Communist Party and try to win the confidence of British pro-German and pro-fascist circles. He gave me the impression that I was joining the

Communist International underground war against international fascism. He also inspired me with the vision of a new world order under communism which would free the human race from exploitation and alienation."

"You talk as if these ideals are all in the past," Cameron interjected.

"This was in 1935 and I was on fire with the idea of saving mankind and believed wholeheartedly that this was the way to go. I could see many things wrong with the Western way of capitalist democracy, which seemed to favour the rich without regard for the poor. And I rebelled against it. I also believed that communism was the only bulwark against the rise of Hitler and fascism."

"So when I met you first on those Arctic convoys, you were already an ardent Soviet agent?" Cameron asked, noticing that his whisky was diminishing rapidly.

"Yes," he answered.

"So what happened to your scruples when the Russians signed the non-aggression pact with Hitler in 1939?"

Cameron put his empty glass down.

"I saw this as a purely political move by Stalin to lull Hitler into a false sense of security, nothing more than that. It didn't prevent me from still believing in the greater cause of world freedom." Anstruther-Plowman, noticing that glasses were empty, went to the drinks cabinet and brought the whisky bottle over to the side table by the sofa. He proceeded to refill the glasses and sat down again.

"When I talked to you on the dockside in Murmansk... do you remember?" Cameron asked.

"Yes, I remember."

"And I told you that I was going to give the Russians some information that would keep them off Anna's back..."

"Yes."

"What were you thoughts, you didn't give me any advice. Did you then tell the Soviets that I was unreliable?" Cameron watched his eyes closely.

"No, not at that time, it was only when you left to go back home that I warned them about the dubious nature of your information."

"Did you ever believe that I also had become a Soviet agent?" Cameron asked.

Anstruther-Plowman looked hard at Cameron, "you did didn't you?"

"I pretended to," said Cameron, "but all the information that I ever gave them was tainted by misinformation."

"Did you not think that they would suspect?" Anstruther-Plowman asked.

"When the war ended, of course, it became a different ball game and I had to devise a new way of doing things. Anna was in Russia and, despite all my efforts through as many channels as I could find, I couldn't extricate her. I continued to send material through, which I hoped would satisfy them sufficiently, so that they wouldn't penalise her in any way, but in 1948 I discovered that she had been sent to a detention camp for 'enemies of the peoplé." Cameron took a long draught of his whisky and put the empty glass down. "It was then that I went to SIS and told them the situation and I became a double agent. I was being run by an illegal here and it became easy to use the work that I was doing to disguise the falseness of what I was giving. It gave me a perverse satisfaction that, in view of what they were doing to Anna, I was doing my best to nullify the effect."

"You, of course, realised," said Ansruther-Plowman, "that the hold the Russians had over you was purely Anna and because of that they wouldn't let her go."

"Yes, of course I did, but I couldn't do anything about it," said Cameron. "I did try to get her on board a merchant ship but it didn't work."

"I know it didn't work because I told them that's what you were trying to do." Anstruther-Plowman threw the statement in like a verbal hand grenade. It blew up in Cameron's brain and scattered his thoughts like confetti.

"You told them... how nice of you." He could think of nothing else to say for some moments, his mind appeared frozen in aspic.

Anstruther-Plowman continued, "It was very easy for me to go ashore in Murmansk, by some curious quirk, the badge of rank on my sleeve, which as you remember, for a lieutenant commander, was one broad gold stripe," here he drew the imaginary line on his lower arm, "above that was a thinner gold stripe and above that the next broader gold band. But, being a medical officer, I also had a scarlet band interposed between the thin and broad band. As it happened, the political officer commissar in the Russian navy also had a scarlet band on his badge of rank and therefore I was very often confused by the various Russian guards as being, somehow, part of their outfit. That was extremely convenient for me, at various times, I can assure you."

Cameron had a vague recollection that he had come to this confrontation with Anstruther-Plowman with the idea that he, Cameron, would have the advantage, both morally and ethically, over his adversary. However, he was now being taught a lesson in control of the moral high ground and was finding how easy it was to be the victim of the confusion that was being spread before him. Anstruther-Plowman appeared completely assured in the situation that he was in. He had obviously convinced himself, from the beginning, that what he was doing was right and that he could rationalise his position without any shift in his conscience.

Cameron collected his thoughts sufficiently to say, "did you never say to yourself that what you were doing was wrong, Brian?"

"Ah, but there is where we differ, you see, I have never considered that. I have always been true to my conscience. I am doing and working for the system that I believe is the right way for the world to go, which, if I may say, is rather better than your dishonest way. You have cheated two systems. I have only cheated one."

Cameron could not suppress a brief, amazed chuckle at the insolence of this remark.

"The worrying thing, Brian, is that I really think that you believe this."

"Look, I know that Orlov has turned and that he has given names, including mine," Anstruther-Plowman appeared to have ignored the jibe and if Cameron had been ultra-sensitive at this point he might have noticed a slight tetchiness in the reply, "but how long have I got?"

Cameron looked at his erstwhile friend; there was a point in their conversation when he had reflected on the way their lives had sustained each other, had converged and then parted. Their friendship had been, he thought, genuine and mutually supportive, but how genuine had it been? How much was it a sham? Could he believe in a friendship that relied on a political faith for its motivation? Brian Anstruther-Plowman had been there for him many times when he needed him, but could he forgive this new knowledge of his treachery towards Anna? How different Cameron's life would have been if he had been able to extricate her out of the tyranny of her homeland. He didn't dare to dwell on the implications of that now. He only felt a consuming desire to terminate something that suddenly was repulsive before him.

"How long have you got? That's an interesting question, Brian; as far as I am concerned I don't really care. I came here to tell you that you had been uncovered and I really wanted to help you and, maybe, find some way out for you. But I now see you for what you are, someone who uses people for your own ends, or for the nefarious ends of your masters in Moscow. You don't really care about anyone, except your own perverted view of life, as you see it, through the dislocated lenses of the myth of this worker/peasant Shangri-la world."

Anstruther-Plowman clapped his hands mockingly, "What a fine statement, you have certainly mastered the rhetoric of your grand democracy."

Cameron rose from his seat and, for a moment, stood there looking down at the friend he once thought he had. "I sincerely hope that we never meet again," he said; he nodded briefly and went out of the room and out of the front door, slamming it behind him. He got into his car and drove off, the anger in his heart burning away the influence of the drink in his body.

May 1966

Two days later Colin Witherspoon rang Cameron at the Kingsbury flat.

"After you reported to me yesterday," he said, "we instituted proceedings against Anstruther-Plowman but, I am not surprised, he is nowhere to be found."

"No, I'm not surprised either," responded Cameron, "have you checked all the ports?"

"All the major ones, yes. If he is still in the country, of course, he could be anywhere. But my guess is that he has slipped out and onto the Continent."

"Yes, I would think that is the case." Cameron replied.

"Incidentally," continued Witherspoon, "Orlov is bringing out some interesting things about our friend, particularly, that he is a colonel in the KGB."

"That high, eh?" Cameron replied. "I am impressed."

"You ought to be," Witherspoon responded, "but I will tell you more when we meet. Can you make next Tuesday?"

"Yes, that will be OK"

He put the phone down and went back into the kitchen, where Nina
and Rachel were having their breakfast. He put some more bread
into the toaster and poured himself out some more tea.
"Are you going into college today?" he addressed himself to Nina.
"Yes, I must, I've got an awful lot to catch up on," she said , smiling at
him. She touched his hand and held it. "Thank you for all that you've
done to bring me back." She looked at Rachel. "And thank you too.
You are the two most wonderful people in the world and I love you
both so much... and Shirley as well, of course."
Rachel got up, "And I must get into work too," she leaned down and
kissed Nina on the forehead, "I love you too, and never forget that."
Cameron got up and embraced Rachel, "I shall have a meal ready for
you both tonight and the first one home gets the gin and tonic."

May 1966

"Do you remember when we were last here?" Cameron and Shirley
were seated in a corner table at the Ritz Hotel in London. He posed
the question as they clinked their glasses of champagne together.
"Yes, of course I do," replied Shirley, "I will never forget it. It was the
evening when you proposed to me in October' 44."
"It was a curious proposal, if I remember. I said I couldn't marry you
but if I could I would, something like that..." he tailed off.
She reached over and took his hand. "It was a marvellous moment
and it really sealed what we had together."
They looked at each other and Cameron felt again that special magic
that she was always able to excite in him.
"I love you, you know," he said, "and I always will."
"And I love you too," she answered. "It's so lovely of you to bring me
here again."
"Well, I reckon once every twenty-two years you will have to expect it."
He smiled.
"Yes, we really are making it a regular fixture." She smiled back.
"I seem to remember that the meal last time was five shillings each,
but we had to pay a supplement to use the dance floor."
"Things change," she said.
"Yes and this is a celebration meal before you go back to Rhodesia. I
wanted to do something special for you... and us."
"It's been an extraordinary time, these last few weeks," she replied,

she looked into her glass as if to try and recollect all that had happened in the bubbles of the champagne.

"Yes, we've found our daughter," he said.

He saw the sparkle in her blue eyes as she responded, "yes, and what a lovely daughter she is, and, I suppose, the fact that we had to rescue her out of something terrible makes her that much more precious."

"I guess, in a way, that applies to a lot of things. I was thinking, the other day about our time in London during the war." He paused as the waiter came to refill the glasses. "Especially that terrible time with the V1s and V2s."

"Yes, it seems a different world now," she replied.

"How London was knocked about and how seemingly every street had bomb damage of some sort." He sipped his champagne, "I couldn't get over the effect of one V1, the explosive damage of one ton of HE. What was it, a crater ten feet deep and blast damage of about six hundred yards? I recall the effect of the V2 that fell on Whiteman Road, it demolished seven houses as I remember."

"Yes, and there were so many gaps in the buildings and the general smell of dust and dirt everywhere," Shirley responded.

"I think by that time Londoners had had enough. Five years of war and for most of that time London was in the front line. They thought that the end of the war was in sight and then they had to suffer from Hitler's terror weapons. No wonder the strain was beginning to show."

"Why are we talking about this?" Shirley enquired.

"Oh, it was the fact of how we were able to bring Nina out of a terrible time and that, somehow, it had a similarity with so many other things. It seems that the worse things get, if you can survive them, the better they will be afterwards."

"Do you remember the film we saw, the first time you took me out, The Gentle Sex and how we talked about it afterwards? About the girls finding out about themselves and the way the sufferings of war brought out the most wonderful things in ordinary people?" Shirley smiled in remembrance.

"Of course I remember, and especially the time we had in the Cotswolds," he held her hand.

"And where Nina was almost certainly conceived," she said and she gave his hand a squeeze.

They gazed at each other, but not into each others eyes, they both knew that to do that would take them into areas that they shouldn't attempt to go.

"I could easily book a hotel room for the night," he said softly.

"I know you could, my lovely," she said, "but I think that would be a bad idea."

"Unfortunately, I know you are right," he replied taking out his cigarette case and offering her one. She smiled and nodded. He put both into his mouth and lit them and gave one to her.

She took it and inhaled deeply through it. She smiled at him, "a remembrance of things past, two cigarettes and one flame that ignites both."

"Yes, how we needed each other then," he leaned back in his chair, "and what we meant to each other."

"We still do," she said, "we have been given back to each other. We meant everything to each other then and what we had cannot be taken away. And the fruit of that is our Nina and the love that will always be ours. But I now have Bill and my boys and you have lovely Rachel. It seems we can move on and take the love that has been given to us and use it to love others with. If I hadn't discovered love with you I don't think that I would be able to love Bill the way I do."

He looked at her and saw again that lovely shining girl that had so mesmerised him in those distant days.

"I love you so much," he said.

May 1966

They said goodbye in the departure lounge of London airport. Rachel, Nina and Ronald embraced Shirley with such emotional vigour that their collective tears were the natural response of what they meant to each other.

"We shall meet again in August," said Ronald.

"Yes we shall," Shirley replied, "because you are all coming over for Nina's twenty-first. That will be a wonderful time."

Nina kissed her, "Thank you for everything, especially for being my mum."

"I love you," said Shirley, those three words being the limit of what her emotions would allow her to say.

June 1966

"Apparently Anstruther-Plowman's 'loyalty' was confirmed to the Soviet Union by them blackmailing him." Witherspoon handed a cup of coffee to Cameron in his office in Whitehall.

Cameron took the seat on the other side of the large desk and offered Witherspoon a cigarette.

"When was this?"

"Round about 1951, when he was becoming a bit lukewarm to the Russian cause. They obviously decided that he needed a boost, shall we say, to his dedication."

"Has Ozerov told you this?" Cameron asked.

"Yes, he's proving very useful. Anstruther-Plowman was part of a trade delegation to Moscow and he was caught in a sexual act near the Metropole Hotel. Did you know he was a homosexual by the way?"

"No, not at all," said Cameron, "I am surprised, he never gave any intimation to me. Mind you, I only once ever saw him with a woman."

"Well, apparently, there is a urinal at the back of the hotel, which is well known as a meeting place for those of that dispensation, shall we say, and he was caught there. An indiscretion of great magnitude, as far as he was concerned."

"Yes, I imagine it was... in a way I feel rather sorry for him," responded Cameron.

"Whatever you do, don't feel sorry for him," interposed Witherspoon, "the more one hears the more it becomes apparent that he was responsible for many of our agents being unmasked, and has many lives on his conscience, if he has a conscience, of course."

Witherspoon handed him a bulky file, "If you have an inclination to feel sorry for him, just read the reports in there. It is pretty comprehensive regarding operations that went wrong and we are just beginning to see that Anstruther-Plowman was the man responsible for the disclosure of those operations to the Soviets. It makes for some grim reading in places."

Cameron flicked through the pages, "Does it say anything about Clarke and why he was disposed of?"

"Only that Anstruther-Plowman was the agent running him. He obviously didn't want Clarke to reveal his identity so he knew the only way was to silence him in a way that would not directly point the finger at Moscow Centre."

Cameron shrugged, "Well, let's hope he is now enjoying his Soviet 'paradise' and being given just rewards for his efforts."

Cameron got to his feet with Witherspoon and they shook hands, "By the way," he said, "you will be getting an invitation in the post to my wedding."

"I shall be very happy for that," said Witherspoon, "and look forward to it greatly."

July 1966

Ronald Boyd Cameron stood up to enthusiastic applause at the end of the wedding breakfast. The guests had all, apparently, enjoyed the meal and were anticipating a speech that would encapsulate a remarkable train of events, of which they were dimly aware, but not certain of.

"I want, first of all, to thank Rachel's parents for their daughter" (applause)... "and for the wonderful reception" (more applause)... "and, you must admit, the beauty of this girl is quite staggering" (applause). "I am the most fortunate of men" (hear, hear-from the male audience.)

"I also want to make a special mention of Rachel's bridesmaid, my daughter Nina, and the truly remarkable story that attaches to her, which I won't go into now, but suffice to say that the miracle of her being here is as amazing as her beauty.

"Most of you are aware of the bare bones of my story, how, during the war," ("Which one, first or second?" some wag shouts out to general laughter) "I will ignore such badinage... I was involved in the Russian convoys and how I met my first wife. Because of that I came to get to know something of the Russian way of doing things. And through my involvement with the Navy and the need to develop particular designs for equipment for ships I made contact with Arthur and Win, Nina's adoptive parents. Arthur was the banker that I thought could be useful in my need for funding. So it was that at a party, arranged by Arthur, I met Nina, not knowing that she was my daughter... extraordinary. I won't bore you with what happened in the next two years" (cries of "Shame"), "but sufficient to say that it was through Nina that I first met Rachel."

"Now comes the part of the story that, I believe, made the newspapers. I needed to find out what had happened to my wife in Russia, so I arranged to go out there in a legitimate party and try to make contact with her. I had heard that she was ill, and I did find her and it was whilst I was with her that she, unfortunately, died. However, this experience left me with a profound distaste for the Soviet system and I will emphasise with all my heart that anyone who still hankers after the myth of the ideal worker/peasant state doesn't know the true state of affairs in that benighted nation. You are attempting to grasp a shadow and it is entirely illusory. As for the grasping of my shadow," he looked down at Rachel and she answered his smile with one of her own, "I can say that this shadow is not illusory, she is the realisation of all my dreams and she embodies, for me, all that I have been searching for all these years. So will you all be upstanding and raise your glasses to toast my beautiful bride."

PS The next day

Colin Witherspoon stood up as Ronald Cameron entered his office. They shook hands and he ushered Cameron to a seat.

"Thank you for yesterday," said Witherspoon, "it was a truly remarkable day, and for you, particularly, it must have seemed the culmination of so much."

"Yes, it was. Rachel and I are going to the Cotswolds for a few days honeymoon, this afternoon, but I just needed to hear the latest news that you had on our erstwhile friend."

"Well, it seems there isn't much else to tell, except to say that he has surfaced in Moscow, as we predicted. It was reported in Pravda, briefly, that a top official had been expelled by us and, judging by the description, it could only be him."

"So that's the end of the matter then," said Cameron.

"Yes, it seems to be, except...."

The End ... or is it?

A Remembrance of Sorrow

'Her beauty was such that it made him halt in his stride.
She said, "You knew my mother once. You gave her irony
instead of understanding; bitterness instead of love; callous-
ness
instead of tenderness."
"When?" he asked.
"When you lived," she smiled sweetly, "I am the daughter you
never had."

JRW

Bibliography

Andrew, Christopher and Vasily Mitrokhin, The Mitrokhin Archive: The KGB in Europe and the West

Mitrokhin, Vasily (ed.) KGB Lexicon: The Soviet Intelligence Officer's Handbook

Jones, R.V. Most Secret War
Wolin, Simon and Robert M. Slusser (eds), The Soviet Secret Police